**FINAL**
The Book Every Preacher on the [...]
Has Been Waiting On!

# PREACHERS GONE WILD!

## Where Do Preachers Go When They Hurt?

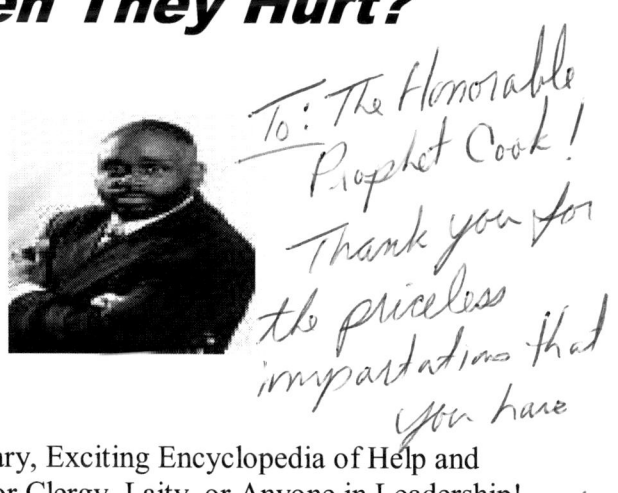

A Revolutionary, Exciting Encyclopedia of Help and Encouragement for Clergy, Laity, or Anyone in Leadership!

By

**Rev. BRENT La PRINCE EDWARDS**

© [2009] [Rev. Brent La Prince Edwards]

All rights reserved. No part of this work may be reproduced, stored in a retrieval system or transmitted in any form or by any means, electronic, mechanical, photocopying, recording, or otherwise, without prior permission in writing from the author or publisher.

[978-1-59712-338-9]


10 9 8 7 6 5 4 3 2 1

Printed in the United States of America

# Dedication
## To My Beloved Parents!

***The Honorable Mr. and Mrs. James Christopher and Gloria La Prince Edwards!*** Where would I be without you? It's your love, prayers, nurture, guidance and wisdom that's brought me this far! YOU GAVE ME LIFE! Without you I wouldn't even exist!

When people hear me, they hear you! Mom and Dad, you've been my sure anchor! How can I say thanks? Inexpressible gratitude and felicitations! People just don't know. The way you reared us has made all the difference! Mom and Dad, little did you know you were rearing nations! YOU ARE GIFTS FROM GOD HIMSELF! Eternal thanks!

And to My Brothers, ***Mr. James Christopher III and Robbins Ulysses Edwards!*** What can I say fellas? You're my history! You're not just my brothers. YOU'RE MY BEST FRIENDS! Oh yeah! Jay and Robbins, you guys are the seasoning in my okra soup. You're the wind beneath my wings. Hey! The 3 Jewels! Thanks for everything!

***To My Sisters, Nieces and Nephews, Montrese, Christa, Claire (Muffin), Henry, Khyla, Robb Jr., Aaron and more to come!*** After all these years, I haven't stopped laughing yet! What a joy! Thanks for everything!

***To Every Preacher and Aspiring Minister*** who feels it's lonely at the top whether serving 5,000 or the faithful 10! To every preacher who sincerely desires to make it in life, establish effective ministry pleasing to God, saving souls, restoring both character and dignity back to the Church. To every preacher who has given up on ministry because of the beating of the rain. To every preacher with a hunger to reach this generation! To every preacher who needs just a little bit of guidance. To every preacher who has forgotten how it feels to laugh again, ***this book is for you!***

# Table of Contents

A Tribute ................................................................................................ 6

Acknowledgments................................................................................. 8

Foreword "The Power and Benefits of Reading This Book"......................... 11

Introduction "Have Preachers Really Gone Wild, Or Is Something Else Going On?"..................................................................................... 26

### SECTION ONE : *LOCATION!*
*"Hearing the Cries and Locating Where We Are As Clergy!"*

Chapter One "Getting Started!" ........................................................ 46

Chapter Two " Ministerial Questionnaire" ........................................ 65

### SECTION TWO: *DISCUSSION!*
*"Where Do We Go From Here?"*

Chapter Three "Taking Off The Mask" ............................................. 82

Chapter Four " Are You Willing To Get Naked" ............................. 101

Chapter Five "Becoming A Good Preacher!" ................................. 125

Chapter Six " Who Are You Accountable To?" .............................. 151

## SECTION THREE: APPLICATION
*"Tips to Healing, Prevention and Recovery!"*

Chapter Seven " Please, Just One More Piece Of Chicken!"
Preachers and Health Issues ............................................................ 204

Chapter Eight " Which One? Lamb Or Lamb Chop?"
Preachers and Sexuality................................................................... 232

Chapter Nine " Lucy And The Offering Plate"
Preachers and Finances .................................................................. 265

Chapter Ten " My Baby Daddy! My Baby Mama!"
Preachers, Marriage, and Family Relationships .............................. 287

Chapter Eleven " Lord, How Do I Deal With Judas?"
The Controlling Minister

Chapter Twelve " Surviving The Church Mafia"
Preachers and Ecumenical Organizational Structures ..................... 325

Chapter Thirteen " The Congregation's Response To the Wounded Leader!" ........................................................................ 331

Chapter Fourteen "Where Do Preachers Go When They Hurt?"
Final Word and Closing Prayers ..................................................... 353

About The Author ........................................................................... 361

# A TRIBUTE!

## To the Honorable
## Rev. Mother Ella Mae Brown!

An old fashioned Holy Ghost filled Mother in Zion only a few years short of 100 whose touch has changed my life! Walking history! President of the renown Holy Ghost Crusader Prayer Band and associate minister of the Greater St. Luke African Methodist Episcopal Church, Charleston, South Carolina for many years.

Mother Brown, what would my life look like without you? You were one of the first who told me I was going to preach although I didn't believe you! Thanks for teaching me the power of prayer, consecration, the importance of integrity and living a clean, sanctified life! You taught me the power of the Holy Ghost and gave me wisdom that money could never buy! You taught me the power of prayer and how through crying out to God we can bring Heaven down to earth! Yes! And who would ever think or believe it's our turn now to carry the mantle?

When people hear me, they hear you too! And I haven't stop praying! I will forever keep this charge given to me by you! It's priceless far above rubies! Eternal thanks!

## In Loving Memory of the Late Honorable
## Pastor Reuben Wright Sr.

My Spiritual Father in the Gospel and to countless others under whose leadership the Lord sanctified and then restored my walk with Christ after a backslidden experience. Wow! A devout educator, teacher and founder of the Household of Faith Evangelistic Church of Jesus Christ, Inc.

What a unique man of God! A modern day Elijah and John the Baptist all rolled into one! He taught us our deliverance makes all the difference and proclaimed to the world Jesus Saves, Heals and delivers! Because of his touch and tutelage, people are being set free from all sorts of bondage wherever I go! To God be the glory! If the world had more role models like him, crime would be less on our streets and the statistics would read differently. Indeed an example of excellence to all! I am forever grateful and look forward to seeing my Spiritual Dad again when the Battle is over! To God be the glory!

**In Loving Memory of the Late Honorable
Pastor Barbara Brewton Cameron
And Pastor Houston Cameron! (Living)**

*Founders of the Community Outreach Christian Ministries and Harvest Center of Charlotte, NC whereas over 52,000 meals are served to the homeless annually! Ain't nothing like it!*

*You believed in me and took me in as your own son! Not only this, you've covered me on the battlefield refusing to let me lose focus on what's really important! You taught me entrepreneurship and when people were saying that my pastorate was too far in the rural area to make a difference, St. Stephen AME Church has now grown to 2 distinct locations! Thank you for teaching me greater evangelism allowing me to minister to the unchurched, streets and homeless in mass! Wow! Thank you for preparing me for nations! I will never forget what you've done for me! You are indeed a Mother in Zion and I am forever grateful!*

*Pastor Barbara Cameron absent from the body but present with the Lord! Missed more than words can say! But she left a legacy! Now the mantle has been passed down to us! Can we impact a generation and turn a whole society upside down to the glory of God like she did? If we don't statistics will continue to alarm us and people die! Let's make the difference today!*

# HEARTFELT ACKNOWLEDGMENTS

**SO MANY PEOPLE** have touched my life I almost don't know where to begin! However, as we'd say in the Charleston vernacular, I feel *"duty bound"* to thank the following. Indeed the African Proverb is true, **"It takes a whole village to raise a child."**

Wow! This is my story!

Let me first begin by giving honor to **my Lord and Savior, Jesus Christ!** Without Him, I, nor this book would exist! Jesus is everything to me yall! He's my life, my joy and I'm forever grateful! He's not only my Savior but my very best Friend. The God of my youth and beyond! Hallelujah!

I want to express unspeakable thanks to every auntie, uncle, cousin and relative on both **the La Prince and Middleton - Edwards** sides of my family! You are my history. Literally! Where would I be without each of you! Thanks for all your prayers, guidance and laughter down through the years!

To my beloved Church family, **St. Stephen AME Church and the Helping Hands Community Youth Development Center!** Wow! Serving you as pastor has been a privilege and blessing beyond words! I can't articulate how much each of you mean to me! Talk about the wind beneath my wings! This indeed you are! We've been through storms together but look what God hath wrought! Every pastor on the planet needs a congregation like you! I'm glad God has granted me the priceless opportunity to serve you. What a wonderful difference you've made in my life! Thanks to all of you! Thank you for believing in me! Eternal thanks!

And **to Bro. Maceo Harris!** Thanks for standing with me like Joshua to Moses and getting me out of all the 9,000 computer and tech jams I've been in. Thanks for helping me with the production of this book! **To Bro. Isaiah, Sis. Merritt, Sis. Kizzie, Mother Dockery, Mother Jessie, Bro. Vernon, Evg. Darin Margaret Taylor, (you've been a bridge over troubled waters!) Rev. Conyers, Bro. Adrian Caple, all stewards, trustees, <u>EVERYBODY</u>!** Thanks!

To my Bishop, **the honorable Bishop and Mrs. Adam J. Richardson,** Presiding Prelate of the Second Episcopal District of the African Methodist Episcopal Church. Wow! Words cannot express how appreciative I am for the exemplary leadership that you and Mrs. Richardson so wonderfully provide for every shepherd under your care! As a young preacher you have touched my life in ways you may never know! It's so wonderful to know that all the real role models in ministry aren't dead! Thank you for all that you've done, your godly wisdom and all that you do! Thank you for believing in the vision at St. Stephen's! May God bless you always!

To my presiding elder, **the Rev. and Mrs. Larnie G. Horton** and all presiding elders, Rev. Benjamin S. Foust, Rev .Bernard Wilder, pastors and laity of the Western North Carolina Conference! When people hear me, they hear you too! Talk about a big family! You know what we say, "the best is in the West!" Huh! God is good! Thanks for everything!

**To Rev. Dr. and Mrs. Conrad K. Pridgen**! My father in ministry! It all started with you! After I transferred from the $7^{th}$ Episcopal District to the $2^{nd}$, I didn't know where to go. Then came you! You and Mrs. Pridgen literally took me in as your own son, covered and raised me in the Gospel. It was under your ministry that I learned ministerial etiquette and protocol. Little did I know that after the Greater Bethel experience I would become a pastor! Thank you for everything. You've been my foundation before many. And wow! Your children, **Joseph and Nefertiti** have become my very own brother, sister and life-long friends! You are indeed a pastor of pastors!

To the honorable **Dr. Aretha Wilson!** Founder of RAW! *Remnant Affecting the World International Gathering, Inc.* and pastor of the Humble Heart Ministries! Dr. Wilson, what can I say? When my spiritual Father, Pastor Wright, passed away, I began to say, "would I ever be able to find such a charge again?" And just before the Lord called him home to Glory, then came you! Thank you for the inexpressible difference you've made not only in my life but also in St. Stephen's! You too have been a bridge over troubled waters. Thank you for presenting me to the late honorable **Mother, Dr. Estella Boyd!** Wow! Since that shot from her my whole life and ministry has catapulted to a height and depth I didn't know even existed! It's a whole new place in God! Thanks for believing in me and every opportunity to serve! Eternal thanks!

To the honorable **Pastors Markeda and Paul Friend!** Founders of Now Faith Holy Church. Wow! What can I say? I met you when I was so wet behind the ears as a Freshman in college around 18 years old. Inexperienced, full of comedy (and even folly) but yet the calling of God was heavy upon my life although I couldn't quite grasp it. Thank you for seeing and nurturing the gifts of God in me and cultivating them to new levels of maturity. **I will never forget you**! I had the anointing but didn't know how to operate in it. Thank you for teaching me and allowing me to make mistakes in your pulpit so I could grow! Eternal thanks!

To the honorable **Bishop George and Mary Searight!** Founders of Abundant Life Family Worship Center! **It took your ministry to get me here**! While I've never been an official member of Abundant, like the Syrophenician woman in the New Testament, I gleaned from the crumbs that fell from your table! It was mandatory by Heaven that I met you! I was gifted but out of balance. Then came you! You two are so important to the Body of Christ world wide. Not enough preachers value the power and importance of marriage and family......balance! And I thank you for the priceless lessons I've gleaned from you as a young man that money can never buy! **I haven't forgotten**. Eternal thanks!

Let me also express my gratitude to the following leaders who in someway have touched my life (list not exhaustive): The honorable Bishops: **Zedekiah Grady, Frederick C. James, Vinton and Mrs. Anderson, Hartford Brookins, Harvey Louis and Mrs. Rice, Anthony L. and Co-pastor Harriet Jinwright, Dr. Yolanda Benjamin, Corletta V. Harris, Elvin and Co-pastor Darlene Mickens. To Rev. Dr. Frank Madison Reid, Drs. Grainger and Joanne Browining, Rev. Phillip R. Cousins, Dr. Lee Washington, Dr. Ann Lightner Fuller, Rev. Dr. Mary Peterson, Rev. Wanda Howell, Rev. Tony Lee, Revs. Tony and Melodie Boone, Rev. Allan Parrot, Rev. Gregory Edmond, Rev. Marion Robinson, Mrs. Robin P. Smith,** Director of Christian Education Second Episcopal District, **Dr. Thomas Currie**, Dean of Union Theological Seminary Presbyterian School of Christian Education**, Dr. Eddie Fox**, President of the World Methodist Council of Churches, **all my teachers and professors via Livingstone College, and the University of North Carolina @ Charlotte,** to pastors**: Robyn and Mrs. Gool, Cynthia Pringle, Apostle Ozella Anderson, Ruth Middleton (aunt), Apostle Saundra Appleberry and every name not mentioned here**, I love and appreciate you all!

To my friends: (Just about all of us are preachers now! Huh! Can yall imagine? Want to start a riot? Get all of us together!) **Desmond and Lady Tanya, Debbie, Helen, Don and Bea, Pastors Reuben and Betty Wright, Pastors Gregg and Lisa Robinson, Lisa, .Millicent, Vincent Sims, Yolanda Martinez, Marcus Chavis, Mother Cheneta Washington, Marquis and Pequetha, Gary and Nikki, Mel and Nikki, Lazar Brown, Rodney Morrison, Sis. Carolyn Wilson, Monica Redmond, Tracy Hammond, Don and Mary Sasa, April and Jellico** (the Hawaiian connection), **Chalice Overy, Shawn and Faye Bell, Jay and Carla Reid Young, Cliff Wilson, Adrian Mc Neill, my spiritual son, Darius Phillips, AND THE 100 OF YOU NOT MENTIONED HERE** UNSPEAKABLE THANKS!

Oh! And special thanks to **Mrs. Tammy Mc Cottry**! How can I say thanks! Thank you for inviting me to be your guest on your television show! WOW! You have made history in my life as the first television interviewer to discuss this book on the air! May God's blessings overtake you and your family beyond measure! I really enjoyed myself!

Finally, TO **JAMES MUHAMMADAND THE DYNASTY PUBLISHING** Thank you beyond measure for coaching me and making my dreams in the world of literature become reality!

Love, Peace and Blessings!
*Brent La Prince Edwards*
Brent La Prince Edwards,
Author

# FOREWORD
## THE POWER AND BENEFITS
## OF READING THIS BOOK!

*"There's one thing I've learned. Watching a preacher and actually being one are two horses of distinct different colors.
The world looks totally different from inside this bubble! Huh!"*
*A Brently Proverb*

*".....How beautiful are the feet of them that preach the gospel of peace, and bring glad tidings of good things!"*
*Romans 10: 15b. KJV*

Hello! I'm Brent. And welcome to sheer joy! I'm honored beyond words to have you as my distinguished guest of highest honor! You are about to embark upon an incredible journey you'll never forget! So 1, 2, 3 let's go! I'm so excited!

## **The Power of This Book!**

### *Revolutionary!*

THIS BOOK YOU'RE HOLDING in your hand has the power to bring great joy, hope, insight, clarity, healing, and transformation to your life!

If you are a preacher, a lay person (non-clergy) actively involved in church or ministry, a public figure, politician, celebrity, professional athlete, a leader of any kind, or just someone who's interested in this subject, this book's for you! Totally revolutionary reading! Globally long overdue!

Today, the ministry of preaching has catapulted to levels and dimensions of greater of expansion than any time in human history. However, when we hear negative reports about clergy, a serious question comes to mind. Have preachers gone wild or is there something deeper going on?

And if so, who's addressing such issues? I mean properly and adequately! And foremost, where do preachers go when they hurt?

Where do shepherds go when it's their turn to cry? WHERE?

This is what this book is about!

Therefore, within these pages we will take an up close, raw and personal look at many very real and candid issues clergy persons face around the world often under-discussed.

We will do this by coming face to face with 15 real life situations called the *9-1-1 Emergency Help Cries*. Secondly I will present to you a *Ministerial Questionnaire* for your own personal perusal and reflection. From here we will move from location, to discussion, then to practical application providing suggested solutions and ultimately victory! I'm excited because finally help has arrived at a level of intimacy where we need it most!

Thus, the goals of this book are four-fold.

## **GOALS OF THIS BOOK:**

- To help each of us to take an honest and personal inventory to locate where we are in life and ministry.

- To help those who are non-clergy see some of the more intimate things we face that are not readily seen across the pulpit. Why is this necessary? Because we're better together and need each other! Everyone's important both the pulpit and pew!

- To help us move from location to solution by providing keys to healing, success, restoration and victory. And foremost, it will provide practical tips on how to avoid unnecessary pitfalls as men and women in ministry as well as congregations.

- When both the pulpit and the pew are whole, we can reach the world for Jesus!

## **Excellent Reading For Non-Clergy Vocations Too!**

While specifically written to hear and meet the intimate needs of clergy persons preacher to preacher, *(I too am inside this wonderful bubble called ministry. Huh!)* anyone can glean from the pages of this book.

In my life's journey, I have several friends and relatives who are not ministers but too are public figures to greater or lesser degrees. These range from judges, attorneys, politicians, teachers in the classroom, NFL stars, Gospel artist, on down to every day moms and dads who may not be in the spotlight of the public but the eyes of their children are always upon them.

While each vocation has its own distinct differentiations from pulpit ministry there's a commonality that exist among most. Even to greater or lesser dimensions. Whenever your work calls you to be in the spotlight there's something peculiar we often face. And what's this?

"PEOPLE ARE ALWAYS WATCHING YOU!"

Yes! Even in the mall! I mean doing something as simple as buying a pair of socks. Huh! I mean going to the grocery store to buy a banana. Mashed potatoes! PEANUTS! Roach spray! (By the way I'm a comedian too!)

I mean you're at an amusement park about to get on a roller coaster and all the sudden someone you've never ever seen before goes,

*"Hi Reverend So and So! Wow! What are you doing here?"*

Then before you know it an unrequested cell phone picture is taken of you before you can even blink! Your hair's nappy! Teeth gone! Corns on your toes and all! Ahhhhhhhh! Oh! This is so real! Huh! And if you're not careful, you'll almost feel guilty about riding the roller coaster. Anybody ever been there? I call it the plight of the never ending audience.

But believe it or not, as funny as this may seem to some this too is a type of pressure. And sadly, there have been many across vocational lines who have crumbled under such a load. Read the news papers!

Therefore, this book provides great reading for a wide diversity of career persons due to similar pressures. With the pulpit being a spotlight vocation, I think the world can learn a lot from the work we do. And guess what's the greatest bonus? There's a blessing in it! Someone may come to know Christ as Savior and Lord! For real Rejoice!

## A Must Read
## For Congregations!

When it comes to congregations and laity, I strongly recommend this book to the highest! It's practically mandatory!

*"There ain't nothing worse and more embarrassing
than a church fight!"*

### FOOD FOR THOUGHT
:
*"The enemy wants the pulpit upset with the pew
and the pew upset with the pulpit.
Together this is a recipe for congregational ineffectiveness!"*

There's one thing I've learned. Satan hates unified congregations! So he comes to divide and conquer! He hates anything that glorifies God and brings togetherness. He wants to make sure the pulpit is frustrated with the pew and the pew is upset with the pulpit. There is nothing worse or uglier than a church fight. And there's one too many going on!

Divided we will get absolutely nothing accomplished. And what's worse? The world laughs at us!

We know Jesus is real! But every time we go around beating up on each other we give God some serious bad PR. (Public Relations/ Advertisement.) We send souls that are hungry a very horrible and distorted message. And God holds us every bit accountable!

Therefore, what this book attempts to do is bring a greater clarity of understanding between the pulpit and the pew so we can win the world to Jesus and fulfill the Great Commission of Christ!

"Go therefore and make disciple of all the nations, baptizing them in the name of the Father and of the Son and of the Holy Spirit, teaching them to observe all things that I have commanded you; and lo, I am with you always, even to the end of the age."Amen.
*Matthew 28: 19-20 NKJV*

**W**ow! But you know what? Ain't nobody getting baptized if Sis.

Watermelon just knocked Bro. Tomato Soup in the head with a brick! Huh! Togetherness in Christ will always put the devil and his works out of business! Thus, it's his chief aim to keep division among the people of God.

## My Heartfelt Passion For Preachers,

## *Why I Wrote This Book!*

Having said all this, I want to tell you where my heartfelt passion to write this book came from. I have 4 reasons.

### *1. I Have A Heartfelt Passion For the Holistic Health of Preachers!*

My first reason for writing this book is because I have a heartfelt passion for the holistic health and well being of preachers. These include the: spiritual, mental, emotional, inter-relational, financial and circumstantial health of clergy!

First and foremost, I'm a preacher myself. So I'm writing this book from inside the world of ministry rather than without. I personally know what the air feels like inside here! One thing I've learned in my years in ministry is watching a preacher and actually being one are two horses of completely different colors. The world feels totally different wearing these shoes! Oh! The joy but the corns! Need a pedicure?

So I want to humbly talk to my fellow clergy brothers and sisters brother to brother/sister, family to family, friend to friend. No judgments. Just talk. As comrades and equals! WE NEED THIS!

> *"We can just chill and take our clergy collars off a moment and just rap about this thing called being a preacher!"*

I mean really pastors and leaders, let's think about this! When was the last time you got a chance to rap to someone about the deeper things you face in ministry with someone who really understands how it feels to be in this spotlight? We don't get to do this often! And how healthy and refreshing this is for all of us! All mask removed. Just friends keeping it raw and simple. No strings attached! We can take our clergy collars off for a moment, chill out, relax and just communicate ourselves to breakthrough about this thing called being a preacher!

This is the first reason why I write!

## _2. I Believe We Can Learn Priceless Lessons From Each Other's Experiences!_

The second reason I wrote this book is because I believe we can learn priceless and valuable lessons from each other's experiences and save ourselves the trouble of having to re-invent the wheel.

I've witnessed (and I know you have too) too many good preachers, brothers and sisters full of unspeakable potential just lose it via the pains and challenges of ministry. Some have never even been able to get their ministries off the ground. It's like being lost at sea crying out for help and no one hears the yell. Many clergy are sincerely called by God but don't have the direction and guidance to perfect the work. I've decided to be a part of the solution.

> *"I've personally felt the painful brush of death through fellow brother and sister clergy leaving this world I believe before the time!"*

And here's something that moves my heart ever so deeply. Particularly between the years of 2000 and 2009, I've personally felt the loss and the painful brush of great preachers and leaders who've actually died and gone home to be with the Lord. I mean great and sincere preachers! Most of these leaders weren't even 70 years old. Some were even very, very young.

In my opinion, I feel some have left this side prematurely in some cases. I know that God is sovereign and we don't always know why things happen but I also believe that many things are preventable! Thus, this too has been one of my greatest motivations for writing!

### *Experience Is Not Always the Best Teacher!*

While I believe experience is a great and awesome teacher not to be compared to, I don't always believe it's the best in every situation. I believe in the power of prevention. I often say it like this,

> *"Experience is good but prevention is better!"*

There are some things we can learn from the experience of others and each other and prevent the hassle. If something can be avoided why make the same mistake just to have a testimony? Is this wise? Isn't prevention much easier on us and everybody touched by our lives? Thank God if we do miss it, God is a God of miracles! But why risk it? There's not always a guarantee that we'll make it out alive! I'm just telling the truth!

The old folks used to say it like this, *"If you play with fire, you'll get burned."* Preacher, you don't have to get burned! Yes!

Preacher King Solomon, who personally knew what it's like to make all kinds of mistakes while leading said it like this,

> "A prudent man foreseeth the evil, and hideth himself,
> But the simple pass on, and are punished."
> Proverbs 27: 12 KJV

My fellow clergy, there's so much drama we can avoid. So I wrote this book with keys of prevention in mind.

## *3. We're All the Body of Christ With Common Needs!*

My third reason for writing is regardless of denominational affiliation, culture and geographical differences, we're all the Body of Christ with basic common needs. We all eat, sleep and drink water. (Or at least should! Huh!)

Over the years I've done tons and tons of work with fellow brother and sister clergy persons from all walks of life crossing denominational lines, cultures and boundaries. Sometimes I feel like a hybrid. Huh!

I belong to the AME sanctified AME Zion Methodist Baptist Episcopalian Lutheran Moravian Pentecostal Reformed Synod Orthodox Evangelical Quaker Non Denominational Presbyterian Church of God in Christ of the Apostolic United Methodist CME Wesleyan Cosmopolitan Temple of Truth Greater Word of Faith Cathedral #4 Ministries! Services Monday through Sunday, Saturday and Sunday! Again: Services Monday through Sunday, Saturday and Sunday at a location near you! Huh! I'm having a time! Oh! We're going to have lots of fun!

Now I'm not confused. I'm just having a good time in our learning process. A riot of joy! I believe laughter is the shortest distance between two people. (I got that from a Chinese proverb) Nevertheless, anybody belonging to that many ministries at one time got it going on more than the 12 disciples! I don't know where you pay your tithes but you got it going on! Huh!

Nevertheless, we're all the Body of Body of Christ! We've got to work on this division thing but we're still His Body! Don't always represent Him well but we're still His Body! Each one of us are inexpressibly significant and carries a needful piece of the puzzle. Now tell me. What would happen if we put all these pieces together? Awesome!

A good friend of mine who passed away a couple of years ago said it something like this.

*"I'm Baptist because I believe in water baptism. - I'm Methodist because I believe there's a divine order in God. - I'm Presbyterian because I believe in the order of presbyters and church government.- I'm Catholic because I believe the Church is universal.- I'm Pentecostal because I believe in the ministry of the Holy Spirit."*

Wow! Compliments of Bro. Jean who's in Heaven today!

Now granted we have different takes on doctrinal views. Sometimes there's error among us. Let's just make sure what we teach is in proper sound doctrine alignment with the Word of God. Nevertheless, we need each other!

> "And the eye cannot say unto the hand, I have no need of thee:
> nor again the head to the feet, I have no need of you."
> *I Corinthians 12:21 KJV*

Are we ready to stop fighting each other now Family? (Let's leave the Family feuds to the game shows!)

Nevertheless, more seriously, working with such a vast group of clergy I've noticed one thing.

*"Regardless of our geography, cultures and denominational differences, the general needs of clergy are basically the same!"*

Yes indeed! There's a commonality that exist among us all! WE'RE FAMILY! Oh! I forgot. To add to my long list of ministries; I've been to Catholic school too! Yeah buddy! ....... And one more thing, I've walked the halls of the Jewish Temples as well. Huh! For real and I loved every moment of it! Yes! Awesome! And Oh! The Spanish Pentecostals! "Gloria a Dios!" That's tongues you know. Huh! (Actually it means "glory to God!") Well it is tongues anyway! Glossolalia!

### *4. I Believe in Recovery!*

Finally, my fourth reason for compiling this work is because I believe in recovery The Apostle Paul writing to Tim said it like this,

> "And that they may recover themselves out of the snare
> of the devil, who are taken captive by him at his will."
> II Timothy 2:36 KJV

Again, where do preachers go when they hurt?

We'll never know how many ministers out there feel they are beyond hope or repair because of some mistake or trespass out there! What I aim to do in this book is not only give keys to prevention but just in case, keys to also getting back up on one's feet!

Now listen. I'm a realist and believe that we should be held accountable and responsible for our deeds and actions! We cannot do things to harm ourselves and others and just act like it's ice cream and candy and not take responsibility for our behavior. This is very unhealthy and indeed a horrible, horrible witness for Christ. As a matter of fact, we can't even get healed until we first humble ourselves and own up to our stuff. Plain and simple!

We might as well practice being accountable now because each of us are going to have to give a strict account before God anyway of every deed done in our bodies whether good or bad at the Judgment Seat!

> "For we must all appear before the judgment seat of Christ, that each one
> may receive the things done in the body, according to what he (or she) has
> done, whether good or bad."
> *2 Corinthians 5:10 NKJV*

Nevertheless, the great and good news is that there's hope! The honorable late Dr. Mother Estella Boyd said it like this,

> ***"There Is a plan of the Lord to redeem you!"***

Yes!

And this is the Gospel that we preach! A message of hope! Therefore, I feel compelled to write because we don't need to lose another minister to the enemy! However, if we don't place the proper resources in place for soldiers to get help when wounded on the battle field, how will the Body remain healthy and how will we ever be able to bring the world to Christ?

So why do I write? Let's review.

## My Reasons For Writing This Book

- I have a passion for the holistic health and well being of clergy.
- I believe in the power of prevention and we can learn from each other's experiences.
- The global needs of clergy are basically the same.
- We need to provide resources of hope and recovery to ministers who have fallen.

### *My Deep Gratitude For the African Methodist Episcopal Church*

While this book is global in perspective and not catered to any particular denomination or affiliation, (we all are part of the Body of Christ) I would be amiss if I didn't take this opportunity to thank the wonderful people and leaders in my own back yard. It's who gave me my first beginnings in ministry and nurturing me along the way.

By affiliation, I serve as a senior pastor in the African Methodist Episcopal Church. I've been serving successfully as a pastor now for 14 years although preaching much longer. And I'm still growing! I haven't arrived yet! To God be the glory!

The AME Church is the oldest and one of the largest Black denominations in the world. Via African Methodism I have been blessed to receive tremendous exposure second to none! I am forever thankful! ETERNAL THANKS to every leader and person that has imparted into my life!

One thing I love and appreciate about the AME Church is it really focuses and prepares pastors and leaders for the pulpit! If you become a minister in the AME Church your stuff is together! Let me tell you what I mean.

Now don't get me wrong. By no means am I bragging. No way! We all have short comings as we are human beings. We're still growing and still bump our heads every now and then. Believe me when I say this! See the knot? See the knuckle? Huh! I'm having more fun here!

However, what I'm saying is how much I appreciate the AME Church for the wisdom of not just sending preachers out there unprepared with no tools! Theological education and training is a priority and preparation for global witness comes with the soup! I'd been lost without these elements! Most of all, as a wee little boy, it was the AME Church that introduced Jesus to me!

That's precious to me. I'm eternally thankful!

Yet my passion for pastors and leaders exploded to a global perspective in 1999. Like the Apostle Paul, I had my own Damascus Road experience pertaining to ministry on a tiny island called, St. Simons Island, Georgia. Let me tell you what happened.

## I Was Inducted Into the World Methodist Council of Churches, Order of the FLAME
*(Faithful Leaders As Mission Evangelist)*

As a struggling new pastor, young, wet behind the ears but excited about ministry, I was in my first 5 years of the pastorate. Via the AME Church through my spiritual father in ministry, the Rev. Dr. Conrad K. Pridgen and the help of Rev. Dr. Roger Reid, to my complete surprise I received a phone call from the office of the World Methodist Council of Churches.

What an honor! This organization is an inter-racial, inter-cultural gathering of pastors from every part of the globe whose ministries have their roots in Methodism. These include male and female pastors from all parts of Africa, the Far East, the Southeast, Central and Southern parts of Asia, the Pacific, Australia, the Caribbean, Mexico and Central America, South America, the United Kingdom and Ireland, all parts of Europe, Germany and of course, North America.

Wow! I was simply blown out the water! So off I went, broke, with little money in a rental car down to St. Simons Island not knowing what to expect.

After arriving, it was as if everyone there was family. Red, yellow, black and white! Lines of division were dropped. There were several workshops, several speakers from different parts of the globe and great food! *(Yall know I had to throw that one in! I was always hungry!)* I even sang on the praise and worship team! However, here's where I had an epiphany.

> "I saw that the Gospel of Jesus Christ was bigger than my own back yard. There were people there from other persuasions who love God as much as I do!"

What blew my mind so was across lines of color and barriers there were people there who loved God just as much as I do! And who said Methodist folk don't praise the Lord??? They were lifting their hands in worship and it was simply phenomenal.

However, the highlight came at the Dedication service. Here, they had bishops from the different branches of Methodism to lay hands on every conference participant and charge us to fulfill our ministries around the world. It was a quiet and holy moment. We heard the preaching of the Word and then the dedicatory service began.

## A Greater Revival
## Broke Loose in My Soul!

After laying hands on each of us we were asked to refrain from talking and quietly and reverently proceed outside. So we did. When we got outside, there was a big, giant, humongous globe showing all the continents of the world. Every preacher joined hands in prayer making a giant circle around that globe facing it. And what was so fantastic was beyond the globe was the Atlantic Ocean only a few yards away! The scenery was phenomenal! It made the service even more relative!

When the prayer was finished, we were asked now to turn and face the opposite direction with our backs now facing the globe. In this way each preacher was now facing every direction outward: north, south, east and west. Then the commissioned was to "Go and share Christ with the world!"

Let me tell you! I will never forget this experience as long as I live!

It wasn't a loud or emotional thing. But in the quietness of my heart a greater revival was taking place in my soul! The presence of the Holy Spirit literally filled my being as He was speaking to me directly about my calling and commitment to preach the Gospel and what I'm supposed to be about. I saw my commitment to spread the good news of Jesus Christ like never before!

"GOD IS GLOBAL!" My spirit shouted!

"I'm called to touch nations!"

I could feel it in my soul.

"People are hurting. And everybody doesn't know this great joy!" And again, "GOD IS GLOBAL!"

Yes.

You know we as Christians go through trials and tribulations just like the rest of the world. But one thing about being in Christ is even in the worst storms, He gives us real peace. Peace is something a lot of people don't have.

I began to think of all the benefits that come with knowing Christ. Then I began to think of how so many people are hurting all over the world. Many are even skeptical about our faith. I began to think about how so many people could benefit from the peace we know in the Lord. But we don't have enough workers!

"People are hurting and we've got to get this great joy out to the masses!" "People are precious and God loves us all!"

"Who's going to get the good news out?" I pondered in my spirit. "This means we've got work to do!" I thought.

"God's not just concerned about my little back yard only. HE'S CONCERNED ABOUT THE WHOLE WIDE WORLD! He wants everybody to know Him!"

My soul was on fire!

It was that day and weekend that I saw my calling to spread the good news of Jesus Christ in a light not known before. An upgrade!

A great and honorable woman of God, Dr. Aretha Wilson,

founder of RAW (Remnant Affecting the World International Gathering, Inc.) says it best like this,

> *"We're not saved to make a living.*
> *We've been saved to make a difference!"*

Rejoice!

And here's further,

**<u>IT STARTS WITH THE PREACHERS!!!!</u>**

It starts with us! Yes!

Let me express heartfelt and special thanks to Dr. Eddie Fox and all leaders of the World Methodist Evangelism for making such a life changing opportunity possible.

## **<u>HOW TO USE THIS BOOK</u>**

Having said all this, we want to now turn passion into insight and practical application. And starting with the preachers we shall! Therefore this book is divided into 3 parts: *location, discussion* and *practical application.*

Chapters 1 -2 deal primarily with location. These involve the *9-1-1 Emergency Help Cries* of clergy and the Ministerial Questionnaire. The sole purpose of such is to help each of us specifically locate where we are in life and ministry. It's an honest assessment of ourselves raw and simple.

Chapters 3--6 are primarily discussion. Here we will discuss avenues on how we can move from location to solution and get the help we may need that we can receive healing, wholeness and restoration. The goal: to experience holistic health both in our personal lives and families as well as in ministry.

Chapters 7 -14 are chapters that give practical wisdom tips and application covering a diversity of topics clergy commonly encounter. These serve somewhat as an encyclopedia of help. Within these chapters, the *9-1-1 Emergency Help Cries* will be addressed.

Then finally, we will close our discussion out with a breakthrough word of prayer and confession of victory!

## I Cannot Counsel You!

*Disclaimer*

Now brothers and sisters, this book is deep! Here we will discuss material that's too often pushed aside or swept under the carpet for one reason or another. Yet if we don't start talking about these issues, more lives will be wounded and lost.

However, please note, I cannot counsel you due to professional and legal reasons. <u>If there's an area of your life whereas you need assistance, please contact the proper professional help in your area.</u> This is so important! This book has been written only to stimulate positive discussion among the ranks of clergy with the hope that more attention and ministry will be developed for those of us who shepherd and lead the people of God!

I'm so excited for the forthcoming victory among us all!

**LET THE JOURNEY OF HEALING BEGIN!**

## INTRODUCTION

# *Have Preachers Really Gone Wild, Or Is There Something Else Going On?*

*"If left to the media alone we'd all look like crooks. Hey! All preachers aren't stealing the money!"*
A Brently Proverb

*"And if one member suffers, all the members suffer with it; or if one member is honored, all the members rejoice with it."*
I Corinthians 12: 26 NKJV

## Up Late At Night!

Now that we've primed the pump, let me tell you about the night this book was actually born.

It's 1:31 AM and I'm up! All is quiet and still with the exception of crickets singing an unusual lullaby outside my bedroom window. The steady sound of a preaching video playing in my living room has saturated my one bedroom bachelor apartment with much inspiration. Sitting on the edge of my bed which rest on 4 cement cinder blocks high as Mt. Everest, I'm feeling quite serene. Finally relaxed, I'm enjoying the quiet but all encompassing presence of the Lord. "WOW! HE'S HERE!" I amazingly think to myself.

I can literally feel the presence of the Lord infusing and saturating my entire apartment like a cool shower after a hot dry summer's day. And oh! How do I need this quiet moment! Simply solitude.

As a newly appointed pastor of a very old rural congregation, I've had to stand eyeball to eyeball with some very serious new challenges. To be truthful, a lot of this stuff has been scary too! I believe I'm the youngest pastor this congregation has ever had. And worse, I'm single! Need I say more? Huh! I've got a zillion stories! Thankfully my single days are coming to an end! Oh!

But here's the equation.
Being Single + Pastoring = Scrutiny!

Yes Mam! Yes Sir!

Do I have stories! I see why the old church mothers used to say to new pastors, "YOU NEED A WIFE!" It sure helps! But even marriage is not a cure all for temptation and traps. Your stuff just got to be together preachers. Folk will try to dissolve the ring!

And with all the traveling I do, I've been offered more wives than Solomon! Both prophesied and wives by force! Get it? BY FORCE! Huh!

"I saw it in a vision preacher!" The familiar cry resounds.

Some of you preachers out there know exactly what I'm talking about! Yeah! Many of you have heard that familiar cry too! I know I'm not alone in this!

Oh!

Nevertheless, God's been so faithful! He's been with me every step of the way and I'm still learning Him. I'm still learning to trust Him more. He's successfully brought me through every test, trial and just points of plain pure stress! And what's more He's made the ministry successful. To God be the glory!

Anyway, besides the pressures of the road, (wife-ology) the congregation that I serve has indeed been the wind beneath my wings. Beautiful people! When people began to say that we're too far in the back woods for anything significant to happen God showed His Hand! Breaking historical barriers, saving souls and having grown from one location to two, the encouraging words of Jesus to the masses are forever true.

> "....with men this is impossible,
> but with God all things are possible!"
> *Matthew 19: 26b NKJV*

So tonight I shout!

As a matter of fact, I feel so good I could go outside this time of night and run a mile! But I better come to my senses. Can't you see the headlines now?

"PREACHER CAUGHT RUNNING AFTER MIDNIGHT IN HIS PAJAMAS. GOES STRAIGHT TO JAIL! DETAILS ON PAGE 6!"

Oops! Reality check! Oh well! Crash that idea. No need to give the annual gossip committee ammunition to chat about.

Nevertheless, in the midst of my newfound relaxation something is deeply disturbing me.

## Preacher Caught in Big Scandal!
*Hot Talk in the City!*

Reflecting back on my day, I recall hearing some very disturbing news. Earlier today, I was told about a preacher in a nearby city who was caught up in a big scandal at a very prestigious church. This church has held a very honorable and credible reputation in the city for years and now this!

Like a snowball rolling down a steep hill the news of this scandal has hit the airways, telephones and media without delay. It's the most current, latest and hottest gossip in town. Scorching!

As a matter of fact, the gossip is juicy. Huh! Hot off the press! Numero Uno. Flourishing! Yea my child! I say unto thee the gossip has gone yea even yea into the very overflow! Huh! I'm having a ball here!

> *"I'm up asking questions
> I have yet to hear
> discussed or answered at levels
> we need them most!"*

However, more seriously the long skinny ancient finger of accusation is now being pointed. People have begun to throw stones everywhere so please be sure to duck! We don't want anybody getting hit in the lip, eye or something. Ouch!

Nevertheless, all hope isn't lost. Like sunshine after the rain, throughout all this drama there is yet some good news. After a period of time this nightmare finally came to an end. The situation at last worked itself out and both the pastor and the ministry are back on course. And thank God!

However, being a preacher myself, (and a young one at that!) all this drama has me up tonight doing some serious thinking. This is how this book came to be! I'm up asking some serious questions I have yet to hear discussed or answered at levels we need them most! Yet like a 9-1-1 emergency call they need to be!

## **Have Preachers Really Gone Wild Or Is There Something Deeper Going On?**

When we hear alarming stories such as these, it brings a very serious question to mind. Have preachers really gone wild or is there something deeper going on? Is there something happening beyond the surface or behind the scenes we're not catching?

I mean what is the root cause behind some of the behaviors and situations we see happening among our ranks? It's always easier to point the fingers of blame and accusation but tell me, what causes us to do what we do? What are the motivating factors? What's the psychology? What spiritual, emotional, mental and even circumstantial things could be in place to evolve into some of the things we hear and see? And foremost, is there a doctor in the house?

*"Pastors have to wear many hats at the same time all on one head!"*

## **The Vocation of A Pastor Is A Stressful One!**

When we consider the vocation of a pastor, it's a unique one anyway. Being a pastor is considered one of the most stressful vocations in the spectrum of careers. It's a 24 hour job that punches beyond office hours and the Sunday morning worship experience. Pastors are always on call whereas the needs of people never cease. Being a pastor is very demanding.

Pastors have to wear many hats and in my opinion the preaching event is the easiest. The real test comes when we put the microphone down! Huh!

Yet check this out. Not only do we wear a bunch of hats, but often at the same time ALL ON ONE HEAD! Can you imagine? People are always pulling on us for this or that.

Not only are we spokespersons for God, we carry out many duties. We serve as the chief business administrators of our flocks. Much deeper we also serve as surrogate fathers and mothers some people have never had. Furthermore, we serve as educators, social workers, funeral directors, community liaison persons, lawyers, teachers, psychiatrist, big brothers, sisters, emergency room specialist, (people call us all times of night for emergencies) hospice servants, referees and the list goes on!

We have to bless the babies, attend tragic funerals, break up gang fights, stand by the bedside of a dying loved one, marry the newly weds, counsel the divorced, cheer the fallen, procure economic growth and development, save the lost, strengthen the believers, visit the sick, break up and resolve church fights, shine as lights to those in darkness, face betrayal and abandonment, attend 2,000 meetings, cry out against injustices, attend graduations, oversee new projects, while still having to manage our own personal lives and families. Most of all, people look up to us for guidance! While these things are indeed our duty, they too are types of pressure. Without help something is bound to get left undone!

Therefore, while ministry is indeed a joy and an unspeakable honor to service still it's nothing to play with!

So again I ask, have preachers really gone wild? Let's plow deeper!

## Is The Media Always Fair?

*"There's a side to the story not being told but needs to be. Everybody's not playing church!"*

Christianity Gets A Lot of Bad PR and I'm Concerned!

My passion is such a burning one because I'm an advocate for preachers and a devout believer in the Gospel and Church of our Lord and Savior Jesus Christ! I feel that Christianity gets a lot of bad PR (public relations and / advertisement) and that the media isn't always fair. Let me explain what I mean.

### *I Studied All the Major Religions of the World!*

During my undergraduate studies, I had to study all the major religions of the world not from a Christian perspective but from an academic, historical, and sociological one. I attended a quite prestigious and secular university I loved it! I got to see the world beyond my backyard! It was great exposure.

It was challenging but a remarkable experience. I got an opportunity to see and hear the world view of countless persuasions other than my own. While maintaining true to my own convictions, such studies have really helped me to better understand the religious and philosophical viewpoints of others cross culturally and internationally. Even if I didn't agree! I know what I believe but it has helped me tremendously in my ministry and relating to people as I often minister and periodically work with those from other faiths.

And you know what? The Lord has granted me wonderful success. And not one time have I had to compromise my beliefs or get in a nasty religious argument. Life has enough problems! Ain't nobody got time for all this fussing and carrying on! We've got too much to do!

> *"As saints we've got to learn how to talk to people with love and respect no matter who they are!"*

When such conversations were over, I've had people from other faiths say things like, "I never thought of it that way." And even, "I've not met too many Christians who could explain this." Or, "I was raised an agnostic but for the first time, this Word touched me!" And you know what? In several cases, I've seen the power of God fall! Yes! I mean upon people who are of completely different faiths!

Am I bragging? By all means no! Am I on some type of mission or something to see who's the greatest in philosophical arguments and debates? No! I'm sharing this with you because I want us to learn something here if we intend to reach the world for Christ. Saints, it's so important that we learn how to talk to people with love and respect even when there are differences of opinion! And foremost, shouting and running around the church is not enough. We've got to study!

> "Study to show thyself approved unto God,
> a workman that needeth not
> to be ashamed, rightly dividing the word of truth."
> *II Timothy 2:15 KJV*

Brothers and Sisters, are we just making a whole lot of noise or do we really know our stuff? And if we know it, can we communicate such lovingly and effectively to a skeptical and angry world?

Huh! Think about this!

Shouting and dancing is good. BUT IT'S NOT ENOUGH! ..............not if we're serious about winning THIS generation! You've got to have information!

Speaking to a mass of pastors and leaders on communication skills, a great bishop once said it this way,

*"You can draw more flies with honey than vinegar!"*

Wow! Take that one to the bank! Let's perfect our skills on talking to people that we may represent Christ well!

And remember, you don't have to compromise!

## **Students and Professors Seemed So Hostile Against Christianity!**

*"People seemed so hostile against Christianity while more tolerant of other religions."*

Nevertheless, in my studies, there's something that always bugged me. In so many of my classes, people seemed to be so hostile against Christianity. Not everybody, but quite a few.

Several students and professors many times seemed more tolerant of other religious persuasions but when issues of Christianity surfaced, it seemed folks started catching attitudes and you could hear quiet and sometimes not so quiet traits of bitterness.

Many times I would ask myself, "What's going on?" I mean, "Who let the dogs out!?" Huh! Some of yall don't know that song! "WHO LET THE DOGS OUT? BOOM! BOOM! BOOM! BOOM!" Ah! That song used to rock on college campuses! Huh! Don't yall look at me funny, I'm still saved! Having a ball here! BOOM!

Nevertheless, upon doing lots of research, I know where some of this hostility comes from historically. (Via crusades, etc. and stuff that long time dead folks have done centuries ago that Christ never told them to do!) However, besides the fact that secular humanism and Christianity don't mix, (we're living in the last days) some of these hostile persons have simply been burned in the church! And they're angry!

Now don't get me wrong. I'm not justifying stuff here. But let's face it. Many times Christianity gets a lot of bad advertisement because sometimes we're the blame. We shoot ourselves in our own toes. Yes we do! We give the world the guns to shoot us with!

Nevertheless, on the other hand, SOMETIMES THE MEDIA

## Don't Throw the Baby Out With the Bath Water!

While serving a great and needful purpose, many times I have issues with the media. Therefore, I've written this book because there's a whole side of this story not being told to the masses and needs to be. Especially when it comes to preachers and the Church! There are always two sides to a coin and for too long we've been throwing the baby out with the bath water!

## All Preachers Aren't Crooks!

Too often we hear wild stories about preachers and they leave the viewer with a lopsided view of Christianity and the Church! What I mean is if it were left up to the media we'd think all preachers are crooks and Christianity is nothing but a big game. This simply isn't true! Everybody's not playing church!

Satan delights in this because he knows it's the Gospel of Christ that will put him out of business. So he loves it when the Gospel is misrepresented and magnifies anything that looks like a stain to untold proportions to keep lost souls captive.

"And the dragon (Satan) was wroth (angry) with the woman (Israel)
and went to make war with the remnant of her seed,
which keep the commandments of God,
and have the testimony of Jesus Christ."
*Revelation 12: 17 KJV*

## Where's the Media When Preachers Do Well?

While it is a dire necessity that we take time to minister to those of us who have fallen, there are thousands of preachers out there who are making a great positive and significant impact in our communities and world. Yet the media is slow to focus on these. Why? Because bad news sells! And if we aren't careful we'd be tempted to believe against the Word of God that all hope is lost. So where's the media when preachers and the saints do well?

The prophet Elijah in the Old Testament thought he was the only one left true to the service of God because that's all he could see. Yet God corrected him. Unknowing to Elijah God informed the prophet that

He had reserved to Himself 7,000 who have not bowed to Baal nor kissed his image.

The same hold true today! WE'RE NOT ALL STEALING THE MONEY AND MESSING WITH THE KIDS! No! There are thousands of preachers out there who walk in integrity!

Why won't the media highlight these as well? Why not do a talk show on these too? TELL US THE WHOLE STORY!

But here's a flip side for you.

What do we do when the media is right?

What do we do when indeed one of our hands has been caught in the cookie jar?

## No Chain Greater Than It's Weakest Link!

Considering no chain is greater than it's weakest link, when just one of us falls where's the doctor?

After all, let's not fool ourselves. Besides all our holy regalia, anointing, accolades, accomplishments, gifts, talents and abilities, what happened in the story I previously mentioned could've been any of us and has been some of us!

*"The truth of the matter is anyone of us could mess up!"*

Now I know some of us out there think we're Superman and Superwoman or even John the Baptist's first cousin. I know some of us claim to have had a cup of hot coffee and doughnuts with Moses and the Apostle Paul. Oh! But the truth of the matter is anyone of us could mess up!

Yet truthfully, through the victory of the Cross and the indwelling presence and power of the Holy Spirit we don't have to mess up. We don't have to fall! It's not mandatory. We're not helpless! We're not pitiful! We're not condemned or doomed to a life of failure and clowning. So let's not treat it as such. WE CAN STAND! CHRIST THROUGH THE HOLY SPIRIT HAS GIVEN US THE POWER TO STAND!

"Now unto him (Jesus) that **is able** to keep you from falling, and present you faultless before the presence of his glory with exceeding joy."
*Jude 1:24 JKV*

"For sin **shall not have dominion** over you: for y are not under the law, but under grace."
*Romans 6:14 KJV*

"**But ye shall receive** power, after that the Holy Ghost is come upon you: and ye shall be witnesses unto me (Jesus) both in Jerusalem, and in all Judaea, and in Samaria, and unto the uttermost part of the earth."
*Acts 1:8 KJV*

"Nay, **in all these things** we are more than conquerors through him that loved us."
*Romans 8:37 KJV*

Wow! Both awesome and encouraging!

So we understand that falling and messing up is not something that has to happen! Remember, we're not powerless!

## The Problem Isn't With God's Provision. We Still Have the Ability to Choose!

However, the problem isn't with the provision God has provided us to walk in victory but rather our cooperation with it! In other words, God never takes away our freedom to choose. And let's be honest, none of us have impeccably always chosen to do the right thing in our lives. We don't always cooperate with God (this is called sin) and if we say we do we're lying! Therefore, we can make the wrong decisions and thus suffer the consequences.

"If we say we have no sin, **we deceive ourselves**, and the truth is not in us."
*I John 1:8 KJV*

Self deception is the worse deception!

This is why the scripture tells us to be careful how we handle the fallen. While we are never called to sanctify iniquity or condone erroneous behavior, there's a right and wrong way to handle such matters. We'll never know when we'll be the ones needing mercy and a shoulder to cry on one day! Nevertheless, we'll discuss this in more detail within forthcoming chapters of this book. .

Paul says it like this,

> "Brethren, if a man (person) **be overcome in a fault**, ye which are spiritual, restore such an one in the spirit of meekness; <u>CONSIDERING THYSELF</u>, lest you also be tempted. **Bear ye one another's burdens**, and so fulfill the law of Christ."
> *Galatians 6: 1-2. KJV*

Oh! If we'd only follow instructions!

Besides, what affects one of us affects all of us!

> "And if one member suffers, all the members suffer with it; or if one member is honored, all the members rejoice with it."
> *I Corinthians 12: 26 NKJV*

Bottom line: Let's drop our stones! Remember what I said, no chain is greater than it's weakest link! It could be you the next time. Or even me! God forbid. But it's real!

What goes around comes around. We'll reap what we've sown. Let's sow good seeds. Let's walk in love and wisdom!

## So, Where Do Preachers Go When They Hurt?

So after sitting up late at night pondering these things in my mind, "Boom!" the baby was born! The billion dollar question! Where do preachers go when they hurt? WHERE? Then later, I gave the baby clothes: *"Preachers Gone Wild!"* I knew this would be an attention getter.

> *"With so many looking up to us for strength, where do we go when it's our turn to cry?"*

Wearing so many hats and with Lottie, Dottie and everybody we know now preachers haven't really just gone wild and something deeper is going on! With so many coming to us for answers and strength, to whom do we go for succor as men and women in ministry when we need a shoulder to cry on? This is not an excuse but it is a reality.

Even when we're facing things that don't have anything to do with sin such as loss, grief, spiritual warfare, serving in geographical regions of poverty, health issues, financial problems, loneliness, etc, my argument is whose doing anything about it? I mean redemptively? Holistically?

I'm talking in a way that will bring relief, clarity, healing, restoration and insight to both the pulpit and pew?

Furthermore, what preventive measures do we have in place so we can avoid such unnecessary pitfalls? And should we fall, how do we recover and not fall victim to repetitive behaviors? Thus, my greatest argument and thesis is this,

"ONE TOO MANY PREACHERS ARE IN PAIN
AND NOBODY'S REALLY TALKING ABOUT IT!"

At least not at significant levels where it's making a global difference to the glory of God! After all, the whole world is watching us! Right? Yes! And you know what else? They're talking too!

## **Going to God Isn't the Issue!**

Having said all this, I can hear someone right now saying, "I know where preachers should go when they hurt! They should go to God!"

"After all, isn't this what you guys teach?"

Ah! Being a preacher myself and having worked with so many fellow clergy crossing over denominational lines, cultures and boundaries, I can easily answer this one. This may come as a shock to you.

GOD ISN'T THE ISSUE! Nor is He the problem.

To answer this question, yes we should go to God but the issue isn't with Him. He's always there! He's faithful. Beyond consistent! Indeed a very present help in trouble and during any kind of season in our lives!

As a matter of fact, it's our going to God and the faithfulness of God that keeps us from cracking up when the storms of life blow their best! The reason we've made it successfully this far and haven't lost it is because of God! Thus, most pastors already know how to walk alone. We know how to make it by ourselves.

Paul said it like this,

"At my first defense no one stood with me, but all forsook me.

> May it not be charged against them."
> *2 Timothy 4: 16. NKJV*

No one stood with the Apostle Paul. Yet being anchored in the Lord he knew how to make it alone. However, even with this it's still not God's best for us. We should be able to go to each other as well when we're going through!

> "And whether one member suffer, all the members suffer with it; or one member be honored, all the members rejoice with it."
> *I Corinthians 12: 26 KJV*

> "Bear ye one another's burdens, and so fulfill the law of Christ."
> *Galatians 6:2 KJV*

We are helpers one to another! Or at least supposed to be!

So the issue isn't with God. He's always there! He does His part! Always!

> "..........for He Himself has said, **I will never leave you nor forsake you.**"
> *Hebrews 13: 5b NKJV*

There you have it! God is not the problem. Hallelujah!

## **The Issue Lies With Us!**

Here's where the problem lies. Us! Yes, THE ISSUE IS WITH US! The family! We brothers and sisters!

Thus, the problem isn't my prayer closet. It's when I come out!

<u>We Were Created For Fellowship</u>!
*We're Better Together!*

Listen. Since the Garden of Eden, God never created us to be solo projects. While we all have our own uniqueness and individuality we're interconnected like the human body.

The human body isn't made of just one organ or part but many. And while every organ in our bodies have their own uniqueness, location, function and distinction, each part is a joint supplier of life to the other.

For an example. Red blood cells carry oxygen and nutrients

throughout the body. White blood cells fight off diseases and infection. We have two different types of cells but each is a joint supplier to the other in some kind of way. The Red blood cells cannot do it's job properly without the white, nor can the white blood cells without the red. God designed the human body that each individual part contributes to the whole!

The Apostle Paul had much to say about this timely comparison in I Corinthians 12.

"For as the body is one, and hath many members,
and all the members of that one body, being many, are one body: so is Christ."

<u>And the eye cannot say unto the hand, I have no need of thee;</u>
nor again the head to the feet, I have no need of you.

...... That there should be no schism in the body
but that the members should have the same care one for another."
*I Corinthians 12: 12, 21 and 25. KJV.*

Now that's off the chain! It doesn't get any clearer than this. But will we obey? Or is it all about us? Remember the familiar saying, "My four and no more?"

No wonder were so divided! Selfishness and insecurities! We've got to come back into unity!

## Why Should I Re-invent the Wheel If You're There?

So now we see again how God isn't the problem but rather the body's willingness to be fellow joint suppliers of life to every part.

Now don't get me wrong. I know and am convinced that God will fix it like He promised whether alone or surrounded by people. But I just need the fellowship! I need the support of my brothers and sisters when riding through a storm!

*"I might be a great prayer warrior.
Anointed with a bag of chips
and all that. But the truth is
I still don't know everything!"*

Listen brothers and sisters, I might be a great prayer warrior but the truth is I still don't know everything!

I may even have some wisdom and find myself very knowledgeable on several subjects. But there's some stuff and things I face as a preacher whereas some solutions are unknown to me! And because the Kingdom of God is never broke there's some brother or sister out there in the Body of Christ whose already faced this stuff having the wisdom I need to keep me from wasting the time trying to re-invent the wheel!

Remember what I said before, prevention is the key and we can trade wisdom with each other and skip the drama!

*"I can learn from you. You can learn from me.
But are we available?"*

Yes. I can walk alone! This is how I've made it this far. But is this God's best? Did He design the family of God to operate this way? What would happen in our physical human bodies if the red blood cells refused to deliver nutrients to the rest of the body? You know what would happen. The body would die!

In the same way, could some of the stuff and things we hear happening among our ranks as preachers been avoided if some red blood cell in the Body of Christ would just deliver? We can learn many lessons from hematology. Whenever we get cut, blood (particularly our white blood cells) rush to the place that hurts the most!

Do we rush to the aid of our brothers and sisters when they hurt or do we reject, criticize and talk about them?

Wonder why Christianity is often ridiculed and not taken seriously? We will give an account to God!

Here's the key.

"**<u>Two are better than one</u>**; because they have
a good reward for their labour.
For if they fall, **<u>the one will lift up his fellow</u>**:
but **<u>woe to him that is alone when he falleth</u>**;
for he hath not another to help him up."
*Ecclesiastes 4: 9-10. JKV*

Preachers, if I as your fellow clergy fall will you help me up? Will I help you? So where do preachers go when they hurt? Again, God isn't the issue, it's us!

Remember the problem isn't God's presence. God was with Adam yet He said,

> "......It is not good that man should be alone;
> I will make him a helper comparable to him."
> *Genesis 2:18 NKJV*

Brothers and Sisters, we're better together!

## **Where Are the Ministries For the Wounded Leader?**

In the Body of Christ there are all sorts of conferences, assemblies, meetings and gatherings that are much needed. We have conferences for singles, the married, women, men, and even youth. We have gatherings on a diversity of subjects and thank God. They're much needed.

But where are the conferences and gatherings for the wounded leader? Now granted, there are indeed some ministry out there for leaders and shepherds and thank God for these. But in my opinion, there certainly aren't enough and more needs to be established! After all, doesn't the health of the Body begin with the head? Yes indeed. It starts with the leadership!

"How then shall they call on Him in whom they have not believed?

And how shall they believe in Him of whom they have not heard?
And how shall they hear <u>WITHOUT A PREACHER</u>?
And how shall they preach unless they are sent? As it is written:

"How beautiful are the feet of those who preach the gospel of peace,
Who bring glad tidings of good things!"
*Romans 10: 14-15. NKJV*

### **FOOD FOR THOUGHT:**
*"Wounded shepherds make wounded sheep.*
*Burned out shepherds make burned out sheep.*
*Healthy shepherds make healthy sheep.*
*Rested shepherds make rested sheep.....*
*When both shepherds and sheep are healthy,*
*that flock can reach the world!"*

## **Let's Stop Fighting!**

Listen if we intend to reach the world for Christ, fulfill the Great Commission (see Matthew 28: 18-20) and see global revival, it ain't going to happen until we stop fighting each other and get together!

*"We've got to stop fighting each other
and start helping each other!"*

Despite doubt and eschatological skepticism, Jesus is on His way back and promised before His return the good news of the Gospel will cover the globe first. We are the instruments He will use in the fulfillment of such. Even in the midst of persecution.

Personally, I believe this is the finest hour for the Church. Why? Because in the midst trouble and Scripture being fulfilled all around us, I believe something wonderful is about to happen in the Body of Christ!

"And this gospel of the kingdom shall be preached in all the world
for a witness unto all nations; and then shall the end come."
*Matthew 24: 14. KJV*

And check this out. Here's the final and ultimate state of the Church.

"Let us be glad and rejoice, and give honour to him" for the marriage of the Lamb (Jesus) is come, and his wife (the Church) **hath made herself ready**."

And to her (the Church) was granted that she should be arrayed in fine linen, clean and white: for the fine linen is the righteousness of saints."
*Revelation 19: 7-8. KJV*

The Church may have its issues now but the end of the Book says,

"We win!"

The Church is going to be alright! Rejoice!

Could it be that our generation will be the one that God uses to bring these things to pass? Let's pull together Family of God!

## **Things to Consider As We Begin Our Journey!**

## **5 Things to Consider:**

- Let's work toward strengthening the holistic health (spiritual, mental, emotional, physical, inter-relational, financial, circumstantial) status of clergy around the world.

- Let's consider establishing more effective Biblical and holistic ministry for both the health and recovery of wounded preachers, families and congregations.

- Let's work toward strengthening our global witness for Christ throughout the world by representing Him well that we may fulfill the Great Commission!

- Let's embrace the power of prevention and ministries of recovery to the wounded leader.

- Let's begin to generate new positive discussions and ministries for the healing and strengthening of under- shepherds among our ranks, within our denominations and ministerial affiliations around the world. Foremost, let's drop the lines that divide us coming together as the Body of Christ!

Now just imagine. If we follow through on these things, revival will surely take place like we've never seen it before!

Let's do it! The payoff is beyond worth it!

# SECTION I

# LOCATION

## "Finding Out Where We Are And Where We Really Live As Shepherds!"

## CHAPTER ONE

# GETTING STARTED
## *"When Preachers Scream!"*

## *The 9-1-1 Emergency Help Cries!*

"Have you ever heard of a silent scream?
It's a terrible thing.
It's an inward urgent cry for help.
However, the agony is not the scream itself.
It's when the cry is made and no one notices!
.......Many preachers are screaming!
*A Brently Proverb*

## A Chapter of Location!
*"Can You Hear the Cry?"*

Preachers, are you ready to keep it real? I am so excited! Hold my mule! Huh! I'm rejoicing because here comes the intimate help we've been talking about! Right where we need it most!

This chapter is a chapter of location. In other words, before we can do anything to propagate health, healing and wholeness in our lives and ministries we must first locate where we are as men and women of the cloth. Many preachers are crying out all over the world and it's time to hear the cries!

Therefore, we are going to begin our journey by first listening to the deeper needs and cries of clergy. This will be done by taking a direct assessment of ourselves and coming face to face with some very real situations and issues that many preachers face all around the globe. These are called *Silent Screams* or *9-1-1 Emergency Help Cries*.

Following these, I will present to you a *Ministerial Questionnaire* in Chapter 2 for your own personal reflection and perusal. Such will help us to move better from location to solution.

However, the goals of this chapter are five-fold. I have listed these here for you.

### **Goals of This Chapter:**

- To generate discussion and help us better locate and understand where we are and what our needs are as men and women in ministry.

- To propel us to seek and find effective solutions that will give us helpful and preventive measures to avoid potential and unnecessary pitfalls.

- To strengthen, encourage, help, lift and restore those who may have fallen.

- To Biblically procure and establish healthy relationships with family and others who are touched by our lives. To establish healthy relationships between the pulpit and the pew producing health, healing, and wholeness in our congregations and overall ministries.

- To advance and restore the joy of ministry!

Ready? Well prepare to celebrate. Breakthrough is on it's way!

## **Preacher,**
## **It's Your Time Now!**

Listen. It's your time now! Not only is it your time but also your turn!

Perhaps you've been out there ministering to everybody else. Perhaps you've been counseling, praying, building, encouraging, serving and preaching to the masses. Maybe you've had to be strong for others while silently and quietly wiping your own tears. Or maybe you're not facing any particular challenges at all but simply desire more wisdom and insight on the subject.

Regardless, you're at the right place at the right time reading the right book! You are valuable to God and the Kingdom! You're priceless and irreplaceable! Now it's your turn to have oil pour into your wounds. So no matter what your circumstances may be, DON'T YOU EVER GIVE UP! God is not through blessing you and what God has called you to do in the earth is a necessity. He still doesn't have enough workers.

"Then He (Jesus) said to His disciples,
**"The harvest truly is plentiful, but the laborers are few."**
*Matthew 9:37 NKJV*

And here's an encouraging bonus.

".....weeping may endure for a night,
**But joy comes in the morning**."
*Psalm 30:5c NKJV*

Preacher, your morning is coming! Hallelujah! Yes!

So let's get the ball rolling by asking a very soul searching question.

## Reverend, Are You Screaming?
*"Understanding the Silent Scream!"*

The route to experiencing health and wholeness will never take place until we are first willing to get "down to the core" honest with ourselves. I like to say it this way, we must become *"gut-bucket honest."*

This means being honest to the bare necessities. 2000% transparent! *"Gut bucket* you say?" Yes. That's using my Charlestonian vernacular. (I'm from Charleston, South Carolina in case you didn't know.) No place like home! Oh! The hot fish, crabs and shrimp! Huh! The mosquitoes!

Nevertheless, if a patient is facing an illness and chooses not to be honest with the doctor concerning his or her symptoms then there will be further complications. It will be difficult for the doctor to do the work or prescribe the treatment necessary. Why? Because telling the doctor what's bugging us gives an informed idea where to begin. Otherwise, a patient can suffer needlessly and even die from something which perhaps could easily be treated.

Thus, we will begin our journey by asking ourselves a very personal and intimate question. Preachers, are we screaming?

### "Somebody Give Me Some Air!"

Now here, I'm not talking about hollering at the end of our sermons when we're most excited. No! I'm talking about something much deeper.

Here comes the comedian.

Let's be honest brothers and sisters. All the hollering we do isn't always because we feel the power. Huh! Sometimes it's because we're out of breath! (I'm about to fall on the floor!) Yall know I'm telling the truth! Come on now. It takes wind to finish a sermon. And when we're out of shape, we're out of breath. That's why we keep water in the pulpit.

> *"It's either sit down
> or fall down!"*

Sometimes our people leave our services saying, "Reverend So and So really preached today!" And that may be true.

But little do they know sometimes our best sermons are delivered struggling for air! (I've got tons of stories!) And when we plop down in our seats, it ain't always because we're under such a heavy anointing. No. It's air baby! The lack of it! Yes! Give me some air! It's either sit down or fall down! Huh! Oh! I'm having a ball!

Nevertheless, yea I say unto thee, the prophetic word yea even for this hour is yea even 8-fold. E-X-E-R-C-I-S-E! Hallelujah! Go ye to the gym! Check with your doctor first. But "Go ye!" You'll preach better.

Now if you're going to go there to get in the flesh, STAY HOME! Walk around the block or something. You got enough problems now. Huh! But if you're serious about getting in shape do some research, find a good gym and fitness program. They're out there! But leave that fat back alone! Not another piece of ham! Oh!

Whoooo! I enjoyed that. Somebody fan me!

NEVERTHELESS, on a more serious note, (told you I was a comedian) there is something called a *silent scream* and many preachers are hollering. Let me explain.

## Defining the *Silent Scream*

According to *Webster's Dictionary*, a *scream* is defined as follows:
1. to utter a shrill, piercing cry as in pain or fright
2. to shout, laugh, etc. hysterically
n.. 1. a sharp, piercing cry or sound

Now let's define the word, *silent..*

1. making no vocal sound; mute  2. not talkative
3. free from noise; quiet; still  4. not spoken, expressed, etc. [silent grief]
5. making no mention, explanation, etc.

Lastly, let's look at the word, *silence..*

3. omission of mention  4. failure to communicate, write, etc.

Using what we've just learned let's pull all these definitions together in one new concise meaning.

*"A silent scream is a cry or call for help that expresses itself in a non-verbal way."*

But here's the addendum.

*"Nevertheless, such screams do have a voice. They speak through actions, behaviors, mannerisms and even circumstances."*

Wow!

A *silent scream* is a subtle cry for help that stems from some type of need in our lives. Silent screams generally express themselves non verbally. In other words such cries for help manifest themselves in our actions, health, behavior, mannerisms, methods of doing ministry, how we interact with others, indulgences, circumstances, family life and the list goes on!

However, the dangerous thing about silent screams is the fact the yell is very easy to overlook or even go unnoticed. If this is the case, when help arrives it could be too late.

I believe many of the things we hear happening among our ranks and fellow clergy are the results of silent screams gone unnoticed or unchecked. What we often see and hear in the news is often the manifestation of that thing all grown up! The seed wasn't arrested in time.

Thus, our first assignment is to arrest such seeds at the root. If we fail to do so, we risk the possibility of not only destroying ourselves but also wounding others who are in some way influenced by our lives.

So before we hear the *9-1-1 Emergency Help Cries*, first there are 2 things I must tell you.

**FOOD FOR THOUGHT:**
*"Pull a leaf off a tree and
it will grow back again.
Get the tree from the root and
you'll see the leaf no more."*

**No Stone Throwing
Allowed!**

The first thing I want to tell you is no stone throwing is allowed. Stone throwing means pointing fingers of blame, accusation and condemnation as we look at a wide diversity of issues we sometimes face as brothers and sisters in ministry.

Therefore, as we get ready to listen to the *9-1-1 Emergency Help Cries* let us do so with the mind set that we are helpers and joint suppliers to one another. Regardless of our differences in geography, nationality, ethnicity, denominational affiliation or whatever our uniqueness, we're all the Body of Christ! We're interconnected. And if we don't help each other, who will? So please no throwing rocks.

Here's a little thought for you. I came up with this one myself.

*"Let us not be so quick to throw stones at others. We'll never know when one of those same bricks will boomerang around and knock us in the eye! Ouch!"*

Huh!

And we know what Jesus said,

> "....He who **is without sin** among you,
> let him throw a stone at her first."
> *John 8:7 NKJV*

Wow!

We know how that story ended. Not one of them could throw a rock because their own consciences told them they'd all have black eyes. Why? Boomeranging bricks! They weren't crazy. They knew the real deal. All of them were guilty of something. Sure enough! One hand would wash the other!

But here's one I think we all should remember. It is our God-given duty to sincerely care for one another. Speaking to the Church of Galatia, the Apostle Paul said it this way.

> "....that there should be no schism (division) in the body,
> but that the members (All Christians)
> <u>should have the same care for one another.</u>
>
> <u>And if one member suffers, all the members suffer with it;</u>
> <u>or if one member is honored, all members rejoice with it.</u>
>
> Now you (all believers) are the Body of Christ,
> and members individually."
> *I Corinthians 12: 25 - 27. NKJV*

Yes my friend, we're all brothers and sisters! So please drop all calloused materials. We're better together!

### FOOD FOR THOUGHT:
*"The unbelieving world is watching us.*
*They are constantly making decisions*
*about what to do with Jesus*
*based on how we treat each other.*
*Especially when we fall!"*

### <u>Are We Treating Each Other Right</u>?

Finally, here's the second thing I want to tell you before we hear the cries of the clergy. Let's make extra sure to treat each other right. This is so important if we want to see global revival among the Lord's under-shepherds! Preachers, we've got to get revived first! Because if we get whole first, the sheep will follow!

Always remember,

> "Healthy shepherds make healthy sheep. When both
> shepherds and sheep are healthy,
> great things will take place in that congregation!"

What a worthy goal to work toward! Can you only imagine?

However, we've got to treat each other right because the unbelieving world is watching us. This is something the Lord has made so real to me concerning how we handle each other especially during difficult times in our lives.

## **People Make Decisions About Jesus Based on Our Behavior Towards Each Other!**

In terms of global evangelism, the world constantly makes decisions about what to do with Jesus by the way we treat each other. Especially when we're down and out! I mean who wants to get beat up on the streets then come in the House of God and get beat up again? We're the only Bibles some people will ever see! So what message are we sending?

### *A Catch 22?*

Now listen. This doesn't mean we're to condone sin and give people a license to kill themselves. No! Should we fall or fall prey to some sin we're never called to sanctify iniquity either. This too is unhealthy!

Paul said it like this,

> "What shall we say then? **Shall we continue in sin, that grace may abound?** God forbid. How shall we, that are dead to sin, live any longer therein?
> *Romans 5: 1-2. KJV*

Bottom line: Two wrongs still don't make a right. Nevertheless, because many don't know how to properly deal with issues of sin, this is where many churches have gone off course. Many times we're either too extreme far off to the left or too extreme far off to the right. Therefore, we end up diluting the delivering power of the Cross! But all the answers we need are in the Word of God!

Many of us have seen ministries abusive to those who have fallen. Not wanting to make the same mistake, and rightfully so we make people feel it's alright to participate in behaviors that will eventually destroy them in fear of not wanting to lose that person. Almost a catch 22.

So we keep the patient which is both wonderful and needed but don't treat the disease. What do you think will happen to a patient who has a comfortable and beautiful hospital room but never gets treated? The condition will worsen and they could die. Needlessly! With help all around! There definitely needs to be more teaching and training on this subject.

*"We can't help peopleif we condone error!"*

We'll never help people if we applaud and condone erroneous behavior. Poison is poison no matter what kind of beautiful jar we pour it in. Yet at the same time we can't crucify people and burn them like pork roast either because of a shortcoming. Who are we to do this anyway when none of us are without frailties!

"For **all** have sinned and come short of the glory of God."
*Romans 3:23 KJV*

However, when we sin (and all of us do!) there's a right and wrong way to handle such matters. And we don't have to wound, hurt or beat people up in the process! Nor do we have to strengthen the thing that will eventually kill us either or is quietly at work within us to take us out! The scripture teaches us how to deal with such matters in a loving redemptive manner. We'll talk about this in greater detail in later chapters.

Nevertheless, we must never forget. Life is funny. It could be you or I needing mercy or a helping hand any day. What then? God didn't call us to be mean and ugly. Suppose Christ was mean and ugly to us when we messed up and needed forgiveness? Where would we be today? It's time to extend the same favor! How soon we sometimes forget!

Remember, we are the only Bibles some people will ever see. So let's make sure we're sending out the right message and not give God bad PR. (Public Relations/Advertisement)

How will we win the world to Jesus? How will the world know that we truly belong to Him? I'll tell you this. It won't be by our holy regalia, gifts, talents, accolades or persona. But Christ said it Himself.

"By this all will know that you are My disciples,
**if you have love for one another**."
*John 13: 35 NKJV*

Wow! That's it my friend. LOVE!

So let's treat each other right. Somebody may come on board when they see real unconditional love in action moving from heart to heart and breast to breast!

Isn't this what real revival is about?

## A Letter From Jesus To You!

*My Beloved Sons and Daughters,*

*"And whosoever shall give to drink unto one of these little ones a cup of cold water only i n the name of a disciple, verily I say unto you, he ( or she)shall in no wise lose his reward."*

*Lovingly Yours Forever,*
*Your Savior and Redeemer*

*Jesus!*
*Matthew 10:42 KJV*

## The 9-1-1 Emergency Help Cries!

### 9-1-1 Emergency Help Cry #1
### Extreme Burnout!

A well meaning, sincere and dedicated preacher who loves his congregation with all his heart dies suddenly and unexpectedly for no apparent reason. The only information that his family and congregation reports is that he worked day in and out for the ministry. However, he never took time for rest or a vacation.

Finally, the autopsy report was completed. The medical professionals concluded that his death was due to extreme burnout. Thus, over time his body shut down resulting in an untimely and unexpected demise.

## 9-1-1 Emergency Help Cry #2
## Drowning In A Sea of Loneliness!

A very popular minister is considered a raving success by colleagues, friends and the world at large. However, this preacher suffers from extreme loneliness. Although always surrounded by people, this minister feels uniquely alone.

While many people claim friendship with this preacher, some only hang around for association and prestige purposes hoping too to get a piece of the spotlight. As a result, this minister is not sure who to trust.

Uncertain of people's motives, this preacher desperately needs someone to genuinely fellowship with. He/she needs someone to talk to without having to wear the mask of keeping up with a certain public image. Just to be human. Finding such a fellowship seems almost an impossible task. Thus, this minister is drowning in a sea of loneliness and frustration.

Practically about to explode for such an outlet, this minister is thinking about ways of relief that could be detrimental to his/her life, family, Christian witness and ministry. Unable to vent, this preacher constantly lives life on the edge.

## 9-1-1 Emergency Help Cry #3
## The Lamb That Became A Lamb Chop!

A young parishioner struggling with his/her sexual identity goes to a well trusted minister for counseling, help and guidance. Unknowing to the parishioner, the minister finds him/her quite attractive and appealing. Eventually as the counseling sessions continue this minister makes sexual advances toward the parishioner.

Shocked, angry and caught off guard, the parishioner leaves the office frustrated, disillusioned, confused. Now bitter, this lamb (parishioner) now feeling like a lamb chop vows never to step foot in another church anywhere or trust another preacher again!

**9-1-1 Emergency Help Cry #4**
**Gender Discrimination!**

A female minister is anointed, effective, gifted, integral, well educated, and most of all called of God to do the work of ministry. However, she is discriminated against because she's a female. Thus, she feels that she is being hindered from what she feels God has called her to do.

Her ministry now stifled, she faces issues and pressures that many of her male colleagues aren't confronted with. Because she's a woman, some of her colleagues still believe her best place of service is in the kitchen! Thus, she lives with anger, bitterness, and great resentment toward men in positions of authority.

As a result, she finds herself spending much time overcompensating to prove her equality. Thus, the atmosphere of her ministry is one of tension and protest that the beauty of her own garden is difficult to be seen.

**9-1-1 Emergency Help Cry #5**
**Persecuted, Diseased and No Resources!**

A preacher in a Third-world country faces great distress whereas something as simple as holding a regular church service is a great challenge. He happens to minister in a country where Christians are persecuted and carrying a Bible could cost a person's life!

Not only this, the country has suffered a great economic collapse and resources are very low. There is famine in the land, disease runs rampant and there is practically no health care. The preacher has pleaded for stronger ministries, missionaries and pastors from other countries to assist but to no avail. Sadly, many people are dying and things continue to get worse before getting better.

**9-1-1 Emergency Help Cry #6**
**Preacher's Kids Who Hate the Church!**

A very sincere and dedicated preacher loves his family and the congregation he serves with all his heart. Not only this, he walks in tremendous integrity, kindness and character.

Having a great vision for the people and community, he places all his time, energy and effort into his work often placing himself last. However, his congregation is very non-supportive. They challenges him on every project that he presents tooth and nail.

When the minister is not around, some parishioners are heard saying mean and ugly things about the pastor and his wife even in the presence of their young children. The children having the greatest love and respect for their Dad quickly become disillusioned.

Over time, they grow to hate the church and church people. They've determined in their hearts after turning 18 years of age, they'll have nothing to do with the church again.

And you know what? They did exactly what they said. They went to the world and became rock stars!

## 9-1-1 Emergency Help Cry #7
## Powerful But Overlooked By the Media!

Several preachers have become disillusioned because the media has been unfair.

A terrible scandal happened at a very prestigious ministry whereas a preacher was found guilty of several alleged charges. The media showed up in full force and several television talk shows joined in to cover this scandal. However, the media painted a one sided picture making it seem all preachers are crooks and hypocrites from this one ordeal.

Needless to say, in the very same community where the scandal happened, there were several churches and ministries in the same neighborhood who've made a wonderful difference in that city and the lives of people. Not only this, but this same community has many sincere pastors and leaders who walk in outstanding character and integrity.

However, when the media was called upon to do a cover story on these, there always seemed to be an excuse why they couldn't come. Thus, a very lop-sided view of the Church has been painted and many wonderful and noteworthy things that the Lord is doing among His people continually goes unnoticed by an unbelieving world.

## 9-1-1 Emergency Help Cry #8
### No Insurance!

An elderly pastor has been preaching well over 50 years. Known for his dedication and hard work down through the years he has gained the respect of many. However, due to his advanced age, this precious minister health fails and dies. Serving a very small congregation, he could not afford health or life insurance.

Therefore, his bereaved wife and family have been left behind with huge funeral expenses and no means of continuing financial support. After 30 days, they have to leave the parsonage because of the new minister's arrival. Because of the lack of insurance and improper financial planning, this family now faces one of the greatest struggles of their lives.

## 9-1-1 Emergency Help Cry #9
### Drag Racing With the Church Down the Street!

A pastor becomes frustrated because his church is located just two blocks from a very large, thriving and popular mega ministry. Fearful of losing members, the minister begins to place his congregation under undue pressure hoping to keep up with the church down the street.

Soon, the sermons on Sunday mornings are no longer relative to the specific needs of their local congregation. Instead, they focus and try to imitate the catchy and attractive ministry style of the big neighboring church down the street.

As a result, the members have trouble relating and are becoming discouraged. Parishioners are starting to leave. Strangely, the congregation has grown smaller than what it's ever been and members leave for the big church down the street anyway!

## 9-1-1 Emergency Help Cry #10
### The Preacher With the Iron Fist!

A well meaning preacher starts his/her ministry off on the right foot with a brand new congregation with a sincere humble beginning. After a period of time, this preacher's ministry becomes overwhelmingly successful and popular. He/she starts to feel that the sound doctrine principles that are responsible for the tremendous growth of the ministry are no longer needed as the ministry no longer has to want for anything due to financial success. Not only this, he/she becomes very controlling and rules the congregation with an iron fist.

By and by, the focus is no longer on Jesus Christ but the minister. Consequently, the congregation is slowly hurled into false doctrine. Members are separated from their own families and total allegiance is required to that minister and ministry alone. Anything less than this is considered blatant disobedience punishable by the laws of that ministry.

Sadly, over a period of time the minister falls and the people fall with him/her leaving only a small remnant of people behind. Those left are now devastated, confused and want absolutely nothing to ever do with God or anybody's church again!

## 9-1-1 Emergency Help Cry #11
### Intimidated By Joshua!

Like Moses and Joshua in the Bible, an outstanding senior pastor has several associate ministers under his/her leadership.

A few years ago, he/she trusted one of them as his/her own spiritual son/daughter. However, this trusted associate minister later splits the church taking several members and started a new ministry. Hurt, the senior pastor is now skeptical about entrusting any associate ministers or secondary leadership with too much responsibility.

Afraid of losing more members, this pastor doesn't allow even those associate ministers who have proven submitted, credible, and trustworthy to utilize their gifts and abilities in the ministry. Even after having the proper ministerial training and character this pastor will not allow them to share the load. He/she has to be in charge of everything that happens in the church.

As a result, many associates feel useless, suppressed, stifled and eventually leave the ministry. So what happens? Associate ministers begin to leave the church again. Once more, this senior pastor feels betrayed, hurt, angry, and stands in the need of counseling.

## 9-1-1 Emergency Help Cry #12
### Anointed But Caught In Sex Traps!

A very sincere, anointed and well meaning preacher does several revivals, crusades, and meetings. This minister is so powerful that many people have been saved, delivered, healed and set free. However, when such meetings are over the minister encounters deep personal struggles. He/she struggles with pornography, sexual fantasies, masturbation and is sexually tormented.

Often spending many hours on the internet, from time to time this minister reluctantly slips out of town having sexual affairs with prostitutes, escorts and other one night stands. To add to the struggle, this minister has become so close with some of the members of his/her ministry staff that secret sexual episodes have occurred with them also.

This minister is really sincere and has a legitimate calling of God to preach the Gospel and help others! However, realizing how far he/she has fallen of course has becoming very discouraging to this preacher. He or she wants to stop but can't seem to find the brakes or the stop button. Unable to break the stronghold of sexual addictions, this preacher plunges into utter frustration, depression and discouragement.

Too embarrassed and afraid to tell anyone what's going on this preacher eventually backslides and decides to give up the ministry altogether.

## 91-1 Emergency Help Cry #13
### No First Lady!

A preacher preaches so well that he brings the house down every time he opens his mouth. However, in the privacy of his home he mistreats his wife. Not only this, his romantic life with her is practically non existent. Although a great preacher, he's a poor father and doesn't spend any time with the children.

The congregation wonders why she doesn't support the ministry or attends any of the tea parties with the other pastor's wives. The gossip committee has taken its place and the congregation has made many speculations concerning her. However, little do they know that she's a battered woman in pain.

## 9-1-1 Emergency Help Cry #14
## The First Lady Who Tore Up the Church!

A dynamic bishop has successfully led a thriving congregation that has impacted the community for years. However, people are beginning to leave this ministry in droves. Why? There are issues with the first lady. The bishop's wife!

This first lady has been with her husband since the beginning of the ministry. Thus, she's seen a lot. She's seen the ups and downs. People coming and going. She's also seen first-hand betrayal whereas it has touched her own marriage, life, and family.

Because of her own fears and insecurities, instead of allowing her husband to take the leadership role as pastor, she often undermines his authority or rearranges the flock. And if anyone appears to be getting too close to the pastor, immediately she steps in to make sure that such ties soon fizzle out.

Thus, what really is a great church has now become a place of confusion. Therefore, people leave. While this first lady really loves the Lord, her husband and even the church, the unsettled issues in her heart causes her to drive the flock away. Meanwhile, the husband never takes time off to properly address the issue and make sure that his family, the $1^{st}$ family of the ministry receives proper counseling and healing.

## 9-1-1 Emergency Help Cry #15
## The Ecumenical Mafia!

A very diligent and gifted preacher serves as a part of a very large and popular denomination. This preacher is sincere, honest, faithful, and works very hard. As a result of his/her labor this preacher has gained national recognition and notoriety. However, some of his/her fellow colleagues are intimidated by such success and sees this rapidly advancing minister as a threat.

Thus, like the Mafia, they begin to put hits out on this minister! How do they do this? Whenever, this preacher's name is suggested to serve in some prestigious leadership role, the ecumenical mafia knocks it down. Boom! Each time they come up with reasons why this preacher shouldn't serve.

Through ecumenical and manipulative politics, they eventually find a way to demote this preacher to a lower position they can both handle and control. Like Judas in the Bible, this preacher feels betrayed at the very hands of those trusted most. Why? He/she was taken out by the Ecumenical Mafia!

Wow!

## Moving Forward!

My brothers and sisters! You have now heard the cries of many clergy throughout the world. It's now time to move forward. The torch has now been passed. What shall we do? What is our pleasure?

Let the healing begin!

## CHAPTER TWO

# THE MINISTERIAL QUESTIONNAIRE
## *"Keeping It Real!"*

*"This poor man cried,
and the LORD heard him,
and saved him out of all his troubles."
Psalm 34: 6 KJV*

*"Hey! It's safe to take our mask off now.
Our relief has come!"*

Hallelujah! God is a deliver! And not only this, He's well able!

**IN THIS CHAPTER, WE WILL UTILIZE** the Ministerial Questionnaire. You have just heard the cries and experiences many clergy face around the world. Now it's time to move to the next step. And what's this? Very simply, <u>keeping it real</u>!

When we talk about keeping something real what we mean is simply being candid and honest. It means being without pretense. And rejoice! This is not a gruesome task.

We rejoice because regardless what we face in our lives and ministries, we're not alone! God never leaves us to face things by ourselves. Therefore, as we confront any issues in our lives we can do so in confidence. Why? God never leaves us to face things as a solo project.

And because we don't have to face difficult times by ourselves, we can have peace. We simply need only to reach out to Him. He's with us in the midst of any and every storm. Thank God!

The Scripture says it like this.

"......For He Himself has said,
"**<u>I will never leave you nor forsake you</u>**."
So we may boldly say:
"**<u>The LORD is my helper</u>**;
I will not fear. What can man do to me?"
*Hebrews 13: 5c-6. NKJV*

And here's one that always brings us great joy, encouragement and comfort.

"Casting all your care upon Him,
**<u>for He cares for you</u>**."
*I Peter 5:7 NKJV*

Yes! Preacher, He cares! Oh yes He does!

And you know what? No matter how long the duration of the trial, you can't give up now. Why? Because it's too soon to quit!

The late Joseph Price, founder of the historic Livingstone College, Salisbury, North Carolina said it this way.

*"It matters not how dark the night,
I believe in the coming of the morning!"*

Preacher, **MORNING IS COMING!**

You can make it through the night!

Rejoice! Hallelujah!

Yes indeed!

**How To Use the
Ministerial Questionnaire**

Now let's get down to business.

The Ministerial Questionnaire will ask us questions <u>that only we as clergy can answer</u>. These questions cover several important categories of our lives and ministries that have the power to make or break us. These questions are totally confidential and are to be answered by you for your private and personal use only for assessment purposes. The categories covered include questions concerning our ministries, personal lives, the people we serve, health concerns, our marital status, family, finances and sexuality. Remember, these are for location purposes only.

When the questionnaire is completed, we won't address any of the answers here. We will discuss such themes along with the previous *9-1-1 Emergency Help Cries* in the forthcoming chapters of this book. Once we can honestly assess and locate where we are in life and ministry, we can move from location to victory. We will know exactly where to begin.

A Gentle Reminder and Word of Caution
(Disclaimer)

However, once again I want to remind you what I said in the Foreword. Please remember, <u>I cannot in any way counsel you</u>. The ministerial questions are solely for your own personal perusal, reflection, growth and development.

Remember, the goal of these questions <u>are only to stimulate positive discussion</u> that will lead to health, healing and wholeness in ministry. They are for your own personal consideration. <u>Your answers to these questions are strictly confidential</u> and need not be reported to me or Dynasty Publishers. In the event you should need help in any of these areas, <u>please contact the proper professional assistance available in your area</u>.

Thank you so much for your thoughtful consideration. Now let's get down to the nitty gritty!

**Golden Nuggets of Victory!**

Before we begin, here are 3 Golden Nuggets of hope and wisdom to strengthen us along the way.

## <u>Steps to Healing and Victory</u>:

### <u>Honesty With Self</u>
(Not being afraid to face our issues in the strength of Christ!)

### <u>Honesty With God</u>
(He loves us <u>unconditionally</u>!)

### <u>Honesty With Others</u>
(Getting the help we need in time!)

Now the Questions!

## <u>Ministerial Questions</u>

I. <u>Your Personal Life and Ministry</u>

    A. <u>You, the Minister</u>!

## 1. YOUR MINISTRY

- Are you convinced that God called you to preach the Gospel of Jesus Christ?
- How do you know?
- How long have you been in ministry?
- Are you licensed? Legally? Are you ordained? If so, by what affiliation?
- Are you affiliated with a denomination or particular organization? Independent?
- Are such affiliations important to you? Why or why not?
- Why are you in ministry? Are you certain preaching is the specific area of service to which you are called? How do you know?
- Are you happy? As a minister? In your personal life?
- Are you excited and optimistic about your calling in life and ministry?
- How do you feel your ministry will assist the fulfillment of the Great Commission of Christ found in Matthew 28: 19-20?
- Where do you see yourself in ministry 5 years from now? 10 years?

## 2. LIFE OUTSIDE THE PULPIT

- What is your life like outside the pulpit?
- How are you when you're not serving? (Via preaching, teaching, counseling, helping) How are you when there is no audience? How are you when alone? When no one's watching? What do you do? Who do you hang out with? What are your deepest thoughts? Concerns? Fears? Anxieties? What do you do for entertainment?
- Do you take time out for relaxation? Renewal? Do you take time out for you?
- When was your last vacation? Did you preach while vacationing? Do you take time to laugh? Smell the roses?
- Are you able to balance the challenges between ministry and your personal life?
- Do you respond to every need and call for your services? Do you ever take on too much at a time? Do you have difficulty saying "no" without feeling guilty?
- Do you delegate assignments when necessary?
- How do you handle difficulty and challenges? Do you see yourself as a winner? An overcomer? Are you optimistic?

### 3. CONCERNING HIGHER EDUCATION

- 
- How do you feel about higher education? Is it important to you? Why or why not?
- Do you feel preachers need to go to school? Why or why not?
- What about seminary? Is it important to you? Did you go to seminary? Plan on going? Graduated? If not, do you plan to finish?
- Do you think a person can be used by God without a seminary degree? With one? Why or why not?
- If you didn't go to seminary, do you feel intimidated by those who have?
- If you did go to seminary, do you feel that those who haven't are belittle to you?
- Seminary or not, are you confident in your ministry?

## B. THE PEOPLE YOU SERVE!

### 1. WHO ARE THEY?

- Who are the people you serve? Are you happy working with them?
- Are they happy working with you and under your leadership?
- Where are they located? Do you live in the same city/town or nearby? Is getting to the site of your ministry easily accessible? Is it a strain?
- Is there an established vision or goal with people you serve? Are you excited about it? Are they? Do you have the necessary resources for such to become a reality?
- What's the general age group in your ministry? All adults? Children? Seniors? Middle aged? Teens? A mixture? More one group than another? Which?
- Are you happy with the generations present in your ministry? If only one age group present are there plans toward reaching the missing?
- What's the culture of the area where you serve? Most people have the same mind set? Diverse? Rural? Urban?
- What style of worship are your people most comfortable with? Traditional? Contemporary? A mixture?
- What worship style are you most comfortable with? If there's dissatisfaction in the pews with your ministry style, how do

you handle such?
- Does it make you feel pressured to go into the unfamiliar?

## 2. YOUR STAFF AND ACCOUNTABILITY

- Did you start your own ministry? Were you assigned? Was it inherited?
- What about your potential tenure there? How long do you think you'll be there? Indefinitely? Not long? Until retirement? Are you itinerant?
- Are you accountable to anyone as a pastor/leader/minister?
- Should you get in a jam doing ministry, is there someone in higher authority who can assist you?
- Is there someone credible in your life who can pour strength positively back into you should you become depleted while serving others?
- If there is someone to whom you're accountable to, are you willing to receive rebuke, correction and guidance from them providing its healthy, sound, and in line with sound doctrine teaching from God's Word?
- What about your staff? Do you work alone or do you have a support staff?
- Do you delegate assignments to them?
- Are they cooperative?
- Do you trust people? Have you ever been burnt by someone you trusted in ministry? If so, how do you deal with such?
- Has it made you bitter? If so, are you able to move on positively? Do you still hold resentment? Has it affected the way you minister?
- 

## 3. WHAT'S YOUR MINISTRY STYLE?

- Are you easy to work with as a pastor/minister/leader?
- How do you handle the business of your ministry? How would you rank yourself as an administrator? Excellent? Good? Fair? Poor? Need further help, training or assistance?
- What's your leadership style in terms of managing people? Is it healthy? Unhealthy? Are you loving? Firm? Bossy? Authoritative? Passive? Demanding? Controlling? Affirmative? Compromising? A mixture? Balanced?

- Understanding? Easy to follow?
- Do you use profanity? If so, why? How do you think it helps your Christian witness? As a pastor/minister/leader? Does your staff use profanity? Do you think they get it or feel comfortable with such from you?
- Do you have any personal insecurities about ministry? Why? How? Or why not?
- When the people you serve do well, do you compliment them? If they don't do well, how do you handle such?
- Within your congregation or the people you serve are you developing future leaders? People who can work well in your absence? Are the sheep totally dependent on you?
- Should for some reason you are no longer able to serve your congregation, how will that ministry survive? Can the sheep stand on their own 2 feet without your presence or assistance?
- Are you skeptical about passing the torch of leadership? Why or why not?

## 4. INTER- RELATIONSHIPS WITH THE PEOPLE YOU SERVE

- How close are you to the people you serve?
- What kind of relationship do you have with them? Professional only? Business? Casual? A mixture? Dependent? Co-dependent?
- Do you get involved with them personally? To what degree?
- Would you consider your relationship with your parishioners healthy? Unhealthy?
- Do you have boundaries established between you and they? If so what are they?
- Do they work on your nerves? Do you work on theirs?
- Have you ever been sexually attracted to a staff member of your ministry or congregation? If so, how did you handle such?
- Has any member of your congregation been attracted to you?
- Either way, have you yielded to such an attraction? If so, what was the outcome? How do you handle the grief and aftermath that often comes with such cases?
- Has professional counseling been sought or needed? For you? For the person involved? Has it become a legal matter? Will you continue to minister?

## II. Concerning Your Health!

### A. Your Physical Health

#### 1. ARE YOU TAKING CARE OF YOUR PHYSICAL BODY?

- How's your physical health?
- Are you taking good care of your physical body?
- Do you get regular check ups? Do you have a personal physician?
- Do you have any known physical conditions? Are you being treated for such? Are you under a doctor's care?
- Do you believe in medical doctors? Do you believe in divine healing? Does visiting a doctor violate your personal beliefs? Does divine healing mean God can't use doctors?
- Do you have health insurance? Life insurance? Can you afford such?
- Does your congregation help you to obtain such? Or is it supplied by your own personal means?
- Do you work a second job outside ministry? If so, is it taxing on your body?
- Have you been able to find balance?
- Are you overweight? Do you exercise?
- Do you get adequate rest?
- What is your average time of going to bed each night? How much sleep do you get nightly? Is it enough? Do you sleep comfortably?
- Are you eating right? Do you eat the right stuff in the right proportions?
- Are you thinking about starting a fitness program? Have you consulted with your physician?
- Do you feel you're beyond the age of starting an exercise and fitness program? Why or why not?

### B. YOUR MENTAL AND EMOTIONAL HEALTH

#### HANDLING STRESS AND OTHER CHALLENGES!

- How is your mental and emotional health?
- How do you deal with pressure? Let downs? Disappointments? Grievances? Anger? Betrayal? Stress in general?
- Do you have a place to vent? Do you have a good buddy or

friend? A confidant? A hang out partner? Or do you walk alone?
- If there is someone, do they add or subtract from your life? Does your affiliation with them make you better? Worse?
- Is there any unforgiveness in your life?
- Are you bitter about anything? Do you find yourself not giving your all towards people due to some past hurt or let down?
- Are you afraid to trust people? Are you afraid of new relationships?
- Besides your public image (our positions and what others perceive and think about us in such light) do you like what you see? Do you like you?

## C. YOUR SPIRITUAL HEALTH, BELIEFS AND THEOLOGY
### 1. BELIEFS ABOUT GOD AND PERSONAL DEVOTIONS

- What are your beliefs about God and Jesus Christ? What's your world view? What do you believe? Is it sound doctrine? Is it in line with God's Word?
- Do you believe the Bible is God's Word and final authority?
- How is your prayer life? Do you set aside quiet time for prayer, Bible study and one on one time with the Lord? Do you fast?
- Is it a priority? Are you consistent?
- When do you seek the Lord? For sermons only and when time to preach or to strengthen your one on one personal relationship with Him? Both?
- Which takes priority? Preaching or Praying? Your works for the Kingdom or your personal relationship with God? Why?
- What are you feeding your spirit? Are you integrating your spirit with religious teachings and other spiritual concepts that are not Biblical or Christian?
- Do you practice yoga? Any other forms of meditation? Are they Biblical? Does it matter to you?
- Are you worldly? Do you indulge in worldly practices and pop trends that don't uphold godly values? What kind of music do you listen to?

### 2. Fellowship with Other Believers and Ministerial Preparation

- Do you fellowship regularly with other Christian believers? Or are you a spiritual loner? Do you isolate yourself? Why or why not? If so, do you think it's a healthy practice?
- Are you allowing other Christian believers to pour strength and encouragement back into you?
- What about preparing for the worship experience? As a preacher, when do you start preparing your sermons for the worship? Months in advance? Weeks? Days? The night before? The morning of? Do you speak extemporaneously? On the spot?
- Do you write your sermons? Do you think it's necessary? Why or why not?
- Are your messages relative? Are they easy to understand? How well do you know your listening audience? Are they inter-generational?
- Are you feeding the people who hear you fresh bread or left overs? If left overs is it because you're finishing up a series? Don't have enough time to study?
- Do you live what you preach and tell others? Do you believe what you preach? Do you preach to impress others? Colleagues? Friends? God?
- Which is more important to you as a minister? Becoming famous? Being respected by colleagues and peers? Becoming a house hold name? Being in right standing with God? Or a mixture?
- When serving or doing ministry in general, do you give all your strength away?

## III. YOUR FAMILY LIFE!

### SINGLE, MARRIED, WIDOWED, DIVORCED AND CHILDREN!

- How's your family life?
- Are you single? Married? Widowed? Divorced? Separated? Whatever your status, are you happy?
- If married, is all well? Should you come to bumps in the road in your marriage, how do you handle such? Is your wife/husband supportive of your being in ministry? Does he or she see the church and ministry as the *"other"* woman or man?
- If married which comes first, marriage or ministry?

- If single, divorced, widowed or separated, how do you deal with being alone?
- Do you desire to marry, marry again or be reunited? Are you happy being single? Why or why not?
- If you've never been married, how do you deal with loneliness? Do you desire companionship? How do you handle such moments?
- Do you find being single and a minister hard? Why or why not?
- Do you have any children? How are they? How do they feel about church? Do they like or dislike it? How do they feel about you being in ministry?

## IV. YOUR FINANCIAL HEALTH!

### 1. YOUR PERSONAL FINANCES

- How is your personal financial situation? How's your money? Is it well? Are you struggling? Are you in debt?
- Are you in full time ministry? Have additional employment?
- What's your annual salary? Are you happy with such? If not, what plans do you have in place to bring improvement?
- Do you pay taxes? Are you current? Behind? If so, what are your plans to correct the situation?
- Do you have credit cards? Are they maxed out?
- Speaking of credit, what's your score? Your FICA score?
- If you are in debt, what's your plan for recovery? Do you have one? Why or why not? Do you have a savings account? Checking? Is anything in it? IRA's? Stocks? Bonds? CD's? Do you have a 401K? Any other investments?
- Do you rent or own a home? Do you have a car? Are you still paying on it? Is it paid for? If you do own personal property, are they properly insured?

### 2. YOUR FINANCIAL PLANS FOR THE UNEXPECTED

- Are you financially covered should the unexpected show up? Do you have a sure financial plan for a rainy day?
- Do you have emergency monies? A financial emergency plan?
- Do you have all the necessary insurances and coverage needed should something happen to you? Can you afford such?

- Do you have a retirement or annuity plan after ministry?
- Is your spouse and family covered?
- God forbid, but if something happened to you and you survived but couldn't preach anymore, how would you and your family survive financially?
- If your church/ministry couldn't pay you for some reason, how would you survive?  How would you make ends meet?
- Do you have a will?  Where is it located?  Do your loved ones know your plans should your demise and know how to access such?
- What about your church?  Should your demise will your congregation be at a loss or do they have clear directions on keeping that ministry on its feet?
- Are your children properly covered?

### 3. YOUR CHURCH BUDGET AND COMPENSATION

- Does your church have a budget?
- Does it operate by that budget?  Is the budget realistic? Practical?
- Are the people integral?  Are you?
- Who handles the money in your church?  You?  Specific officers?  Members at large?  Who are the persons that handle money accountable to?
- Are your church financial books in order?  Are they IRS compliant?
- Do you have a certified public accountant? Do you need one? Why or why not?
- Are you a full time minister?  Do you have other employment?
- How are you compensated for by your ministry?  What and how's your salary?  Do you get benefits?  Housing? Insurance? Travel? Education? Other benefits?
- Have you ever received a raise?  Feel entitled to one?  Is your ministry financially able to do so if desired?
- Are you a tither?  Do you believe that tithing is for today?  Is your congregation a tithing one?  Why or why not?
- Does your church/ministry have the proper insurance coverage needed should an emergency or situation requiring such arises?

## V. YOUR SEXUALITY!

### 1. YOUR PERSONAL VIEWS

- What are your views on sexuality? Are they governed by the Word of God or have you determined your own views?
- How important is walking in sexual integrity and purity to you? Very important? Important? Little importance? Not at all?
- How does your sexuality and views affect your ministry? The people you serve? Your Christian witness?
- If not married do you practice abstinence? Is it difficult? Walking in victory? A struggle?

### 2. Marriage, Romance and Sexuality

- If married are you faithful to your spouse? Why or why not? If there are problems, are you seeking professional counseling? Is your spouse open to counseling?
- How is the communication between you and your spouse? Excellent? Good? Fair? Room for improvement? Poor?
- If poor, are there unresolved issues that contribute to such? If so, how are they being handled? Need help?
- If married do you spend quality time with your spouse laying aside the duties of the ministry? Do you take time to minister to your spouse in romance or are you too busy?
- Do you take time to make sure your spouse is happy at home? Satisfied?
- Is this a priority? Are you committed to this? Why or why not?

### 3. Risky Sexual Enticements

- Married or single, do you ever find yourself attracted to any of the people you serve? If so, how do you handle such? Do you think such attraction is wise? What about someone outside your ministry?
- Do you struggle with pornography in any of it's forms? Do you periodically sneak out to hot spots like strip clubs and other places to fulfill secret fantasies and frustrations that may torment you? Do you secretly surf the internet? Met with someone off the internet? Are you flirtatious?

- Do you have any sexual addictions? If so, how do you deal with such? If fallen prey to any, how do you deal with such? Do you feel discouraged or guilty? Cover it up and preach over it? Find yourself extremely critical in your ministry against people that are doing what you're secretly struggling with?
- If fallen, do you get depressed? Abandon ministry altogether? Confess, repent, get counseling and keep moving forward? None of the above?
- Do you believe that there is hope for ministers who are sexual offenders? Should they continue in ministry? Why or why not?
- What about a minister who's just having the normal human struggle with the appetites of the flesh? Should they continue in ministry?
- Do you believe in deliverance? Do you believe God can set any captive free? Should such persons who've received deliverance be readily trusted?
- Do you think society is always fair concerning ministers who have fallen in these areas? What about the church? What positive solutions can you think of concerning such matters?

Wow!

**Bringing It Altogether!**

What a questionnaire! Whoooo! We've got a lot to both think and talk about. This is so good! Why? Because we're locating where we are! Now we know where to apply the healing balm.

Having completed Chapters 1 and 2, we are now ready for discussion!

# SECTION II

# DISCUSSION

# "Where Do We Go From Here?"

## CHAPTER THREE

# TAKING OFF OUR MASK!
## *"The Power of Talking!"*

"Confess your faults one to another, and pray one for another that ye may be healed. The effectual fervent prayer of a righteous man (person) availeth much."
*James 5:16 KJV*

## No More Masquerades!

Wow! Now that we've completed Chapters 1 and 2, we can begin our discussion to healing and victory.

In this chapter, we're going to talk about how to position ourselves for the help or breakthrough we may need. The *9-1-1 Emergency Help Cries* in Chapter One are very real! The Ministerial Questionnaire helped us to particularly locate where we are as individuals. Now it's time to propagate the healing, health, restoration and wholeness we may need in our lives and ministries. And how shall we do this? By keeping it real! In other words, it's time to take off our mask. In other words, no more masquerades!

### What's A Mask?

<u>Mr. Webster</u> defines the word *mask* this way.
 1. *A covering to conceal or protect the face.*
 2. *Anything that conceals or disguises.*

In the same way, a mask is anything we may use to cover or hide what's really going on with us. It could be our positions, titles, gifts, accolades, accomplishments or any behavior or persona we project to others to hide or blanket our pain, fears or insecurities.

And you know what preachers? Many times we wear mask. And what's really funny is often when we all get together in conventions, conferences, meetings and such we have masquerade parties! A masquerade is a gathering or party where costumes or fancy mask are worn. It's when we act under false pretenses. Oh! This is going to be good!

Let me further explain.

## The Public and Private Selves
*Dr. Jekyll vs. Mr. Hyde!*

As a kid growing up I remember a cartoon called Dr. Jekyll and Mr. Hyde. Do you? (We're telling our age! Huh! I'll always be 25. Even next year this time!) Nevertheless, this story was about one man who had two completely different personalities. The personality that was most dominant would be determined and triggered by whatever altering circumstance that provoked such.

During my undergraduate studies, I took a course in criminology. And how I loved it! This was one of my most favorite classes! It was one of the most informative classes I've ever taken especially in terms of human behavior.

In this class we studied the psychology behind criminals and investigated potential causes to why people do what they do. This class has helped me tremendously in my ministry particularly as I minister to persons from all walks of life and those involved in street life, gangs and other life styles considered as "at risk" behaviors.

One day in class our professor introduced a concept that talked about the two aspects of a person's character. These are not limited only to criminals but we all have them! They are called the *public and private selves*. Simply revolutionary information! This is gonna bless you real good!

### The Public Self!

The *public self* refers to our outward person and image. It's our positions, careers and titles in life. It's what people see. (i.e.: doctor, lawyer, judge, minister, teacher, politician, church member, professional athlete, gospel artist, hip hop artist, custodian, celebrity, gang leader, dope dealer, etc.) It is what we are, what we do and how we are perceived and interpreted by others.

### The Private Self!

Then there's the *private self*. This part of our character is who we are without our titles, positions, accolades and when no one is watching. It is who we are as a person, plain, naked and simple! It's who we and what we'll do when we're all alone after the stage lights have been turned off and the audience goes home. It's the real us in the raw!

Thus, here's the equation. The public self deals with *what* we are. The private self deals with *who* we are!

*"It's the public self that puts
food on the table
and gets the bills paid!*

*It's generally the mask!"*

Now it's the public self that generally serves as the mask. Why? Because how we are perceived by others and our positions in society puts the food on the table, pays the bills, takes care of our families, and gives us the needed respect among our peers and greater communities. Therefore, the public self fights for dominance because it secures our survival, livelihood, and quality of living.

*"While the public self
fights to maintain survival.
Sometimes the private self
is in secret pain."*

But check this out. Here's where the battle comes in. The Dr. Jekyll vs. Mr. Hyde syndrome!

While the public self is needed to maintain survival, many times the private self is quietly in pain. And guess what? Although wounded, many times the private self will bend over backwards <u>to its own discomfort</u> to make sure the public self doesn't collapse! Why? 2 reasons:

1. Without the public self the private self would go hungry.

2. Some personal issues are so delicate, the private self needs the public self as a cloak to hide its nakedness from the potential scrutiny of the outside world.

And what do we get from this? An anonymous person says it this way.

### *"LEADING WHILE BLEEDING!"*

Wow!

See, here's the struggle. The private self can get away with things the public self could never do! The public self has to be refined, distinguished, having it all together and on top of things.

The private self on the other hand can let it all go! It doesn't have to wear make up for the cover shoot of the latest and hottest magazine out there. It doesn't have to wear a Botany 500 suit for the prestigious job interview. It doesn't even have to comb its hair. Why?

It's private.

Yet without the public self, the private self won't have a roof over its head! So even when the private self is worn to shreds because of some internal struggle or difficulty, if it doesn't muster up enough strength to keep the public self up, the whole building will come tumbling down. The result? A leader whose personal life doesn't seem to match his or her public ideals. Or a leader whose personal ideals matches the public but he or she is wounded in other areas.

So the public self serves as the mask. However, there's something we must never do.

**FOOD FOR THOUGHT:**
*"Whenever we refuse*
*to take off our mask,*
*we set ourselves up for the*
*9-1-1 Emergency Help Cries to become*
*a reality in our lives!"*

## Don't Let Your Pride Kill You!
*Take Off the Mask!*

Listen. Pride is when we value our image more than our own health, families, peace of mind and safety. Let me tell you a story.

When I was a young brother in my late teens or so, I thought I was one of the most handsomest dudes around! Truly a ladies guy. Thought I had it going on like most young teen boys trying to impress the girls. I valued clothes and the way I dressed.

One day I had a brand new shirt that I wanted to wear that was quite fashionable and a serious fit. So I wanted to sport it to school. But here's the problem. It was cold outside and I didn't want to wear a jacket.

So getting ready to walk out the door, my Mom stopped me and told me about my need for a coat. I knew I needed a coat but if I placed one on it would hide the sheekness of my new shirt. I wanted to show my physique. (Yes, I was in the flesh! Huh!) Then my mother made a statement I'll never forget. She said something like,

***"Don't let your pride kill you!"***

Huh! I'll never forget this to this day. How foolish I was thinking as a lad. I'd rather go outside in pneumonia weather with no coat on all in the name of trying to impress the girls! I'd rather risk catching a cold and getting sick just to look good for a few school hours. Does that make sense? No!

So preachers, I say the same thing to you my mother said to me.

*"DON'T LET YOUR PRIDE KILL YOU!"*

GET THE HELP YOU NEED! The Bible says it like this,

> "Pride goes before destruction,
> And a haughty spirit before a fall.
> Better to be of a humble spirit with the lowly,
> Than to divide the spoil (plunder/goods)
> with the proud."
> *Proverbs 16: 18-19 NKJV*

In other words, the recognition or false sense of security that we might gain by trying to look strong for others while we know our lives are in disarray simply ain't worth it!

Preacher, why sacrifice your soul just for a few hot moments in the spotlight? Let's remember the powerful words Jesus said;

"For what profit is it to a man(person) if he( or she)gains the whole world, and loses his (or her) own soul? Or what will a man (person) give in exchange for his (or her) soul?"
*Matthew 16: 26 NKJV*

Let's move to victory brothers and sisters!

### FOOD FOR THOUGHT:
*"When our private self
is in pain,
it's time to take the mask off!
That's a sacrifice
we need not make!"*

## Knowing When To Quit!

In each of our lives we must know when to quit. Here I'm not talking about quitting our relationship with God (Why would we do that?) or even ministry. Rather, I'm talking about <u>knowing when to</u>

stop and get help!

Listen. When our private self (who we really are) is in pain it's time to take the mask off! "Take the thing off Ida Mae!" (Fictitious names) "Take the thing off Sam!" "Don't make me get ghetto up in this piece!" Huh! I'm having a ball here! (Too many movies!)

*"I'm not saying
we should resign
from our careers or positions."*

Take the thing off! Oh! I'm about to fall out my chair!

Nevertheless, on a more serious note don't get me wrong. By no means am I saying we must resign from our careers or positions especially if not necessary. However, there are times when such may be necessary but we must make sure we have the wisdom to know the difference. Nevertheless, there may be times we may need to take a breather but resignation isn't always the answer! So don't jump to this conclusion hastily.

As a matter of fact, it's the enemy's goal from the get go to shut you up and stop you from preaching the Gospel of Christ! He wants to silence all of us anyway because he knows our obedience to God will put him out of business!

Our obedience to fulfill our callings makes the world a better place to live!

"You are the salt of the earth; but if the salt loses its flavor,
how shall it be seasoned? It is then good for nothing but to be thrown out
and trampled underfoot by men."
*Matthew 5:13 NKJV*

Listen. With all our imperfections and shortcomings, we bring flavor, seasoning, healing, preservation and taste to a world often void of such elements. WE'RE SALT!

Awesome! Do you know who you are?

Thus, because of our potential the enemy is angry and wants to shut us down!

> "And the dragon was enraged with the woman,
> and he went to make war with the rest of her offspring,
> who keep the commandments of God
> and have the testimony of Jesus Christ."
> *Revelation 12: 17 NKJV*

Therefore, Preachers we must understand we have one of the most important jobs in the universe! People won't know if we don't show! Our obedience or lack of it will affect souls for eternity!

> "How then shall they call on Him in whom they have not believed?
> And how shall they believe on Him of whom they have not heard?
> And how shall they hear <u>WITHOUT A PREACHER</u>?
>
> And how shall they preach unless they are sent?
> As it is written:
>
> "How beautiful are the feet of those
> who preach the gospel of peace,
> Who bring glad tidings of good things!"
> *Romans 10: 14-15. NKJV*

Wow! Reverend, don't stop preaching!

Nevertheless, should it ever become <u>ABSOLUTELY NECESSARY</u> that we must resign from our positions to get better, then we've got to do what we've got to do! But this is a last resort and often in extreme cases. This is why I'm writing this book. <u>PREVENTION</u>! I'm hoping to share some practical things with you so we'll never get to this point. And if you have, IT'S NOT OVER! So keep looking up!

So don't go out there and say I told you to get out the pulpit! Huh! Understand what I'm saying! We want to make sure we <u>fulfill</u> our ministries to the glory of God!

Yet realistically, sometimes we do need to take a seat. If so, we can always seek restoration. If this is the case, let's do just that. Get restored! Get back up! But let's not get back up making the same mistakes over and over again. Let's not continue to be repeat offenders! After all, what's more important? Having a title or having our life together?

Speaking to the church of Sardis in the book of Revelation, Jesus said it like this,

*"These things says He who has the seven Spirits of God and the seven stars: "I know your works, that you have a name that you are alive, but you are dead. Be watchful, and strengthen the things which remain, that are ready to die, for I have not found your works perfect before God. Remember therefore how you have received and heard: hold fast and repent. Therefore if you will not watch, I will come upon you as a thief, and you will not know what hour I will come upon you."*
*Revelation 3: 1-3. NKJV*

If our public images, careers and what people think about us is keeping us from getting the help, assistance and breakthrough needed we're skating on thin ice. We're sitting in a very dangerous spot.

So think about it. What's really most important to you? Trying to be all that and a bag of chips but drowning or getting the help and deliverance we need so we can truly enjoy the chips?

Listen. God wants us to enjoy the chips.

Baked of course! Huh!

### FOOD FOR THOUGHT:
*"The anointing is not who we are,*
*that's what we have.*
*Our callings aren't who we are,*
*that's what we do.*
*Behind all our gifts and holy regalia*
*we're still human beings."*

**Mask Are Never Healthy!**

The truth of the matter is mask aren't healthy from the beginning. God never intended that we should cover up the beauty of what He has created.

Mask aren't healthy because they block the sun from shining where we need it most. They keep light from getting in and air from getting out. Thus, we grow stale. They keep us in dungeons of gloom and heaviness while trying to carry on the work of ministry. Whenever we refuse to take off our mask, we set ourselves up for the *9-1-1 Emergency Help Cries* to become a reality in our lives.

My fellow clergy, this is not God's will for us! Jesus has already paid the price for our victory so WE DON'T HAVE TO BE SLAVES ANYMORE TO ANY BONDAGE! And not only bondage, but also we can have victory via all life's ever challenging circumstances.

Christ said it like this,

> "The Spirit of the LORD is upon Me,
> Because He has anointed Me
> To preach the gospel to the poor; brokenhearted,
> To proclaim liberty to the captives
> And recovery of sight to the blind,
> To set at liberty those who are oppressed;
> To proclaim the acceptable year of the LORD."
> And He began to say to them,
> "Today this Scripture is <u>FULFILLED</u> in your hearing."
> *Luke 4: 18-19,21. NKJV*

Yes indeed!

Claim Your Victory Today!

Because of what Christ has done for us, our exit papers have been signed and we can claim our victory!

Notice I highlighted the word, *"fulfilled."* Preacher's this means <u>it's already done</u>. This means our stuff has been paid for and our warfare accomplished! Whatever we need to be successful in both life and ministry has already been provided by Christ! We've just got to claim it!

So rejoice! Go ahead and get your praise on! You're about to get both your life and ministry back! Celebrate! Dance my brother! Dance my sister!

Why dance? Here's why!

> "Therefore if the Son makes you free, you shall be free indeed!"
> *John 8:36 NKJV*

Yes! Hallelujah! I feel my shout coming on! Brothers and Sisters, WE'RE ALREADY FREE! We just have to reach for it!

Anybody got an organ and some drums out there? A tambourine? A guitar? I feel a praise swelling up in my soul!

Christ has made us free! Yes! But here's a serious question.

..............Then why do we still struggle???

**We Get Rid of Our Mask
By the Power of Talking!**

Reverend, It's Time to Talk!

Now here's how we get to the next level in our breakthrough. Talking!

If we have truly been made free by Christ, then why do we still struggle? There may be several reasons. But remember, the presence of problems and challenges doesn't mean we haven't been liberated by Christ. No! When we truly decide to follow Christ in Christian discipleship there will be some bumps in the road. Indeed, some of these can certainly be avoided but there will be bumps!

Christ said it like this,

"These things have I spoken to you, that in Me you may have peace.

In the world <u>you will have tribulation</u>; but be of <u>good cheer</u>,<br>
<u>I have overcome the world</u>."<br>
John 16:33 NKJV

Yes! And because Christ overcame, we are overcomers too!

"Talking is the means<br>
by which we remove our mask!"

So the problem with liberation is not the Cross. However, one of the main reasons I feel we struggle and many times needlessly is because of the lack of communication. We don't talk! If we embrace this concept, I believe it will help tremendously to cause things in our lives and ministries to fall into better perspective.

So Preachers it's time to talk. And I don't mean constructing a sermon! We do that well. Rather, I mean simply communicating what's going on with us. Talking is the means by which we remove our mask!

While some things that happen to us are circumstantial, many can be avoided if we just open up and lay it on the table. However, we must be 110% willing and honest. We must be willing to come clean concerning what's going on with us both within and outside the pulpit. Remember, experience is good but prevention is better!

## A LESSON FROM THE PENTECOSTALS!

Let me share something with you that will bless you.

I'm a Methodist pastor but I've had much experience and exposure in the Pentecostal - Holiness church. Growing up as a boy, most of my family were Methodist. (African Methodist Episcopal) However, segments of my family were also Pentecostal so I got exposed to both! I feel the fire burning right now! Huh! Ain't nothing like it!

Nevertheless, pertaining to our discussion there's a powerful lesson I learned from the Pentecostals that has revolutionized my life and provoked me to health, healing and wholeness down through the years.

I remember years ago visiting a Pentecostal church standing at the altar praying for a breakthrough. I really wanted to be free from some things that were nagging me. Afterwards, the pastor's wife came over to me and said something I'll never forget. She said,

*"If you want to get rid of the devil, "TELL ON HIM!"*

Oh! I'll never forget this! "Tell on him!" In other words, cry out and get help!

Little did I know the wisdom in what she was saying.

The scripture says it like this,

> "He who covers his sins will not prosper.
> But whoever confesses and forsakes them will have mercy."
> *Proverbs 28: 13*

Sure enough!

Thanks Sis. Wright! It works!

People that keep stuff bottled up inside will soon explode!

## The Devil is Like A Roach!

See, the enemy of our souls is like a roach. Let me explain. Are you ready to laugh again?

Once upon a time I was in a home where I got up out of bed in the wee hours of the morning. Everything was pitch black dark and still. (This is a true story! Get the roach spray ready! RAID!)

*"There were so many roaches
they looked like they were at a party.
The roaches were break dancing!"*

Going to the kitchen, I immediately turned on the lights so I could see. And what did I find? Right there in the middle of the floor were roaches upon roaches all over the kitchen floor! They were everywhere! Big roaches. Small roaches. Roaches that were pregnant! Roaches on the stove. Roaches that could fly! I ain't kidding yall!

Oh! I'm having fun with this!

Don't act like yall don't know nothing about roaches! Especially living in inner cities! Huh! Some of you have had roaches to crawl out your pocketbooks! Huh! Right in the middle of an interview! Yall know! (Somebody please catch me as I fall out my seat!)

And you know what's really funny? Cock roaches! THEY CAN FLY! They'll wait until your company comes and sit on your couch. Then, ZOOOOMMM! Your company screams! Ahhhhh! New movie: *"The Battle of the Flying Roaches!"* Huh!

But I'll never forget it. There were so many roaches in that kitchen it looked like a roach party or festival. The roaches were break dancing! They were having a ball!

But something very peculiar happened that I won't forget. I TURNED ON THE LIGHTS!

Immediately The Roaches
Began to Scatter!

As soon as I turned on the lights, every roach in that room began to scatter and take cover! They were getting out of there fast! Why? BECAUSE LIGHT EXPOSES! Where there is light stuff can be dealt with! Why? BECAUSE WE CAN SEE!

### FOOD FOR THOUGHT:
*"Anything we allow
to fester too long in our hearts
will soon become
contaminated."
"God is light.
And talking is the light switch!"*

Now let's apply this to our situation.

See, God is the light. And talking is the light switch! Light scatters darkness. God provides the inspiration and the resources that we need to be free (already paid for by Christ) and talking places the order in!

"Ask, and it will be given to you;
seek, and you will find;
knock, and it will be opened to you."
For everyone who asks receives,
and he who seeks finds,
and to him who knocks it will be opened."
*Matthew 7: 7-8. NKJV*

Reverend, have you placed in your order?

I John says it like this,

"This is the message which we have heard from Him and declare to you, that <u>God is light and in Him is no darkness at all</u>."
*I John 1:5 NKJV*

And no matter how dark our situation, God has all the light we'll ever need! But we've got to start talking about it!

The late Joseph Price, founder of the historic Livingstone College located in Salisbury, North Carolina said it like this,

*"It matters not how dark the night,
I believe in the coming of the morning!"*

Preacher, again your morning is coming! Let's open up!

Failing to talk will cause stuff to fester in our hearts. Anything that festers too long will soon become contaminated. And what's contaminated in us will eventually affect and spill over into other areas of our lives and everything we touch. Even people and those influenced by our lives!

The familiar saying is true,

*"Wounded shepherds make wounded sheep!"*

Wow! Think about that. We'll talk about this in more detail later.

Reverend, are you wounded?

## Darkness Helps Roaches Maneuver Undetected!

So as long as there's darkness roaches can really thrive. Now don't get me wrong. They'll come out in the daylight too. But they do their best work at night! Night time helps them to better maneuver undetected. In the same way, if we're facing problems in our lives and refuse to properly address them they'll get worse before better.

In the same way, the enemy of our souls is like a roach. He thrives in darkness. This is why he's called, *"The Prince of Darkness."* And if there's darkness in us, the enemy will always have someplace to sit in our lives.

"....Nor give place (an opportunity) to the devil."
*Ephesians 4:27 NKJV*

"The prince of this world cometh and finds nothing in me."
*....NewTestam.*

*"Clergy, have we provided a place for the enemy to sit?"*

So preachers, are we giving the enemy a place to sit in our lives? Are we making him comfortable? Could it be that many of the things we go through are a direct result of the continual compacting of pain, hurts and disappointments we don't talk about? When we're caught in a sticky situation, find ourselves in some "at risk" behavior or in a rut, could it be because we've allowed things to fester so long that what people hear, read, and see on the news is the explosion of such?

Let's turn on the lights so we will be able to see clearly how to properly deal with our stuff, issues AND LIVE!

PREACHER, <u>GOD WANTS YOU TO LIVE</u>! WE NEED YOU! You're priceless to God, us and the world itself! PREACHER, YOU'VE GOT TO LIVE! So don't give up! It's too soon to quit! I don't care how long the battle!

Therefore, in the Name of Jesus Christ of Nazareth, I speak the life of God into you! COME OUT OF THAT GRAVE! COME OUT OF THAT CAVE! COME OUT OF THAT DESPONDENCY AND DEPRESSION! YOU'RE NOT A FAILURE! GOD'S NOT THROUGH BLESSING YOU! <u>LIVE</u>!!!

<u>LIVE MY BROTHER! LIVE MY SISTER! LIVE</u>!!!!!

Be encouraged!

LIVE!

Rejoice!

**Final Keys To Victory!**

Having said all this, let me give you 3 keys to victory.

First, we must be honest with ourselves.

> "If we confess our sins, He is faithful and just
> to forgive our sins and cleanse us from all unrighteousness."
> *I John 1:9 NKJV*

And remember, not only do we need to be honest about our shortcomings but also any situation we may face that may not even have to do with a trespass.

Secondly, we must be honest with God and come to Him in sincerity knowing that His love for us is unconditional. No matter what we're facing in life He won't ever turn us away.

"All that the Father gives Me will come to Me,

and the one who comes to Me I will by no means cast out."
*John 6:37 NKJV*

And thirdly, we must be honest with others in order to get the help we may need in the time we need it! Otherwise, we can wait and wait too late!

God still indeed does miracles in the $21^{st}$ Century but why push the button? Why wait till that point? Is this wise?

Brothers and Sisters, let's be prudent!

## A QUICK REVIEW OF CHAPTER 3!
### "Taking Off Our Mask!"

- Mask are anything we use to conceal what's really going on with us.
- The public self is what we do and our outward image to ourselves and others.
- The private self is who we are and what we do when no one's watching.
- Mask aren't healthy because they block what we need from getting to us.
- We remove our mask by talking and being honest about ourselves and situations.

Finally,
### "WE'RE BETTER TOGETHER!"

"Two are better than one;
because they have a good reward for their labor.
For if they fall, the one will lift up his fellow:
but woe to him that is alone when he falleth;
for he hath not another to help him up."
*Ecclesiastes 4: 9-10.*

And here's one that summarizes everything we've talked about so far.

"Confess your faults one to another,
and pray for one another that ye might be healed.
The effectual fervent prayer
of a righteous man (person) availeth much.
*James 5:16 KJV*

**PREACHERS, LET'S START TALKING!**

**NOTES:**

# CHAPTER FOUR

# ARE YOU WILLING TO GET NAKED?

## *"Why Preachers Don't Talk!"*

> "And they were both naked,
> the man and his wIfe,
> and were not ashamed."
> Genesis 2: 25 NKJV

**IN CHAPTER 3 WE TALKED ABOUT** mask. We discussed how to get rid of them to start the path to breakthrough. Now we are going to plow deeper! We are getting ready to launch out into the deep and catch some big fish! Croaker to be exact! Can't you taste some nice hot juicy croaker fish right now?

Where my Charleston people at? (I know that's broken English. But yall understand? Can't be proper all the time! Huh!) Hot croaker and red rice! With some cold slaw on the side! Oh! Let me stop right now. I don't want to have to put this book down in the name of a juicy fish sandwich! Don't try me now!

Nevertheless, in this chapter we're going to talk about issues of nakedness. In other words we're going to discuss what makes talking uncomfortable for some clergy and even persons of other vocations that places them in the public eye.

From the previous chapter we've learned that talking is the first step towards healing and wholeness. However, many of us don't do it! Having worked ecumenically with so many preachers crossing over denominational lines, you know what I've found out? Our general needs are basically the same! Just different locations and some twist in theological perspectives. But we all breathe air, eat and drink water! Unless you're from Pluto of course! Let me stop! We all desire love and acceptance just like any other human being on the planet.

But nevertheless, when we do talk it won't bring us the victory we need unless we're willing to get totally naked! Totally!

**Preacher Are You Willing
To Strip!**

Now here comes more comedy! I'm really, really going to have fun with this one! And no! I have not backslided! No! Still saved, sanctified and holy. And you know what else? Do speak! Huh! Yall heard me? Do speak! Huh! Hallelujah! I feel peculiar! Oh!

Yall ever been in church where the people emphasize the,

*"Do speak!"*

Your testimony's not complete without it! Please hold my mule! Ain't nothing like church!

Now when I speak of nakedness and stripping, by no means am I talking about taking off our physical clothes! Whaaaaaat??????? No way! Please keep your clothes on at all times. Please! Because if you go to jail I can't get you out. No, not even in Jesus' Name! Ah! Hallelujah!

You'll have to take up an offering for your own freedom and then be on the 6:00news! Then your parishioners are gonna want to know why the extra offering!

We're not talking about taking off our physical clothes! I told yall earlier in this book I come from the AME sanctified Pentecostal Temple of Truth Baptist Presbyterian Lutheran Episcopal Church of God in Christ Non-denominational Moravian United Methodist Institutional Church of the Greater Faith Tabernacle #4 at a location near you! So sanctified folk don't strip! (or at least not supposed to! Huh!)

But can't you hear those old mothers of Zion now,

"Cover up child! Cover up!"

And I agree!

Huh! Those were the days! Cover up! ...... And ladies, don't forget your prayer doily.

If we we're talking about nakedness literally then we could really say *Preachers Have Gone Wild* sure enough! You would need to close this book and run! So I'm not talking about dancing at the pole! Loose here! Call 9-1-1 for real! Somebody needs deliverance! Can't you hear the people now, "Miss. Lucy, the church has really gone to the dogs!"

"I know it's so Sister Earthalene." The gossiping soul responds. "Child, Rev. So and So was at the pole!"

"Mercy no! Girl let me call the Committee now!"

Oh! I am really having fun here!

Nevertheless, more seriously for the record, the Bible says such behaviors are dangerous!

> "Flee sexual immorality. Every sin that a man (person)does
> is outside the body, but he who commits sexual immorality
> sins against his (her) own body.
> Or do you not know that your body is the temple of the Holy Spirit
> who is in you, whom you have from God, and not your own?
>
> For you were bought at a price; (the Cross of Christ)
> therefore glorify God in your body and in your spirit,
> which are God's."
> I Corinthians 6: 18-20. NKJV

## FREE COMMERCIAL!

*"There's no such thing as safe sex.
There's some things contraceptives can't stop.
Why? Sex goes beyond the physical.
It's also a spiritual, emotional and mental experience
whose effects continue long after
the bedroom experience is over!"*

"Stay off the Fornication Committee!" Huh!

Wow! That's a free-bee preview from an upcoming chapter.

Nevertheless, here's the bottom line: Some things are a no -no!

However, when we talk of stripping and nakedness, we're talking about telling the truth without pretense. We're talking about being transparent.

### Nakedness defined:

Let's consider *Webster's* definition of nakedness.

> 1. completely unclothed; nude. 2. without covering
> [a naked sword]
> 3. <u>without additions, disguises, etc.; plain</u>
> <u>[the naked truth]</u>
> 4. unaided by any optical device [the naked eye]

The definition that I like most here is #3. It says to be naked is to be without additions or disguises. In other words, no coverups! It goes back to what we've said before, being honest. Telling the truth boogers and all!

**Nakedness,
An Uncomfortable Issue!**

*"When we're naked
we can't hide anything.
We're seen "as is!"*

Nakedness has always been an uncomfortable issue since the beginning of human history! And because nakedness or becoming transparent is uncomfortable so is talking in many instances.

When we're naked we're in a position where we can't hide anything. Everything's exposed. All our rust, dust, lumps, bumps and other things we dare not mention! When we're naked we're seen *"as is."* All imperfections revealed. No make up, jewelry, or clothes to cover or hide what we don't want people to see or find out about us.

The embarrassment of nakedness came *after* the Fall of Adam and Eve. Prior to the Fall they were both naked and unashamed. They didn't have anything to be ashamed about because they were without sin! No imperfections! Even their physical bodies! No cellulite or love handles! Every detail of their lives was in order! They were in such a wonderful place and had such a communion with God they didn't even know they were naked.

"...And they (Adam and Eve) were both naked, the man and his wife,
<u>and were not ashamed</u>." NKJV
*Genesis 2:25.*

However, after the Fall their perspective and views of their unclothed condition immediately changed.

"The eyes of both of them were opened,
<u>and they knew that they</u> were na<u>ked</u>;
and sewed fig leaves together and made themselves coverings.
And they heard the sound of the LORD God
walking in the garden in the cool of the day,
and Adam and his wife <u>hid themselves from
the presence of the LORD God</u> among the trees of the garden.

So he said, "I heard Your voice in the garden,
and I was afraid because <u>I was naked</u>; and I hid myself."

> And He said, "<u>Who told you that you were naked?</u>
> Have you eaten from the tree of which I commanded you
> that you should not eat?"
> *Genesis 3: 7-11. NKJV*

Wow!

Now there's a lot of meat in this passage. But notice. When things were going well in Adam and Eve's life they weren't embarrassed about their naked existence. Remember, it was God who placed them there naked and God doesn't make mistakes! There was purity in their nakedness. Adam nor Eve had issues with this at all.

But when they sinned and disobeyed God, not only did they try to hide their nakedness from God but also from each other! And the same happens today. Isolation! Separation! Division! We become so embarrassed about our failures, inadequacies and short comings that we isolate ourselves from each other! It's happening all over the world and we've got to fix this.

Take a moment and think about that.

*"We don't just hide from God but each other!"*

Wow!

I believe the root cause Adam and Eve responded like such was because of embarrassment and fear of rejection. They knew they'd done wrong and brought an avoidable, unnecessary trial and heartache upon themselves by disobeying God.

Yet even in their trespass, God still took care of them and made sure their needs were met although expelled from the Garden of Eden and the Tree of Life. He didn't just throw them aside like we often do each other when we blow it!

> "Also for Adam and his wife the LORD God made tunics of skin,
> and clothed them."
> *Genesis 3:21 NKJV*

And even greater, God won humanity back to Himself by sending Christ to bear in completion the guilt of Adam's sin making it possible for all to take of the Tree of Life in Paradise restored!

> "For God so loved the world that He gave His only begotten Son,

that whoever believes in Him should not perish but have everlasting life."
*John 3:16 NKJV*

"And the Spirit and the bride say, "Come!"
And let him who thirst say, "Come!"
And let him who thirst come.

Whoever desires, let him take the water of life freely."
*Revelation 22:17 NKJV*

"He who has an ear, let him hear what the Spirit says to the churches. To him who overcomes <u>I will give to eat from the tree of life,</u> which is in the midst of the Paradise of God."
*Revelation 2:7 NKJV*

Hallelujah! What a mighty God we serve!

Wow! We can get back to the Tree! Even in our mess God never left us hanging and He wants us to extend the same example!

"Now all things are of God, who has reconciled us to Himself through Jesus Christ, <u>and has given us the ministry of reconciliation,</u> that is, that God was in Christ reconciling the world to Himself, not imputing their trespasses to them, <u>and has committed to us the word of reconciliation</u>."
*2 Corinthians 5: 18-19. NKJV*

The beauty of it all? Even when Adam and Eve messed up and tarnished the beauty of their nakedness, (purity) <u>GOD NEVER STOPPED LOVING THEM</u>!

And further more, He did something about it!

What about us? Do we stop loving our brothers and sisters because of a trespass?

What if God treated you this way how would you feel? Where would you be today?

Think about it. This is serious stuff!


## <u>Many Preachers Won't Talk Because of Fear of Rejection and Betrayal!</u>

Therefore, because nakedness is such an uncomfortable issue due to open exposure, most preachers won't talk. I believe this is so because of *the fear of rejection* and *betrayal*.

### FOOD FOR THOUGHT:
"It's not that some preachers
don't want to talk but
rather it's a trust issue!"

To be rejected means to be declined, cast off or forsaken according to *Mr. Web*. Rejection simply says, "I won't be accepted, embraced or treated with dignity because of a flaw."

Betrayal on the other hands means to win one's confidence then lead astray specifically to seduce and desert. It's to reveal or disclose unknowingly. To breach one's confidence and trust. In laymen's terms I call it, *"flipping the script!"* Huh! Betrayal hurts!

### QUESTION?
*"If I become transparent
and tell you what's really going on with me,
will I hear it again on the 6:00 news?
Will you put my stuff in the street?"*

Having worked with clergy persons from so many different walks of life and being a preacher myself, I've discovered many are reluctant to talk about their deeper personal issues because of feelings of vulnerability and fear of betrayal. All this can be placed under the banner of rejection.

Here are some examples.

### Why Preachers Won't Talk!

#### 1. Breach of Confidentiality

"If I take off my clothes, become transparent and tell you what's really going on with me, will I hear it again on the 6:00 news? Will it be posted in the Sunday morning bulletin? Will it be repeated in the morning announcements? Will you tell my secret?"

*"Since I'm not sure, I'll just keep it to myself and just tell God."*

### 2. Fear of Betrayal

"If I open up to you and tell you my personal business concerning my battles within and without the pulpit, how do I know you won't use this information against me? How do I know you won't use this information to bring me down and discredit my reputation?

"Judas betrayed Jesus. How do I know you won't betray me? Will you change on me? Will you still be my friend if you find out I'm not as strong and courageous as you deem me to be?"

### 3. Fear of Abandonment and Rejection

"I confess. I'm hurting and really do need to talk to someone. I'm even willing to do so! But if I open up my heart will you lose your respect for me after what I have to say? Will you treat me the same or distance yourself? Will you leave me to face this alone?"

"Will you annihilate your association with me because of the depth of my situation? Will you look at me funny? Will you become ashamed to be seen with me in public?"

### 4. Fear of Losing Loved Ones, Positions, and Loss of Respect Among Peers and the Community

"Hey I'm going through but I've got to tough this one out on my own. I would talk about what I'm facing but I'll lose my wife! I'll lose my husband! This info will kill my marriage and then the publicity! I couldn't take it."

"Worse, my children would be devastated. And let's not talk what the congregation might think. No! What they'd do!"

"My ministry is my means of keeping food on the table and paying my bills. If I flunk this I'd lose my credibility among my peers and the community. Then what? That's too risky a price to pay so I'll just suffer through it. Hopefully, with prayer things will get better. I'll just keep trying."

Wow!

**PREACHERS THIS IS REAL!**

And you know what happens? We stay quiet to our own hurt. Then, BOOM! An explosion happens in our lives at the most unlikely moment.

People are in a state of shock at the news but the truth of the matter is that it's been growing silently all the time. What is seen publicly is only an outward manifestation of seeds planted inward that were not uprooted in time.

**Preacher,
God Doesn't Want You in Pain!**

Listen colleagues God does not want us living in pain like this. It's even very difficult for me to write this without my heart being moved with great empathy just discussing this matter!

As fellow clergy, we all perhaps can share story after story about leaders who go through this. Not only ministers but also people from other vocations in life! Furthermore, I can give you my own testimony.

Let me share this with you. I pray it will encourage your heart to keep on keeping on and to know that you are more than a conqueror through Jesus Christ! And trust to know, nothing can separate you from the love of God in Christ and the victory that comes with such!

"Yet in all these things we are more than conquerors through
Him who loved us.

For I am persuaded that neither death nor life, nor angels nor principalities
nor powers, nor things present nor things to come,
nor height nor depth, nor any other created thing,
<u>shall be able to separate us from the love of God
which is in Christ Jesus our Lord.</u>"
*Romans 8:37-39. NKJV*

Preacher do you believe this! The Apostle Paul who went through all kinds of stuff knew what he was talking about.

Remember, you're more than a conqueror. And because of this, YOU CAN MAKE IT!

**My Testimony!**

So here's my story.

As a young man (again, I'll always be 25!) the Lord has blessed me and allowed me to do quite a bit of traveling and sharing the Gospel. By His grace and mercy He has afforded me opportunities to minister in some of the most unusual places and great platforms. God uses imperfect people! I give Him all the glory! I still pick my nose. Huh! Got you there didn't I? Even when picked up from airports in limousines. Huh! I'm not impressed with flashy stuff. No! I'm a down to earth southern boy. (Now if I come to your ministry, don't be looking in the rearview mirror to see if I'm picking. I'll be delivered by then!) Oh!

Sometimes when people hear me or see me they inquire about the anointing on my life as almost if I've just got it made or something. As if I was born in swaddling clothes. Huh! If only they knew! " Miss. Lucy and Uncle Bob, I barely paid my phone bill last week." Yall better know! But swaddling clothes?

Even to the point one day, I was exercising outdoors and a fellow preacher friend suddenly took my hand and placed it upon his forehead as if the anointing could be simply transferred to him just by one touch. (I wanted to slap him but I changed my mind. Ah!) I told him it wasn't that simple. A NFL star asked me the same thing.

The anointing of God comes through Jesus via the presence of the Holy Spirit in our lives. However, the anointing still has to be developed as each of us are at different levels in Christian maturity.

I told him that the anointing in my life has been and still is being developed through years of walking with the Lord, (I got saved at age 11) growing in that relationship with Him, studying His Word, learning His voice, submitting to godly and healthy leadership, serving others, via trials and test I've been through and check this one out: THOUGH MISTAKES, BLEEPS, BLOOPS AND BLUNDERS I'VE MADE!

Yes. When you've bumped into a few walls you'll get the wisdom after while! You learn firsthand which hall ways to pursue and which to avoid.

While God does use the ministry of laying hands, (however, you can't just take someone's hand, place it on your head and think you're going to just walk in power) you've got to die to self and daily take up your Cross! The anointing isn't cheap. You can't go to the store or conference and order the anointing like a cheese burger!

> *"I personally know what it*
> *feels like to lead while you bleed!*
> *Yes, I do!"*

However, in my ministerial journey, I've been tried by fire! I know what it is to look all polished with nice suits and you don't have a dime but you have to keep on preaching. I know what it is to be a senior pastor and your apartment is so cold that fog is on the inside because you don't have enough money to pay the bills. Thus, you're so embarrassed you hope no one comes by to visit you so they won't see you living in that condition. Then, there's not a drop of food in the cabinet and only an old jar of water in the refrigerator. And that came from the sink! Bottled water? What? Whose going to pay for it? I personally know what it is to lead while you bleed.

I know what it is to be the senior leadership of the house and your car is so tore up you have to hitch a ride with the sheep while being embarrassed because you want to set a better example. And then when the church blesses you with a new car, the community calls you, "Jim Jones!" And then God tells you to keep loving them and keep preaching anyhow!

I know what it is to have helped so many and the very one's you've helped (I mean miracles!) when no one else wanted to reject, scandalize and abandon you. I know what it is to feel the brush of death when an unexpected young person affiliated with your ministry suddenly dies and you're trying to figure out why?

I know what it is to have a great vision but the resources are almost non-existent and because of pioneering in a region that's never seen advances in economic development, people talk about you, lie on you, accuse you of inappropriate behaviors when it's not so and then blackmail your church telling the community never to attend! Yes!

I know what it is to be stung with the scourge of jealousy because you've decided to obey God and the Lord prospers that decision beyond measure. I know what it is to have fellow preachers and colleagues to smile in your face as if celebrating you and say all kinds of wicked things about you behind your back.

I know what it is to have people and friends ignore and abandon you because they consider you "strange" because you don't fit the mold like everyone else because you choose consecration, holiness and to wait on the Lord for your wife rather than sleeping around. Thus, if you're not married you're either sleeping with all the women or you have deviant sexual desires as if holiness and integrity aren't possible. While they themselves are guilty of the things they accuse you! Huh!

They can't or couldn't keep themselves sexually so they think you can't either! Ah! They're loose so they think you must be loose too because they themselves don't know how to practice sexual integrity and keep their pants up! So if you're single you must be in the same boat! You've got to be doing something! THEY WOULD!!!

They worry about why you're not married and they themselves are cheating on their wives or can't stay with their husbands working on their $3^{rd}$ divorce! Three! Don't mess with me today! I'm a nice guy but yall know I keep it raw! Want to know where the anointing in my life comes from?

> *"I've learned how love*
> *and forgiveness*
> *will set you free everytime!"*

But you know what? I also know what it is to love and love those who you know don't really care about you from the heart. I also know what it is to forgive. Even when people never ask for your forgiveness and probably never will! I've personally learned how agape love and forgiveness will set you free and keep us from becoming slaves to the offender!

I've also learned how to endure. Yes! I've learned how to stay focused on my goals and purpose and not allow the noise from the sidelines distract me from crossing the finish line. And you know what? I'VE SEEN GOD SHUT THE ENEMY'S MOUTH! The very thing people said could never happen, GOD DID!

I've learned how to be patient. And you know what? My trials in ministry actually worked out for my good. They helped me to become a "better me." The heat of the flames showed me that there was still some traces of pride left in my life so I learned how to humble myself and stay there! The abandonment by others whom I've helped in ministry has taught me that the sheep don't belong to us no how. They belong to God! My job is only to be a witness for the season God would have me do so in their lives. God will take good care of them and I don't have to make that happen. Stray sheep do come home. And even if they don't, God may have even better plans for their lives.

I've learned via working with people that only the Holy Spirit can convert a soul. That's not our job. We're only called to be witnesses. All He requires is that we do our part and He will do the greater. Paul said it like this,

> "I have planted, Apollos watered; <u>but God gave the increase</u>."
> *I Corinthians 3:6 KJV*

Yes! And today, I'm free! I can go to sleep at night.

So wonder where the anointing in my life come from? I've been marinated through a wilderness experience!

### I Wasn't Afraid To Get Naked!

But there's one more thing. Out of all the things I've mentioned to you concerning the fires I've experienced in ministry, I made it this far because I never was afraid to get naked! I had people in my life that I made myself accountable to. I had people in my life who weren't caught up on my gifts, anointing, prestige or abilities but would tell me about myself plain, simple and in love! I got rebuked! I got encouragement. I got loved.

So much thanks to my spiritual father in the Gospel, the late honorable Pastor Reuben Wright Sr. (This man could see straight through you and would literally cast the devil out of you if you had one!) Thanks to the honorable Mother Rev. Ella Mae Brown, Pastor Markeda Friend, Dr. Conrad Pridgen, the late Pastor Barbara Brewton Cameron, bishops and presiding elders over our ministry, and most of all, my parents!

This is the key! With all the arrows being shot at me during ministry I would have crumbled under the load if I refused to drop my pride and get help and back up! Mother Brown used to say it like this,

*"You can't row this boat by yourself!"*

Yes indeed!

So it's by no goodness of my own that the Lord's blessed me to come this far. I HAD HELP! And because I wasn't afraid to get naked, I was able to weather the storm.

### It's Either Get Naked Or Stay Sick!

Bottom line preachers, it's either get naked or stay sick!

## If We Refuse To Take Off Our Clothes, The Doctor Can't Help Us!

As a former health care technician in mental health, I've learned some powerful things. Any health care professional will tell us unless we're honest and are willing to talk about our symptoms, getting the right kind of help and diagnosis may become extremely difficult. Even if a health care professional is the best in his or her field! A doctor can't get to the source of the problem if we won't take off our clothes.

Remember, talking removes our clothes.

## A Lady in Peril

Just only 2 days ago I decided to go for a morning exercise at a big park in my area at the lake. As I was walking around several laps, there was an elderly lady before me that had an accident. Unfortunately she suffered a terrible fall that bruised very badly almost rendering here unconscious.

Moved with a sense of urgency, I and several other bystanders went to her rescue to assist her until the paramedics came.

When they arrived, the first thing they had to due was cut her clothes off. She was wearing a very nice and good looking jacket. Thus, they asked her husband if it was ok.

Granting the permission, if they didn't cut her jacket off they would've not been able to properly apply the neck brace needed to lift her into the ambulance. But because of she and her husbands willingness to cooperate, they were able to apply the neck brace, lift her to safety and take her to the hospital.

The problem with clothes is they have a way of blocking what needs to be seen and prevent the proper instruments from getting to the source. They obstruct the view of the part of the body that's affected or needs examination. This can hinder the treatment plan, diagnosis or the prescribing of the proper medicine. In worse cases, a person can actually die needlessly from something that could've been easily treated.

Preachers, if we want to be made whole, we must be willing to take off our clothes.

## Clothes We Sometimes Wear As Preachers:

- Pride
- Positions and Titles
- Accolades and Accomplishments
- Our Public Image
- Concerns About What Others Think of Us
- Insecurities and Feelings of Vulnerability
- Anger
- Distrust
- Fear and Fear of Betrayal
- Other

My fellow clergy, it's time to strip!

**FOOD FOR THOUGHT**
Which is easier?
Uprooting a tiny seed
or chopping down a 30 ft. tree?

## Don't Wait Until You Need A Miracle To Get Help!

My brothers and sisters, we rejoice in that fact that God can and still does miracles. Even in the 21$^{st}$ Century! However, don't wait until you need a miracle before you start crying out for help. Waiting until we need a miracle is not His best.

*"Do we want to live?
Or do we want to die?"*

While many times we don't talk because of fear of betrayal and rejection, we have to ask ourselves a serious question. Do we want to live or do we want to die? Do we continue to suffer internally and even externally because we're afraid of what people might say?

Let me tell you. People are going to talk about us anyway! They talked about Jesus! You can wash folks car, cut their grass, baby sit the kids, pay their light bill and after all that some folk will still talk about you. SO WHAT?!!! Don't give people this much control over your life!

So should we refuse to get help because what people may say or do? That's giving people too much power! A power they should never have!

Let's keep it real. Grant it. When you do go for help people may talk. You might get betrayed. Somebody might put your name out as trash on the streets. But you know what? You'll live! You'll see the victory. You'll walk in health. You'll walk in freedom.

And I'll tell you. Life is funny. Sometimes those same persons who've put you out there like trash will have to come right back around and acknowledge that God is in you of truth! And even if they don't, LIVE!

## A Lesson From
## *The Color Purple!*

It's like *Miss. Celie* from the famous movie, *The Color Purple*. After leaving her extremely abusive husband called, *Mr.*, he spewed out some very ugly and painful words toward her as she finally decided to leave the nightmare to victory. Thinking he was crushing her self esteem, Miss. Celie said some very liberating words to him. She said,

*"I might be black, I might be ugly,*
*BUT I'M HERE!"*

Huh! Ain't no movie like *the Color Purple*. "You told Harpo to beat me!" Oh! Do you remember?

But here's my point. Miss. Celie said something powerful. She said, "I'm here!" Meaning indeed there were seemingly negatives stacked against her but she finally had come to a place in her life of real breakthrough! And where was her accuser, Mr.? He was left standing on the porch!

## God Will Take Care of You!

My fellow clergy, let's start talking! Now of course, we have to use wisdom. We need to make sure we're getting the right kind and professional help we need. Don't go to quacks or someone who hasn't proven properly certified or qualified in the assistance we need. Do your own research before getting assistance and of course, pray for God's guidance.

King David said it like this,

> "Blessed is the man(person) <u>that walketh not in the counsel of the ungodly</u>, nor standeth in the way of sinners, nor sitteth in the seat of the scornful."
> *Psalm 1:1 KJV*

And always remember, GOD WILL TAKE CARE OF YOU! No matter who betrays, flip out, or forsake you. Never forget, people aren't your source, GOD IS! While indeed God will use people to help us, the ultimate provision comes from Him. So no longer be afraid of rejection and betrayal. Why? BECAUSE GOD'S GOT YOUR BACK!

Growing up as a little boy in Morris Brown AME Church, the people of God used to sing a powerful hymn that's forever etched in my memory about the covering and keeping love and care of God. The words were written by Civilla D. Martin and the tune by W. Stillman Martin. Let these words breathe new life, hope and encouragement to your spirit.

### "Be Not Dismayed"
*(God Will Take Care of You)*

*Be not dismayed what -e'er betide,*
*God will take care of you;*
*Beneath His wings of love abide,*
*God will take care of you,*
*God will take care of you,*
*Through every day, o'er all the way;*
*He will take care of you,*
*God will take care of you."*

Isn't that beautiful? What a wonderful, tender and loving God we serve.

Just take a quiet moment, pause and think about this promise.

Now quietly lift your hands and your heart towards Heaven and worship Him. Tell God how much you love, appreciate, and adore Him!

Yes my brother! Yes my sister! You have the victory!

Get help!

Therefore, there's a powerful word of encouragement I want to share with you. If you don't remember anything else from this book remember this.

### NO MATTER HOW DEEP YOUR SITUATION, YOU ARE NOT BEYOND REPAIR!

In Psalm 23, King David, a leader of God's people knows the pain of messing up after receiving the call of God on his life. Yet through his experience, he pens to us this following word of hope..

> "He <u>restoreth</u> my soul....."
> *Psalm 23: 3a*

I've been doing a study on shepherding. David was a real shepherd before becoming King of Israel. The 23$^{rd}$ Psalm was written out of David's experience with real sheep. However, in this Psalm, David is now the sheep and the Lord the Great Shepherd!

To restore something means to bring something back to its original position. It's to recover that which was lost and bring it back to its rightful place. But check this out. In my studies, when the phrase, *"He restoreth my soul"* is used it's referring to fallen sheep being placed back up on their feet again. And dear preacher,

### <u>"THE LORD IS ABLE TO PLACE YOU BACK UP ON YOUR FEET AGAIN REGARDLESS!"</u>

Rejoice!

Then that's not all! It gets even better. Not only is He able to restore you, He's going to give you new and clear direction for your life!

> "....<u>He leads me in the path of righteousness</u> for His name's sake."
> *Psalm 23: 3b*

Wow!

In other words, after the Lord restores you, He's going to take you off the path that will cause destruction and place you on the one of righteousness which leads to victory! Yes! And why is He doing all this? Not because we've been so great, holy or wonderful but for His very own Name's sake! Wow! In other words, <u>HE JUST LOVES US LIKE THAT!</u>

Worship Him!

## Preacher, You Can Talk Now!

So preacher, you can talk now! No longer will we fear rejection and betrayal! We're going to mount up on eagles wings and receive all the healing, wholeness, restoration and breakthrough God has for us! Why? Because God's involved to help us in our struggles!

## A Prayer of Blessing and Declaration of Encouragement For You!

In leu of all that we've learned and shared so far, let's make this declaration of hope and prayer of victory together over our lives and ministries. Take a quiet moment and <u>make this confession aloud</u> with me together!

## <u>Declaration of Hope and Victory!</u>

*I, (Say your name here)     , in the Name of Jesus Christ of Nazareth humbly accept the fact that I am priceless to God and the Body of Christ. I am needed. And even the world needs to hear my voice! I decree that I have now been set free from the chains that have held me bound by the power of God's Word. I am free to become all that God has called me to be, accomplish all that He has called me to accomplish and do all He has called me to do!*

*I thank God that today I receive new strength where there is no strength, hope where there seems no hope, encouragement where encouragement seems gone, clarity of direction where confusion seems paramount, and refreshing from the Holy Spirit on High! Yes, I can make it! In Christ, I will make it! My best days are in front of me and like Father Abraham regardless my age!*

*No longer will I be bound by the spirit of fear, fear of rejection, fear of abandonment, and the fear of betrayal. For 2 Timothy 1:7 says, "God has not given us the spirit of fear but of power, and of love, and of a sound mind." And if I am indeed rejected by people, Jesus took care of that too because Ephesians 1:6 decrees that I have been accepted through Christ in the Beloved. Yes, I am the beloved of God with all rights and privileges entitled as joint heirs with Christ. (Ephesians 1:6-7) Therefore, I am never alone! I make no apologies for God's love for me and my fellow brothers and sisters in Christ and the whole wide world itself.*

*No longer will I be held in constraints and captivity in my mind because the nightmares of my past. If shortcomings are in my life, I'm willing to take responsibility, own up to them and make whatever amends necessary if needed and possible. I am willing to forgive all those who've wounded me even as Christ has forgiven me. I am not resistant to any needed repentance for I realize it destroys all Satan's legal rights to harass, torment and stay in my life! I am willing to give up all legal grounds, acts of disobedience, rebellion, handling accursed things, making unwise decisions, movies that defile, unforgiveness, failure to pray and study God's Word, not taking care of my health or anything the enemy uses to cling to my life.*

*No longer will I let my past, mistakes or sins of yesterday keep me enslaved from reaching for higher ground, fulling my God-given destiny and goals in my life. For God has decreed in His Word in 2Corinthians 5:17, I am indeed a new creature in Christ. Old things have passed away and all things are new! I will no longer allow people who remember the mistakes of my past cause me to hold my head down in shame especially if I've made the necessary amends and God has forgiven me!*

*According to Ephesians 1: 17-23, through the power of the Holy Spirit, I receive freely from God the much needed wisdom, strength, encouragement and revelation knowledge in Christ I need to be successful in my personal life, marriage and family relationships, and the ministry God's assigned to my hands. I rejoice now that the power of God is released to me to surmount like eagles through every storm, challenge, temptation, victory over sin and anything I face in my life. My total dependency is upon God alone.*

*<u>Therefore, I will no longer be afraid to reach out and get any help I may need understanding that the payoff of wholeness and victory in my life will far out</u>weigh any ridicule, rejection or scandals the enemy may bring. In the midst of all my challenges, <u>I CHOOSE LIFE</u> and therefore, I shout the victory because in Christ, <u>MY BEST IS YET TO COME</u>!*

Wow! If you believe this declaration of hope take a moment and in your own way begin to give God praise! He inhabits (dwells, take a seat, functions and moves in) the praises of His people!

Let's move forward my brothers and sisters. I am in agreement with you concerning this prayer and declaration of hope and victory in Jesus' Name!  Amen!

And what's more, we're no longer afraid to talk now!

Celebrate!

**Chapter Review**

Let's do a quick review of what we've learned in this chapter.

### ARE YOU WILLING TO GET NAKED?
*"Why Preachers Don't Talk!'*

- Getting naked is not the physical removal of clothes but things we hide behind to hide our real issues.

- Nakedness has always been an uncomfortable issues because of unrestricted exposure.

- Most preachers don't talk because of fear of betrayal, exposure and rejection.

- If we refuse to get naked, we hinder the help we need.

- There's no situation beyond God's repair.

- We must get help from the right sources and not the opposite.

- Talking will take us to victory!

**Notes:**

## CHAPTER FIVE

# BECOMING A GOOD PREACHER!

*"Good preachers are like pancakes.
They aren't born but made.
They must be fried on both sides before they're done!"*
*A Brently Proverb*

Let's have some more fun here.

**IN THE APOSTLE PAUL'S LETTER** to his spiritual son Timothy, he shares some great advice and admonishment that would cause any young minister to experience success in the vineyard. He writes,

> "If thou put the brethren in remembrance of these things,
> <u>thou shalt be a good minister</u> of Jesus Christ,
> nourished up in the words of faith and of good doctrine
> whereunto thou hast attained."
> *I Timothy 4:6 KJV*

Prior to this passage, Paul spends much time advising Timothy about several things. Such include: staying true to sound doctrine, the importance of intercessory prayer, the necessity of church protocol, the importance of good character among aspiring overseers and leaders, the eschatological falling away from the faith in latter times, and the overall passing of the mantel of great leadership. Then in verse 6, he tells Timothy how obedience to such would make him a *good minister* of Christ.

Today with all that's going on in our world and society, God needs and wants to raise up some good preachers. He desires men and women who will arise to the occasion and make a difference in a dying world.

### Is It Possible for Anyone to be A *Good* Preacher?

*"We may be called to preach
but preachers are human too!"*

After all we've discussed so far, considering that we all have our own frailties, shortcomings and the like, someone may have some serious questions about this *good* preacher stuff. After all, we may be called to preach but preachers are human too! And with our imperfections is it possible for anyone to become a *good* preacher?

## God Sees In Us What We Can't!

As a kid, I never wanted to preach although I knew the hand of the Lord was upon my life. My career choice was to become a medical doctor. A brain surgeon to be exact! As a matter of fact, I majored in pre-med biology when I first went to college to pursue such. Yet in the back of my mind I felt ministry on my life but I didn't want to preach mainly for 3 reasons.

### **Reasons I Didn't Want to Preach:**

- I felt the life of a preacher was boring and restricted.

- Preaching places one directly in the spotlight and I wasn't sure if I could always live up to the pressure. (What if I had a non-Hallelujah moment and feel like sinning then what?)

- You don't have to be a preacher to go to Heaven. We're saved by grace. There are so many other ways of serving the Lord.

These were my youthful thoughts against pursuing ministry.

Needless to say, I'm preaching today! Yet in spite all my youthful fears, doubts and inadequacies about ministry, there's something I really love about the Lord that always blows my mind. God has the ability to see us as great vessels of His even when we're in a jacked up or imperfect state.

*"God is a master for perfecting diamonds in the rough!"*

He always sees the priceless beauty and potential in each of us even when we or others can't discern, believe or recognize it ourselves! He sees us for what we can become even when people have often counted us completely out! He's a master for perfecting diamonds in the rough. Otherwise, none of us would make it!

Paul, speaking about the calling of God on Abraham says it like this,

".....who gives life to the dead <u>and calls those thing which do not exist</u>

> <u>as though they did</u>: who contrary to hop, in hope believed,
> so he became the father of many nations, according to what was spoken,
> "So shall your descendants be."
> *Romans 4:17b, -18. NKJV*

Awesome! God sees in us what we can't always see! And guess what more? YOU ARE ONE OF ABRAHAM'S' DESCENDANTS!

Rejoice!

### Defining the Term, *"Good!"*

Therefore, when we use the term, *good* we're not talking about immaculate perfection. Nobody holds this honor but God! So we're not talking about being incapable of making mistakes. So don't be discouraged if you've had some bumps in the road along your journey. Growth bring bumps and sometimes blunders and bleeps too. God is not through with you yet so don't be discouraged.

However, the bonus is many bumps, bleeps and bloops can be avoided! As previously discussed, as preachers we don't have to camp out or live in a world of continuous mishaps. God has made provisions so we don't have to keep hitting brick walls over and over again!

> *"Good doesn't mean settling
> for average. We're called to be
> exceptional people!"*

Also, when we use the term *good*, we're not talking about settling for mediocre, average or doing just enough to make it by. God has called us to be exceptional people! However, the context in which we use the term good here comes form the Greek usage of the word found in our text rather than today's English vernacular. I will explain this in just a moment.

**So What Is A
*Good* Preacher?**

In the English language, the word *good* means several things. According to *Mr. Web*, it means to be suitable to a purpose, beneficial, healthy or sound. It's to be valid, dependable, thorough, virtuous, devout, kind, dutiful, skilled, etc. It also refers to being benevolent.

In our text found in I Timothy, the Greek word for *good* here is *kalos*. This word expresses beauty that' harmonious, in proper proportion, completeness and balance.

So Paul was telling Timothy if he hearkened to the sound wisdom that he was giving him, his life and ministry would be in proper alignment with the things of God. It would be well pleasing to God, not out of sync, in harmony with the truth of the Gospel, embracing sound doctrine, balanced and in proper proportion. In other words, he'd represent Christ well to a dying world!

*"Being a good preacher
means being on point for Jesus!"*

So when we use the term, *"a good preacher,"* we mean our lives and ministries are in proper alignment with God, the truth of the Gospel, representing Christ well to a dying world. It does not mean some false sense of spirituality, superiority or being pious. Nor does it mean the absence of trouble, temptation or challenge. I like to say it this way. Being a good preacher simply means being on point for Jesus!

*"Becoming a good preacher
is attainable!"*

Foremost clergy, becoming a good preacher is attainable! What does it take? A simple "yes" to God's will, Word and way!

## God Uses Ordinary People!

And here's one more thing. God uses ordinary people! Yes, God uses ordinary people to extraordinary things! Let this be a source of great encouragement to you!

Always remember, the glory always goes to God. Not us! God chooses to use us! Even in our humanity! Otherwise, who could relate to us? This Gospel that we preach would seem foreign and non applicable to the lost because we'd be too impeccable for them to relate to. Unattainable!

Ordinary people simply refers to regular human beings who breathe air, drink water, need food, clothing, shelter and have feelings just like the rest of the world. I think this covers all of us! It does not mean matchless perfection. Ordinary people make mistakes!

When people can look on us and see how God has brought us from nothing to something, from sin to forgiveness and cleansing, from failure to lives of success and victory, it sends a powerful message of hope and redemption.

By watching us, it let's the person whose down and out know that they can come out the dumps. By watching us, it let's the person whose facing a terrible storm in their life know that they too can make it! When people can look on us and see that we didn't always have it together but watch how Christ delivered us, it sends volumes of hope to the person who may feel they are so far gone that they are beyond help.

God using ordinary people says to the world,

> "IT'S NOT WHERE YOU COME FROM
> BUT WHERE YOU'RE GOING
> that makes the difference!"

A famous hymn says it this way,

> *"It is no secret what God can do!*
> *What He's done for others, He'll do for you!*
> *With arms wide open, He'll pardon you!*
> *It is no secret what God can do!"*

What good news! Takes the pressure off doesn't it? GOD INDEED USES ORDINARY PEOPLE! Be free from feelings of worthlessness today in Jesus' Name!

You're priceless.

Rejoice!

And here's one more thing. God is so down to earth and believes so much in the power of ordinary people that guess what He did!

He became human too just to save us all!

> "In the beginning was the Word, and the Word was with God,
> and the Word was God.
>
> ......And the Word was made flesh, (human) and dwelt among us, (and we beheld his glory, the glory as the only begotten of the Father,) full of grace and truth."
> John 1: 1 and 14. KJV

There is nothing stuck -up or arrogant about our Savior! He made Himself attainable! Aren't you glad?

## Not An Overnight Process!
### *Are You Willing to Wait?*

In my little *Brently Proverb* at the top of this chapter, I said something I want you to consider. I said,

> *"Good preachers are like pancakes.*
> *They aren't born but made.*
> *They must be fried on both sides before they're done!"*

Success in ministry and becoming a good preacher is a process. And it involves the discipline of waiting.

Let me explain what I mean.

### We Don't Reach Maturity
### In Ministry Overnight!

Just on yesterday, I was looking at myself preach on several DVD's at various services where I ministered in different parts of the country. And guess what? Are you ready? I didn't like everything I saw! I mean I know my head is round and big but that wasn't just it. Huh! (They used to call me *"Cabbage Head!"*) Oh! Can you imagine? Those were the days!

Nevertheless, I always use my tapes, CD's, and DVD's as personal learning tools for reflection, assessment and growth. My sincere desire is to be pleasing to the Lord and to represent Him well. While people sitting under my ministry during these recordings may feel the messages were powerful, I saw little mistakes in my presentation or things that could've been done a little to a lot better.

Many of the DVD's I watched were recorded years apart. So I could go back to my past and come up to the present. That's one of the blessings of modern technology. So I was able to see my ministerial journey, seasons of immaturity, seasons of growth, seasons of greater stability. My point is developing maturity in our ministerial journey is a process and not something that just happens overnight!

### FOOD FOR THOUGHT:
*"Never get to the place
in your ministry
that you're so anointed and appointed
no one can tell you anything!"*

Just like we grow in our salvation into greater Christian maturity and discipleship, it's the same with ministry. I'm quite sure many of us can say who've been preaching for quite sometime can look back and see areas and things we used to do when first starting out that perhaps we don't do now. Why? Because we have more wisdom and experience than when we first begun! Time somehow has a way of teaching us better ways of doing things.

However, a key to growing into ministerial maturity is that we should never get to a place that we feel we've arrived. It doesn't matter how greatly we're used of God! We should never get to a place where we're so anointed, appointed and prosperous that no one can tell us anything. This is dangerous and a sure enough way to not remain in ministry long! It's a sure way for us to fall flat on our faces. Sermons and all!

A very wise church mother said it like this,

*"Even the birds flying high
have to come down and get water!"*

WOW!

Thank you Mrs. Albertha Prince! You hit a home run with that one! I haven't forgotten.

Remember that preachers. "Even the birds!" Huh!

## The Issue of Waiting!

Today, many people have a problem with waiting.

To *wait* means to remain in a state of expectation until a desire or need is met. It also means to serve. Waiting requires much patience because it means we won't always get what we want right away.

*"Modern technology has taught us impatience!"*

Today we live in a very fast technologically advanced society whereas we have become accustomed to getting what we want instantly. Thus, as a whole people are generally more impatient than years gone by. If ever the familiar saying, "patience is a virtue" has some serious validity it's now. Modern society has acclimated us to getting whatever we want quick, fast and in a hurry!

Technology is so advanced that the need for human interaction is becoming less and less. Here are some examples.

To mail something years ago you had to go the mailbox or post office. Today, just e-mail it and never leave the comfort of your home.

Need gas? Why get out your car and walk inside the gas station? Just go to the pump, swipe your credit or debit card, skip the long line inside and conveniently drive away.

And what about paying bills? Why drive all across town to multiple locations fighting traffic and weather conditions? Simply get on the internet, pull up the site, key in the right numbers, pay your bill and it's done!

While many of these modern conveniences are a great help, waiting is soon becoming a thing of the past. Our society has become accustomed to getting what we want, when we want it quick, fast and in a hurry as a preacher friend of mine once put it. <u>AND SOMETIMES WE BRING THIS SAME SPIRIT INTO THE MINISTRY</u>! Waiting issues!

Wanting everything now!

But there's something very powerful that happens when we wait. Especially when we wait on God! The prophet Isaiah says it like this,

> "Even the youths shall faint and be weary.
> And the young men shall utterly fall,
> <u>but those who wait on the LORD</u>
> Shall <u>renew their strength</u>;
> They shall <u>mount up with wings as eagles,</u>
> They shall <u>run and not be weary,</u>
> They shall <u>walk and not faint</u>."
> Isaiah 40: 30-31 NKJV

Wow!

Preacher, are you willing to wait?

## FOOD FOR THOUGHT:

<u>4 Things That Happen
When We Wait On God</u>:

- Our strength will be renewed.
- We will soar like eagles! (Think about the powerful things eagles can do!)
- We will be able to work in the Kingdom and find satisfaction. (We will be mature enough and ready to handle the responsibilities that come with blessings and promotion.)
- We will be able to work in the Kingdom without burnout.

Lord, teach us how to wait!

### Don't Flunk the Process!

Thus, waiting involves a process. <u>Mr. Web</u> defines *process* this way.

" A series of changes by which something develops."

In other words, a *process* is something that takes time. Just like a caterpillar doesn't become a butterfly overnight so it is with the development of our callings and ministries. There's a process to go through.

Years ago, a great bishop speaking on this matter said it something like this in a sermon.

He said,

> "What makes you think you can
> fall down a blunder and wake up a wonder?
> It doesn't work that way.
> There's no instant success in God.
> It's going to take some prayer, fasting and going through
> to make it in God."

Wow!

Thanks Bishop Brown! All these years I remember this sermon.

> "Anybody can get a platform.
> But it's definitely going to take
> character and discipline
> to keep you there!

Therefore, when it comes to ministry, you don't just accept the call to preach, go to bed, wake up and now you're some overnight success! It ain't happening! And if it does, it won't last because the major ingredients to sustain life will be missing. Anybody can get a platform but it's definitely going to take character and discipline to keep you there!

You don't just go to a hot worship service, have somebody pray for you, fall out on the floor and get up as *"Super Pastor!"* No! Now don't get me wrong. I'm a firm believer in the gifts of the Holy Spirit and the power of God available to this generation. (See Acts 2:39!) I too operate in such as the Spirit wills by the grace of God. However, while the gifts of the Spirit may prime the pump and get us a jump start it's going to take some serious discipleship, discipline and follow through to become the kind of leaders God has called us to be! But *Super Pastor?*

> *"Faster than Apostle Paul!*
> *stronger than the Red Sea!*
> *It's a bird!*
> *It's a plane!*
> *No! It's Super Pastor!*
> *Here I come to save the day!"*

Sorry! It doesn't work like this! Super characters are only for cartoons and movies. It would be nice though. I'd be Superfly! Huh! That's back in the day!

> **FOOD FOR THOUGHT:**
> *"Too many preachers
> have gotten off the potter's wheel
> too soon!"*

## Is the Flunk Monkey Sitting On Your Shoulder?

Let's have even more fun here. I have a question for you. Is the *Flunk Monkey* sitting on your shoulder?

I have a good preacher friend that once talked to me about the *Flunk Monkey*. I had never heard this term before. One day he was talking about a preacher doing a sermon and said the Flunk Monkey was sitting on his shoulder during his whole presentation.

With the comedian that I am, all I could do was imagine a monkey holding up the letter "F" on the preacher's shoulder while the preacher was up there giving his sermon. Oh! I thought it was so funny! I said to myself, "that ain't no monkey, that's a demon!" Somebody needs to rebuke that demon monkey and bind him up in the Name of Jesus! Oh! Cast the monkey out! (I took it to the next level.) Huh!

But more seriously, I think the Flunk Monkey makes a good example. The Flunk Monkey is when a preacher gets up and flunks. Either he or she didn't take the time to adequately prepare his or her sermon and the delivery (homiletics) of the message crashes. Or it could be some behavior or action the minister does that discredits his or her ministry. The Flunk Monkey! Oh!

For example, years ago I was told of an anonymous preacher who once got up to preach and the audience started booing. I mean they started booing as soon as this minister mounted the pulpit for sleeping with multiple women on a college campus! I mean at the top of the sermon. It was a riot! They didn't want to hear anything the preacher had to say. Oh! I tell you, ministry is nothing to play with! The Flunk Monkey was doing cartwheels. No, somersaults! Oh!

Nevertheless, in school when a student flunks, this means he or she has failed or didn't pass. If a student doesn't pass, they can't get to the next grade. PREACHERS, GOD WANTS US TO PASS!

## Some Preachers Have Jumped Into the Pulpit Too Soon!

The truth of the matter is some preachers have gotten off the potter's wheel too soon! Some preachers have jumped into the pulpit too early before ever making sure they received any necessary deliverance, ministerial training, and breakthrough in character issues first. This doesn't mean that such are not genuinely called of God either! The calling is not the issue! Remember God calls us in our imperfect state. But here's where we go wrong. Timing! There's a difference between being called and sent! And like my cousin used to say,

*"......Some just went!"*

God bless you Pastor Rosalyn Weathers!

*"Being called to preach doesn't mean we're ready to preach!"*

We can truly be called of God but go a few seasons too early. Being called to preach doesn't mean we're ready to preach. It doesn't mean we're ready to get up front and lead people yet! This is where the waiting and process comes in! This is excellent discussion for dialogue in our route and quest to becoming *"good"* preachers. This is why ministerial candidates need the right kind of guidance.

The Apostle Paul said it like this,

"Not a novice (a person on probation or a beginner)
lest being lifted up with pride he fall into the condemnation of the devil."
*I Timothy 3:6 KJV*

This is why I believe those who ordain ministers need to take a closer look at ministerial candidates before sending them to the people. How can a new born baby drive a tractor trailer without causing an accident or even without injuring him or herself?

Does that baby have potential? Yes! Will that baby be able to drive a tractor trailer one day? Yes if it grows up and take lessons. Is that baby ready to drive one now? No! Why? Because it's <u>underdeveloped</u>! Its arms and legs aren't long enough to steer the wheel or reach the brakes at the same time. Foremost, the baby can't see over the wheel and you know what happens when the blind lead the blind? In the same way, though many ministerial candidates have potential, time and maturity is the issue. Is it time to entrust the lives of people into their hands?

Speaking of the deaconate, Paul said this.

> "And let these first be proved; then let them use
> the office of a deacon, being found blameless."
> *I Timothy 3:10 KJV*

Let the training begin!

## The Power of Attending Seminary

When you're leading people's lives you've got to know what you're doing! This too is why I believe in addition to character issues ministerial academic training is important before getting in the drivers seat as well. I believe in seminary training. Now some people don't but I do. Some folk call it the cemetery. But I beg to differ.

Yes God has used countless people down throughout history without a formal education or seminary training. So in no wise am I arguing that a minister cannot be effective without such. I've seen it with my own eyes! While I am the product of great leaders who have attended seminary, I am also the product of several great world changers in Christ who haven't! Both groups of persons were mightily used by God and God got the increase! Hallelujah!

However, just like the Apostle Paul told Timothy that leaders must be proven first before being placed in office the same holds true for us. While the 12 disciples with the exception of Paul did not have a formal education they still had to be taught! Anything less would've been a disaster! Every disciple had to sit under the teachings of Jesus for at least 3 years <u>before</u> He could entrust them to ministry. That's about the same time it takes to get a Masters of Divinity. Huh! Interesting.

Listen my friend ministerial training is important. Just like an attorney has to go to law school before practicing law, a surgeon to medical school before performing open heart surgery on someone, or even an airplane pilot to aviation school before being entrusted to fly a passenger plane full of people, SO MUST MINISTERS BE TRAINED!

Well someone might argue, "There are some seminaries out there that teach some off the wall stuff." Well that's where you do the research before matriculating because there are many good seminaries out there! Nevertheless, at any seminary you will encounter exposure to doctrines, philosophies, etc. that you may not agree with and don't have to. The Bible teaches us not to be ruined by doctrines and philosophies that are after the rudiments of the world and not after Christ. (See     Colossians 2:7-8)

Such studies may be too meaty for a babe in Christ.

"For though by this time you ought to be teachers, you need someone to teach you again the first principles of the oracles of God: and you have come to need milk and not solid food.

For everyone who partakes only of milk is unskilled in the word of righteousness, for he is a babe.

But solid food belongs to those who are of full age, that is, those who by reason of use have their senses exercised to discern both good and evil."
Hebrews 5:12-14. NKJV

Bottom line: seminary may not be for everybody. However, in my opinion exposure to such is a necessary part of training for ministers because we're leading people. Also it prepares us for the real world should our parishioners or anyone ask questions we couldn't answer otherwise. We live in an information age and if we intend to reach this generation without compromise we cannot be afraid to tackle issues our parishioners may struggle with in the pews! This is why many cults and strange doctrines are successful in winning new converts. They study! Many are willing to deal with stuff and issues we sweep under the rug!

A good and dear friend of mine said it this way when it comes to matriculating in seminary. She said,

> *"Your anointing comes from your prayer closet.
> What seminary does is give you information!"*

Wow! Thanks Rev. Monica Redmond! Girl you know you're a preaching somebody!

See, we don't go to seminary to become anointed that comes from our personal relationship and walk with the Lord. Nevertheless, seminary and ministerial training enhances and enlarges our scope of understanding so that we can become more effective in Kingdom service.

## God Holds Us Responsible For the Souls!

Therefore, because leading the lives of other people is such a serious job you can see now why ministerial training is a must. Besides, God holds us responsible for every soul entrusted under our watch care. And we're certainly held responsible for every soul shipwrecked at our hands! Shepherds, if we have wounded or caused any soul to go astray, let's repent today! People's lives are priceless! This is why Jesus died and rose. To save lives!

Preachers, it's a dangerous thing to mess over God's sheep! Consider this passage.

*Ezekiel 34: 7-10* KJV

> 7. Therefore, ye shepherds, hear the word of the LORD:
>
> 8. As I live, saith the Lord God, surely because my flock became a prey, and my flock became meat to every beast of the field because there was no shepherd, neither did my shepherds search for my flock, but the shepherds fed themselves, and fed not my flock;
>
> 9. Therefore, O ye shepherds hear the word of the LORD:
>
> 10. Thus saith the Lord GOD; Behold, I am against the shepherds; and I will require my flock at their hand, and cause them to cease from feeding the flock; neither shall the shepherds feed themselves any more; for I will deliver my flock from their mouth, that they may not be meat (food) for them.

> 11. For thus saith the Lord GOD; Behold, I, even I, will both search my sheep, and seek them out."

We must always remember, the people are not our personal property. They belong to the Lord and God requires them at our hands.

See how serious ministry is? This is why we must make sure we wait and allow the Lord to process us before jumping into the pulpit!

## Talent and Education Alone Won't Cut It!

*"A lot of preachers have gotten into the pulpit off talent alone."*

Now while seminary, ministerial training, and education are certainly important it won't cut the pie alone. A lot of preachers have made it to the pulpit strictly off talent, resources and education alone. Now don't get me wrong, we need all three. I'm certainly a devout advocate for higher education. However, we cannot exclude what I feel is the most important piece of the puzzle. <u>CHARACTER!</u>

Character is the forerunner before any education and resources come in. Why? <u>IF OUR CHARACTER IS TORE UP THE FLUNK MONKEY WILL SIT ON OUR SHOULDERS</u> with our PhD's accolades and all! And you know what? Our accomplishments or schooling won't keep us out of jail or off the 6:00 news!

Let's be honest. We can have degrees and still be rude. We can have tremendous pulpit etiquette and still be nasty. We can know how to handle all the business and transactions of the church and ministry and still be full of lust! We can even preach the grease out of a biscuit but don't know how to talk to people!

We can have the faith to raise the dead, lay hands on the sick and people legitimately get healed but not exercise enough resurrection faith for our own loved ones, marriages, children and families. As a result, we open the door for our children to hate or grow indifferent towards church and ministry.

And what's this fad going on with cussing preachers?

We've got preachers cussing and using foul language as if we never met the Lord. And when someone corrects us on it we call it "being too deep." Yet we want people to respect us in spite of a dirty mouth!

There's nothing worse than a cussing preacher. (There are some things worse but you get the point. Huh!) How can we cuss and then prophesy? All out the same mouth? Then want to lay hands on people. And speak a word over their lives!

Just because we hear some leaders do it doesn't make it right. And we say because we're in the 21$^{st}$ Century it's an excuse?

How are we any different from the world? They already know how to cuss. Believe me! When are we going to show them something different? No wonder many worldly folks and people from other religions take us like a big joke and non-authentic.

And you know what? If the people and sheep we serve start cussing and using "A-F" words, (Most of them already do! Huh!) we can't say a word to them. Perhaps they're only FOLLOWING THE LEADER! We've got to practice integrity first!

James said it like this,

> "Out of the same mouth proceedeth blessing and cursing.
> My brethren, these things ought not so to be.
>
> Doth a fountain send forth at the same place
> sweet water and bitter?"
> *James 3: 10-11. KJV*

Wow!

Come up higher we say? To what? What are we calling the world up to? To show them how to do what they're already doing?

Could it be possible we're laying hands on people and getting minimum results because we need to tighten up on our personal integrity?

Well I'll tell you this, character is more important than any gift we can offer at the altar. And if we humble ourselves and allow the Lord to carry us through our developmental process, we'll be alright.

And you know what else? If we do these things, we'll never have to worry about the Flunk Monkey!

**FOOD FOR THOUGHT:**

*Keys to Avoiding the Flunk Monkey:*

- Pray and seek God above all else.
- Wait on your ministry.
- Be accountable and don't neglect ministerial training (seminary) and preparation.
- Value the power of good character!

## Struggle Is Good For the Caterpillar!

In terms of becoming a *good* preacher, I remember a story that I once read that has stuck with me down through the years. I believe it will help us to understand the power of process even better. It's a story about a little boy in a science class and a caterpillar.

The story talks about a little boy in a science class who had the project of watching the stages of a caterpillar becoming a butterfly. The caterpillar had now gone through several stages and now was in the last which is being trapped inside a cocoon.

Patiently and more patiently the boy waited in sheer excitement or seeing this great miracle of transformation taking place right before his eyes. Then finally, the moment of truth!

*"To deny the process of struggle is to kill the future butterfly!"*

All the sudden he saw the cocoon shake and vibrate! He knew the caterpillar was about to emerge. Full of excitement but no impatient, the little boy thought he would help the caterpillar out much faster by cutting open the cocoon with a knife.

Thus, he proceeded to cut the cocoon open only to realize that his efforts killed the new butterfly that was almost ready to emerge.

Saddened, what he didn't know scientifically was that struggle is good for the butterfly. When the metamorphosis is complete, God through nature designed struggle to get the "used to be" caterpillar out the cocoon. To deny the caterpillar this process is to kill the future butterfly.

## Let God Make You!

In the same way, let God make you! Let me tell you something from experience. When God makes you, you shall be made and it's something no one can take away from you.

<u>Mr. Web</u> defines the word, *"make"* the following way:

"To bring into being; build, create, produce, etc.
To cause to become. To prepare for use. To amount to.
To have the qualities of."

Preacher, check this out. God's about to:

- <u>Bring you into being</u>!
- <u>Build your life</u>!
- <u>Create and open new avenues and doors</u>!
- <u>Cause you to produce</u>!
- <u>Cause you to become a precision instrument in His Hands for His glory</u>!
- <u>Prepare you for greater service</u>!
- <u>Your ministry will make a mark in the earth that cannot be erased for the eternity of eternities</u>.
- <u>You will possess and have all the qualities of the Kingdom with all rights and privileges thereof</u>! *(See Ephesians 1st chapter!)*

All you've got to do is remember the caterpillar and be encouraged! Becoming a good preacher and developing excellence in ministry is so similar. So whenever it seems like things aren't happening for you as fast as you'd like, remember this story. YOU'RE ABOUT TO EMERGE! Hallelujah!

Now that's good news!

Shout about it! Yeah!

## The Path to the Prize
## Is Greater Than the Prize Itself!

In retrospect of what we've discussed here's a golden nugget that will change your life and ministry to greatness you've never seen. A very honorable, successful pastor (in the true sense of the word) full of faith, wisdom, experience and most of all character and integrity said these powerful words in one of his sermons.

He said,
> "The path to the prize is greater
> than the prize itself!'

AWESOME!!! Simply off the chain! Thanks Pastor Gool! I've never forgotten.

**FOOD FOR THOUGHT:**

> *"In ministry and life,*
> *HOW we obtain something*
> *is more important than*
> *WHAT we obtain."*
> *A Brently Proverb*

In other words, how we obtain or pursue something is even more important than what we actually obtain. Let me explain.

Let's go to the world of sports. A person can be the greatest athlete in the world. A track star can be so fast that he or she out runs every opponent in a race in record breaking time. He or she may even cross the finish line first. But guess what? If caught cheating they will be disqualified and rightfully so!

Paul said it this way,

> "But I discipline my body and bring it into subjection,
> lest, when I have preached to others, <u>I myself should become disqualified</u>."

*I Corinthians 9:27 NKJV*

We don't want this to be our plight. We've come too far!

Worse, Jesus said it will be like this for some.

> "May will say to Me in that day,
> Lord, Lord, have we not prophesied in Your name,
> cast out demons in Your name, and done many
> wonderful works in Your name?'
> "And then I will declare to them, 'I never knew you;
> depart from Me, you who practice lawlessness!"
> *Matthew 7:22-23 NKJV*

Brothers and Sisters, it ain't worth it. Let's not cheat. Remember the path to the prize is greater!

## **Don't Get Recalled!**

Whatever we do, we don't want to be like a brand new car purchased off a lot but on recall. This has happened several times in the automotive industry. Brand new cars have been recalled by the manufacturer because post purchase it's been discovered an important part has been missing or some other defect. To continue to drive a car in such a state could end in an accident.

God is too wise to send us onto the battle field half dressed and unprepared. He may call us to ministry in an unready state but trust when He sends us, we'll be equipped before going out! So whatever you do, let God dress you. Fully! Let Him fix you up for the journey and you'll be so glad you did in the long run.

And you know what? Sometimes through the trials of life we do get recalled back to the manufacturer's shop. I know I have! If this is your case, let God do it! Go back to the shop and let God fix you! This is a smart person who is wise to cooperate with God's leading. I'd rather be recalled so I could get everything placed in me that I need to be successful than to keep traveling in pride and get demolished on the road.

There was a time in my life whereas I got gravely off course and I got called back to the Manufacturer's shop. It was the best thing that could've happened to me at that time. If I hardened my heart,

I don't believe I would've lived to write this book to you! So walk in wisdom and obey God!

However, still remember prevention is still better. I would've never been recalled if I'd listened to the voice of the Holy Spirit from the beginning. But thank God for mercy!

> *"God wants whatever you're called to do
> to be effective and last!"*

Listen. Whatever God has called you to do, He wants it to last! Yes! God wants your ministry to last. God's about longevity. He wants your works to stand! It's that important! Somebody will find life because of the work God has called you to do!

Jesus said it like this. Here's Christ desire for your ministry.

> "Ye have not chosen me, but I have chosen you,
> and ordained you, that ye should go and bring forth fruit,
> <u>and that your fruit should remain</u>: that whatsoever ye shall ask
> of the Father in my name, he may give it you."
> John 15:16 KJV

Let God dress you today!

**Ready to Become
A Good Preacher?**

So far, I've given you some good food for thought. I feel someone who felt like throwing in the towel is having revival right now in the quietness of your heart. Whatever you do, don't faint, quit or give up. Your best is yet to come! So here's the big question, are you ready to become a *good* preacher?

If you've been preaching for a while you know that ministry brings new and diverse experiences every day. If you're just taking your first steps in ministry know there's a wonderful wide diversity of experiences before you.

> *"The wonderful thing about
> being in ministry is that it's not
> a solo project but rather a*

*partnership with God Himself!"*

While the awesome call to preach and serve the people of God is indeed a joy unspeakable, it yet carries both highs and lows complete with both mountain top and valley experiences. But guess what? God will be with you every step of the way! One of the most comforting things I love about ministry is it's not a solo project but a partnership with God Himself! We take the light hand and He takes the heavy hand!

And oh! What a wonderful partnership! Mark says it like this,

> "And they went forth, and preached everywhere,
> <u>THE LORD WORKING WITH THEM</u>, and confirming the word
> with signs following."
> Mark 16:20 KJV

Wow! Yes! Celebrate!

We don't do ministry alone! The CEO of the Universe and all creation works intimately and directly with us! To God be the glory! Hallelujah!

This means we can go to sleep at night! We don't have to do the work of the Holy Spirit. Our calling is only to be obedient to His voice, love the people and be a witness for Him. It's His job to provide all the miracles!

I heard a wonderful pastor and mother of one of my friends saysit something like this,

*"You do what is possible and trust God for what is impossible!"*

Thanks Pastor Cynthia Pringle! You are such a blessing!

Visiting one of our AME churches, an old mother stopped me and said something to me I'll never forget. With one of the sweetest smiles in the world she said,

*"Let go and let God. He can do a much better job than you!"*

Very encouraging!

So we've learned in this chapter that becoming a good preacher is so attainable for all of us no matter how many mistakes, bleeps, and blunders we've made. God is so awesome all we have to do is have a willing heart. And like the little boy who gave Jesus his tiny two fish and five loaves of bread, Preacher God will take your sacrifice and feed multitudes for His glory!

Take a moment and celebrate a new beginning in your life!

Let's review.

## **<u>CHAPTER 5 REVIEW</u>**
*Becoming A Good Preacher!*

- God needs good preachers to reach today's world and generation.

- Being a *good* preacher doesn't mean perfection but being on point for Jesus! No matter our past and frailties becoming a *good* preacher is attainable!

- There's no such thing as overnight success and there's power in the discipline of waiting.

- The pathway of process will place our ministries on a solid foundation and keep us from being disqualified.

- Good character is superior to any gifts, accolades or resources we can bring to the table.

- We never have to fear doing ministry alone because we minister in partnership with God!

And there you have it! Preacher rejoice! You're about to be made by God Himself!

It's celebration time!

**Notes:**

## CHAPTER SIX

# WHO ARE YOU ACCOUNTABLE TO?
## "*The Dangers of Being A Lone Ranger!*"

*"Even the animals can teach us something. The lonely sheep is always easiest for the wolf to snatch. Stay with the herd!"*
A Brently Proverb

"Obey them that have the rule over you, and submit yourselves: **for they watch for your souls**, as they that must give account, that they may do it with joy, and not with grief: **for that is unprofitable for you**."
Hebrews 13:17 KJV

IN THIS CHAPTER WE'RE going to talk about the power and blessings of accountability.

> *"Many preachers have fallen prey to all sorts of pitfalls and hurt because of not having someone to be accountable to!"*

To be accountable means to be held liable. It's to be held responsible or explainable to. It means giving a report of our actions, deeds and stewardship. It's to allow someone of credible standing to peep into our world. To allow someone to check us out and make sure we're alright! There is power in being accountable! Many preachers have become victims of all sorts of hurt and have suffered many pitfalls because of not having someone to be accountable to.

## A Lesson From the Animal Kingdom!

Since I was a little boy, I've always loved animals. If it had more than two legs, crawled, flew or looked strange it had my full attention. If I couldn't catch it or put it in a jar, I'd try to take it home or do something to keep it in my memory. And even to this day,
I still love animals! Therefore, the Animal Channel is one of my favorite networks.

One day I was privileged to hold a baby tiger cub in my arms. It was love at first sight. This was about 4 years ago or so. It was the most beautiful creature I ever held. Its coat was a beautiful orange with black stripes. I even took pictures with it. I didn't want to let the thing go. Then I got to thinking. "He's cute today, but I might look like dinner to him tomorrow!" "Preacher Prime Rib Deluxe to be exact!" Then I'll have to shoot the thing! Huh! I'm just teasing.

But oh! How I would love one as a pet. Can't you see it now? All the boys from the Hood walking around ever so proudly with their pit bulls on leashes then here I come with a 1,000 lb plus tiger! "Who's your Daddy now?" "Who's your Daddy now?" Huh! "Who's your Daddy?!!" Nevertheless, reality check! I think I'll save the tiger thing until I get to Heaven. Then I'll know it's safe.

Can't you see the news paper clippings now?

"PREACHER EATEN BY TIGER. THOUGHT HE WAS BACK IN THE GARDEN OF EDEN! DETAILS ON PAGE 3!"

Oh! I'm not going to make the same mistake people make on the movies!

However, there's so much we can learn from the animal kingdom. Especially when it comes to issues of preachers and accountability!

Let me explain.

## There's Safety in Numbers!

I can recall watching the animal channel one day looking at thousands of wilder beast running through a vast African wilderness in an attempt to cross a river. Now preachers if you think we have problems and rivers to cross, check out these animals! They make our situations look like cake and pie. Talk about a troubled congregation. These animals go through!

*"They all attend the*
*Holy Wilder Beast Temple of Faith*
*Ministries #4.*
*A mega ministry!*

*"Even the enemy realizes*
*there's safety in numbers!"*

What amazes me about this whole thing is as powerful as the enemies of the wilder beast are, even they realize there's safety in numbers. For example, when these creatures are running or grazing in the vicinity of lions, it seems the lions always try to catch the ones that are alone or straggling alongside the herd. Or if they move into a moving herd, they try to catch one that's with the group but not so locked in that the catch would be difficult.

While a lion can easily tear anyone of these animals apart, it realizes that it's not so easy to do when a would be dinner is surrounded by it's brothers and sisters!

Here you have thousands upon thousands of these animals trying to get across the wilderness (represents for us life's challenges) in search of new grazing grounds. To get to their destiny, they have to watch out for all types of predators (for us things that will cause preachers to fall) ranging from hyenas, to lions, to cheetahs, to tigers, to hungry vultures (news reporters. Huh!) just waiting for just one of them to die!

Then here's where it really gets exciting. When they finally get to the river! If they could just cross this river, their destiny is on the other side. But here's where it gets hot!

There are tons of humongous hungry crocodiles who aren't afraid to jump up at anytime and snatch one of these wilder beast between their teeth ending their lives forever.

But you know what? I really admire these animals. Because they're fearless! They know they're surrounded by enemies on every side but they never let such challenges stop them. They keep moving forward. And they believe in unity too. They always stay in a group because they know there's strength and safety in numbers. They know it would be foolish to try to cross such a dangerous wilderness alone without backup. Preachers, let's learn something here!

The wider beast are animals of faith because they never stop reaching. They are always in movement towards their goal. As a matter of fact they all attend Holy Wider Beast Temple of Faith Ministries #4! Dr. Hurry Let's Run Wilder Beast is the senior pastor. Truly a mega ministry! It's the fastest growing congregation in the wilderness. And you know what? They have an international television broadcast too! That's how I can tell you this story, I saw it myself. The animal channel! Huh!

Having a ball with this but here's the twist.

**Preacher, Don't
Let the Lions of Life Get You!**

Wow!

Fellow colleagues, now the story of the wilder beast will preach! However, whatever you do, don't let the lions of life get you. Or the hyenas, cheetahs, vultures or whatever your challenge may be. We all have them but don't isolate yourself. Find someone <u>credible</u> to be accountable to today! There's safety in numbers!

The Bible says it like this,

> "Be sober, be vigilant; because your adversary the devil, <u>as a roaring lion</u>, walketh about, <u>seeking whom he may devour</u>: Whom resist stedfast in the faith, knowing that <u>the same afflictions</u> are accomplished in your brethren that are in the world."
> *I Peter 5: 8-9. KJV*

Preacher, are you going to let the enemy devour you? Remember the scripture says, "whom he *"may"* devour." That means he can't do it unless we open a door and give him permission. Remember, this is what this book's about; prevention and recovery!

The enemy just can't walk up and swallow you. He has to size us up and see if we are giving him something to work with. (Remember the wilder beast!) And because *"the same afflictions"* or the fact we all deal with similar challenges as the Body of Christ happens to us all, we're better together! There is so much strength and wisdom we can draw from each other.

Again always remember,

*"The lonely sheep is a wolf's easy prey!*
*Stay with the herd!"*

Get accountable and skip the drama! It's worth it!

## It's Dangerous To Do Ministry Alone!

My brothers and sisters, the truth of the matter is it's dangerous to do ministry alone and not be accountable to anyone. God never called us to be lone rangers.

I know we have our own uniqueness, differences in personalities and all that. We can keep these things! Yes indeed! Our uniqueness, and individuality in ministry comes from God thus, these are not the issue. Be yourself! You're at your best being you!

However, the problem comes when we isolate ourselves and close ourselves off into our own private worlds not allowing anybody in. Even those who care about us most. Thus, we become trapped in our own worlds not allowing any fresh air in or out.

> *"Developing an isolationist mentality*
> *and closing ourselves off into our own*
> *private worlds of ministry*
> *sets us up for horrible explosions*
> *to happen in our lives!"*

Now everything falls on us alone. Everything becomes about us alone. "It's my ministry!" We cry. " It's what God told me to do!" We adamantly convince ourselves.

"Can't nobody tell me how to do this because God gave the vision to me!" We resist defending our territory.

"It's time for me to branch out and do my own thing anyway." "I've been sitting under other people's leadership long enough now." "I've got a ministry too!"

Then becoming afraid that outside help will somehow destroy or weaken our vision, we cry, "I don't need nobody to help me! I can do this by myself!"

Thus, we start developing an isolationist mentality and risk becoming easy prey to the lion's of life. First the chain wraps around our thinking and perception of things.

Secondly we become worn out and tired by having wasting time and energy trying to recreate a wheel that's already been invented. And because we've made ourselves solo projects, we have to be all sufficient rejecting the many available resources that God has made available throughout the Body of Christ. Why? Because we fear asking for help.

Finally, because we've closed ourselves off into our own worlds doing our own thing, several negative seeds begin to take root. After a period of time we find ourselves becoming overprotective of our grounds, sometimes intimidated by others, indifferent, bitter, and eventually grow stale. Then "BOOM!" The explosion happens. We turn on the television and hear the news;

## *"PREACHER CAUGHT IN SHOCKING SITUATION! DETAILS AT SIX!"*

## Important Questions To Breakthrough!

This is real colleagues! Listen. This lone ranger stuff isn't healthy at all! A very wise preacher who knows what it's like to blow it in ministry said it like this. Please consider this with all your heart.

> "**Two are better than one**;
> because they have a reward for their labor.
> **For if they fall, the one will lift up his fellow**:
> but woe to him **that is alone when he falleth**;
> **for he hath not another to help him up.**"
> *Ecclesiastes 4: 9-10. KJV*

No more lone rangers!

This is a 9-1-1! Reverends, please listen! It's happening right now even as you read this book! Even within the ranks of non-clergy vocations! THEREFORE, in leu of what we've discussed so far, I have a few questions to ask you pertaining to these matters. Please answer these for your own personal reflection and perusal. Answer them honestly so you won't become meat to the lions of life!

Here's for starters.

Reverend, are you a loner? Are you trying to do ministry all by yourself?

Please check one: _____ YES, _____ NO

Are you open for help and assistance if available?

Please check one: _____ YES, _____NO

If your answer is no, why not?

_____

_____

_____

    Here's my second question.

Preacher, should you fall (God forbid!) or experience some unexpected blow in life, do you have someone to help you up?

Don't answer saying, "God!" Remember in the foreword of this book we learned that God is not the issue here! He's always faithful! But He's made us the Body of Christ. We have a responsibility to each other as brothers and sisters. Remember? God wants His Family to get along! This is where real revival will begin! Therefore, what credible and responsible person/s in the Body of Christ are you accountable to?

Please write name/s here:

_____

_____

_____

If you haven't found someone yet state so here:

_____

_____

_____

    Here's my third question.

Preachers, should a fellow colleague, brother or sister come to you for help during a time of crises, are you too high or too exalted in your ministerial, ecclesiastical, ecumenical, social or global status to help?

Check one: _____ YES, _____NO

Are you willing? \_\_\_\_ YES, \_\_\_\_NO, \_\_\_\_\_Maybe Later, \_\_\_\_\_ Depends on what the problem is, \_\_\_\_\_Too Busy, \_\_\_\_\_ Not my problem or responsibility, \_\_\_\_\_ I'm trying to overcome my own issues, \_\_\_\_\_ "I had to get mine on my own let them get theirs!"

\_\_\_\_\_Yes with great joy!
\_\_\_\_\_ Not sure if it's safe for me to get involved,
\_\_\_\_\_ I have to first find out if I have the proper credentials and training to provide assistance, \_\_\_\_\_ I have other reasons for not providing assistance.

## Something To Consider:

*Jesus Was Never Too Grand
To Help Us In Need!*

"Who being in the form of God,
thought it not robbery to be equal with God:
**But made himself of no reputation,
and took upon him the form of a servant**,
and was made in the likeness of men;
And being found in the fashion as a man,
he **humbled himself**, and became obedient unto death,
even the death of the cross."
*Phillipians 2: 8-10 KJV*

Wow!

Suppose Christ was too important or busy to save our souls? Where would we be?

*"If Christ could humble Himself,
who had bragging rights if He wanted to,
yet reached out and helped others,
what's our problem?*

Sadly, some of us have become greater than Jesus! Now yall know I'm going to tell the truth! It's the only way to see real revival! Aren't you ready for real revival and refreshing from on High? It's time!

> "Repent ye therefore, and be converted that your sins may be blotted out, <u>when times of refreshing</u> shall come from the presence of the Lord;"
> *Acts 3: 19 KJV*

Sounds good to me! Let's obey.

Let's never forget where we came from! Never! Remember, even the best of sky scrappers can collapse! And we'll never know what bridges we burn we'll have to cross again. Life is funny. With all our money, prestige, fame, glory or whatever, we'll never know whom we'll have to ask for a drink of water! This is so serious! We're better together!

Remember what Mrs. Prince said earlier,

*"Even the birds have come down to get water!"*

Remember?

Finally, here's my last question.

If a fellow preacher comes to you and shares their personal problems, will you put their business out in the streets?

Please check one: _____YES, _____NO, _____Depends on the circumstance.

For any answer you gave, please write your explanation for doing so:

_____
_____
_____
_____
_____
_____
_____

Do you think God would be pleased with this response? _____YES, _____NO

Can you support such with scripture? _____YES, _____NO
If yes, which one/s? _____

Is it the right exegetical interpretation? _____YES, _____NO, _____Not sure

How do you think the colleague who shared with you would feel?
Check one: _____good, _____bad, _____wonderful, _____helped, _____betrayed, _____disappointed, _____hurt, _____wounded, _____exposed, _____relieved.

How would you feel if the tables were turned and the responses you gave were turned on you?
_____

Colleagues, we've got to do.

### **Wisdom Reminder**

Let us also remember <u>should we not have</u> the professional training, expertise and credentials to assist in certain issues, it's important to REFER people to the right professionals who do. Although sincere in our efforts, <u>we can do more damage than good</u> if we're not qualified to plunge into specified areas of people's lives. Also such can result in terrible legal matters affecting both you the preacher and the ministry you serve.

> *"As a pastor over many years,*
> *I've seen many people delivered*
> *and set free. I've learned when*
> *and when not to work!"*

As a pastor over several years, the Lord has blessed me to help and see many people delivered and set free. However, I've always honored boundaries! Thus, the Lord has blessed me to not have any casualties doing ministry. And believe me, I'VE HAD SOME VERY SERIOUS AND PECULIAR CASES! Oh! But the secret is I've learned when I can and cannot work. I've learned that we don't have to be everything to everybody. Yet at the same time we can serve as tremendous vessels of support, encouragement, and strength <u>as we stand with others (not abandon) who are in trial.</u>

First and foremost, as leaders we should follow the leading of the Holy Spirit. The Holy Spirit is intelligent! Yes! (see John 16: 13-15) Secondly, we must also know how to work with others who have the professional expertise in various areas to get the job done. Preachers, don't be afraid to delegate when necessary! Let's get out the "re-inventing the wheel" mentality! However, should delegation be the call of the day, there are still so many other things we can do to help others as systems of support without crossing boundaries.

And let's remember, "we'll never know when it will be our turn to cry!"

Concerning being there for each other, Paul said it like this,

> "As we therefore have opportunity,
> let us do good unto all men, (people)
> <u>especially unto them who are of
> the household of faith.</u>"
> *Galatians 6: 10 JKV*

Remember, the unbelieving and very skeptical world is watching us. They will make decisions about what to do with Jesus based on how we treat each other! Let's give God the right **advertisement!**

## Every Pastor Needs A Pastor!

Now that we've laid some criteria for integrity in helping each other, we're now ready to discuss our next phase that will deliver us from the lone ranger syndrome.

A couple of years ago, I heard a great woman of God say something I'll never forget. She said these powerful words,

*"Every pastor needs a pastor!"*

And now that I'm a pastor, I see the wisdom in this like never before!

Thanks Bishop Corletta V. Harris! If we can really grasp a hold of this, what greater things we'll accomplish in the Kingdom of God!

*"Who's to stop the people
from drinking poison Kool-Aid
when the meeting is over?!!!!"*

Yes! Every pastor needs a pastor! A preacher once said;

"Who's to stop the people from drinking poison Kool-Aid and blowing their brains out when the meeting is over?"

"Who's to stop the people from being abused at the hands of the presbytery?"

"Who's to pull the gifted leader in when success has gone to the head that he or she starts teaching strange and erroneous doctrines and the people are now suffering from spiritual food poison?"

"Who's to encourage the pastor when he or she is so entrenched in the work of ministry that the marriage now suffers, the children gone astray and one's private self is in tremendous agony because the public self has swallowed up all the gas?"

"Where does the pastor go when he or she needs a shoulder to cry on, or *wisdom advice* from the voice of one who's already traveled down the road they're presently on?"

"Where can a pastor receive encouragement coming from the voice of one who has the experience and proper oversight to speak correctly without error or fraud from apostolic and prophetic realms ordained by God for servant-leadership?"

"If a ministry is set up where all the money goes into the pastor's pocket, and that pastor is the final authority in that house, then who ranks to make sure that pocket doesn't have holes?"

WE'RE EITHER GOING TO GET IT RIGHT OR ST
THE NEWS! No! JAIL!!! No! PRISON!!!!!

Again, every pastor needs a pastor! And if you're a movie star, celebrity, public figure, politician, professional athlete or anybody who risk being tempted to get beside yourself via success, you need one too!

Drama is to be prevented! Save it for the theater!

Integrity is the key!

**We Need to Be Accountable
To Somebody on Earth!**

I don't care how anointed, gifted, talented or popular we are, there's not a preacher, bishop, apostle, prophet, evangelist or whatever on this planet that should be without a covering and somebody to be accountable to................ON EARTH! Not just Heaven, EARTH!

*"When our stuff is right,
we don't mind the lights being turned on.
When we use God as an excuse
for our lack of accountability,
we can get away with murder!"*

Remember let's not use God as a scapegoat. Sometimes we misuse spiritual things and God as a copout. Often this is because there's something in us that's rebellious with all our "hallelujah's" and claims to deeper sanctification. We don't want to be exposed! We don't want to be accountable to anyone so we can do what we do when we do undistracted. I'm preaching now! Somebody hit A flat on the organ! Drums! Shout!

When we use God and Heaven as our excuse for not being accountable to each other we can get away with murder!

We can steal church money, mess over people's kids, (horrible!) sleep with the members, demand from our parishioners things God never requires making them feel guilty just because "the pastor said it!"

Because we've decided to remain a law to ourselves, though perhaps sincere, we remain stuck and left to our own way of thinking. Thus, we never get the proper counsel, correction and confrontation needed so both we and the people we serve can be healthy and prevent further disaster and ministerial catastrophe from taking place!

So turn on the lights so we all can see what we're doing so the people won't be abused! I'm telling you every leader needs to be accountable to somebody ON EARTH! HERE AND NOW!

See, when our stuff is right, we don't mind the lights being turned on! There's nothing to hide. It's when we're not ready to give up the grounds the enemy uses to keep our lives in bondage that we run from accountability.

Jesus said it like this,

> "And this is the condemnation,
> that light is come into the world,
> and men (people) <u>loved darkness
> rather than light because
> their deeds were evil</u>.
>
> "For every one that doeth evil hateth the light,
> <u>neither cometh to the light, lest his (her) deeds
> should be reproved</u>.
> <u>But he that doeth truth cometh to the light</u>,
> that his (her) deeds may be made manifest,
> that they are wrought in God."
> *John 3: 19-21. KJV*

Oh!

God knows our proclivities this is why He's the one that established the system of accountability. I'll explain this in a moment. But check this out! This will really bless you!

## If Jesus, God in Flesh Had to Be Accountable to Ordinary Human Beings, Then What About Us?

Now here I come!

If Jesus, God in flesh, the Creator of all things and life itself, had to humble Himself and be accountable to ordinary human beings <u>who are not perfect</u>, then what about us? First let me prove to you from Scripture that He was indeed "God in Flesh!"

Let's go to Bible Study Class 101.

### Jesus, More Than A Prophet or An Angel!

Here's the account.

> "In the beginning was the Word, and the Word was with God,
> <u>and the Word was God.</u>
> The same was in the beginning with God.
> <u>All things were made by him; and without him was not any thing made that was made.</u> In him was life;
> and the life was the light of men.
>
> ....<u>And the word was made flesh,</u> and dwelt (lived) among us,
> (and we beheld his glory, the glory as the only begotten
> of the Father,) full of grace and truth."
> *John 1: 1-4, 14. KJV*

God wouldn't have it any other way! There aren't 2 saviors, only one! And that's God alone! He loves us so much He came to earth Himself to do the job. (See John 3:16) Also note: the term, *"begotten"* means taken from or derived from the same substance. Christ was *homoousious,* a term taken from Greek which also means of the same substance.

Oh this is good!

From the Old Testament, God declared that He's the Only Savior!

> "Tell ye, and bring them near; yea, let them take counsel together;
> who hath declared this from ancient time? Who hath told it from that time?
> Have not I the LORD? <u>and there is no God else beside me;</u>
> <u>a just God and a Savior; there is none beside me.</u>
> Look unto me, and be ye saved,
> all the ends of the earth:
> <u>for I am God, and there is none else;</u>
> I have sworn by myself,
> the word is gone out of my mouth in righteousness,
> and shall not return, <u>That unto me every knee shall bow,</u>
> <u>every tongue shall swear."</u>
> Isaiah 45: 21-23. KJV.

Now, so the people wouldn't be confused, thousands of years before the advent of Christ, God foretold us via Israel that He would be the Messiah coming in flesh.

> "For unto us <u>a child</u> is born, unto us <u>a son is given</u>:
> and the government shall be upon his shoulder: and his name shall be called
> Wonderful, counselor, <u>The mighty God, The everlasting Father,</u>
> The Prince of Peace.
> Of the increase of his government and peace
> there shall be no end, upon the throne of David,
> and his kingdom, to order it, and establish it
> with judgment and with justice from henceforth even forever.
> <u>The zeal of the LORD of hosts will perform this.</u>"
> Isaiah 9: 6-7. KJV

Wow! Folks got it wrong. Jesus is more than a prophet! Many beautiful and sincere people just don't understand the wisdom of the plan of God in bringing salvation to humanity.

God becoming human just to save us may seem too good or too wonderful to be true to some! That's some serious love! Think about it! A God who cannot die, letting Himself die to feel our pain and legally whip death on our behalf. Then rise again bodily from the dead so that every thing God intended for us to have in the Garden of Eden can be eternally restored plus some! And remember, no one else could do this but God or they would be the Savior!

Wow! Besides, there's not another being in the universe capable of doing such anyway. Not even the angels. Why? Because no one can forgive sins but God alone! (see Matthew 9:6)

> "For unto which of the angels said he at any time,
> <u>Thou art my Son, this day have I begotten thee</u>? And again,
> <u>I will be to him a Father, and he shall be to me a Son</u>?
> And again, when be bringeth in the first begotten into the world, he saith,
> <u>And let all the angels of God worship him</u>.
> And of the angels he saith, Who maketh his angels spirits,
> and his ministers a flame of fire.
> But unto the Son he saith, <u>Thy throne, O God</u>,
> is for ever and ever: a sceptre of righteousness is
> the sceptre of thy kingdom.
> Hebrews 1: 5-8. KJV.

Remember, worship belongs to God alone. Jesus was not an angel!

Finally, remember Isaiah 45: 21-23? Now consider this verse and compare the two.

> "Who, <u>being in the form of God</u>,
> thought it not robbery <u>to be equal with God</u>:
> <u>But made himself of no reputation</u>,
> and took upon him <u>the form of a servant</u>,
> and was made in the likeness of men:
> ......Wherefore <u>God also hath highly exalted him</u>,
> and given him a name which is above every name:
> <u>That at the name of Jesus every knee should bow</u>,
> of things in heaven, and things in earth, and things under the earth:
> And that every tongue should confess that
> <u>Jesus Christ is Lord, to the glory of God the Father</u>."
> Phillipians 2: 6-7, 9-11. KJV

Wow! No wonder the devil hates the Name of Jesus so and does whatever he can to make sure that name is sanctioned from being mentioned in public or television shows! You can talk about any religion or religious leader in the world and be tolerated. But say something about Jesus! Folks start looking at you funny. Why? Because behind the scenes in the invisible world (which most people are ignorant of) Satan and his demons knows who whipped them! And their worse fear? They know

He's coming back again! So hush the Name of Jesus. Even if very sincere people don't understand why!

> "Thou believest that there is one God; thou doest well:
> <u>the devils also believe, and tremble</u>."
> James 3:19. KJV

### *Jesus Had To Be Accountable!*

Now here's the main point I want us to understand about accountability.

> *"What I love about the Lord is
> He never requires of us
> anything He won't do Himself!"*

My reason for showing you the *"Godship"* of Christ is because I want us to see how God always leads by example. What I love about the Lord is that He never requires from us anything He won't do Himself! That's so awesome!

Now if God who is ubiquitous, omnipresent, omniscient, and omnipotent can humble Himself in Christ and then hold Himself accountable to people whom He Himself created, what is He telling us about "healthy" submission and accountability?

Let's consider the account of Jesus when he was a lad teaching in the temple.

### **Luke 2: 40 - 51. KJV.**

40. And the child grew, and waxed strong in spirit, filled with wisdom: and the grace of God was upon him.

41. Now his parents went to Jerusalem every year at the feast of the passover.

42. And when he was twelve years old, they went up to Jerusalem after

the custom of the feast.

43. And when they had fulfilled the days, as they returned, <u>the child Jesus tarried behind in Jerusalem; and Joseph and his mother knew not of it.</u>

44. But they, supposing him to have been in the company, went a day's journey; and they sought him among their kinsfolk and acquaintance.

45. And when they found him not, they turned back again to Jerusalem, seeking him.

46. And it came to pass, that after three days <u>they found him in the temple, sitting in the midst of the doctors, both hearing them, and asking them questions.</u>

47. And all that heard him were astonished at his understanding and answers.

48. <u>And when they saw him, they were amazed: and his mother said unto him, Son, why hast thou thus dealt with us?</u> Behold, thy father and I have sought thee sorrowing.

49. And he said unto them, <u>How is it that ye sought me? wist (knew) ye not that I must be about my Father's business</u>?

50. And they understood not the saying which he spake unto them.

51. And he went down with them, and came to Nazareth, <u>AND WAS SUBJECT TO THEM</u>; But his mother kept all these sayings in her heart."

Wow!

*"Mary and Joseph pulled
Jesus out the pulpit to go home with them!
What volumes of wisdom lessons
this is for us!"*

Jesus was accountable! So accountable that his parents pulled him out of the pulpit to go home with them! Imagine that! And did Jesus rebel? NO! He knows and understands the power of accountability and order! He created the universe! We'll talk about this in a moment. However, for those of us who are so anointed, revelatory, important and gifted that we feel we don't have to listen to ordinary human beings who have faults just like us, CONSIDER JESUS!

Your anointing is never greater than His! He saved our souls, not we His. He didn't need any saving! Remember, He's the potter and we're the clay. Not the other way around!

If we only listen life and ministry won't be so hard!!!!!

## My Personal Testimony of Accountability in My Life!

Very quickly let me give you my personal testimony of how being accountable and submissive to healthy, credible, responsible leadership and others has benefited my life.

I've come from a mighty long way in my Christian journey and ministry. Wow! Be sure to purchase my next book!

As mentioned before, the Lord has opened doors for me in life in ministry that I could never, ever open for myself or even dream of. But it didn't come easy. I had to sit my hips down, get under good leadership, take advice, <u>wait my turn</u>, become a servant from the heart and listen! Let me tell you, accountability works!

## The Blessing of the Quarterly Conference System in the AME Church!

For starters, I've learned personally that it's dangerous as mentioned to assume a pastorate and you're out there all by yourself. Thus, I'm ever so thankful for the Quarterly Conference (meeting) system in the AME Church.

The AME Church has globally 5 conferences or meetings. They are as follows:

## Conferences of the AME Church

- The General Conference. This is when all the churches come together globally every 4 years to establish global or connectional leadership throughout the denomination for both clergy and laity. Here bishops and general officers are elected for the global church and policies are discussed, examined, reevaluated, or pursued.

- The Annual Conference. This is a smaller meeting that composes all clergy and laity within a given local region of an Episcopal district. These regions are called conferences. An Episcopal district is a given region under the oversight of a bishop which is made up of such conferences. At the Annual Conference, clergy and lay leadership come together annually to give an account and update of annual stewardship. Also it's where pastors and lay leadership are appointed and assigned to various ministerial charges.

- The District Conference. Because the AME Church is so large, Annual Conferences are divided into smaller segments called Presiding Elder Districts. A presiding elder is a minister who serves as the overseer or *"middle-management"* between the local pastor, ministerial charge and the presiding prelate of an Episcopal district. The AME Church has currently 20 Episcopal districts (regions) throughout the world. The District Conference is a smaller annual meeting with the presiding elder and his or her district. This meeting prepares the presiding elder district for the annual conference. From here new persons taking their first steps in ministry are sent to the Annual Conference to begin their ministerial journey.

- The Quarterly Conference. (In my opinion most helpful to a pastor on a more intimate level.) This is where the presiding elder meets with each local pastor and his or her congregation 4 times a year on an intimate and up close level. Here, the presiding elder is able to hear both the concerns of the pastor and the local congregation. It's not a meeting where the presiding elder tells the pastor how to run the church like some believe. No! Rather, it's a meeting of accountability and stewardship and proven a tremendous help to leadership.

- The Church Conference. This is a local meeting with a congregation called by the pastor of that charge. It can be called by the pastor as needed giving the parishioners ample notice to attend.

Now I realize that everybody doesn't belong to the AME Church and there's so many of us that are reading this material from various other denominations and organizational structures. Thank God we're all the Body of Christ! Hallelujah! But I'm sharing this with you because regardless of your affiliation or even if you're in an independent status, there's something we can all glean from this.

While I love all the conferences of our denomination, the one I find most helpful as a pastor is the Quarterly Conference. The simple reason for me is you get the detailed individual attention your ministry needs proven to be so helpful for both the pulpit and the pew. It's like a daily tonic that helps you stay on top of things as you move forward in ministry. Also it plugs you into so many resources and gets you ready for the larger meetings.

As a formerly new pastor, (I'm not new anymore! Huh!) I would've been lost without the voice of an experienced minister there to provide the support and guidance I needed. As a result of such leadership, the ministry I serve has grown and has even received global recognition because of the souls that have been saved, delivered, set free and the miraculous advancement in economic development. We're now in 2 locations in a rural area. This is a new concept among any ministry in our given area.

The Quarterly Conference has helped me not to have to waste time re-inventing the wheel and also avoid many foolish and harmful mistakes I could've made as a brand new pastor! Let me take this time to honor the wonderful presiding elders who have mentored me and always told me the truth during my first 14 years of pastoral ministry. These are the honorable; late Rev. John R. Crutchfield, the Rev. Benjamin Samuel Foust and the Rev. Larnie G. Horton. How can I say thanks!

Now let's plow deeper. Oh! Get ready for this one! It will bless you real good!

### My Spiritual Father Wouldn't Let Me Preach Because I Was About to Fornicate!

Now I want to show you something about the power of

accountability on an even deeper level. Throughout my life and Christian journey, from childhood to now, I've had many wonderful mentors. Foremost, my parents! I would not be here today without them! Eternal thanks Mom and Dad! You've reared us well. To God be the glory! My parents still don't play with me to this day! What??? Huh! I thank God for them.

However, before I moved to North Carolina my spiritual Father in the Gospel was the late honorable Pastor Reuben Wright Sr! Founder of the Household of Faith Evangelistic Church of Jesus Christ, Inc. The Lord literally sanctified, delivered and cleaned up my life living under his ministry. My soul was set on fire!

Pastor Wright was Pentecostal Deliverance and a great friend and colleague of my Dad! They were both devout educators in the school system and profound opera singers. Together they'd blow you out! Both were accomplished baritones and starred in George Gerswhin's famous folk opera, *"Porgy and Bess!"* Pastor Wright played the role of *Porgy* and my Dad played the role of *Robbins* from which my baby brother gets his name. My mother, an alto also acted and sang in the opera.

### *"He was a man of power and integrity that didn't play!'*

Nevertheless, what I loved about Pastor Wright was integrity was his middle name and he didn't play! Pastor had 10 children. Yes, ten! And you know what? He taught us how to be men indeed and the women ladies of character and power! If the world had more people like Pastor Wright, I guarantee the prisons wouldn't be so full with our young men and women nor crime rampant on the streets. Pastor Wright was a major soul winner and would cast the devil out of you before you could blink. He was like a modern day John the Baptist and the Prophet Elijah all wrapped up into one! Under his ministry real miracles happened. People were healed in their physical bodies and I saw with my own eyes people delivered from all sorts of demonic bondage! Those were the days!

He was my foundational father in the Gospel prior to my North Carolina experience and even supported me when I relocated. He was a "Body" Christian. In other words, like some he wasn't bent on what denomination you were in as long as you know for certain that you are in the will of God and sat under sound doctrine teaching. He didn't send you to Hell because you didn't belong to his church! Not once has he ever tried to pull me out of the AME Church and even frowned when I told him

I was thinking about leaving during a season in my life. He rebuked me rapidly shaking his head and said,

> *"Before you ever think about doing something like that,
> you call down here first so we can pray!
> You're anointing can only function best where God has called you!"*

Wow! He wasn't trying to gain "personal converts." He was only concerned about the proper development and maturity of the Christian believer. Oh! We need more leaders like him! <u>SECURE</u>! NON-JEALOUS, NON-POSSESSIVE OF SHEEP, NON - INTIMIDATED!

Nevertheless, let me tell you about the fornication. This is juicy!

Being a single pastor, I've committed myself to abstinence and made a quality decision to save my body for my upcoming wife! Prior to even becoming a pastor, I had been committed to abstinence for a long time until the time I backslid in college. Back then I was one of the presidents of the Fornication Committee! Yes. And periodically with a Bible in my hand! Don't yall look at me funny, some of you preachers out there are still fornicating! Yes! Nasty! Don't let me open up the gift now! You know I'm a prophet! Huh! Oh! I'm having a time with this! Let the laughter roll!

> *"Booty has gotten a lot of
> us preachers in trouble!"*

Nevertheless, if there were awards given out for a brother who got the record for staying out the bed for the longest time, I believe I'd win hands down! I mean I denied myself from all types of booty! Barbecue booty! Roasted booty! Booty on ice! (I know you're about to fall out your seat! Huh!) Booty! Booty! Booty! Booty! Oh! Booty has gotten so many of us preachers in trouble. Booty! Reverends, we need to talk about this! There needs to be more teaching on the power of booty! Booty! It keeps us on the news!

Booty! Oh!

…………..Booty!

I'm telling you, I'm about to fall out my chair writing this! Huh! ……….. Booty! One preacher said, "Cursed Booty!" Now that's a sermon. It will make you act like you don't have no sense at all! Make

175

you forget your assignment, purpose, and goals. "Cursed Booty!" It'll make you forget your Mama! Oh! Now that's cursed! ……….Booty!

Nevertheless, on a more serious note, I mean, to God be the glory I don't think I'm a bad looking dude and I've always had an influx of women coming on to me telling me the Lord said I'm their husband. Yet God never told me a word! It's a booty call! We'll talk about this more in a later chapter, stay tuned!

Nevertheless, staying out the bed wasn't really that hard for me because of 7 reasons.

### <u>7 Reasons Why I Stayed Out the Bed:</u>

- I was serious about my decision. <u>I respected my relationship with God, my witness for Christ and I respect the sisters</u> so much that I didn't want take anyone of them on a joy ride that forever ended in hurt. (Been there done that!)

- <u>Sex is like a drug</u>. The more you get the more you want. It's hard to turn off the switch once it's been activated. So like the old saying goes, "let sleeping dogs lie."

- I knew there's really no such thing as "safe sex" as sex goes beyond the physical <u>and has long lasting</u> spiritual, mental, emotional and even physical ramifications after the bedroom act is over.

- The more a person sleeps around, <u>the harder it becomes for God to send the one He really has for you</u>! (Learn something single preachers!)

- <u>I decided I wanted to be a prize to my wife when I get married</u>. (Don't yall sisters out there get no ideas. Don't call me! <u>Save yourself the rebuke</u>! I get enough of this. I'll find my own wife. Thank you! <u>She's already coming down the aisle. Sorry.</u> Yall know I love yall. )

- I had enough tail(sex) in college to last me until I get married. <u>I needed the break.</u>

- <u>I knew how to access the power of the Holy Ghost and walk in victory when my flesh wanted the wrong kind of attention!</u>

(Thanks to the power of God and excellent deliverance teaching from Pastor Wright!)

Yeah! I was faithful to this too! Now let me tell you the other side of the story.

## I Started To Feel I Was Worthy At Least One Slip Up!

So like I told you, I believe I'd win the abstinence award for men! Until...... one day! I was in probably my third year of being a senior pastor. I was walking in integrity and devout holiness. I was Mr. Abstinence USA. And I really was. I was more than serious about my walk with God. I wasn't playing! All my accountability pieces were in place. I and the ministry were known for being a house of genuineness and integrity. I didn't do foolishness in church or even outside as a matter of fact.

For some reason I had to go out of town for something. I think it was a pastor's conference. (This is really going to help you!) Going to a pastors conference is a good thing! So it wasn't like I was going to a party or a strip club. I didn't do clubs! It wasn't my appetite. Again, I was committed to spiritual integrity. Even behind closed doors. I really loved the Lord!

*"My biggest mistake was traveling to the pastors conference alone with no one riding with me."*

The big mistake I made was traveling to this conference alone with no one riding with me. So after driving for a long period of time, a couple of hours, I hooked up with some old friends from guess where? College! Yes. I was in a city where a lot of my old undergraduate buddies lived. Does it feel like a set up brewing yet? Huh!

So excited about the meeting, I made a few phone calls. And let me tell you, fornication and all that stuff was the farthest thing from my mind. I hadn't seen my college buddies in years so I was excited and decided to do so after one of my ministerial sessions was over.

So I hooked up with one of my lady friends from school who was a devout Christian. We had a great time and there was not problem there.

After so many years, she still remained a godly woman of integrity. I felt no alarms going off in my spirit from the Lord as our fellowship was indeed a joy and we had a great and wholesome time.

> *"...I played it off almost wishing
> I didn't have to be a preacher
> for the moment!"*

But then I went to see one of my buddies who was not committed to Christ nor trying to be. AT ALL! The alarm in spirit began to go off telling me to be careful. However, I ignored it feeling that I of course was strong enough to deal with whatever atmosphere he surrounded himself with.

So it was good to see the brother. We talked and laughed about the good old college days and absolutely nothing went crazy at all until, "BOOM!" Some chick he knew walked through the door and was simply slamming! Built from head to toe! Fine I tell you! Just what the doctor ordered. Exactly my type! So you know the devil had pre-orchestrated the whole ordeal through my own willful cooperation. And guess what? If you look good you just look good. I'm keeping it real!

The alarm in my spirit was now screaming. "DANGER AHEAD!" DANGER AHEAD!" "GO BACK TO THE HOTEL!" "I REPEAT. GO BACK TO THE HOTEL AND GO BACK ALONE!!!"

So, I kept my cool. I told my flesh to shut up and chill. Holiness is right! So I played it off very well almost wishing I didn't have to be a preacher for the moment! But oh! What an inner battle! Preachers I know many of us with all this power and anointing have been there!

So I didn't say much to this chick whom I'll call for this story's sake, Mary Ann. No. That sounds too sacred. (see holiness is in me yall.) I'll call her, Bo' Queesha! Huh! Yea! She was a Bo' Queesha! No. Let's call her Cheryl. We'll call her Cheryl!

So I didn't say much to Cheryl and Cheryl didn't say much to me. But our eyes met. This is so real. I'm being transparent for a reason! And after a period of time, I finally left. And you know what? Nothing went wrong. I didn't say anything out the way nor she to me. And I went back to my hotel unblemished and fornication free. But guess what? I got her phone number! A seed!

When the conference was over and I got back to my hometown, I called. This chick was too fine to let slip through my fingers like that! After all, it's been so long since I've been on the fornication committee, surely I wasn't going to mess up now. "Spiritually, I can handle this!" I thought. Besides, how many men my age could say that they've practiced abstinence successfully as long as I have and not be lying? Surely God understands and wouldn't mind just one slip up? I mean. I wasn't going to backslide like I did in college. Just have a little fun.

*"We decided to make the connection. But one problem. I had to preach at my spiritual Dad's church that Friday night! Oops!"*

So Cheryl and I talked and to my surprise, as sophisticated and polished she acted while I was at my buddy's, everything I was thinking she was thinking too! Oh! I was the man! I caught a big fish with her! Feeling I was more than faithful to my integrity not for months but years, I decided I was going to get on the Committee and repent later! Cheryl was off the chain! Why not have some fun? I've brought so many souls to Christ! To God be the glory!

So we decided that we would hook up and not for prayer either! However, there was one big problem. I HAD TO PREACH THAT FRIDAY NIGHT AT MY SPIRITUAL FATHER'S CHURCH!

Now you got to understand what kind of church I was preaching at. This wasn't some church where the preacher is living a double life style, playing with the Lord and the people playing drenched in carnality. This wasn't some church where the pastor smokes cigarettes and the deacons drink liquor and sleep with the girls! Oh no! <u>THESE PEOPLE IN THIS MINISTRY WERE THE REAL THING</u>!

And worse, the gifts of the Holy Spirit operated in this church just like in the Book of Acts. In other words, this church was full of seers. I mean the very ushers at the door! They'll put the Blood of Jesus on a demon in a minute! I ain't kidding! You weren't coming up in there with a bunch of foolishness! Oh no!

The gift of discerning of spirits was mighty in this house. Satan never has been able to creep up in Household of Faith unnoticed and I knew it! THIS CHURCH WAS THE DEVIL'S NIGHTMARE! The power of God was in there for real so much you could feel Jesus on the outside of the church before you even get in! And I had to preach there. In the wrong state of mind!

So there I went leaving North Carolina and going back to my hometown to preach. Cheryl was on my mind every step of the way. Yet I'm contemplating how I could escape being discovered about my secret internal plans to fornicate without it being supernaturally revealed in the Friday night service. See, Pastor Wright had absolutely no idea of my previous whereabouts in North Carolina. No one did. Not even my buddy where I met Cheryl. He didn't even know the elements of my telephone conversation with her.

*"The House was packed
and Pastor Wright
was looking at me sort of funny."*

So off to Household of Faith I go. And guess what? THE HOUSE WAS PACKED! Standing room! People heard that I was back home in town and wanted to hear what this young anointed relatively new pastor had to say.

There I went with a serious good looking suit on, a brief case, shoes polished and my sermon ready and available. I went through a fake repentance in my heart just to shut the voice of my conscience down. I was determined that as soon as I get back to North Carolina Cheryl and I were going to hook up......regardless!!!

However, I noticed while Pastor Wright was indeed glad to see me back home, he was looking at me sort of funny. And if any of you reading this have a spiritual father or mother watching over your soul, you know when you're in trouble even when others don't!

Pastor Wright took a long time to invite me to the pulpit which is sort of unusual. Then finally he called me up. I was starting to feel that even the congregation knew that something was wrong. I still felt like I was in trouble. I hadn't discussed anything with my Man of God but we all knew Pastor Wright could see straight through you no matter what the disguise!

*"The house was packed
and he wouldn't let me preach!"*

Then finally, the moment of truth came. It was time for the sermon. It was time for the Word. Instead of telling me to mount the podium, guess what happened? HE DID! And guess what he said? With a deep, raspy baritone voice he said,

"Brother Brent, I think I'll be preaching tonight!"

Oh! Pride slapped me right in my face! THE HOUSE WAS PACKED! The people came to hear me! Now I know they know something is wrong!

And guess what else? Guess what this Man of God preached on?

EVERYTHING I WAS GOING THROUGH AND THOUGHT ABOUT DOING!

Like the Apostle Peter with lying Ananias and Sapphire, God supernaturally revealed to Pastor Wright <u>ALL MY BUSINESS</u>! I wasn't shocked at all because I've sat under his ministry for years since early high school and knew first hand that the Holy Ghost was in that church for real! All kinds of signs and wonders used to follow God's Word in that house. But see, I couldn't get out the engagement because I had already committed.

And guess what else? It's not over yet. As soon as his sermon was over while I sat in the pulpit in front of all the people and cringed, guess what he said?

"Pastor Brent come down to this altar front and center!" He spoke with all the authority and love of Heaven backing him up.

He said,

"God told me not to let you go back to North Carolina in this condition!" He spoke by supernatural God given insight.

"Son, God has invested <u>TOO MUCH IN YOU</u> and <u>you've come from too mighty a long way</u> to allow the devil to take you out like this! I've got to set you free TONIGHT!"

Then before I knew it, he raised those big hands in the air and laid them upon head.

He began to take authority in the Name of Jesus over every seducing and foul spirit that was on assignment from Hell to make me stumble, lose the ministry and even my life and commanded them to flee! And before I knew it, I started coughing up stuff and the enemy didn't get to sabotage my life nor ministry as intended through a demon called, *pleasure!*

Somebody ought to shout right now! Thank God!

God loved me enough not to allow me to fall into a snake pit even when I was going to do so anyway with my eyes wide open! However, while the revelation of my struggle was supernaturally revealed to Pastor Wright, a long time ago I had already put my accountability pieces in place.

## Are Your Accountability Pieces in Place?

This is what accountability does for us! See, when I first became a pastor, one of the first things I did was to make sure that certain credible, responsible, godly, and integral people were in place in my life. I knew I was entering ministry as a single pastor which opens the door for even greater challenges especially from the opposite sex. The anointing doesn't stop them from coming! As a matter of fact, it makes you more attractive!

Besides, when you're single you have to face issues of loneliness to another degree. No shoulder to come home and cry on. I mean no one to cook dinner. No one to socialize with you don't have to be a shepherd to. These are serious issues. So single pastors, take heed! Married too! We're in a hour where people don't care what your marital status is! Let's be real! Yet I'm a witness that you can walk in steadfast victory and integrity as a single pastor. I've done it successfully for 14 years! However, I didn't do it without paying a price. Trust me it won't fall out the sky! It's a decision. And you will need backup.

*"Don't get upset when the
people you hold yourself accountable to
rebuke you!"*

    The people that I've placed in my accountability system were people who I knew for sure loved me and had my best interest at heart without jealousy. (People who are jealous of you will have tremendous difficulty covering you.) These were people that I could trust and at the same time knew they loved me enough to tell me the truth and get in my business even if unwanted! Uninvited!

    When God places people in your life that you hold yourself accountable to, never get upset with them should they start asking you tough questions that tap into your personal business. It will help you in the long run although it doesn't always feel comfortable. Remember, unlike some, these persons aren't here to assassinate you or put your business in the street. <u>They are safeguards from impending danger</u>. We must always remember, while God is merciful, there's no guarantee that we won't have to pay a terrible price for a careless mistake.

    Remember the lesson we learned from the wilder beast in the animal kingdom. There's safety in numbers! The scripture says it better like this,

> "And if one prevail against him, two shall withstand him;
> and a threefold cord is not quickly broken."
> *Ecclesiastes 4: 11-12. KJV*

    Remember, a lot of the things we see happening among our ranks is because too many of us are lone rangers and aren't accountable to anyone!

**FOOD FOR THOUGHT:**
<u>How to Establish Your Own Accountability System:</u>

- <u>Pray, Ask and Seek God first for guidance</u>.
- <u>Submit to the governing spiritual leadership already over your life and ministry</u>.(make sure healthy sound doctrine leadership)
- <u>Make sure your system is wholesome, godly, credible, responsible, integral, and

- have your best interest at heart. (A devious, wicked person can't watch for you. Don't get counsel from the ungodly! See Psalm 1:1)
- Make sure you have people in your system with wisdom beyond yours! (This is a must but not all exclusive. There are people who can help watch for you who don't have all expertise but they mean business concerning your life, ministry and well being.)
- Make sure your system has integral people who will tell you the naked truth and are not stuck on your anointing, gifts, popularity or accolades.
- Make sure you are willing to allow your system to do it's job without getting upset when they ask you important questions you deem private.
- Don't hide from your system! Check in immediately when you feel you're in at risk situations and even before honoring prevention!

While I had absolutely no discussion with Pastor Wright about what happened at my buddies house with Cheryl, although in 2 different states, he was always praying covering me in the spirit while pastoring in North Carolina. Then on top of this, in North Carolina I had the covering leadership of senior ministers in my own denomination. Greater still, I deliberately surrounded myself with prayer warriors both within my local congregation and beyond to always keep me covered when out ministering on the road. This is so important!

*"Preacher, whose praying for you
when you're out doing ministry
on the road?"*

And to this day I never travel alone, (Especially being single! Nobody's that anointed!) I never go anywhere without proper prayer coverage, (I've trained my parishioners how to pray for me when on the road) and most of all I set up my accountability system way before I board any airplane or ride in someone's car. My system of accountability knows and can answer the following questions.

## Questions My System of Accountability Can Answer

- Where I'm going?
- How to contact me if an emergency!
- The occasion? (My reason for going)
- My departure and arrival times going and returning?
- My method of travel and accommodations? Is all secure?
- The person/s traveling with me and their character?
- Whose picking me up from the airport, hotel, etc.?
- The physical address of the hotel, numbers, etc. and the quality of housing?
- What time will I actually begin to minister? (I often have people back home praying for me the exact time I'm preaching. I've seen phenomenal success in the preaching event doing this!)
- How do I fare after the ministry event is over? (Health, tiredness, warfare, etc.)

I'm telling you it works!

I've heard some preachers say that having all this and adjutants isn't necessary. Whaaaaat????? There are so many Biblical examples to refute such a statement beginning with Exodus 18: 13-26! And when you travel as much as I do, as far away as I do, as often as I do, you better have some back up! Every city has its own unique personality! And so do people in every region! And even if you don't do a lot of extensive travel, you still need someone to be accountable to! It's God's order! It's healthy!

## Don't Get Upset Should Your System of Accountability Rebukes You!

Now setting a personal system of accountability is only for people who are really serious about being integral and avoiding pitfalls. If you've got a lot of play in your game and a lot of sneak in your streak, you're going to have some major problems. However, when you do set up your personal system of accountability don't get upset when that system rebukes you!

    Now when Pastor Wright didn't let me preach, opened my files and called me publically to the altar (The intensity of my situation called for immediate public prayer. I didn't give you all the details of the story just enough so you'll get the point.) my flesh didn't like it. I didn't know I had so much pride until I was sat down from my regal horse.

    Although Pastor Wright is known for great love and tact even when he rebukes you, my little pride was hurt. It was a packed house. But you know what? My spirit was leaping and jumping up and down rejoicing because what he was saying was so true and I really loved God! I wanted to make it in life and ministry! I wanted to be successful! I enjoyed the peace of having clean hands and drama free living. I didn't want to be one thing in the pulpit and something else at home! Living clean has so many more benefits than being controlled and driven by the ugliness of the lust of the flesh!

    Thank God for a pastor in the Kingdom who could care less about my popularity, education, gifts and accolades. Thank God for a leader who didn't think that I was so anointed that I was exempt from being told the truth! Thank God for rebuke! IT SAVES LIVES!

    The book of Hebrews says it best this way,

> "And have ye forgotten the exhortation
> which speaketh unto you as unto children,
> <u>My son, despise not thou the chastening of the Lord,</u>
> <u>nor faint when thou are rebuked of him</u>:
>
> For whom the Lord loveth he chasteneth,
> and scourgeth every son whom he receiveth,
>
> <u>If ye endure chastening God dealeth with you as with sons;</u>
> <u>for what son is he whom the father chasteneth not</u>?
>
> But if ye be without chastisement, whereof <u>all are partakers</u>,
> then are ye bastards, (not really His) and not sons.
>
> "...Now no chastening for the present seemeth to be joyous,
> but grievous: nevertheless afterward it yieldeth

> the peaceable fruit of righteousness
> <u>unto them which are exercised thereby</u>.
>
> <u>Wherefore lift up the hands which hang down,</u>
> and the feeble knees;
>
> and make straight paths for your feet,
> lest that which is lame
> be turned out of the way; <u>but let it rather be healed</u>."
> Hebrews 12: 11-13. KJV

Thank God for the love of our accountability systems and correction! So please. Don't get upset when your accountability system rebukes you. Such love and concern can save your life............ and ministry!

Rejoice!

## Your Anointing Is Not Who You Are!

There's something as pastors and leaders we should always remember.

> "Our anointing <u>is not who we are</u>.
> <u>That's what we have</u>.
> Our callings are <u>not we are</u>.
> <u>That's what we do</u>!
> Behind all our holy regalia
> is still a normal human being
> <u>subject to falter</u>
> <u>if blown by the right wind!</u>"
> A Drently Proverb

Yes indeed.

What is the anointing? In essence, it's a fundamental awareness of the presence of God. It's God's divine presence, power, and ability upon us through the Holy Spirit that enables us to do exploits! The anointing is indeed a precious and priceless gift from God to be valued and treasured.

However, as great as God's anointing is upon our lives it's still not our person. I may have the anointing of God upon me and even in me through the indwelling presence of God's Holy Spirit. However, I still have my own will, feelings, intellect and emotions. I still have my freedom of choice. I can either obey the leading of the Holy Spirit or disobey. God never forces us to obey Him. He leaves the decision totally up to us!

Thus, the anointing is a precious gift from God like oil, yet it's not who I am as a person. Neither are our callings, gifts, talents, abilities, accolades or accomplishments. These are no more who we are than a beautiful suit coat a person wears. They are blessings and tools given to us to help us fulfill our assignment on the earth and fulfill our destinies. A person can have all this and still go to Hell. Why? Because what we operate in only assist and equips us to do ministry. <u>They are not the person</u>!

Jesus said it like this,

> "Many will say to me in that day,
> Lord, Lord, have we not prophesied in thy name?
> and in thy name have cast out devils?
> and in thy name have done many wonderful works?
> And I will profess unto them,
> <u>I never knew you</u>:
> depart from me, ye that work iniquity."
> *Matthew 7: 22-23. KJV*

This is cutting it close yall! We better re-examine ourselves and motives. The Word can't lie, THIS WILL HAPPEN!

Besides it's our relationship with the Lord Christ that gets us into Heaven and not our works anyway. We get rewards for our works, we were created to do them, (see I Corinthians 3: 10-15.) but good works don't save! It's the blood of Christ that makes the atonement for the soul.

> "For by grace (unmerited favor)
> are ye saved through faith;
> <u>and that not of yourselves:</u>
> <u>It is the gift of God:</u>
> <u>Not of works</u> lest any man (person) should boast.
> For we are his (God's) workmanship,
> created in Christ Jesus unto good works,
> <u>which God hath before ordained</u>
> <u>that we should walk in them</u>"

*Ephesians 2:8-9 KJV*

"Much more then <u>being now justified by his blood,
we shall be saved from wrath through him.</u>
For if, when we were enemies, we were reconciled to God
by the death of his Son,
much more, being reconciled
<u>we shall be saved by his life</u>."
*Romans 5: 9-10. KJV*

<u>Keys to victory</u>: "Value your relationship with God more than your ministry and your ministry will always be successful in every sense of the word!"

## Our Positions Don't Stop Us From Being Tempted!

If Jesus who is our anointing through the Holy Spirit was tempted by the devil where does that leave us? Indeed, Christ never yielded to temptation or sinned one time. But there's no guarantee we'll do the same. This is where the power of accountability comes in.

Now don't get me wrong. According to Jude 1:24, He's able to keep us from falling. Also Hebrews 4: 14-16, let's us know that we have help during times of temptation and need. But still, our receiving the benefits of these promises rest on our willingness to cooperate with the Holy Spirit in our lives! What if we refuse? Now let's be honest. Do we always cooperate with God? No! As a great preacher once said,
*"Let's take our halos down!"*
Oh!

Let's take them down and place them under the pews and cry, "Mercy!" At some point all of us have messed up. Even if we're better now! We didn't get here overnight!

And we better watch it. A bishop once said it something like this,

*"Until we get behind the Gate, hear God tell us, "Servant of God well done!" and He place a crown upon our heads,
WE'RE NOT THROUGH PRAYING!"*

Huh!

Let's act like we know! None of us have arrived. Maybe have come a long way, but not arrived.

Failure to cooperate with God is called sin and we all have been guilty.

"For all have sinned and fallen short of the glory of God;"
*Romans 3:23 KJV*

"If we say that we have no sin, <u>we deceive ourselves,</u> and the truth is not in us."
*I John 1: 10 KJV*

Therefore, none of us can throw rocks. Besides, self deception is the worst deception!

However, through the victory of the Cross of Christ, His resurrection from the dead, and the indwelling of the Holy Spirit in our lives, it is possible to live a life of victory without falling. (See Acts 1:8, Romans 6:11-14, 22.) Remember, we're not some helpless little creatures in these matters. No way! We are overcomers and more than conquerors!

However, people even preachers are at different levels of commitment to God, stages of Christian growth, spiritual maturity, and handle the many blowing winds of life differently. Thus, we need each other regardless

## A Lesson From
## the Human Body!

In terms of being accountable, there's nothing that explains it better than the human body. The human body is a prototype of how we're supposed to function in the Body of Christ. Worldwide! Individual organs of the body can't function alone.

Let's turn on the TV and consider the old sitcom, <u>The Adams Family</u>. Remember? I'm telling my age. Told you I'll always be 25. Even next year! Huh!

Nevertheless, the Adams Family had an amputated hand called, *Thing*. And what's strange was *Thing* was alive. Now don't yall go and tell people I'm condoning horror movies and stuff. I'm just using this as a popular example. Huh!

However, this amputated hand could do all sorts of stuff without the body. As a matter of fact, the hand was a renegade because no one knew where the rest of the body was! Nevertheless, this hand could walk without legs, write without a mind, participate in all kinds of conversations and here's a good one. It could even see! Without eyes!

Thing didn't need nobody! It was all self sufficient and whatever it wanted to do, it did it. Even if it meant carrying out bodily functions that belong to other parts alone. Oh! There's so much revelation in this!

However, in the real world we know this is unrealistic and fictitious. Biologically, a hand cannot operate by itself much more an amputated one! Get it? Amputation! That means it was cut off. Preachers, have we cut ourselves off from the rest of the body?

In order for a hand to function it has to have bone, tissues and muscles. Muscles can't move without nerves. Nerves can't send signals without a brain. The brain can't function without oxygen. Oxygen can't get to the brain without the lungs and blood. Blood can't carry oxygen to the brain without the heart. The heart can't get oxygen and nutrients throughout the body without veins and arteries.

Veins and arteries can't receive nutrients without a digestive system. The digestive system can't work without a mouth. (except in cases of intravenous feeding etc. which is not the body's norm) The mouth can't break down food carrying nutrients without enzymes and teeth. Teeth can't stay healthy without hands to brush them, floss, and gargle. And on and on it goes.

But notice how we started out with the hand and ended back up with the hand? In order for a body to remain healthy, every part must submit and be accountable to the other or the whole thing will shut down!

## We Are All Parts
## of the Same Body!

In the 12<sup>th</sup> chapter of I Corinthians Paul has much to say about the wide diversity of gifts, administrations and operations within the Body of Christ. To give the Church at Corinth a better understanding, he used the connectedness of the physiological human body to give better clarity of how we function. Though some may be Baptist, Methodist, Pentecostal, Lutheran, Episcopalian or whatever, we are all needful parts of the same Body!

> "For by one Spirit are we all baptized into one body,
> whether we be Jews or Gentiles,
> whether we be bond or free;
> and have been made to drink into one Spirit.
> For the body is not one member, but many.
> If the foot should say, Because I am not the hand,
> I am not of the body;
> is it therefore not of the body?"
> *I Corinthians 12: 12-15 KJV*

Bottom line: Let's start celebrating our uniqueness but tremendous unity we have in Christ. We no longer have to reinvent the wheel. Whatever we need to function is already in the Body!

## Blood Rushes To The Place
## That Hurts Most!
*(The Body is Set Up to Heal Itself!)*

Let me give another example.

The human body is set up to heal itself. In the same manner, so is the Body of Christ!

Prior to matriculating in ministry, I was a pre-med biology major. I was studying to become a medical doctor. I loved it and still use lots of biology in my sermons today! However, there's something I've learned. Our blood rushes to the place that hurts the most! Blood represents life! (There's great revelation in this concept too! I'm excited!)

In our blood we have two types of cells. Red blood cells and white blood cells. Red blood cells carry nutrients and oxygen throughout the body. White blood cells fight off diseases and infections.

Let's say a person stomps their toe and cuts it. Watch what happens.

First, the nerves in that toe immediately sends a message to the brain that a part of the body is in trouble. The nerves run back to the muscles in that toe and scream, "PAIN!"

Pain, the messenger of the nerves, speaks to the muscles in that toe to remove it from the site of danger. The nerves also alert the eyes so they can look down and see where the trouble is. Further, the nerves tells the foot to freeze until the pain subsides. Then the whole body is alerted and whatever that person is doing stops until the situation is corrected. Oh preachers! When just one of us goes through, what if we worked together like our human bodies?!!

Now here comes the blood. The Bible says, the life of the flesh is in the blood. And Jesus shed His blood for us!

When a person gets cut and you see pus, that's not a negative thing. The pus is a sign that the white blood cells are at work doing a microscopic job of fighting off foreign invaders designed to bring the body infection.

The red blood cells are constantly at work giving the body the strength it needs to win the battle. Then the blood works together to create a clot at the site of the wound to by closing the door of entry to invaders and prevent the loss of more blood. What's happening? THE BODY IS HEALING ITSELF!

And how is this possible? Each organ is accountable to the other creating order. Order now being established paves a smooth route for healing and recovery. When the body has been healed and recovered the person lives!

Preacher, God wants you to live!

### How the Body of Christ Is Set Up To Heal and Protect Itself!

Now just like the human body has specific organs that carry out specific duties, so does the Body of Christ. Now remember, every organ is important whether great or small. So there are no "Big I's and Little You's!" No! Not in the Kingdom! For an example, teeth are small. But get a toothache and see if it won't cause you to go somewhere and sit down! Huh!

My point: EVERYBODY IS SOMEBODY AND CHRIST IS ALL! Yes!

However, I want to use this time to expound on some organs or resources that God has placed in the Body of Christ to keep us from being shipwrecked and that we may have the order to function in peace, unity and properly.

According to Ephesians 4, when Jesus rose from the dead, He ascended on High to the right hand of God and gave Gifts to the Church to keep us healthy, on point and in line until He returns for us again.

The scripture says it this way.

> "Wherefore he saith, When he ascended up on high,
> he led captivity captive, <u>and gave gifts unto men.</u>
> *Ephesians 4: 8. KJV*

This is where the theological term, *"ministry gifts"* comes from. They are also called by some the *"Sonship Gifts"* because they are given by Christ Himself. These gifts are not to be mistaken with gifts of the Holy Spirit found in I Corinthians 12. Rather, these refer to specialized duties and functions given to different types of ministers. Like the organs of the human body, each has a specialized assignment to fulfill in the Body of Christ and the world itself!

Now it doesn't stop here. Let's move down to the 11th verse.

> "And he (Jesus) gave <u>some apostles</u>; and some, <u>prophets</u>;
> and some, <u>evangelists</u>; and some, <u>pastors</u> and <u>teachers</u>...."
> *Ephesians 4:11 KJV*

Notice the scripture says, "some." This means everybody's not called to the pulpit. Nor is everyone called to the pew. God needs one of us in every position to establish completeness.

Moving on, ministry gifts are preachers with specific duties. Let's review them.

## Functions and Duties
## of Ministry Gifts!

### I. Apostles

These are special messengers. They establish new works and territories in the Kingdom. This ministerial grace also carries a special anointing to establish governmental order in the Body of Christ in larger dimensions. They have a grace to perfect leadership within the Body whether clergy or laity including other apostles, prophets, evangelist, pastors and teachers. The apostolic anointing is both an establishing and sending anointing. All apostles in the New Testament have seen Jesus! Even the 2 new ones, Matthias (Acts 1: 20-26.) and Paul. (I Corinthians 9:1)

While I believe the work and office of the apostle continues to this day according to Ephesians 4:13, the idea of contemporary apostles are often a very controversial subject in several theological schools of thought. However, for sure according to Scripture, everybody is not an apostle only "some." And those who claim to be need to be very careful.

*"I know thy works, and thy labour, and thy patience,*
*and how thou canst not bear them which are evil:*
*and thou hast tried them which say they are apostles,*
*and are not, and has found them liars."*
*Revelation 2:2 KJV*

Wow!

Now this doesn't indicate that the apostolic office ceased to exist but certainly hints that there are certain qualifications necessary in order for one to be pronounced as an apostle. Those professing this office around the Church of Ephesus flunked the test. While the office didn't stop with the original 12 disciples, (remember 2 were added post resurrection) one thing all 14 New Testament apostles had in common is that they all seen Jesus. Have you seen Jesus? Does this make you or I an apostle? Ah! This is some good stuff to go back and study on! And here's another question. If the work of the apostle has ceased since the passing away of the early disciples, then how can the Church survive without such an important job being fulfilled considering what the term *apostle* really means?

On the other hand, a bishop (meaning overseer) is not necessarily an apostle although bishops indeed do apostolic work. Yet an apostle can be a bishop simply because the bishopric is an elected office whereas apostleship is a calling. (See I Timothy 3:1, I Corinthians 1:1) Deep huh? A little meaty isn't it? Please don't just take my word for it or come out with some new doctrine! We have enough of these. It's just something interesting to think about and to pursue further in depth study. One thing's for sure, it's certainly nothing to argue over! It's only something to consider.

## II. Prophets

The prophetic office mainly deals with direction for the Body of Christ. Prophets are preachers who have a special grace and gifting to pronounce, speak out and proclaim the mind of God or the direction He would have us take as His representatives in the earth. They are seers who proclaim new frontiers, judgment and are known to cry out against spiritual, social, and political injustices.

## III. Evangelists

The ministerial office of the evangelist is a very powerful and needed one. This gifting is very important because without this office, the Church cannot grow! The grace given to this office specializes in winning the lost and reaching persons who are outside the Body of Christ. The evangelistic office specializes in spreading the Good News of the Gospel so lost souls may come into the ark of safety.

## IV. Pastors and Teachers!

While evangelist bring those from without, the office and function of the pastor and teacher perfects those within the faith of Christ. In essence, the *pastor-teacher* nurtures, trains, equips and develops those who have been brought in. More so, another name for the word *pastor* is protector or shepherd. Thus, the main assignment of the pastor is to watch and care for the souls of the sheep.

Some schools of theological thought separate the pastoral office from the teaching. In other words, while both nurture and train, the pastoral carries the weightier part. The teacher trains and that's it. But the pastor trains, equips, nurtures, watches over and protects.

Other schools based on the language of Greek consider them one office but simply 2 extensions of the same. Thus, when it comes to the total overview of all the Sonship gifts or ministerial gifts it's called the 4-fold ministry rather than the 5. However, in most schools of thought such ministerial gifts are called the 5 -fold ministry.

> *"Out of all the Ministry Gifts,*
> *the pastoral is considered*
> *the most stressful and demanding."*

Out of all the ministerial gifts, the pastoral office is considered the most unique and the most stressful. Why? It's because this office is nurturing in nature. Out of all 5 ministerial functions it's the baby sitter out of the group. The apostle establishes, the prophet points, the evangelist gathers, and the teacher trains. BUT THE PASTOR HAS TO CHANGE THE DIAPERS! Huh! Yes! Not only this, it has to be available throughout all the stages of a sheep's spiritual growth and development. This especially is not easy when a shepherd has several sheep to tend to at the same time! However, without this precious office, the Body of Christ would be severely handicapped, malnourished and become serious prey to all the wiles of the enemy.

This office is so weighty that the Apostle Paul said this concerning the treatment of pastors,

> "Let the elders that rule well be counted worthy of double honour, especially they who labour in the word and doctrine."
> II Timothy 5:17 KJV

Nevertheless, like the human body Christ place these ministerial functions it the Church and even for the world that we might walk in holistic health in every facet of the world. To deny ourselves accountability, teamwork and submission to such when healthy and in order is to deny ourselves wholeness!

Paul said these functions have been established for these reasons.

> "For the perfecting (maturing, equipping) of the saints,
> for the work of the ministry, for the edifying (building up and strengthening)
> of the body of Christ.."
> Ephesians 4:12 KJV

There will develop at least 3 things in us.

### 3 Things We'll Be Via the
### Ministry Functions:

- We'll be equipped and solid in our personal relationship with Christ and just knowing Him as Savior and Lord alone.

- We'll be equipped to handle and face the vast many challenges of ministry and to be effective in doing such.

- We'll be grounded enough in our own personal lives that we will be able and have what it takes to strengthen and encourage others!

And like the blood works to clot infected sights sealing future doors of invasion, let's consider how such functions protect us. Consider this next verse.

"....That we henceforth be no more children **tossed to and fro, and carried about with every wind of doctrine**, by the sleight of men, and cunning craftiness whereby they lie in wait to deceive...."

But speaking the truth in love, **may grow up into him** in all things, which is the head, even Christ:"
*Ephesians 4:14-15. KJV*

Hey. God wants us to grow!

## Chapter Review!

Wow! What a rich and meaty chapter! Did you enjoy your meal? I hope so! It's so important that we understand that we can make it and if we rid ourselves of the lone-ranger syndrome we can miss tons of preventable, unneeded and hurtful pitfalls!

Refusing to be a lone ranger in ministry, I can personally testify how the Lord has blessed my life by holding myself accountable to leadership, waiting my turn, and serving my best from the heart with no wicked ambition or hidden agenda in mind. If I never get any promotion, everything I do I strive to do it as unto the Lord and not for a Grammy Award or some type of praise or recognition.

As result of listening and submitting to healthy, sound doctrine, integral and godly leadership, doors I could never opened for myself have been released and I give God all praise. And what's more, by the grace of God I've never had to compromise my integrity for any promotion! Every thing that has happened in my life happened on my knees first in my prayer closet and following the instructions of God's Word. While I have made mistakes along the way, keeping myself accountable has been the source of every victory. And even today, it doesn't matter how high God takes me, (I say this with great humility and groundedness because only God knows the future) I refuse to be out here without an accountability system! It's so unwise, risky, and dangerous. Remember the wisdom of the wilder beast! Huh! Those animals can really preach!

Thus, as we prepare to move now to the last section of this book which is practical application, I trust that something said in this chapter has encouraged your spirit, mind, heart and soul to pursue excellence, never give up on yourself or ministry and embrace the power of accountability! May God bless you always until we meet again in Chapter 7!

## Chapter Summary:
## "Who Are You Accountable To?"
### *The Dangers of Being A Lone Ranger!*

- To be accountable means to be liable and to allow someone to help watch for your life.

- Many preachers have suffered and fallen into pits needlessly because of not having someone to be accountable to.

- God has not called us to be lone rangers.

- We can learn from the animal kingdom as the lonely sheep is always an easier catch for the wolf.

- To destroy the lone ranger mentality among us, we must be willing to help others in need without betrayal becoming serious systems of love and support to those going through yet knowing our boundaries wise to refer to professional assistance should we not have the professional expertise.

- Your accountability system needs to made up of people who are godly, credible, responsible, having your best interest at heart, non-jealous, not moved by your persona, gifts, popularity, anointing or talent but will call you to the carpet and tell you the naked truth!

- Don't do ministry without people praying for you.

- Jesus Himself was accountable to people.

- If we're not serious about integrity and safety, we'll have problems with accountability.

- Never get upset when your accountability system rebukes you.

- Order and peace cannot come into being without accountability.

- The human body is a perfect example of how

<u>accountability and order work together</u>.

- <u>Christ has establish Sonship or Ministerial Gifts, (or functions) to make sure all of us remain well nurtured, protected and able to produce successful ministry</u>.

Find your system of accountability today!

Celebrate! A fresh new start is coming your way!

**Notes:**

# SECTION III

# APPLICATION

Tips To Reducing Hurt
And Maximizing Breakthrough
Through Practical Wisdom
Nuggets of Prevention, Health,
Wholeness and Recovery!

*"Remember,
Experience ain't always the best vocalist.
Prevention can out sing experience
many days. Let prevention sing!"
A Brently Proverb*

*Celebrating New Beginnings!
Yes Indeed!*

# CHAPTER SEVEN

# "PLEASE, JUST ONE MORE PIECE OF CHICKEN!"

## *"Preachers and Health Issues"*

"Sometimes our eyes are bigger
than our stomachs.
Don't dig your grave with your teeth."
Wisdom Compliments of the honorable
Mr. James C. Edwards, Senior II

"Or do you not know that your body is the
temple of the Holy Spirit who is in you,
whom you have from God,
and you are not your own?"
I Corinthians 6: 19 NKJV

[This chapter addresses 9-1-1 Emergency Help Cries 1, 2, and 8.]

**WHAT AN IMPORTANT CHAPTER!** God is concerned about our physical bodies! In my opinion this is one of the most important chapters in this book. Yes! The health and well being of our bodies!

*"Without a physical body, all the wisdom,
and know how God has invested in us
to bless generations
has to get up off the earth!"*

Why is our health so important? It's simply because our phyical bodies are our *"earth suits."* Therefore, it doesn't matter how gifted, anointed, or even wise we are. Without a body, WE CAN'T PREACH! Foremost, without the capsule of our bodies all the wisdom, talent, ingenuity, and know how God has invested in us to bless generations has to get up off the earth!

Thus, in this chapter, we are going to address the importance of holistic health. This covers our total person: body, soul (mental and emotional health) and spirit. (the real eternal part of us that never dies.)

Listen. God is concerned about the well being and preservation of our entire being!

"Now may the God of peace Himself sanctify you completely;
and may your whole spirit, soul, and body be preserved blameless
at the coming of our Lord Jesus Christ."
*I Thessalonians 5:23 NKJV*

"Beloved, I pray that you may prosper in all things and be in health,
just as your soul prospers."
*III John 3:2 NKJV*

Well, let's get this ball rolling!

**FOOD FOR THOUGHT.**
*"Someone once said,
"Most preachers die from a heart attack,
stroke, and broke!
Let's make the necessary corrections
we need in our lives today!"*

## My Passion For the
## Health of Preachers!

I write this chapter with great feeling because I have a deep passion for the holistic health and well being of preachers. In my opinion, too many great leaders have died seemingly way before their time! Throughout the years of 2000 -2009, I have personally felt the loss of great men and women of God who have influenced and touched my life more than words can say. Such have gone on to be with the Lord seemingly before the completion of their work. Most of these were men and women of God who went on to Glory before reaching the age of 70.

Listen. These were not men and women of God who were fakes or goofing off. These were honorable Generals in the Kingdom of God who really loved God, His people, walked with great integrity and power having turned whole communities, regions, and even nations upside down to the glory of God! They were all powerhouses in their own right. Awesome! And because my life has been tremendously touched and transformed by these, I write with great passion and urgency.

Now I'm very careful when I say, "these men and women of God seemingly passed away before the completion of their work" because in our finite minds we don't always know how God views our work from a heavenly perspective. We don't always know if God only intended for us to carry a work to a certain point and then has a greater plan of someone else picking up from where we left off to take it to the next dimension. From our vantage point we may see a work as being incomplete. However, what we see is only a piece of the puzzle. God sees the whole picture even if we don't!

Speaking to the Church at Corinth the Apostle Paul said it like this,
"For we know in part and we prophesy in part."
*I Corinthians 13:9 NKJV*

So tell me, what's the part that's missing or unrevealed?
Then the prophet Isaiah says it this way,

"For My thoughts are not your thoughts.
Nor are your ways My ways,' says the LORD.
"For as the heavens are higher than the earth,
So are My ways higher than your ways,
And My thoughts than your thoughts."
*Isaiah 55:9 NKJV*

Let's face it. We just don't know everything!

However, even though we don't always know every iota or detail of the awesome plans of God, He does let us know in spite of all the wonderful things He has in store for us, we can make the wrong choices and cut our lives short! As anointed and powerful we may be, we can leave something uncorrected in our lives and it takes a costly toll on us!

> *"I've learned if Satan*
> *can't get us to backslide,*
> *the next thing He'll try to do is kill*
> *us via our health!"*

When it comes to people that are totally sold out for Jesus Christ and are catalyst for positive global change, I find the enemy of our souls does this. If Satan cannot get us to backslide and return into a life of sin embracing the things of the world, the next thing he'll try to do is kill us! He wants all the laborers of God off the field! And what greater way to accomplish this than attacking our health! Many times through doors we ourselves have opened.

While Christ has given us authority and power over Satan and all the works of darkness, (see Luke 10:19) the enemy of our souls still can take a child of God out if we play with his toys!

Consider the wisdom of this passage.

> "For the scepter of wickedness shall not rest
> On the land allotted to the righteous,
> <u>Lest the righteous reach out their hands to iniquity</u>."
> *Psalm 125:3 NKJV*

Wow! This means we can open the door ourselves for stuff and things to happen to us!

According to this scripture, as long as we're doing what we're supposed to be doing we're covered. It's when we start tipping trouble lurks at the door. I know! I've been there!

Nevertheless, with all being said, I still don't claim to know or fully understand why some great and awesome preachers and leaders have passed from labor to reward in the time they have. I'm not God. However, we thank God the devil still loses! However, being a preacher myself, I'm very concerned more so now than ever before about the health of people of God and we who mount the pulpit.

## The *"All You Can Eat"* Buffets After Church Have Gotten Us in Trouble!

As a boy growing up I had an appetite out of this world! If you could cook it, I'd eat it! My kindergarten teacher used to call me the "Cookie Monster" and a former minister used to tease me saying I had a bottomless stomach.

My father used to say something as a boy that makes so much sense to me now. He used to say,

*"Your eyes are bigger than your stomach.*
*You're digging your grave with your teeth!"*

Huh! How I was so tickled by this as a kid. However, now a grown man, my Pops was on to some serious revelation about our health care and eating habits.

### Many Preachers Like to Eat!

I've noticed most committed Christians are on much guard about living right, against sin, and disobedience. We can spot a demon 40 miles away! But here's where many of us get the flunk monkey. We're not as committed when it comes to our health! The "all you can eat" buffets have gotten so many of us in trouble and if you're like me, many preachers like to eat!

We can cast every spirit out except the one called gluttony! Huh! And now we're so heavy we can hardly breathe doing our sermons and folks think it's the anointing. No! <u>WE'RE OUT OF SHAPE</u>! I'm writing this to save somebody's life!

We'll preach the horns off a Billy goat or the grease out a biscuit and then go right to the "all you can eat" buffet after service. Then we do this all in the name of "fellowship!" Yall know I'm talking right! And guess at what time? 10:00 PM at night or later! Then go straight to bed and sleep on all this stuff. Oh the gas! Glory halitosis! Huh!

**FOOD FOR THOUGHT:**
*"Did you know that many times
heart conditions, strokes and diabetes
are diseases of the fork?"*

And because we don't get enough fiber in our diets it doesn't all come out in our waste. Much of this stuff remains trapped in our bodies. So where does it go? Where does it hide? It remains in our bodies building up and building up just waiting for the right time to do us in! It will wait right until we're at the peak of success in our ministries and then explode. It will wait right until we're at the door of the greatest breakthrough we've ever seen in our lives! God forbid! And I'm not talking about passing gas either! Oops, I went there! I'm talking about heart attacks, strokes, and diabetes! I heard a great preacher say it like this, "Diseases of the Fork!"

Some of us will sing on the choir. Work as ushers. Serve on various committees and boards in ministry with love and due diligence. All these things are good and even needful at times. But where's our due diligence when it comes to eating right, exercising, getting the proper rest, and dealing with stress properly? Are these foreign words to us?

When was the last time we had a physical from head to toe? When's the last time we visited the doctor and it wasn't an emergency? I know God can heal supernaturally, yes! But why use the supernatural as a cop out when so much can be prevented just by doing simple things? Besides, God is not Santa Claus or our genie! This is not witchcraft or hocus pocos. He's too great for that! Remember there's a difference between faith and foolishness!

Why must we skip over "the known" to get to "the unknown?" Sometimes we use spirituality as an excuse for laziness and end up giving God a bad name! We cause people to think we're out to lunch!

God does and will do miracles. I believe in miracles and the power of God! Yes! But the Holy Spirit is also intelligent! In my opinion, miracles should be our last resort. We should look for miracles <u>after</u> we've done all we can do!

A wise woman of God said it like this once on her voice mail.

*"You do the possible. Then trust God for the impossible!"*

Thank you Pastor Cynthia Pringle, I'll never forget!

Some of us haven't done the possible yet.

### If It's to Be, It's Up to Me!

The bottom line is this. When it comes to making positive and needful improvements in life it's not up to God. It's up to you and me. The decision to walk in better health starts with us. It's our choice.

Joshua says it like this,

"This Book of the Law shall not depart from your mouth,
but you shall meditate in it day and night,
that you may observe to do according to all that is written in it.
For then <u>YOU WILL MAKE YOUR WAY</u> PROSPEROUS,
and then you will have good success."
Joshua 1:8 NKJV

There you have it! Our success in life isn't up to God nor the devil. It's solely up to us and the decisions we make. God provides and gives us everything we need to be successful. Satan tries to hinder our doing the right thing. However, our overcoming is totally up to us and the attitude about life we carry!

### They Used to Call Me Reverend Gu-Butt!

Now here's one to make you laugh! I can talk about all this health stuff because I know what it's like to be on the wrong side of the fence. Let me tell you! They used to call me Reverend Gu-Butt! Do you know what that stands for? *GUT AND BUTT!* Yes! That's what my buddies called me in New Jersey. Reverend Gu-Butt! Those were the days! And while I could pull the ladies Huh! I was searching for a wife but my big stomach always deducted points as far as appearance goes in my opinion at that time. Sometimes we are always our own worst critics. Yet a young lady from the Bahamas even told me so! I mean she said it with pin point attitude. Oh!

Nevertheless, I wasn't obese but I was well on my way. I was a chunky preacher with a belly the size of a basketball and I won't talk about the other aspect. Huh! However, I was indeed overweight!

> *"I'd shout so hard
> I'd fall slap out! 'BAAMMM!"*

    I can talk about trouble breathing, heart palpitations, and not having enough wind to properly finish sermons not because of someone else but because for a moment I was there! Yes! I could preach the grease out a biscuit and then had to sit down. Not so much because of the anointing but rather because I was out of shape! And I was young too!

    I was a Methodist shouting preacher! What a hybrid! I would praise God with great fervor and enthusiasm. I was very sincere about it too! I meant business. And although I had tons of Pentecostal and non-denominational friends, I could out shout and out dance all of them! I'd shout so hard I'd fall slap out! BAAMMM! I was on the floor! Folk thought I was powerful! No brothers and sisters! I needed water! No! AIR!!! Somebody get me some air! Oh! I'm having a ball! Somebody needs some air right now! Huh!

    And while I'm riding this horse, come on preachers. Let's be real! Let's be honest. Now some of yall know you plunked down in that chair on Sunday morning not because you finished your sermon! You were tired! Huh! I know the people were up shouting and getting their praise on while you were preaching. But come on Reverend. You know it was either sit down or fall down because you know it takes wind to finish a sermon! YES WIND! And you hadn't been to the gym since...............? Oh! I'm just teasing now. But come on............ good preaching takes WIND!

> *"I noticed I was getting
> bigger and bigger
> and my breath was getting
> shorter and shorter!"*

    NEVERTHELESS, now that we've got our laugh on, on the serious tip I can talk about the all you can eat buffets because that's what I did! After attending some of the most powerful life changing services, I and a whole tribe of us would go and plant ourselves in mass at one of these eternal food restaurants regardless how late the hour! However, as time progressed I noticed I was getting bigger and bigger and bigger and my breath was getting shorter and shorter. And worse, I was only in my late twenties to early thirties!

## I Had 3 Wake Up Calls
## That Brought Me to Fitness Reality!

However, in spite all my humor and jubilation, I had 2 wake up calls that slapped me into reality motivating me to take control over my health situation. Here's the first.

### 1. I was hospitalized
### for 2 days due to pains in my chest.

One day, although a young man I thought I could've possibly been having a heart attack. I had been preaching over the land, earth, sky and sea getting very little rest and absolutely no exercise while yet eating every and anything that could be cooked or baked. I was sincere and faithful in what I was doing loving God and the people with all my heart. Yet, I felt something was going on with my ticker.

Not wanting to take any chances, I had one of my parishioners to take me immediately to the emergency room to be checked. To my surprise, they hospitalized me! Outside of doctor visits and minor outpatient surgery, I'd never been hospitalized before in all my life! They kept me for 2 days simply to run test on me making sure everything was ok.

During my stay, the news of my hospitalization reached one of my dear ministerial colleagues. Coming to the cardiac floor to visit, she asked me the most thought provoking and agitating question that I'll never forget to this day. Noticing my room was in the cardiac wing she said,

"Reverend. What's the average age of people on this floor?"

Finding this a peculiar question with some unknown catch I answered something like,

"Probably 60 and up." I said somewhat reluctantly.

Then she said with a voice of concern and rebuke, "THEN WHY ARE YOU HERE????!!!!"

Ouch! She stung me!

And as quickly as she asked, guess what? She walked out the

room, went home not giving me much time to answer!

Now I'm going to tell you. I was angry with her. Yes. Reverend Gu-Butt was angry. I was angry because she cut me to the core and landed right where I lived. Then she was abrupt about it. Yet I knew the genuine concern she had for me as a fellow colleague and sister in the Gospel for many years.

Nevertheless, her sharp rebuke worked wonders like a medicine. I got to seriously thinking about my health. Why was I there? At age 30 something? All I was doing was ripping and running all over the country side doing a good work but using a poor method. Burnout! This experience was my first wake up call and from this day forward I started taking my health more seriously and began to seek out an exercise program.

Thank you Reverend Lisa Marshall! God always uses you in some of the most unusual yet spectacular ways! Thanks for making a difference in my life. I'll never forget!

## 2. Working with NFL players provoked me to do better!

Through the honorable and recently late Pastor Barbara Brewton Cameron, founder of the outstanding Community Outreach Christian Ministries and the Harvest Center of Charlotte, North Carolina where over 52,000 meals are prepared for the homeless annually, I met several NFL players.

Pastor Cameron saw something great in me that I didn't necessarily see in myself and entrusted and appointed me as the Tuesday afternoon speaker for the Harvest Kitchen. This created an opportunity for me to speak to the homeless in mass as well as to countless others who frequented the center. Having volunteers from all walks of life, crossing over cultures and racial barriers from the rich and famous, on down to former prostitutes and dope dealers, I encountered many wonderful people. However, my connection with several fellas from the NFL seemed paramount.

*"I was invited to be a premier speaker at a NFL and celebrity gathering in Miami, Florida."*

One year a NFL star requested and invited me to be the premier speaker at a gathering of several professional athletes and youth in Miami, Florida. Being honored and even overjoyed by the request I consented to go. It was a remarkable trip although I thought the airplane was going to crash! Huh! Talk about a rough flight! However, I thanked God for the experience as I got to see aspects of what it's like to be a NFL star that I could've never experienced just by watching a football game on television. We had a remarkable time!

So one night on this trip, all the players, other guest and myself went out to eat and a very nice restaurant. I was so glad all meals were being paid for by the host because no one knew how broke I was on this trip! Oh! I was broke yall! I only had enough money for Bojangles Chicken and that was it! Nevertheless, because the meal was on the house we could order whatever we wanted. So I pigged out!

All the sudden, I noticed how it seemed everybody at the table was in excellent physical shape but me. I mean all the brothers were buff and cut with no bellies hanging over and when we entered the restaurant people started cheering! So since I was with them I tried to act like I too was of the team. You know how that goes! Oh! Yet not a soul asked for my autograph. Huh! I wonder why?

As the evening progressed I noticed something else. Every NFL player at our tables ate right! I mean they ate a lot but it was all the right kind of stuff! I was the only one at the table who ordered a whole slab of pork ribs or some kind of fattening meat. I don't remember specifically what kind of meat it was. I just remember it wasn't too healthy. I mean I had all the grease all over my face and if I wasn't among such a distinguished group of brothers and ladies, I'd chew the bones! That meat was good! Besides, the food was free! So I thought I'd just live it up!

Then all the sudden one of the players sitting across the table spoke to me. He asked me something like,

"You're a pastor?"

Not knowing him as well as I knew some of the other players I said reservedly, "Yes." I didn't broadcast the fact that I was a pastor as everybody didn't know I was scheduled to speak at the celebrity Sunday morning service. I never was big on waving a title around. I didn't think it was that important. I was just glad to be there.

Then he began to talk to me about another mutual pastor we both knew. Now here comes the punch line. Like Reverend Marshall he said something ruffled my feathers too. He said something like,

"You know, most of you pastors don't take care of your health! I tell my pastor all the time he needs to take care of his health! You pastors got to take care of your health!"

I said to myself, "I know he ain't rebuking me!" Actually it was my pride that was a little disheveled with rib grease all over my hands.

Then he went on and continued to expound on the subject of preachers and health while all I could see between he and I was the living remains of an animal that I just slaughtered on the table. I ate like I hadn't eaten in months. While he was talking all the guilty evidence of gluttony lay before me. Huh! I ate like I was eating for three hungry people! I knew he was checking out my plate. The full but healthy meals ordered by the other team players brought quick rebuke to my adverse and radical plate! It stood out like a soar thumb.

Nevertheless, like Reverend Marshall's words, it was another positive cut. But again, it became another turning point for me! God used these NFL brothers to inspire me to get in shape and I'm thankful too! They even helped me. From time to time several brothers would periodically give me some serious healthy tips on how to get started on a healthy fitness program from a professional point of view and not just something that would give you a heart attack from throwing your body into shock! And even when I began to work out, lose weight, change my diet, and started developing new muscle formation they'd always encourage me helping me to stay focused when people would criticize and say some of the ugliest things about my weight loss. Thus, I was reaching my goals!

A heartfelt thanks to Sasa, Mike, Derwin, Leonard, Ismael, Purcell, Eddie and to every player whom God used to inspire me that preachers can be fit too! Unspeakable thanks! It's changed my life!

Needless to say, the glory and power of God fell in that Sunday morning service. It's one we'll never forget! To God be the glory!

### 3. I had a supernatural experience while preaching!

Finally, the thing that really motivated me and pushed me into consistency with not cheating with my fitness program was an unusual experience I had while preaching. I had started to cheat with my fitness and was gravitating back to my old unhealthy ways.

Right there in Charlotte, North Carolina I was invited to preach at a convention hosted by a ministry from Atlanta, Georgia. It was located at a great hotel and was indeed an awesome service! I was the afternoon conference speaker and oh! The power of God was all in that place.

Right in the midst was an organist who could really play the organ. I believe the organ was a Hammond B-3. Anybody who knows something about organs knows this thing can put out a serious gospel sound. So there I was preaching and this brother could really play and flow with the message. (Preachers you know how refreshing it is to have someone who can compliment your message with an organ and not distract it!) Nevertheless, it was a tremendous time!

> *"Like a dark fog I saw in a vision things the enemy wanted to do to stop me from preaching such as heart conditions, diabetes, and other illness that are associated with poor eating and heredity."*

Well right in the middle of the message I had an unusual experience. I was preaching with all my strength and for some strange reason it seemed like I could see myself preaching while I was preaching! How this happened it's difficult to explain. The power of God was on me and it was like I was at two places at one time.

Nevertheless, I was preaching hard and I could see myself doing so! Then I heard a question.

"You see how hard you're preaching?"

I didn't answer because I could see and feel myself clearly.

"If you want to continue to be able to preach with strength you're going to have to bring your body into its proper alignment!"

Then I saw right in the middle of my sermon like a dark fog things the enemy wanted to do to stop me from preaching that had a history in my family such as heart conditions, diabetes, and other illnesses that are associated with health and eating habits.

> *"Preacher, the devil wants to shut you up!*
> *Don't let him do it!*
> *Practice good health today!"*

Let me tell you. This was the motivation that walked me over the bridge. The message was clear. Either take care of my health or complicate life and ministry with tons of problems down the road! I told you if the devil can't get us to backslide the next thing he'll try to do is kill us if possible through our health! Why? Because preacher your ministry is going to encourage and cause somebody perhaps about to throw in the towel to live!

> "....How beautiful are the feet of those who preach the gospel of peace,
> who bring glad tidings of good things!"
> *Romans 10: 15b NKJV*

Preacher, the devil wants to shut you up! Don't let him do it! Practice good health today!

> "The thief (the devil) does not come except to steal, and to kill, and to destroy,
> I (Jesus) have come that they might have life,
> and that they might have it more abundantly."
> *John 10:10 NKJV*

I will never forget this service. It was at this point that I dropped all my excuses and decided not to cheat anymore and be consistent with physical fitness, diet and nutrition, and learning how to properly handle stress. And guess what happened?

## I Got A Brand New Body
## ......On Earth!

Let me tell you what happened. I got a brand new body! Not in heaven (I'm waiting on that too one day! See I Corinthians 15:50-58! Hallelujah!) but here on earth! Yes!

Instead of encouraging me, several people started to criticize me about my weight loss thinking I was sick and one person even said my head was too big for my body! And to be honest, it certainly looked that way! But I never gave up. I knew I was in a physical transition that wasn't yet complete. People didn't know or understand the professional fitness goals and process I had undertaken. It was a price I had to pay to get to my goal.

### FOOD FOR THOUGHT
*"Whenever you make up your mind*
*to do the right thing, look for opposition.*
*Sometimes from the most unusual places!*
*But keep stepping and moving forward!*

Some said I looked like I was a crack addict and others even began to spread vicious rumors about me saying I had some type of deadly disease. I mean church folk unfortunately! Some of my own colleagues! But I refused to let such ignorance stop me! Let me encourage you. Be mindful many times when you make up your mind to do the right thing look for opposition. Sometimes from the most unusual places but keep stepping! You'll be glad in the end that you persevered and will feel horrible if you don't! The opportunity may not come again!

And you know what's funny? Some of the same people who were most critical of my weight loss could use losing a few pounds or even tons of it themselves! Yes! I guess for some folk it's their way of saying, "I should be doing what you're doing but I'm too lazy!"
Oh! Told yall I believe in keeping it real!

But guess what? THE HARD WORK PAID OFF! In my late thirties I had the body of a 24 or 25 year old with all the energy too! Now I'm in my early 40's and still the same holds true. I could take my shirt off at the beach and not be ashamed. And I'm not talking about using such as an occasion for the flesh either!

Guess what else? My cholesterol levels became normal and no more heart palpitations! I could run as far as I want to and no longer get out of breath. Thus, such as made preaching and doing ministry so much easier! And here's a big bonus: WHAT A STRESS RELIEVER! Yes! With all the challenges that come with ministry, exercise and eating right does wonders for stress removal.

*"YOU CAN DO IT TOO*
*regardless of your age if you*
*get serious and try!"*

And here's another thing. My clothes fall on me so much better! I can fit once again into my college pants. I've moved from a size 38-40 waist to a 34! Why? Because I obeyed the Lord, brought myself under discipline and He gave me a new body on earth!

Am I bragging? BY ALL MEANS NO! I'm sharing all this with you as a testimony that YOU CAN DO IT TOO IF YOU TRY REGARDLESS OF YOUR AGE! You've got to do it because it will make all the difference in your ministry plus benefits! God forbid, if you go Home to Glory let it be because God called you and not because you didn't make the necessary corrections you needed to while on earth. Remember, you can't preach without an "earth suit!"

When you serve God, He promises to do this for you:

> "Who redeems your life from destruction,
> Who crowns you with lovingkindness and tender mercies,
> Who satisfies your mouth with good things,
> <u>So that your youth is renewed like the eagle's.</u>"
> *Psalm 103:4-5 NKJV*

Listen. At any age, God will restore your youth if you let Him.

Rejoice!

Don't believe me? Ask Abraham and Sarah! Abraham impregnated her at 100 and Sarah was 90! Huh! (Genesis 17:17) With God nothing is impossible! All you got to do is believe!

## 4 Principles To Start A Health and Fitness Program!

Well Preachers, it's time now! Let me give you a few principles of success on how to start a fitness program. Remember, you are investing into your own life, family, ministry and destiny!

### 1. You must learn to feel good about yourself no matter what shape you're in or size!

This is so important! This is most important! This is the first step. The starting point!

If your self worth is based on your physiological size you're going to be in a lot of trouble! While we all should desire to come down to our ideal healthy weight, it has nothing to do with the value and beauty of we are as individuals and Children of God! Remember, who you are is more precious and deeper than that.

Valuing who you are regardless of shape or size is important because life is funny. It doesn't matter how much we exercise and work out, God forbid, so many different things can happen to us to alter our physical appearances at any time. Then what do we have? This is a fact of life.

While we should strive for optimum health, if our self esteem is based solely on our outward appearance we're headed for a life of emotional ups, downs, and instability as every season in our lives brings different changes as we grow older. Nevertheless, feeling good about ourselves fat, skinny, or in between will do wonders to start off any workout program because you'll enter such free from the anxiety of undue self torment.

And please, do remember! The quickest way to unhappiness is to compare yourself with someone else. You have your own story and uniqueness! Celebrate that! Refuse to be a carbon copy!

## 2. Never start a fitness program without consulting your doctor first!

This too is so important. Never begin a fitness program without consulting your doctor first!

I have heard horror stories of well meaning people trying to start a fitness program to get in shape and becoming seriously sick and even falling dead on the spot because of putting their bodies into shock!

Always remember that all our bodies are on different levels of tolerance as each of us are unique. Every fitness program should begin small and gradually and then building from there. Your doctor can professionally tell you what your body is capable and not capable of doing.

And let me say this. <u>YOU CAN EXERCISE AT ANY AGE</u> even if you're 99! Professionals have now coordinated appropriate exercises for every age group that exist. Even with several health conditions. However, still you must first check with your doctor or risk the consequences!

### 3. After being approved to begin a fitness program get a certified professional fitness trainer.

This too is important because a certified (not a jack leg or quack) professional fitness trainer can tell you set you up on the right program to target and reach your desired goals. Also they can tell you what exercises would be most appropriate for you to accomplish such. And greater still, they can show you the proper way to use the equipment and when to stop.

Using the right amount of weight and having the proper form is everything in an effective fitness program. Failure to have these characteristics could result in serious injury and even death in extreme cases. Also having a professional fitness trainer can assist you and teach you how to monitor and chart your progress which is very key to seeing real results.

Now never fear. Getting a professional fitness trainer does not have to be difficult or expensive. While there are some that are, most gyms have representatives on hand who can at least get you started on a program at little or no cost at all if you cannot afford a consistent trainer. Nevertheless, I encourage you. It's good to take your first steps to health and physical fitness with one. The education and things you'll learn from them you can eventually use down the road when you grow to the point where having a trainer may not be necessary.

### 4. You cannot have an effective fitness program without a proper nutritional program.

Now here's a biggy! You cannot establish an effective fitness program without a proper nutritional guidance!

> *"It doesn't matter how hard you sweat in a gym. If you don't eat right you'll lose everything you worked so hard for!"*

The saying, "you are what you eat" is so true! It doesn't matter how hard you labor or sweat in a gym if you don't eat right you'll lose everything you worked so hard to achieve. Ask me how I know? Been there! Done that!

In my journey of weight loss, I never dieted. They don't work for me! They're tormenting and normally don't last long. So I just changed what I ate and the portion size. However, I learned this information from nutritionist.

Therefore, it's important that you consult a professional nutritionist (most gyms have these on site) to give you proper nutritional guidance as you work out. Let me tell you why.

Whenever you work out or expend physical energy, it's important that you replace that energy with the necessary nutrients, proteins, and vitamins lost during the exercise. Without such your body cannot repair itself or grow properly resulting in loss of needed gain and advancement. Also, if you're seeking to start a fitness program and have some type of physical illness, health condition, or the like, you'll definitely need to know what foods, liquids, supplements, and quantities are necessary for you so you'll never place your body and health in at risk situations or danger. Especially if you're on medication! (In such cases your doctor along with your nutritionist should be notified.)

### The Benefits of Using A Gym!

Now let me say this. With all that's been discussed there are tons of benefits of utilizing a professional gym. While anyone can also effectively workout at home, the benefit of using a professional gym can be summed up in one word: RESOURCES!

Your local gym will have resources that you may not have at home, current updates and equipment that's regularly serviced, several group classes to help you reach your goals, and so many other features that may not be readily available in your home. And most of all, the atmosphere of the local gym inspires motivation. For some people, working out at home requires a whole lot of diligence and discipline because the only motivation you may have is yourself. However, the atmosphere of a local gym often encourages you to push to your goals.

Now let me also say this, because many of us are clergy and are followers of Christ, when you choose a gym membership you may see all kinds of stuff that aren't godly. However, remember we have to live in this world till Jesus comes. But it doesn't mean we have to participate in any foolishness. Just stick to your focus and reasons for working out and you will do well.

"I do not pray that You should take them out of the world,

> but that You should keep them from the evil one."
> *John 17:15 NKJV*

However, if this is an issue for you, do research prior to signing up for gym membership and find one that's comfortable for you. They're out there!

**The Benefits of Working Out!**

Now that we've discussed 4 keys to starting a fitness program, let me share with you a few wonderful benefits of working out. Please note: This list is not exhaustive. However, I also added what working out and fitness can do!

## **Benefits of Working Out!**

- Better overall health
- Adds years to life
- Improved self esteem
- Relieves stress
- Increases ability to fight off disease and infection
- Improved digestion
- Increased energy and stamina
- Better sleep
- Healthier skin
- Improves the removal of toxins from the body
- Improves sexual performance (I'm talking to married folks! Huh! Get off the Fornication Committee single people! Get off! Oh!)
- Improves overall appearance
- Improves water retention
- Strengthens bones, increases flexibility
- Advances and strengthens muscular development
- Decreases aging
- Lowers bad cholesterol
- Improves circulation
- Reduces high blood pressure, cardiovascular disease, stroke, and some forms of diabetes
- Improves brain functions and ability to think and process
- Improves and advances your quality of life and living!

Wow! And there's so much more!

Preacher, can you afford not to exercise? Sounds exciting to me!

Get with your doctor and start a fitness program today!

Now here are some benefits specific to clergy.

### Benefits of Working Out For Preachers and People in Ministry!

*" It keeps the sanctuary from becoming your mortuary!*
*Need I say more?"*

- Increases ability to hear from God by removing sluggishness and tiredness!
- Helps you to preach better by placing your body in a better condition
- Allows you to be able to do more in ministry enlarging your territory, expanding your borders without excessive taxing on the body
- Helps prolong your life in this world giving you a greater opportunity to fulfill your total destiny, fulfill the Great Commission of Christ, complete your assignments, enjoy your family, live to see the fruit of your hard labor, get things in order with clear directives for those coming behind you should you die, leave a living will, inheritance, and legacy for the generation to come!
- Helps relieve the many mental and physical stresses and challenges that come with ministry. Keeps the sanctuary from becoming your mortuary!
- Helps you fit better in your robe! Huh!
- Great stress reliever when the sheep are working on your nerves and you can't tell them!
- Helps married clergy to keep the fire burning in their marriage
- Helps single clergy to be in shape should they decide to marry and even if not giving more energy to enjoy life and smell the roses along the way!
- Gives you more stamina to endure spiritual warfare!
- Helps you to do better sermon preparation
- Clears the fog away from our minds helping us to dream great dreams and establish greater vision and destiny for the Kingdom of God!

Reverend, I think it's time to hit the gym today!

## When It Comes to Total Fitness Remember Healing is Good But Being Made Whole Is Better!

Remember I told you in the beginning in this chapter how God is concerned also about our mental, emotional and spiritual health and well being also? This too is so important! So far we've talked about getting in shape through beginning a fitness program. However, no program can be complete until we understand the importance of holistic health which also includes soul and spirit! Without such we cannot call ourselves completely healthy or whole in the full sense of the word. Let's discuss this.

### FOOD FOR THOUGHT
*"The healing ministry of Jesus*
*extended far beyond the mending*
*of physical discomfort.*
*He always embraced the power of wholeness."*
*A Brently Proverb*

### Why Wholeness Is Better!

When a person is healed that means something is fixed. A person can be healed and still not be whole. For example, a person can be healed from a physical condition and still struggle with issues of low self esteem, inferiority complexes, or even guilt form past mistakes and failures. The list could be infinite.

And guess what? If a person is troubled in spirit and soul, it will in turn still affect the body. For example stress can lead to an elevated blood pressure which could lead to headaches, lack of sleep, heart attack, stroke, and other alarming physiological affects if not corrected. See why wholeness is better?

### Wholeness Deals With Issues From the Root!

Please understand both wholeness and healing work together. Healing sometimes is an extension of wholeness but not always in every case. Wholeness deals with issues from the root.

The word *whole* means to be complete. One. Undivided. Without fragments or parts. Unified. To be sound. Healthy. Not diseased. In the words of a preacher, it's to have "nothing missing nothing broken."

Thus, while healing places broken things back together, wholeness goes to the source AND THE REASON! Let me give you two examples from the New Testament.

### The Paralytic!

In the New Testament, there was a paralytic who was brought to Jesus for healing. However, there were skeptic religious leaders who had issues with Jesus claiming power to forgive sins. Thus, when He performed the miracle upon the paralytic, he also forgave the man's sins. This miracle shows the holistic healing ministry of Christ proving it to be far greater than just mending physical discomfort.

> "But that you may know that the Son of man
> has power on earth to forgive sins"
> then he said to the paralytic,
> "Arise take up your bed, and go to your house."
> *Matthew 9: 6 NKJV*

### Wholeness is Better Because Healing Can Be Lost If Root Issues Aren't Dealt With!

Now here's the second example.

Because wholeness deals with the root, cause, and reason, healing can be lost if such aren't dealt with. Consider this passage!

> "See, you have been made well. Sin no more,
> lest a worse thing come upon you."
> John 5:14 NKJV

Here we see that staying well of healing carries responsibility from the recipient. In this particular passage, while the scripture does not give clear indication how this man's condition originated, we can assume that sin had something to do with it by the response Jesus gave. Thus, in this case, the maintenance of this man's healing would be based upon his willingness to stay out of sin!

Now the scripture makes it clear that all sickness is not caused by sin! (See John 9:2-3.) So please don't go around misdiagnosing people with screwed up theology that's not of God! Some things are caused by sin and some things aren't! Know the difference!

However, I lift this text simply to show that if we intend to procure holistic health body, soul (mind/emotions) and spirit, it cannot be done if we neglect even just one part of our person!

So preacher, GOD WANTS YOU WHOLE!

If we're not whole colleagues in areas of soul and spirit or even in our bodies here's what we must do. Talk about it! Begin to tell what's bugging us so we can get the help that we need. We've already discussed the importance of talking, how and who to talk to in a previous chapter. However, if we follow through holistic health is on its way!

## So Can I Have Just One More Piece of Chicken?
## Chapter Review!

The answer is yes! However, only if in moderation and not too close between! Nevertheless, in this chapter we talked about preachers health and wholeness. We've said several things. However, while the main focus of this chapter has been on physical health, we also learned that the body is only one aspect of total well being as every part of us is interconnected to the other.

> *Our bodies as temples*
> *of the Holy Spirit*
> *goes beyond issues of fornication."*

We must always remember when the Bible says "our bodies are temples of the Holy Spirit" that such goes beyond issues of fornication. (all illegal and unlawful sex in the eyes of God)

When the Apostle Paul said that *"our bodies are temples of the Holy Spirit"* he was addressing issues of fornication among believers and why such shouldn't be. God is Spirit but He indwells and uses our physical bodies to carry out the present day ministry of Jesus Christ. And because He lives in our bodies, when we fornicate, we're messing with the holy presence of God in our bodies! One of the quickest ways to pick up demonic bondage is through unlawful sexual practices. We'll talk about this in the next chapter. However, if we read all that Paul had to say about our human bodies we'll see that our bodies are simply the dwelling place of God period.

The Holy Spirit not only lives in our spirits but also our bodies! So it's good if we're not married that we strive to avoid fornication. But married or not, we need to also focus on keeping our bodies strong and healthy for the glory of God!

Nevertheless, Paul in his discourse to the Corinthian church made it clear that our physical bodies aren't the only aspect of our beings we should present to the King of Kings and Lord of Lord's. We also must never forget our souls and spirits too!

> "For you were bought at a price;
> therefore glorify God in your body and in your spirit,
> which are God's."
> *I Corinthians 6:20 NKJV*

Besides, our bodies are like taxi cabs for God! You'll never know when He'll need a ride to bless someone through us! Yeah!

I borrowed that one from a great woman of God!

Thanks Mrs. Gool!

## Chapter 7 Review
## Preachers and Health Issues!

- The physical health of clergy is of utmost importance because our bodies are our "earth suits." Without such we can't preach.

- To stay on the earth we must have physical bodies therefore, we must take care of them.

- God is concerned about the holistic health of clergy. This involves body, soul (mind/emotions/will) and spirit. (the real eternal part of us that never dies)

- If we don't take time to correct habits, ways, and things in us that destroy good health, we can leave earth before the time leaving our ministries unfulfilled and generations behind us groping.
-
- Healing is always a good thing but being made whole is even better!

- It's important that clergy pursue a professional fitness program to advance holistic health.

- When a person decides to pursue health and fitness he or she might encounter obstacles but the rewards are far worth it!

-

## A Final Encouraging Word!

Wow! How I enjoyed this chapter! This is my bread and butter! Colleagues if only we follow through watch the great things we'll accomplish in our lives and ministries!

Here's a final word I want to share with you. It comes in the form of a famous old Negro spiritual sung all over the world. It's so encouraging. Especially during times things get rough in our lives and ministries and we feel like giving up. May it encourage you heart exceedingly and abundantly!

### *"Ain't Got Time To Die!"*
*By Hall Johnson*

*"Well I keep so busy praising my Jesus*
*Keep so busy praising my Jesus*
*Keep so busy praising my Jesus*
*Ain't got time to die!*

*When I'm feeding the poor*
*I'm praising my Jesus*
*Feeding the poor*
*I'm praising my Jesus*
*Feeding the poor*
*I'm praising my Jesus*
*Ain't got time to die!*

*Cause it takes all of my time*
*to praise my Jesus!*
*All of my time*
*to praise my Lord if I don't praise Him*
*the rocks gonna cry out!*
*Glory and honor!*
*Glory and honor!*
*Ain't Got Time To Die!"*

Celebrate and rejoice!!!!

# CHAPTER EIGHT

# LAMB OR LAMB CHOPS?
## *"Preachers and Sexuality"*

*"If you're human like the rest of us,
every now and then we feel the fire burning
and it's not always the Holy Ghost!"*
A Brently Proverb

"Flee sexual immorality. Every sin that a man (person)
does is outside the body, but he who commits sexual
immorality sins against his own body. Or do you not know
that your body is the temple of the Holy Spirit who is in you,
whom you have from God, and you are not your own? For
you were brought at a price; therefore glorify God in your
body and in your spirit, which are God's."
I Corinthians 6: 18-20. NKJV

" Preacher, what do you do when the lambs you serve
look like lamb chops?
What do you do when you know
that church member
looks good?
Christ told us to feed the lambs not eat them!" Huh!
A Brently Proverb

[This chapter addresses 9-1-1 Emergency Help Cries 3, 12, 13, and 6.]

**NOW HERE'S A HOT ONE!** Literally! Huh! Hot! Get it? Preachers and sex! What a topic! Sadly, second to accusations of stealing money and misappropriating funds, this is one of the biggest topics keeping us on the news! Ecclesiastical sexual misconduct!

Now while it's very unfair to slander all the pulpits of the world with accusations of sexual misbehavior, we know this is indeed a very real issue that exist among us meriting our healthy discussion. Certainly there's not enough talk about this matter among our ranks! Maybe if we talk more on sex and the pulpit we won't have so many casualties!

*"Politicians, celebrities,*
*and people of other vocations feel the fire too.*
*So let's not limit this to clergy alone!"*

Nevertheless, let's be fair. Let's not isolate or limit this matter to clergy alone! How many politicians, celebrities, athletes and just people from all walks of life deal with this same issue? Sexual desire is a part of the human nature and clergy aren't excluded! Therefore, let's open up the floodgates of understanding and healing up in here!

Therefore in this chapter, we are going to talk about ministry and proper attitudes about sex. We will discuss tips to sexual integrity within and without the pulpit, recovery from failures, and prevention. In other words, how to avoid falling into needless sexual traps and pitfalls that can easily ensnare the non-watchful minister every time!

And preachers let's be honest. Because we're human like the rest of the world, every now and then we feel the fire burning and it's not always the Holy Ghost! Yes! Sometimes it's that other fire! Yes! It's that natural fire of human passion that desires companionship and intimacy in physiological ways which can't be met through serving in the pulpit. And even sometimes, it's that strange fire pushing and edging us like Adam and Eve to eat fruit from forbidden trees of desire God never intended for us to touch. Ever! So here's my question. What do we do when we come to moments such as these? Let's be real. IT HAPPENS!!!!

Because this chapter is so deep it's divided into 3 sections to take us where we need to go. I have listed these for you.

## Divisions of Chapter 8

- Section 1. Lamb or Lamb Chops? *Clergy and Sexual Temptation*
- Section 2. *Developing Proper Attitudes About Sex*
- Section 3. *Tips to Sexual Integrity From the Pulpit*

I'm so excited because we ain't talking about this yall! Not like we should or at levels where needed. It's a hush - hush among us. And you know what Reverends? Our silence has caused us to lose one too many soldiers on the battlefield! Let the revival begin!

**SECTION I.**
**Lamb or Lamb Chops?**
***Clergy and Sexual Temptation!***

**FOOD FOR THOUGHT**
*"Listen. Preachers desire sex and romance too!*
*We're human! However, the problem is*
*when we go to the devil to get it! Huh!"*
*A Brently Proverb*

Listen. Preachers get tempted too! Sometimes we get tempted from one night stands, to booty calls, struggles with porn, to slipping out on spouses. IT AIN'T RIGHT BUT IT HAPPENS! And since there's not a human being on the planet who doesn't get tempted, whether we've done these things or not, all stones have been dropped chapters ago! Remember the woman caught in adultery in the New Testament? Remember how Jesus responded?

"...He who is without sin among you, let him throw a stone at her fist."
John 8: 7b NKJV

And serves them right! She didn't commit adultery by herself. Why didn't they report the man? See how hypocritical we can sometimes be? God forbid!

And check this one out! What do you do when the lambs we serve start looking like lamb chops? Ah! Preachers what do we do if that sister in the congregation is just gorgeously hot or ladies that brother just got it going on and his eyes are dead slap on you? And not just for the Word either! Reality check: IT HAPPENS! And we've got to talk about this or we'll have more casualties!

Jesus told Peter,

> "So when they had eaten breakfast, Jesus said to Simon Peter,
> "Simon, son of Jonah, do you love Me more than these?"
> He said to Him, "Yes, Lord; You know that I love You."
> He (Jesus) said to him, "<u>Feed My lambs</u>."
> John 21: 15 NKJV

Like Peter, as under-shepherds we are commissioned by Christ to serve the flock of God by feeding His lambs until He returns. However, have you ever been in a situation where one of those lambs started looking like a delicious meal to fulfill some appetite unsanctioned by God or common sense? If so how do we handle such moments? Oh! I know this may be an uncomfortable but this is some real stuff! So let's talk about it and get the victory!

Colleagues, even if this is not your situation if it affects one of us it affects all of us so let the healing oil and balm be poured! It's time for us to embrace sexual integrity, healing, wholeness, deliverance, and sanctification once again in our pulpits. And I'm not being super spiritual either! Bedroom holiness is possible! Pulpit holiness is possible! Having healthy relationships between shepherds and sheep is possible without crossing boundaries! Yes!

The same God who can open the Red Sea and raise Lazarus from the dead is able to help each of us to walk in sexual integrity regardless to any bondage, addictions, bleeps, and bloops from our past! Yes He is! Rejoice! His power is available to us today!

> "Now to Him who is able to keep you from stumbling,
> and to present you faultless.........."
> *Jude 1.24a NKJV*

Listen. I'm a personal witness that He's able! With all the traveling I do I've had all kinds of lamb chops thrown at me! Talk about the leg of lamb! Huh! Oh the stories! None of us are exempted! Yet I'm a first hand witness that God is able and yet knows how to keep us in integrity and in the ark of safety. But we've got to start talking about this stuff.

Not only do politicians, celebrities, attorneys, athletes, and other human beings go through this, preachers we certainly aren't battle zone free. Now we may not all find ourselves in such situations but if we're not careful we could be! We're only one step away by the grace of God. Now

I certainly don't believe in roasting the lambs we're called to serve but I too know the heat of the kitchen! Hell's kitchen baby! Oh! Having a ball here!

Rejoice!
### "Colleagues, We've Got Work To Do!"

Nevertheless, we've got to talk about this stuff in a healing and healthy manner because we've got work to do. So as you read this chapter don't draw back breakthrough is coming. In my opinion, there's nothing more damaging than shepherds who become intimate with the sheep they serve or vice versa. I call it *"spiritual incest"* and walking on very thin ice and dangerous ground. We are called by God to feed the lambs not turn them into lamb chops!

Now again. Don't close this book because it's coming down your street or someone out there! Your breakthrough is coming! You might close it just a second before your miracle breakthrough arrives! Keep reading! We've got to talk about this or we'll sink like the Titanic!

We are held accountable to God for every lamb, sheep and person damaged at our hands. Consider these powerful passages of scripture.

"My people have been lost sheep.
<u>Their shepherds have led them astray;</u>
They have turned them away on the mountains.
They have gone from mountain to hill;
They have forgotten their resting place."
*Jeremiah 50:6 NKJV*

"Woe to the shepherds who destroy and scatter
the sheep of my pasture!" says the LORD."
*Jeremiah 23:1 NKJV*

This is why character before ministry is so important no matter how well learned or gifted we are. When a life is ruined at the hands of the pulpit, it's a terrible thing and one that often takes a sovereign move of God to fix! As leaders, we can never play or trifle with people's lives! This is why we need to make sure we've allowed the Lord to thoroughly purge and deliver us if needed and get our foundation right before trying to build a ministry on top with shaky hands.

Dear colleague, if you are struggling with unhealthy sexual addictions, get help today! It will pay off in the long run. Don't sit there because of pride and ruin people's lives! Don't be discouraged but get help!

Hey! Let's not be so quick to jump into ministry if we know the spiritual tires of our cars aren't bolted in tight. Wait on God and seek professional godly counsel!

Consider this passage.

> "My brethren, (ladies included) let not many of you become teachers, knowing that we shall receive a stricter judgment."
> *James 3: 1 NKJV*

In other words, "to whom much is given much will certainly be required." Look before you leap! We can't lead people until we lead ourselves. Secondly, if we cause any of God's lambs to stumble, we have to answer to God Himself.

> "But whoever causes one of these little ones
> who believe in Me to sin,
> it would be better for him (or her) if a millstone
> were hung around his (or her) neck and he (or she) were drowned
> in the depth of the sea. "Woe to the world because of offenses!
> (enticements to sin) For offenses must come,
> but woe to that man (or person)
> by whom the offense comes!"
> *Matthew 18: 6-7 NKJV*

Wow! This is Jesus talking here!

> *"Listen. It's not just the preacher.*
> *Some of you sheep are hot too!*
> *Some of us will drop it like it's hot in a minute! Huh!*
> *Let's get it together yall!"*

Why is the penalty so severe? Because people's lives are beyond price! And let me say this. If you're reading this and you've fallen short in any of these areas, listen! Still never give up! GOD IS STILL IN THE RESTORATION BUSINESS!

However, let it also be known that this doesn't apply to preachers alone. There are some hot sheep too! Yall know it! Some of you sheep will drop it like it's hot in a minute! Huh! And then blame everything on the preacher! Sisters coming to the House of God with those tight dresses like you're going to a night club pretending like you don't know you're figure is all that! Then gonna sit all up on the front row with just enough of your thighs to show to distract the preacher. And my brothers! Using the sanctuary as a place for hook ups and connections. Judgment Day is coming! Let's get it together yall! Don't got to Hell with a Bible in your hand! Don't go to Hell at all!

Yall know I'm telling the truth. Somebody say, "Amen!" Give me a B flat on that organ! We've got work to do!

### Preachers Are Human Too!

Nevertheless, while we make no excuses, nor should ever support, condone, justify, sanctify iniquity or any erroneous behavior, we must also remember that like you, preachers are human too! And just like you or any other human being, we too are built with the capacity for love, companionship, sex, and the capacity to reproduce. AND IT'S A GOOD THING AND NOT EVIL! Especially when we handle the God's gift of intimacy following the wisdom of God's Word in the commitment of marriage.

However, before we enter this discussion, let me share 4 reasons why I feel the temperature for sexual temptation among clergy is so high along with several other vocations that cast the soul into the spot light of popularity.

**4 Reasons For Increased
Sexual Temptation
Among Clergy!**

1. <u>**Being in the spotlight exposes us to greater degrees of pressure and isolation**</u>.

Someone made the statement, "it's lonely at the top." And if you know anything about mountain climbing, the higher up you go, the thinner the air becomes.

Being at the top brings pressure because when everybody knows your name and look to you for guidance, it's almost as if we're held hostage to our "public selves." It's like we have to remain one step above being human although the rest of the world doesn't have to. They can make all sorts of failures without the pressure of excessive scrutiny by the public and media. Just one mistake. Just one and "BOOM!" You're out of there although our shortcomings happen among human kind everyday.

Such pressure leads to isolation. As mentioned in a previous chapter when people in the spot light aren't so sure how people will respond if we reveal our personal struggles and battles, we internalize. If stuff stays internalized too long like a volcano it will explode! Thus, because of scrutiny concerns, when actually facing a crises some clergy are reluctant to cry out for help. Therefore, stuff gets pent up inside instead of being released.

When stuff is pent up on the inside of us this places us in the danger zone. And if not careful this is where sexual temptation get's it's strength. It's a proven fact by science that sex brings physiological relief and reduces stress. Thus, when a preacher is going through the corridors of pressure and isolation, if not anchored in his or her resolve, IF NOT CAREFUL he or she becomes more vulnerable than at other times to get caught up in sex traps and nets.

### 2. **People Are Often Attracted To Authority Figures And People of Notoriety**!

Here's another avenue that raises the temperature gage of ecclesiastical temptation. There are some people who watch us and are seriously attracted to persons in the spot light or authority figures. Celebrities, politicians and professional athletes go through this all the time.

People in general have different agendas whether good or bad. So I dare not attempt to speak for everybody. However, there are some people attracted to authority figures for the following reasons. (Not limited to these!)

- A sense of identity and desire to associated and recognized with persons who appear successful.

- For financial security reasons.

- For personal gratification, other motives and agendas. Sometimes even obsession. (It can get spooky sometimes. I've got stories! Oh!)

- Some people feel connecting with an authority figure ensures that they will be treated right with respect, dignity, and the promise of a prosperous future.

- Other

Thus, with all this going on sexual temptation increases because connecting with people in the spotlight almost seems like a grand prize to some. In worse cases, some will even throw themselves at you sexually. And can I be honest? All temptation doesn't look bad at all! (Oh! I can tell you stories!) As a young preacher there have been many times I've just had to ............... RUN! I hope this discussion is helping you!

### 3. <u>Sometimes clergy persons have deep, hidden sexual wounds and addictions never discussed</u>.

Now let's plow a little deeper. Sometimes public leaders have deep seated sexual addictions that are never discussed but preached over and covered by community service. These are the most dangerous more than the previous two reasons for increased sexual temptation among clergy already discussed. It's more lethal because when temptation comes from without, it's more manageable. But when temptation comes from within it's another story.

> *"None of us were born preachers.*
> *We became preachers. Therefore, in spite our sincerity,*
> *sometimes there are issues from our past that have*
> *followed us to the pulpit."*

We must remember, none of us were born preachers. We became preachers. Thus, beyond our sincerity and love for God and community service, sometimes there are wounds and things from our past some have never been able to shake. Sometimes clergy and persons from other vocations have had sexual wounds, experiences or addictions that have followed them to public service making sexual enticements so much easier to fall prey to! Why? Often that's what's quietly been at work in them on the inside.

Always remember. Temptation works best at what we desire. If we don't desire it, it's not much of a temptation to us. The scripture says it this way.

> "But each one is tempted when he (or she)
> is drawn away by his own desires and enticed.
> Then when desire is conceived, it gives birth to sin;
> and sin, when it is full-grown, brings forth death.
> Do not be deceived, my beloved brethren"
> *James 1: 14-16. NKJV*

However, the good news is we rejoice that if this is our situation, we are not condemned or confined to living the rest of our lives in prisons of sexual addictions and bondage! Christ is able to set any captive free! However, we must be willing to cooperate with God's instructions and the breakthrough ministry of the Holy Spirit. We'll talk about this in more detail later. But for now always remember you're not a slave to your yesterdays!

Jesus said it like this concerning your situation!

> "Therefore if the Son makes you free,
> you shall be free indeed."
> John 8:36 NKJV

Celebrate!

## 4. <u>Loneliness</u>!

You may be surprised to know how many preachers struggle with issues of loneliness. I mean preachers that have thousands of sheep following them as well as those who may pastor the faithful few! It's not the size of a congregation that matters in these situations.

Such loneliness is not one where there's an absence of people. A preacher can be married and still be lonely. Rather, it's a loneliness that comes from being found on a peculiar plane in life and place that speaks a language only known by a few inclusive of rivers that only you can cross alone. It's like what I said earlier about actually inhaling air that's much thinner at higher altitudes on a mountain that at its base.

Two people can be talking by way of a cell phone with one on the top of the mountain and the other at the base thousands of feet apart. The commonality is that they both are on earth and are breathing air. However, although communicating, their actual experiences of the feeling of breath going in and out of their bodies will be significantly different. These differences create different feelings and needs. This explains the type of loneliness and peculiar language I'm talking about.

What is real to the person breathing an atmosphere of thinner oxygen levels may not be as real to the person below. This is a type of isolation.

Some studies have shown that there are many pastors who have tons of difficulty just finding someone to call "friend." I don't mean someone who just hangs out in the sanctuary all day but someone whereas we can remove the covering of our public image as senior leaders and just be down to earth human without all our grandiose titles, etc. etc. A friend who accepts us for the person we are plain and simple, short comings and all without scrutiny.

When this cannot be found, it is so much easier for leaders in this position to fall into the arms of a stranger in the night. This too is a potential cause for the increase of sexual temptation among clergy. Because we are human, there are times we want to let our hair down too!

Nevertheless, it's a trap! So let's consider some avenues and principles to help enlighten and strengthen us in such matters.

## SECTION II.
## Proper Attitudes Towards Sex!

**FOOD FOR THOUGHT:**
*"Sexual intercourse was God's idea!"*
*A Brently Proverb*

HAVING DISCUSSED 4 REASONS why sexual temptation is often so high among clergy and vocations of the spotlight, let's get down to the nitty gritty. We've got to first understand and make sure we have the proper attitudes towards sex and sexual behavior. There are 3 important things we need to know here.

First we must understand that sexual intercourse was and is God's idea not the devil's. Secondly, we must know that there is no such thing as "safe sex" outside God's instruction manual. And thirdly, we must understand as clergy regardless of our sexual past, God has made provision for us to walk in sexual integrity. And thirdly, Oh! This is going to be good! Let's get started!

## 1. Sexual Intercourse
## Was God's Idea Not the Devil's!

Let's begin by considering the origin of sex. Sexual intercourse and intimacy is not dirty or filthy. It's a gift from God! It was God's idea and creation not the devil's. Sex is a wonderful thing! Amen! It only becomes unclean and defiling when not used in the confines of its original design by God its manufacturer, originator and abused.

Note: the word, *defile* means to contaminate, pollute, corrupt or make dirty.

Sex is Celebration!
*"Sex is the highest physical pleasure
a human being can naturally have.
The very act speaks it's own sermon!"*
A Brently Proverb

God created sex as the highest physical pleasure a human being can experience naturally. Drug addictions don't count as they will mess up your mind and kill you!

God not only created sex for procreation but celebration! Yes! Celebration! And even more FUN! (For those of you preachers who've forgotten how to laugh!) While intercourse in marriage is sacred, intimate, and holy, it's also FUN!

A Chinese proverb says it this way,
*"Laughter is the shortest distance
between two people!"*
Oh!

With the divorce rate climbing everyday, how wonderful it is for married couples to keep laughter in marriage! We need to see more of this in the Body of Christ. Our children need to see this! It will heal nations! We'll talk about this more in a forth coming chapter. However, let me say this powerful 3 letter word again. Married couples get it in your spirit.

**"FUN!"**

It will keep your marriage together and full of joyful spontaneity. Fun!

Rejoice!

When was the last time you and your honey laughed? Fun!

*"The celebration of sex preaches a sermon without words!"*

Nevertheless, sex is so powerful it's a gift to married people only! Sorry! I'll tell you why later. Don't close this book! Remember, your breakthrough is coming!

Sexual intercourse in marriage is celebration because the very act itself preaches its own sermon without words. When two people get married, they're exchanging. Now only do they exchange vows but are exchanging their very lives.

Thus, the celebration of sex was created by God to seal and celebrate such an exchange. This is called consummating the marriage. In some circles, a marriage isn't complete until it's been sealed by the physical sexual exchange between a man and a woman. Why? Because nothing could be more deeper. When people have sexual intercourse their entire being is involved, spirit, soul (mind/emotions) and body!

Therefore, sexual intercourse is a physical way of celebrating and a wonderful picture of showing what has taken place between a man and woman as husband and wife mentally, emotionally and spiritually! Two worlds have now become one and the coming together of two physical bodies closes out the event.

When a man and a woman become one in marriage, God joins them together spiritually. Two separate distinct worlds become one world. It's something that cannot be seen with the naked or physical eye. Marriage is spiritual. That's why people buy wedding rings. It's a physical reminder of a spiritual union unseen by the physical. The circle of the ring represents a never ending relationship until parted by death. (Huh! We won't talk about divorce in this chapter. Oh! Too much for now.)

However, in marriage God makes a man and a woman "one flesh."

"Therefore a man shall leave his father and mother
and be joined (cling) to his wife,

> <u>and they shall become one flesh</u>."
> *Genesis 2:24 NKJV*

This is awesome!

Even biologically the structure of our physical bodies gives clue to the power of the celebration of sex. This may be a bit deep for persons under 18 so parental guidance is admonished.

> *"When a man gives the woman receives.*
> *When the woman receives she give back!*
> *What powerful exchange!"*

When a man enters a woman *he's giving her something*. Everything about the male sex organ shows that it's designed to give. This is the reason for its shape, appearance, and scrotum sack that houses what will be given. The seed of life! It's the chromosomes within the seed of the male that even determines the sex of a child!

When a woman receives the male organ *she's getting something*. Even the phenotypical and physiological structure of her sexual organ says everything is built to receive. Nothing in her body is designed to give seed. Only receive. Her body even knows how to lubricate itself without the assistance of outside help because it was pre-designed to receive from the man.

Now here's the equation. When a man gives the woman receives. When the woman receives she gives back. Thus, the celebration of sex is the serious coming together of exchange! And what are they exchanging? Their lives! And what does the woman give back? A baby! Even babies are living gifts and testimonies of the power of two worlds becoming one. A new life has begun!

So see, sexual intercourse is so powerful it's for the married only. However, I still haven't entered this discussion yet. But for a moment, let me encourage every preacher out there, learn to enjoy the gift of sexual intercourse with your wife or husband!

There's not enough healthy talk about this among our ranks and for this reason 9-1-1 Emergency Help Cries 3, 12, 13, and 6 occur all the time! So married folks, remember romance in marriage and holiness is God's gift to you. Consider these passages of scripture.

## God Wants Married Couples To Enjoy the Gift of Romance!

### To the Man

"Let your fountain be blessed,
And rejoice with the wife of your youth.
As a loving deer and a graceful doe,
Let her breast satisfy you at all times;
and always be enraptured with her love."
*Proverbs 22: 18-19 NKJV*

### To the Woman

"He brought me to the banqueting house,
And his banner over me was love.
Sustain me with cakes of raisins,
Refresh me with apples,
For I am lovesick.
His left hand is under my head,
And his right hand embraces me."
*Song of Solomon 2: 4-6. NKJV*

"Behold, you are handsome, my beloved! Yes pleasant.
Also our bed is green.
The beams of our houses are cedar,
And our rafters of fir."
*Song of Soloman 1: 16-17. NKJV*

[Note: The Song of Solomon is a dichotomy because it speaks of both human love and also uses such to declare several meanings of spiritual significance.]

### A Warning To the Unmarried Who Are Sexually Active!

"Marriage is honorable among all
and the bed undefiled;
but fornicators and adulterers God will judge."
*Hebrews 13: 4 NKJV*

Embrace God's gift of romance God's way and skip the drama!

[Note: Fornication in it's root meaning refers to any and all forms of sexual activity outside marriage. Not limited to heterosexual sex only.]

## God Created Sex, Satan Perverts It!

Now check this out. God created sex but Satan perverts it.

The word, *pervert* simply means to change, twist, or alter something from its original order and purpose. This is what the enemy of our souls does for the sole reason of getting back at God for losing his eternal position with Him and to bring our lives into bondage!

> "Therefore rejoice, O heavens, and you who dwell in them!
> Woe to the inhabitants of the earth and the sea!
> For the devil has come down to you, having great wrath,
> <u>because he knows he has a short time</u>."
> *Revelation 12:12 NKJV*

Now this first passage of scripture is eschatological (the theological study of end time events) in its writing but I highlighted it here just to give example how the enemy is really angry at God and His creation because He's eternally lost out.

> "The devil, who deceived them,
> was cast into the lake of fire and brimstone
> where the beast and the false prophet are.
> And they will be tormented day and night
> forever and ever."
> *Revelation 20: 10 NKJV*

This hadn't occurred yet otherwise we'd have peace on earth.

> "Be sober, be vigilant; because your adversary the devil
> <u>walks about like a roaring lion,</u>
> <u>seeking whom he may devour</u>."
> *1 Peter 5. 8 NKJV*

Nevertheless, it's coming. And the enemy of our souls knows it! Thus, one of his greatest ways of bringing people under demonic bondage and addictions is through the act of unsanctified, illegal or perverted sexual acts. It's something that not even soap can wash away. Only Jesus can deliver from such strongholds.

God created sex for wonderful and divine purposes. However, the enemy wants a good thing to be misused because he knows sex is that powerful! People are having all forms of sex not sanctioned by God all over the world. And indeed, sex sells! Even our youth are experimenting and engaging in real heavy duty sexual activities whereas whole lives are being transformed for the negative!

Sexual intercourse is so intimate, sacred, and special that God requires this beautiful gift be handled in utmost care.

Now is God being mean or trying to crash our party? NO!!! Instead, He's given us this commandment so we can really have a good time in Him and in life! He's given us sexual guidelines to procure our holistic health, safety, prosperity, and success in life to the fullest sense of the word. Anything outside of this, we're headed for trouble. Which brings me to my $2^{nd}$ point in our discussion.

## 2. There's No Such Thing As *"Safe Sex"* Outside God's Instruction Manual!

### FOOD FOR THOUGHT:
*"Sexual intercourse represents exchange whether we're married or not. Is it wise to receive exchange without the commitment of marriage?"*

Concerning being sexually active outside marriage someone might argue. "If people are two responsible consenting adults, what's wrong with having sex? I mean especially if it's practiced safely and with mutual respect?"

Let me answer this question for you.

In today's society with all the sexually transmitted diseases being spread abroad at alarming rates, we hear much talk about practicing "safe sex." But here's my question. Is there really such a thing as "safe sex?"

Now in writing this book, I've decided to be transparent and am not ashamed to say that there was a time in my life after becoming after becoming a believer I was sexually active. After walking with the Lord close to some 14 years, I backslided, went the way of the world, and sure enough got my groove on! But thank God for restoration and deliverance. However, I share this with you just to let you know that I'm talking from experience as well. I learned tons of valuable lessons from the season of sowing wild oats in the deceptive fields of sin and temporary thrills.

> *"If sex was just limited to the physical,
> then maybe we could talk. But there's no
> such thing as safe sex outside God's instructions
> because sex goes way beyond the physical!"*

I say there is no such thing as safe sex outside of God's instructions because sex is more than a physical experience! As mentioned previously, sex is exchange. If sex was just limited to the physical, then maybe we could talk. However, sexual intercourse is also mental, emotional, and spiritual with long lasting ramifications way after the bedroom act is over! In other words, there are some things the birth control pill and condom can't stop!

I said when people have sex they are both giving and getting something both physically and spiritually. Even if it's a one night stand! And no, one might not get pregnant but we will certainly take on the spirit of the person/(s) we have sex with! Do we want this?

> *"There are some things condoms
> and birth control cannot stop!"*

For example, this is why often when people commit adultery it often becomes so exceedingly difficult to enjoy their married partner sexually after the act without being challenged. Why? Because such an act causes them to take on the spirit of the person they've cheated with and that spirit goes to bed with them even when they're resuming a sexual relationship with their married partner. Again, soap can't wash this off! So instead of there being two in the bed, now there are three and even more in some cases!

This is real folks! While a husband and wife are trying to have marital relations, here comes the memory of smells, odors, comparisons, intimate feelings, and many things we won't discuss here competing in the heart and mind right in the middle of the married couple's bedroom experience! And please, don't call out the person's name! WAR!!!! Oh! But where did all this come from? It was transferred during the act of sexual intercourse. Why? Sex goes beyond the physical. See why God requires us to walk in sexual integrity now? Told you He wasn't being mean or a party crasher!

> *"They won't tell you this on TV,
> magazines or web sites!
> They'll advertise the pleasure
> but never the pain!"*

The partner tampering with infidelity may even have visual flashes of the person's face right at the most peculiar times with their married partner! This is how serious and deeply powerful sexual intercourse is EVEN IF IT'S CASUAL! They won't tell you this on TV, magazines or web sites! They'll advertise the pleasure but never the pain!

Thus, when God says, *"Thou shalt not commit adultery"* (Exodus 20:14) or any other sexual sin, He wasn't being mean I say! He's showing us how to avoid needless drama because any sexual activity carries long term effects simply not worth it. Not to mention the lives of others we touch who aren't even involved! ( i.e.: our children, families, witness for Christ, reputation, effectiveness at work, credibility, etc.)

> *"While we can be forgiven,
> why play with fire?"*

Now someone might say, "Well God will forgive me!" And this is true especially when we come to Him in sincerity, confession, and repentance. However, how much will our forgiveness cost?

If I go in a grocery store and steal a ham and get caught, I can ask the Lord to forgive me and He will if in true repentance. But guess what? I'M STILL GOING TO JAIL! Did God forgive me? Yes! But guess what? I'm a forgiven person in jail! Cause the cops ain't hearing it! Remember the TV song? "Bad boys bad boys! What you gonna do? What you gonna do when they come for you?"

In the same way, why play with fire? Why chance it? How much will your forgiveness cost? HIV? Jail? A broken marriage? New and advanced sexual addictions? Again thank God He's a deliverer and a miracle worker but why risk it? Who promised us that we'll always be able to escape?

The Bible says even if we sleep with a prostitute there's an exchange that will take place and transfer in the spirit between sexual partners. Even if we don't know each other! It could be in the dark!

Some theologians call these *"soul ties"* or deep emotional, mental, and spiritual bonds of attachment to greater and lesser degrees. Consider this passage of scripture.

I Corinthians 6: 16-20.
*Amplified Bible*

16. Or do you not know and realize that when a man (person) joins himself to a prostitute, he becomes one body with her? The two, it is written, shall become one flesh. [Gen.2:24]

17. But the person who is untied to the Lord becomes one spirit with Him.

18. Shun immorality and all sexual looseness [flee from impurity in thought, word, or deed]. Any other sin which a man (person) commits is one outside the body, but he who commits sexual immorality sing against his (or her) own body.

19. Do you not know that you body is the temple (the very sanctuary) of the Holy Spirit Who lives within you, Whom you have received [as a Gift] from God? You are not your own.

20. You were bought with a price [purchased with a preciousness and paid for, made His own]. So honor God and bring glory to Him in your body."

Wow!

Chew on that for a moment.

When we commit sexual immorality we're not just sinning against our selves and own lives but against the Holy Spirit who lives within us. This is not the unpardonable sin of blasphemy against the Holy Spirit but we are certainly defiling His temple which is the dwelling place of God. Lord help us!

And you know what else? Whenever we practice sexual intimacy without commitment .... I mean a real commitment in marriage it equals hurt!

I was once hosting a local television show talking about Christian views and pre-marital sex and a good NFL buddy of mine said it something like this,

> *"Fire in a fire place is good.*
> *But fire uncontrolled is trouble on your hands."*

Thanks Pastor Gray! That was a powerful show!

Preachers, it's time to recover!

Finally here's my last point in our discussion.

## 3. Regardless of Our Sexual Past, God Has Made Provision for Us To Walk in Sexual Integrity!

Preachers! Now it's time to put into practice the message of hope we share with others! It applies to us to!

In the beginning of this chapter I shared 4 reasons that escalate sexual temptation among clergy and people who hold vocations that thrushes them into the spot light or public eye. In a moment I'm going to give you several helpful tips that will help us to maintain sexual integrity both within and without the pulpit. However, before doing so you might be reading this material and find yourself stuck in some sexual addiction or rut. You may even feel that all hope is lost but I stopped by just to tell you God's not through blessing you and THE BEST IS YET TO COME!

So look up! Be encouraged and hold on! Why? Because regardless of any failures in our sexual past, God has made provision for each of us to walk in sexual integrity! Yes! Rejoice!

### God Is Able
### To Place You Back on Your Feet Again!

I'm quite sure most of us are familiar with the $23^{rd}$ Psalm. Especially the verse that says,

> "...He leads me beside the still waters,
> <u>He restores my soul</u>."
> *Psalm 23: 2b, 3a NKJV*

David who wrote this Psalm was a shepherd before becoming King of Israel. Isn't that just like God? Always making sure we have the proper experience needed so we may be totally equipped for our destiny!

Nevertheless, David wrote this Psalm concerning God's wonderful love, protection, and provision for us using the detailed care an earthly shepherd uses taking care of his sheep.

Now check this out. When he recites, *"he restores my soul,"* we know that David's talking about God's ability to renew and refresh our broken or wearied lives anew again. However, I heard an interpretation of this passage that set my joy bells to ringing and heart to singing.

It's been said shepherds utilized the term, *"restoring the soul"* as a term used when sheep for some reason or another had fallen. Thus, in this context when the term, *"He restores my soul"* is used, it's been said this means, *"He places me back up on my feet again!"* Wow! And dear colleague I just stopped by to tell you regardless of any sexual addictions, wounds, hurts, struggles, habits, or any problems you may have had, <u>GOD IS ABLE TO PLACE YOU BACK UP ON YOUR FEET AGAIN</u>! So get ready and rejoice! Don't you dare give up on God!

As a matter of fact, why not pause, take a quiet moment and worship Him now for His unconditional love for you, mercy, and grace!

When Christ said, "He'll never leave you!" He meant that!

And guess what? Your emancipation papers from being a slave to sexual addictions and vices have been written and decreed over 2,000 years ago! You no longer have to be a captive to your past or any sexual vice. Your emancipation papers from such read this way!

Read this and celebrate!

### Our Emancipation Papers and Rights of Deliverance From All Sexual Vice and Bondage!

\*\*\*\*\*\*\*\*\*\*\*\*

*"Do you not know that the unrighteous*
*will not inherit the kingdom of God?*
*Do not be deceived.*
*Neither fornicators, nor idolaters, nor adulterers,*
*nor homosexuals, nor sodomites, nor thieves, nor covetous,*
*nor drunkards, nor revilers, nor extortioners will inherit the kingdom of God.*
<u>*AND SUCH WERE SOME OF YOU. BUT YOU WERE WASHED,*</u>
<u>*BUT YOU WERE SANCTIFIED, BUT YOU WERE JUSTIFIED*</u>
*in the name of the Lord Jesus and by the Spirt of our God."*

*I Corinthians 6: 9-11. NKJV*

****************

Preacher, you have been emancipated! Go get your life back! You're not a slave to your past. Begin your journey to sexual integrity today!

Celebrate!

## SECTION III.
## Tips To Walking In Sexual Integrity Both Within and Without the Pulpit!

**FOOD FOR THOUGHT:**
*"If you're hungry and a lamb looks good to you, run!*
*Don't mess up your ministry or its life.*
*Acknowledge where you are*
*and let someone else pray for the sexy sheep!"*
*A Brently Proverb*
I'm telling you it works! Run!

JUST A MOMENT AGO, I told you that God is able to restore you from any sexual vice as a clergy person, leader, or even someone in another vocation that thrushes you to the forefront. Now I'm going to tell you how. And even if you're not in the forefront but have had sexual challenges of your own, this information is good for you too!

In a moment I'm going to give you 8 suggested tips to help us establish sexual integrity from both within and without the pulpit, recover from any pitfalls experienced, and most of all provide tools needed for prevention to skip the drama and save it for the theater! I hope you'll find these helpful.

*"Sexual integrity won't just happen by chance.*
*There's a price to pay.*
*Pay the price, you'll stand.*
*Don't pay the price, you'll fall.*
*It's as simple as that!"*

By the grace of God, the Lord has allowed me personally to see great success in this area. He's blessed me to serve my congregation with consistent integrity never turning lambs into lamb chops! So pastors and leaders, I'm telling you sexual integrity is not only a must it's possible! And guess what? I'M A SINGLE PASTOR! So you know I've got stories! Especially with all the traveling I do! And it's not like I was born in swaddling clothes either! It's not like I don't know what it feels like to fall prey to sexual temptation. I too feel the fire burning every now and then! However, there are several principles to victory I've learned to embrace.

By the grace of God, (not my own merit) I can personally testify that God is a keeper even behind closed doors. Having chosen abstinence until marriage, I'm a witness of this first hand. But please ladies. Let me make you laugh. No more marriage prophecies. Huh! I get enough of these. Spiritually forced brides! "I'm gonna make you marry me! Even if you don't want to cause I saw it in a vision!" "It's just not real to you yet. I'm holding on!" I ain't kidding yall! This stuff really happens. "The devil is only trying to hinder cause I refuse to believe I missed God on this one! I'm fasting and praying brother! I'm fasting and praying! Even if it means I have to wait all year! I'm going to manipulate until you come around!" Somebody really needs to rise up and do some serious teaching on this type of behavior. It's dangerous but that's another book!

Anyway, I praise God my marital situation is already taken care of hallelujah! I said it's already taken care of! So the prophecy is wrong. Come off the fast. Eat! Huh! And my lovely "God sent" bride ............ Oops! That's my business! Sorry!

And mothers..... stop putting your daughters up to this stuff! Stop trying to relive your life through your child! Stop putting stuff in your daughter's head about how to get a man setting her up for disaster. God doesn't work like this! "HE THAT FINDETH A WIFE!" Not she! Let the man be the man! If he doesn't come after you on his own free will stop acting desperate and go on with your life! Don't wait on him either. You don't have time. You've got too much to live for! To much to do! Raise up your self esteem! Have you forgotten you're a Child of God? Parents what are we teaching our children?!!! What???

I feel better now. That tangent was a commercial. Oh!

However, my point is sexual integrity is possible for all of us male or female even if our calling and vocations places us in glass bubbles of unique pressure and loneliness with unrequested audiences! But let me say this, NOT WITHOUT PAYING A PRICE!

> *"I'm no super man or super pastor.*
> *Nor do I claim to be.*
> *But I've made it this far only because*
> *I wanted to!"*

Listen. I'm no super man or super pastor nor claim to be. But I've made it this far only because I wanted to. In my position, and just being an ordinary human being I get tempted all the time! And sometimes the temptation looks better and better! And the more you have materially they become more convenient and accessible too! Professional athletes, celebrities, and politicians, yall know what I'm talking about! Let's help each other here!

But the secret is I've learned to count up the cost. Is it worth losing all I've worked so hard for in life over a few moments of temporary pleasure? I don't think so. Sexual integrity doesn't happen by chance. It doesn't just fall out the sky no matter who or how gifted we are. There's a price to pay. Pay the price, you'll stand. Don't pay the price, you'll fall. It's as simple as that!

Look. Your destiny and what you become in life is totally up to you!

.........Not God. Or even the devil. You!

Make the right choice today!

## 8 Principles to Sexual Integrity Both Within and Without the Pulpit and Beyond!

Pastors and leaders, I have 8 principles that have worked successfully for me all these years without reproach. I hold fast to them for dear life! I trust in some way these will be helpful to you too!

As a young boy growing up in the African Methodist Episcopal Church, we used to sing a hymn in response to the Decalogue (the Ten

Commandments) every Communion Sunday. Never before have these words carried so much meaning to me as we finalize our discussion. Written by George Heath, consider the wisdom warning they give us.

> *"My soul, be on thy guard;*
> *Ten thousand foes aries;*
> *And host of sin are pressing hard*
> *To draw thee from the skies!"*

Wow! Isn't that the truth!

Eternal thanks Mom and Dad for exposing us to fine music and keeping us in the House of God. Special thanks to Bishop and Mrs. Zedekiah Grady for laying such a wonderful and solid foundation of solid Christian theology in our lives as young boys growing up in Morris Brown AMEC. Wow!

Doesn't this hymn speak volumes?

Nevertheless, colleagues, enjoy these principles. Remember, I cannot counsel you. Get professional help if needed.

Let the healing begin!

## PRINCIPLES TO SEXUAL VICTORY!

1. <u>Be willing to own up, identify, admit, and acknowledge any sexual struggles you may have refusing to act like they don't exist.</u>

This is the first step to victory. Acknowledgement and confession!

God, yourself, nor anyone can do anything to assist you until you first admit where you honestly are and have a problem. Remember, one of the most lethal deceptions is self deception. If you're struggling with some type of sexual struggle, stronghold, or addiction and pretend like it's not happening you're only deepening the wound and opening yourself up to further hurt. Refuse to let pride, arrogance, embarrassment, or the opinions of people stop you from getting help. You're not from Mars because you may be experiencing sexual battles, only human. But acknowledgement and confession are the first steps to healing.

> "He (or she) who covers his sins will not prosper,
> But whoever confesses and forsakes them will have mercy."

2. <u>We must be willing to give up the grounds or disassociate ourselves and allegiance to the thing that gets us in trouble or makes us fall.</u>

If we intend to walk in sexual integrity and victory we must be honest enough with ourselves to refuse to keep toying with the thing that got us in trouble the first place. This is called *giving up the grounds!* For some, this may mean going certain places, hanging around certain people, watching certain movies or programs, keeping certain phone numbers in your call log, listening to certain types of music, wearing certain types of clothing, visiting certain web sites on the internet, getting involved in certain types of conversations, hanging around old playgrounds and places of the past, embracing certain types of negative attitudes or anything that serves as a trigger to make us fall, we must be willing to let go and avoid it. Like constantly picking a cut on our hand refusing to let it heal failure to give up grounds of trigger points will keep us in a relentless cycle.

Always remember, there's a progression to falling. Things that serve as triggers in our lives are like undeveloped seeds to behaviors we seek to avoid. Giving up the grounds pulls these triggers up at seed level.

> "Therefore, since we have this ministry,
> as we have received mercy, we don not lose heart.
> But we have renounced the hidden things of shame,
> not walking in craftiness nor handling the word of God deceitfully,
> but by manifestation of the truth commending ourselves
> to every man's conscience in the sight of God."
> *2 Corinthians 4:1-2. NKJV*

3. <u>Know that God is a deliverer and be willing to get godly counsel and professional help and assistance if needed.</u>

Now this is a big one! For many people even giving up the grounds may be a serious challenge.

If your struggle with sexual integrity is a difficult challenge, call for back up. But be careful. Make sure it's professional help. In other words, people who are certified and have the proper credentials to assist you in you area of need. i.e.: psychiatrist, psychologist, social worker, attorney, etc. Do research and avoid all quacks!

Also make sure you get "godly" counsel. When I say godly counsel I'm referring to healthy, wholesome, safe, counsel from a person such as a fellow pastor, etc. who is qualified in his or her right and won't give you garbage but sound doctrine encouragement and support from God's Word. While some pastors may not be legally able to counsel you in certain situations, they can serve as serious and helpful backbones of support and uplift as you receive help from professionals who can.

And remember, when it comes to sexuality we don't do things like the world. What I mean is a lot of stuff society is doing and the way the world trifles with such a powerful thing as sex has caused millions of people to suffer untold tragedies. The Bible gives us some good advice how not to fall into this dilemma.

Consider this passage.

"Do not love the world (it's wicked system of doing things)
or the things in the world.
If anyone loves the world,
the love of the Father is not in him. (or her)
For all that is in the world— the lust of the flesh,
the lust of the eyes, and the pride of life
is not of the Father but is of the world.
And the world is passing away, and lust of it;
but he who does the will of God abides forever."
*1 John 2:15-17. NKJV*

Always remember. Just because it's popular and everybody's doing it doesn't mean it's right or safe. So be careful!

4. <u>Make sure you have done steps 1-3 and have been delivered before assuming ministry.</u>

Now here's where patience comes in. Always remember, "roast cooked on a slow fire in the oven tends to always come out better than a fast job!"

While none of us are perfect, make sure your foundation is right before taking the driver's seat of the flock! This is so important. Why the rush? The first soul you must save is your own! You don't have anything to prove to anybody. And when you know that you have properly taken time to minister to yourself, when it's time for you to get back up in that pulpit you'll get up in power! And not only this, you'll feel good too!

You'll be free from all condemnation. Why? Here's a slogan of mine I'll share with you.

> *"We cannot enjoy our present or move into our future until we've come to peace with our past!"*

That's one of mine yall!

Otherwise, we risk suffering ministerial and life head on collisions!

5. <u>In spite of spiritual growth and advancement always remember none of us are beyond falling into sexual vices, pitfalls, and traps</u>!

The quickest way to fall is to think that you can't!

None of us are exempt from falling no matter who or how gifted we are even if we're married! For every anointing and advancement in God, there's an anti-anointing the enemy of our souls will try to use to nullify what God is doing in our lives. So never get cocky and besides ourselves. Let's stay grounded in our approach to life.

While Jude 1:24 tells us that Christ, *"is able to keep us from falling"* be mindful we have to first be willing to cooperate with his lead. Failure to heed the wisdom of God, warnings and prompting of the Holy Spirit will always land us in a ditch! Remember, under no circumstances will God ever take away from us the freedom of choice. I don't care who we are! If something looks like fire, don't play with it! Our best strategy against the enemy is not to flirt with danger! You might get burned. Even beyond recognition! God forbid!

When God has delivered you from sexual pitfalls in the past, you must recognize that at some point the enemy will try you again. (See Matthew 12: 43-45) Be honest with yourself and don't forget how to recognize your personal triggers to stumbling and avoid them. Remember trouble is so easy to get into and so much harder to get out! The enemy not only wants your anointing and witness, he wants your life!

6. <u>Never cease to keep yourself accountable as a preacher!</u>

This is one of the greatest things that has kept me down through the years in ministry. I never tried to be Super Man or Wonder Pastor! I realize I'm not above stumbling! And how this principle has made the difference!

Remember Chapter 3? The lonely sheep is easy prey still! Always keep people around you who have your best interest at heart without hidden agendas who aren't afraid to ask you personal and tough questions even if you get upset. Even if you feel you've outgrown the danger zone!

Never travel alone or do ministry by yourself. There's strength in numbers. And if you do have to travel alone, increase your accountability system on down to knowledge about your physical location, housing, schedule, and whereabouts. If you really mean business you won't shrink from tough questions from your accountability system. Nor will you view it as control or trying to get all in your business. Thus, you won't be reluctant to honestly share what's really going on with you. However, if there's some creeping and tipping in you and you've resolved it to be so, you'll just do what you want to do and inherit your own consequences.

### 7. Do not minister to people you are attracted to (the opposite sex) especially alone!

Now here's a river that only you can cross because nobody knows what's going on in your heart and mind but you and God! This one requires total honesty on your behalf.

If in ministry you encounter someone you know you are attracted to and feel a sexual pull towards, refer them to another qualified person to minister to them. Especially if you're struggling in your flesh and have not completely overcome past struggles in your own sexual experience! If you proceed anyhow, what may start off as Jesus, Jesus, Jesus, can end up as bedroom, bedroom, bedroom! This is real! Know your limitations and boundaries.

It's best to let women minister to women and men to men to avoid risky situations. Opposites still attract even with Bibles in our hands! Remember you can cross boundaries, get sued, go to jail, ruin a life, and some cases even get killed! People aren't playing these days!

And here's a deeper twist, because we live in a world whereas homosexuality and lesbianism have become a growing issue, if you have been delivered or being delivered from such and have the same attractions for a ministerial candidate as above, refer the candidate for ministry to another qualified person who is able to minister so that boundaries won't be crossed and mess occurs. Crossing lines with people we're supposed to be helping is a dangerous thing with often many unseen long lasting ramifications.

In any situation, if you know you're struggling with any attraction to a candidate for ministry, be honest with yourself. Don't even call on the phone. Let someone else take the assignment. It's a set up! This applies to e-mails, and text too! However, if it's a situation where it's unavoidable and you have to minister to a candidate, take someone with you and refuse to do it alone. However, in all actuality, sexual integrity boils down to your own personal integrity, character, and commitment to the Lord.

## *8. Additional Keys to Avoiding At Risk Situations*

- Never minister when you're physically tired. It opens doors.

- If doing home visits, never go into a home alone with the opposite sex or where you know an attraction lies either with yourself or the other person towards you.

- If in an office, never close the door with just you and the opposite sex alone. If something happens it's their word against yours!

- Never counsel or minister to a married person of the opposite sex without involving the spouse. Watch what you say in terms of advice and counsel. Try to bring the couple together for accountability purposes. If this is not possible, include a credible witness. And remember, stay in your grade. Don't counsel if you don't have the credentials to do so! Refer the candidate to someone who can!

- Never go on long trips with the opposite sex alone nor stay in the same hotel room or even close by. May sound old fashioned but it works! Don't overstep boundaries in the name of "doing ministry."

- Never keep ministry going into the wee hours of the night alone with the opposite sex. The Bible may turn upside down! Huh! Remember, a preacher once said, "There's nothing open after 11:00 PM but legs!" Unless you work 3$^{rd}$ shift! Oh!

- Stay professional with the people you minister to. Don't overstep boundaries and become playmates or buddies. Familiarity still breeds contempt!

- A great Mother in Zion once said, "Stay out these people's cars. Stay out these people's houses. And stay off these telephones and you'll do alright!"

- And finally. Never do ministry without the covering, oversight, counsel, and approval of your senior leadership such as your bishop, presiding elders, or governing body to whom you hold yourself ministerially accountable. In the multitude of counselors there's still safety. My ministry has catapulted to untold greater dimensions today because I honor this principle!

## CHAPTER 8 REVIEW
## Lamb or Lamb Chops?
*Preachers and Sexuality*

Wow what a chapter! Did it help or inspire you any? May God use it to provoke and start positive and healthy healing discussions on the pulpit and the pursuit of sexual integrity among us all over the world! Thank God He never throws us away in our struggles and His grace is always available in times of need.

Here's a quick review of what we've discussed.

### A Quick Review!

- Preachers are human too and shouldn't find it strange that we have sexual desires.

- There's not enough healthy talk about sex and the pulpit among our ranks therefore, we've lost many beautiful soldiers to often preventable casualties.

- Sexual intercourse is a gift from God and is so powerful with long lasting ramifications it's for the married only.

- There's no such thing as "safe sex" outside of the instructions of it's originator, God!

- Clergy, and people of vocations that thrust their lives into the spotlight of the public often encounter higher pressures of sexual temptation.

- No matter what our sexual past, mistakes, or failures, God's love for us never ceases and He is able to restore and place us back on our feet again.

- The quickest way to fall into sexual temptations and vices is to pretend that we can't.

- Through Christ, honesty, seeking professional assistance, having a willingness to give up dangerous grounds of triggers, and keeping ourselves accountable, we can walk in both sexual integrity and victory!

I enjoyed this chapter!

Rejoice! Let the victory begin! Yeah!

# CHAPTER NINE
# LUCY AND THE OFFERING PLATE!
## *"Preachers and Finances!"*

*"Bring all the tithes into the storehouse,
that there may be food in My house,
and try Me now in this, says the LORD of hosts,
If I will not open for you the window of heaven
and pour out for you such a blessing that there
will not be room enough to receive it."*
*Malachi 3:10 NKJV*

"A new preacher was sent as a new pastor of a
well established congregation.
His first words to his new parishioners was this,
"PAY ME SO I WON'T STEAL!" Huh!"
*Anonymous*

[This chapter responds to 9-1-1 Emergency Help Cries 5, 6, and 8]

**NOW I KNOW RIGHT NOW** somebody is wondering who is

Lucy and you know what? I can't tell you either! Huh! It just sounded good for this topic. But for real though. Anybody seen Miss Lucy? Lucy? Where are you? Miss Lucy??? Oh! Lucy girl! Where you at! LUCY!! Nevertheless, I want to take a moment to talk about preachers and finances. Miss Lucy that you? Oh!............. .................. Lucy!

However, on a more serious note, I mentioned two chapters ago how it's been said that many preachers die from a heart attack, stroke, and broke. I want to take a moment and talk about the "broke" part. Now like preachers and sexual issues, the way we handle money too is a major thing that keeps us on the news. Why the preachers got to steal the money? Let's talk about this. But remember what I told you. Despite the media, all preachers aren't crooks.

## People Get Antsy When It Comes to the Church and the Offering Plate!

I will never forget this as long as I live! I was a teenager sitting in a big giant mega church during a Sunday morning service and it was time for the offering.

The service was slamming, the saints were singing, and the offering plates were being passed out. I was so excited and decided to sit close to the old mothers in the Amen corner at the front right part of the church under the surround balcony.

Oh you should've seen it! The ushers who were receiving the offering in perfect uniform and decorum were strutting down the aisles receiving needful money from the saints. And the dollars were dropping.

Then after they left, another set of ushers came with huge drop bucket baskets to receive another offering.

With the music slamming another offering basket was being passed to us from another group of ushers for whatever reason.

*"Mother did not care if she was a distraction to the service! She didn't care!!!"*

On and on this went until I believe if not mistaken six sets of offering plates had been received. Then all the sudden, a middle aged mother perhaps in her sixties just yelled out loud in stern rebuke to the last set of ushers. I mean she just blurted out not caring who heard her or why! Loud! She did not care if she was a distraction to the service. SHE DID NOT CARE! Oh! I'm telling ain't nothing like church! Hollywood has gone to the wrong place looking for actors! I'm telling you Mother went off!

Sitting right next to me let me tell you what Mother said. She said sternly rebuking the usher,

> *"Don't come to me no more with another offering plate!*
> *THIS MY WATER BILL MONEY!!!!!"*

Oh! I was wounded! Mother stung me. I was about to fall out my seat with laughter! Mother was wondering why in the world they had to take up so many offerings. I guess she was counting the times different sets of ushers came around like I was. It was very noticeable. So Mother got tired. Mother wondered about that thing So Mother cried out! And guess what? She was not on the program! This would've been great material for a movie scene!

However, I shared this humorous story with you to express how when it comes to preachers, churches and money, antennas go up. Especially the IRS!

## God Ordained that the People of God Support the Work of the Ministry!

Now when it comes to the work of the ministry and the support of the Church, God ordains both in the Old and New Testaments that it's the people of God's responsibility to support the work of the ministry. Otherwise, how will it be supported? And secondly, we must remember that money is only a tool that God uses to get His work on earth done.

> "And you shall remember the LORD your God,
> <u>for it is He who gives you power to get wealth,</u>
> that He may establish His covenant which He swore to your fathers,
> as it is this day."
> *Deuteronomy 8: 18 NKJV*

Don't tell me God does not want us to enjoy wealth. I didn't say covetousness. Just wealth! Especially when we use it for His glory! He gives us power to get it! So go get it!

### FOOD FOR THOUGHT:
*Have you ever heard of "the wealth of the Lord?"*
*It's a term I coined to express the holistic aspect*
*of being wealthy before God.*
*It goes far beyond money although money can come with it.*
*But the wealth of the Lord is having God Himself*
*as your inheritance! And out of this*
*there's nothing missing, nothing broken in your life.*
*It doesn't mean life comes without challenge but rather*
*you're walking in complete peace, joy, and wholeness.*
*And guess what else?*
*You've got some bling bling too! Huh!*
*A Brently Proverb*

While we're thankful for the benefits of governmental assistance, God's original plan is that the local membership of the congregation be able to support itself via the system of tithes and offerings. Not dependence upon the government although helpful. The biblical text sharing God's system of financial congregational support is quoted in the heading of the chapter found in Malachi 3:10. Tithes are 10% of our earnings or any increase and offerings are anything we desire to give after that.

In God's eyes, when He has blessed us with resources and we do not tithe and share back our portion of financial responsibility to keep His work in operation, He says we're robbing Him like a thief directly.

"Will a man (person) rob God?
Yet you have robbed Me!
But you say,
'In what way have we robbed You?'
In tithes and offerings."
*Malachi 3: 8 NKJV*

Whenever the people of God don't financially support the work of God it keeps that ministry from being able to do and accomplish all that God has commanded.

In the New Testament we are commanded by Christ to preach and spread the good news of the Gospel, feed the hungry, clothe the naked, visit the sick, visit those in prison, cheer the fallen, care for the widows, weep with those who weep, rejoice with those who rejoice, and be the "salt of the earth" bringing healing, preservation, flavor, seasoning, and taste to all who may lack these elements. In other words, the ministry of Christ is about helping to make the world a better place to live making a better quality of life for all.

However, these wonderful things cannot be done without financial support and resources. And when the people of God don't give, the work becomes stifled. Thus, God who chooses to operate through people becomes hindered. Thus, failure to give after He's given so much to us is direct robbery against Him!

The same situation happened again in the Old Testament in the book of Haggai whereas the congregation of Israel had become so self absorbed in their own personal prosperity and advancement that taking care of the House of God was the last thing on their list. Thus, the House of God was falling apart in both lack and ruins.

Consider the report.

"Go up to the mountains and bring wood and build the temple,
that I may take pleasure in it and be glorified," says the LORD.
"You looked for much , but indeed it came to little;
and when you brought it home,
I blew it away. Why?" says the LORD of hosts.
"Because <u>of My house that is in ruins,
while every one of you runs to his own house</u>."
Haggai 1: 8-9. NKJV

Again, the people of God allowed the work of the ministry to be hindered and go into lack.

Dear pastor, leader, or congregant, are you letting the work of God suffer lack due to inconsistency or lack of giving? Can God trust you to bless Him financially as He always blesses you?

No. God does not personally need your money. He's God! But His work does! He Himself has chosen to work through the hands or ordinary people...... His Church!

"When did we see You a stranger and take You in,

> or naked and clothe You?
> Or when did we see You sick, or in prison,
> and come to You?
> "And the King (Jesus) will answer and say to them,
> 'Assuredly, I say to you, inasmuch as you did it
> to one of the least of these my brethren (ladies included)
> you did it to Me."
> Matthew 25: 38-40. NKJV

Wow!

## Why People Are Reluctant to Give!

Now when it comes to giving money to a church or ministry, many people are reluctant to give. I can think of at least 12 reasons why.

- Some people are afraid their money will misused, abused, and go to the wrong purposes. Financial mismanagement and appropriation.

- Some people think a church or ministry doesn't need money to operate. Especially if it's a ministry that's apparently prosperous.

- Some people don't believe in paying tithes considering it an "Old Testament" principle.

- Some people think all the money will go to the pastor who seemingly doesn't need it.

- Some people have a bad taste for giving to ministries based on scams and bad reputations about some ministries by the media.

- Some people have never been taught the proper Biblical principles of financial stewardship in terms of supporting ministry.

- Some people don't have the money to give.

- The past due bills of some people makes giving to ministry a greater challenge.

- Some people are simply apathetic.

- Some people think giving to ministry is a loss of money that they'll never see again.

- Some people will give but are reluctant to give to programs they don't support or believe in.

- The personal interest of some people takes priority over giving to ministry.

Wow!

**Developing Proper Attitudes Towards Giving!**

Unfortunately, time does not afford me opportunity here to deal with each of these reasons exhaustively. However, there are 3 things I'd like to encourage and say. We must develop proper attitudes toward giving.

**1. We are commanded by God to support the work of ministry at the local congregational level.**

I do want to say once again that we are commanded by God to financially support His work for the advancement of the Kingdom and the betterment of the people. Once again, if we don't support such who will? And even if there are thousands who are already giving, God requires from us our own personal stewardship.

Now where you plant your financial seeds are up to you but the first line of duty is to support the ministry or congregation where you belong and are being spiritually fed. Failure to do so is like going to a restaurant, eating the food and refusing to pay your bill.

Somebody might say, "Well I give to other ministries and charities." This is ok but it's still not God's divine order. Charity begins at home! While it's wonderful to give wherever you want to give providing it's a ministry or organization of integrity, you don't feed the kids across town while your own children are starving to death! Does this make sense? Take care of home first then go out and be a blessing!

In both passages in Malachi and Haggai, the Israeli congregation were required to support the ministry right where they were! It might be Old Testament but the same principles spill over into the New! Ask the Apostle Paul! (See I Corinthians 9:9-14.) If we don't take care of our own backyard who will? And even if we hire someone, we still have to pay them!

## Preaching Costs!

While the Gospel of Christ is free, the means to getting the Word out to you and others isn't! Ask me how I know!

Not only am I a senior pastor of a church and director of a youth center, I also preach and am in covenant with a ministry that feeds thousands of homeless persons a year as well as provide transitional housing, health care assessments, GED programs and the list goes on. I'm here to tell you operations like these cannot run off, "Thank You Jesus!"alone! IT EVEN TAKES MONEY TO CARE FOR THE POOR! Plus food has to be purchased, the power bill has to be paid so we can have lights, air, and heat. Vans have to have gas to pick up the homeless from different parts of the city plus staff members have to be paid to keep the operation going. And don't forget about maintenance and incidentals!

Once I had to do a humongous service at a convention center and due to a lack of integrity, the people didn't want to pay me an offering. Now don't get me wrong. I'm not about money. I've done and still do tons and tons of volunteer work and joyfully not get paid a dime. I love to serve. So I'm not about money. However, in this situation an offering was due me. I spoke 4 times when only scheduled to speak twice. So I didn't bring adequate clothing for the additional requested services. I sweated out everything I had. Plus I had to go into my own resources for additional supplies to do proper on the spot presentations. And because the additional speaking wasn't on the schedule, I had to further inconvenience the staff person who traveled a great distance to accompany me who had a wife and young child left at home.

When the meeting was over and I inquired about the offering which they were reluctant to pay, a lady said this to me.

*"Your treasure is in heaven."*

And then I responded.

*"Yes. This is true. But my bills are on earth!"*

*"Let this be a lesson to all of us.
Let's stop spiritually raping each other
when it comes to giving!"*

She became silent. And what's worse about this situation is that this convention was a multi-million dollar convention and still didn't want to give. It wasn't like they were broke! I wasn't even charging a fee! I just needed financial help to cover the expenditures I had to put out to make "their" event possible!

Let this be a lesson of financial integrity to all of us! Let's stop spiritually raping each other when it comes to giving!

While the Gospel of Christ is free, that's not what we're paying for. It's the expenditures that surround making the event possible that requires our financial gifts.

With nothing being new under the sun, the Apostle Paul said it this way.

"<u>If we (ministers) have sown spiritual things for you,
is it a great thing if we reap you material things</u>?

If others are partakers of this right over you,
are we not even more?
Nevertheless we have not used this right,
but endure all things lest we hinder the gospel of Christ.

Do you not know that those who minister the holy things
eat of the things of the temple,
and those who serve at the altar
partake of the offerings of the altar?
<u>Even so the Lord has commanded
that those who preach the gospel
should live from the gospel</u>."
I Corinthians 9: 11-14. NKJV.

Wow!

**Don't Shortchange Your Church**

### If Your Ministry is Small!

Having said all this, again remember if we don't support our own who will? And let's remember, even if are ministries are small it's still not reason to shortchange such financially.

Actually in God there are no small ministries! All of us to Him are of equal value! However, a ministry may be considered small numerically. Even if your ministry or congregation is such that may not have a lot of extensive outreach programs that ministry still needs your financial support! We should never want to see any ministry struggling to carry out the Great Commission of Christ because of lack and insufficient funds!

So if we refuse to give and support the local church where we attend don't complain if that ministry isn't able to carry out its vision. We're starving it to death!

But if we give and sow into the work of God with the right motives, integrity and stewardship there's no limit to our blessings. Which brings me to our next point of discussion.

### 2. We Can Never Beat God in Giving!

While I'm still not able to deal with all 12 reasons why some people are reluctant to give let me share this word of encouragement with you. We will never be able to beat God in giving! He'll always have the lead!

There's a popular hymn that says,

> *"Count your blessings!*
> *Name them one by one.*
> *Count your many blessings*
> *See what God has done!"*

If you could count all the blessings that God has given you I promise you you'll never be able to finish because they're so many! And I'm talking beyond having money!

God commands us to take care of His work here on earth. And He knows this isn't always easy. He knows our financial struggles, day to day bills, and all the challenges of our lives we face on a daily basis. And because He knows, He never forgets.

Thus, when we give and do what He requires concerning our giving He releases blessings upon us we could never dream of. Therefore, like a preacher colleague of mine says every time he leads in receiving an offering, he always tells the people to say to their financial seed sown,

*"I'll see you when you get back!"*

Why? Because God has promised to do what He said when we give to the work of God.

May the following passages of scripture both encourage and inspire you!

"Now to Him who is able to do exceedingly abundantly above all that we ask or think, according to the power that works in us."
Ephesians 3:20. NKJV

"And God is able to make all grace abound toward you, that you, always having all sufficiency in all things, may have an abundance for every good work."
II Corinthians 9:8. NKJV

"Bring all the tithes into the storehouse,
That there may be food in My house,
And try Me now in this,'
Says the LORD of hosts,
"If I will not open for you the windows of heaven
And pour out for you such blessing
That there will not be room enough to receive it.
And I (God) will rebuke the devourer for your sakes,
So that he will not destroy the fruit of your ground,
Nor shall the vine fail to bear fruit
for you in the field,"
Says the LORD of hosts;

"And all nations will call you blessed,
Fro you will be a delightful land,'
Says the LORD of hosts."
Malachi 3: 10-12. NKJV

"Give, and it will be given to you:
good measure, pressed down, shaken together,
and running over will be put into your bosom.
For with the same measure that you use,
it will be measured back to you."
Luke 6:38 NKJV

"So let each one give as he (or she) purposes in his (or her) heart,
not grudgingly or of necessity;
for God loves a <u>cheerful</u> giver."
II Corinthians 9: 7 NKJV

### 3. We Should Always Make Sure We're Giving into Good Ground!

Finally, I'd like to say that in the giving process we should always look before we leap and make sure we're giving into good ground.

What is good ground? It's rich, nutrient filled soil that if a seed is placed there it will return a harvest. For example, if I take some apple seeds and drop them on concrete they won't grow. But if I place those apple seeds in fertile ground and nurture such they will bring forth a harvest.

With all the skepticism in the world, still we want to watch where we give. In addition to supporting our own ministries, give to works that are integrity led and are doing the works of Christ. And you know what? It's ok to inquire and ask how your money is being used.

Any ministry or organization of integrity won't have problems sharing with you the whereabouts of your financial seed. Most ministries keep written accounts of gifts you've sown and you should be able to request those at any time. If a ministry or organization is reluctant to express how your money is being used then that's a red flag and you may need to do more investigation.

### 4. When Ministers Steal!

Alright preachers let's take this to the next level. I cannot blame one soul for being skeptical about giving if we as leaders aren't walking in financial integrity! Actually, it's really a shame and a reproach that we have to even address such an issue when we're the people of God! This is why my prayer is that this book will stimulate positive discussion among our ranks that will bring global revival and respect back to the Church! Jesus is sure enough real but we keep doing things to give Him and Christianity a bad name! Lord, help us all!

We're the light of the world but we're clowning!

> "You are the light of the world, A city that is set on a hill cannot be hidden."
> Matthew 5:14 NKJV

It's time for the whole Body of Christ to have global repentance so real revival can occur! I know it's going to happen one day, the Bible says so!

> "Let us be glad and rejoice and give Him glory, for the marriage of the Lamb has come, and His wife (the Church) has made herself ready."
> Revelation 19: 7 NKJV

So we know the Church will be alright and finally get there!

Nevertheless, why do some preachers steal the church people's money?

I made a quote of a real situation at the top of this chapter of a new minister being sent to an established congregation as the new pastor. At his first meeting with his new parishioners he told them,

*"Pay me so I won't steal!"*

Now this too is a funny story but it actually happened. Here's one thing however, at least the minister was straight up! He told them what he was going to do if they didn't pay him.

But as humorous as this story is, I find a lot of revelation in what he said. Let's review.

## "PAY ME .....
### so I won't steal!"

Although there's never any excuse for stealing, I see something in this. The man had needs (bills, expenditures, a life outside of church) and the way he was going to meet those needs is by getting paid a salary fit his worth. If the congregation refused to pay him, his needs wouldn't get met. If his needs aren't met, this throws his life into lack. And if he falls into lack he'll start losing stuff. If he starts to lose stuff then this means he'll move into tribulation and want. Therefore, rather than going through all this, he'd forcefully take what he feels he deserves even if he has to do it without proper authorization. Now he may end up in prison and of course lose both his reputation and his ministry. But I guess that's a risk he was willing to take. Unless he was only kidding when he made this opening statement to his congregation!

**FOOD FOR THOUGHT**
*"When we're needy and in lack,
we're more open to financial temptation
and mismanagement."*

But check this out! The point I'm trying to make here is I believe people do things in life because of a root reason. After working in mental health services and the ministry of counseling folk so long I've noticed that every behavior can be traced back to a cause. I didn't say justification but rather, *a cause*. If we can get to the root cause of stuff that causes us to react the way we do in certain situations especially when it comes to the pulpit and finance, I believe we'll be well on our way.

And here's one thing I've learned. When we are needy and in lack, we're more open to financial temptation and mismanagement. For real! Just like a stale cracker may look good to a starving man or woman who hasn't eaten for days, when the bill collector is knocking on our doors and we don't have the money, the spirit of desperation can drive us to put the fire out in some very risky ways if we're not careful. So the key to financial victory is making sure our financial foundation and basic needs are covered. We'll discuss this in a moment.

Now I'm no financial expert! So please go see a financial expert or go see Prophetess Suze Orman! Suze's the girl! She gives great financial advice! And will tell it like it is all on national TV! I'm a Suze fan! However, from my little experience in ministry and watching fellow colleagues I want to share only 10 simple wisdom suggestions about preachers and finance with you.

## 10 Wisdom Tips to
## Financial Stability Among Clergy!

In 9-1-1 Emergency Help Cries 5, 6, and 8 we see 3 situations occurring among our ranks. One was a pastor in a third-world country facing great distress because of very poor resources. The second was a well working pastor whose congregation was very non-supportive although an integral and dedicated leader. And then lastly, we see an older minister who passes away with absolutely no will, life insurance or anything. Thus, his grieving wife now a widow is left behind to struggle with no on-going means of financial support or housing!

Let's see some basic and general things we need to set in order financially as clergy. Always walk in financial integrity at all times never

ever abusing or manipulating your congregation.

1. <u>Be honest. Sit down with your congregation and discuss where you are financially, your financial compensation package, and making sure they are giving you all the necessary resources needed to fulfill your duties as their senior minister without stress.</u>

This is important because unless you have the proper tools to do your job you will have difficulty meeting the expectations of the pastorate.

Some questions to ask may cover the following areas: (not limited to these)

- salary
- pension
- retirement
- housing allowance
- travel allowance
- health insurance
- life insurance
- disability
- self employment tax
- professional liability,
- continuing education
- any other compensations related to official duties

Not all congregations are financially set up the same per administration and denomination. Some may or may not include all these in their pastoral benefit package but should. In the event this is not possible, discuss and seek other means of sustenance. Smaller congregations may not be financially able to provide a total package. In such cases sometimes second employment may be necessary to supplement your financial needs for survival.

2. <u>Must be able to see beyond our financial present and plan and prepare for the unexpected.</u>

However, your package is set up make sure you can see beyond today and prepare for the unexpected like health care emergencies, flooding, storms, death, or any situation whereas your employment stability can be interrupted. As an insurance agent once said, "Failing to plan is planning to fail!" 9-1-1 Emergency Help Cry 8 is a sure example of what can happen to a preacher and his or her family if he or she doesn't prepare for unexpected changes of life in advance.

3. <u>If you are the sole provider for your home (and even if you're not) make sure your spouse, children, and loved ones can survive should you no longer be able to work and perform your duties and senior minister.</u>

Again, what will your spouse, children, loved ones and family do and how would they survive if you passed away or lived but become physically unable to perform the duties of ministry and be the sole provider for your home? This is real! Don't wait until a storm hits to plan.

Here are a few more questions:

- Do you have a written will? Is it legal?
- Do you have life, health, auto, dental, rental, home, and any other insurances to cover you and your family in times of crises?
- If so, where are the documents? Where are they kept?
- What is the extent and boundaries of that coverage? Who all does it cover?
- Who has the power of attorney should you not be able to speak and act for yourself?
- Where will your family reside if something happens to you?
- Who will handle your funeral arrangements should something happen to you?
- Is this information in writing? Is it kept in a safe place?
- What sources of income are available for your spouse and children in the event of your demise for them to survive?
- Concerning your ministry, who will make important decisions for your ministry should you pass away or if you are not physically able to handle the affairs of the church?

While most of these questions are worse case situations as we look for life, yet we will make life difficult if we don't bring closure to these things while we're able and in our right minds. These are only a few of the many questions we need to ask and prepare for <u>WHILE THE SUN IS SHINING</u>! I've seen too many great leaders who were powerful in their own right but forgot to fulfill this aspect of their lives.

Remember, the Bible encourages us this wise.

<u>"A good (wise) man (or woman) leaves an inheritance to his (or her) children's children,</u>

But the wealth of the sinner is stored up for the righteous."
Proverbs 13: 24 NKJV

When a person passes away it's hard enough our loved ones are left to grieve. It is even harder when all our business though anointed is out of order.

4. <u>Stay on top of things with the IRS and make sure you and your ministry are IRS compliant at all times.</u>

Failure to comply with the IRS will send you straight to prison! And if you or your ministry is receiving any funds from the government please make sure such is handled with the utmost expertise, integrity, and proper execution without deviation. Get a CPA (certified public accountant) or someone who knows how to handle such funding especially if you and your ministry don't! Providing professional training for your staff by professionals is certainly a plus.

5. <u>As pastor never every handle the finances of your church or ministry. You can oversee but hire someone of integrity and expertise in this area to do such for you.</u>

It's good for pastors never to touch the money. It's the best way to avoid mess from happening in your ministry. While each ministry is set up properly, find the proper, integral persons with the expertise to handle such and assignment. If no one is available, get a CPA! Don't go to jail!

6. <u>While living in a parsonage has some benefits, seek to own your own home</u>.

Someone said, "the first step to wealth is home ownership." Actually it may not be the very first step but it sure is a powerful one! You'll never own an apartment. The money you pay rent for an apartment per month could buy you a serious home!

Living in a parsonage has some benefits especially as most are close to the church. However, most parsonages are owned by that congregation. If something should happen to you and you can no longer serve as senior minister, where are you going to stay? And what about your family? Invest in your own home today!

If you are in itinerant ministry and are not certain of your next location, you can still purchase a home and it work out for you. Seek professional real estate counseling on this and make further determinations from there. But nevertheless, seek to own your own home!

7. <u>Learn the power of making investments that can pay you back in the future but the right kinds. If not knowledgeable of how investments such as stocks, CD's etc. operate, go get professional financial counseling.</u>

All money has the power and potential to grow. But the lack of knowledge will bring us into lack. Find out as much as you can about investments that can benefit you and your family in the future. Seek professional financial counseling so you can know what's safe to pursue, and safe to avoid.

8. <u>Do all you can to get out of debt and improve your credit standing.</u>

Bad credit has some serious side effects and some of them long term! If in debt, work to get yourself out even if beginning one step at a time. Also apply the principles of the Word of God concerning finance and practice good stewardship, financial discipline, and watch your spending habits. Before you know it, you'll look for the mountain of debt and it'll be gone!

9. <u>Always walk in financial integrity before your congregation and never lie to them about your financial situation. If there are problems be honest. Respect the opinions of the executives on your financial board considering their value and weight before making a drastic financial move.</u>

The worse thing a preacher can do is lie about his or her financial situation! DO NOT LIE! Be honest, clean, and clear cut about your finances with your congregation and they will respect you more. Do not put false burdens of finance upon your people! Never manipulate or prophet-lie them to give a certain amount of money. It's both a disgrace and a reproach! Just tell them what you need. And if they aren't able to give it do not punish your people financially for your lack of discipline in your spending habits!

Be a pastor your people can reason with. We know the oversight of the flock is given to you but never to foolish inclinations! Remember your people don't belong to you but to God Himself purchased by Christ very own blood whereas you must give an account! Your people may not be the pastor but as officers in your ministry they may be aware of some blind spots concerning the finances of the ministry that don't readily meet your eyes.

Remember, we are servant-leaders not dictators. Be able to make compromises when making a compromise is wise. Then set a proper plan in place that both you and your congregation can work with together to reach a financial goal should there be set backs. I'm telling you, it works and the people will have a greater respect and appreciation for you not because of your sermons but because you know how to respect and work kindly with the people you serve with both dignity, humility, and excellence.

10. <u>Be a good steward over all the increase that God has placed in your hands and He'll entrust you with more.</u>

I tell people this all the time.

> *"If God can't trust you with 5 dollars*
> *, He won't be able to trust you with 50.*
> *If He can't trust you with 50 dollars,*
> *He won't be able to trust you with 500.*
> *If God can't trust you with 500 dollars*
> *, He won't be able to trust you with 5,000.*
> *And if He can't trust you with 5,000, why should*
> *He trust you to handle 5 million?*
> *We will spend our money on whatever is going on in our hearts!"*
> A Brently Proverb

I'm a firm believer if we can show God that we're faithful, dedicated, and integral to handle the small stuff, He'll graduate us to greater and higher dimensions! Big things are made up out of small things. So don't play small things cheap! It's your training ground! Yes! Be a good steward over the money your church gives you Preacher! Be faithful to stick to the budget your church has established for the year in all it's projects. Handle your financial stewardship like you're doing it for the King Himself and watch where the King will take you! God delights in the prosperity of His servants.

He's looking for someone to bless!

> "For the eyes of the LORD run to and fro
> throughout the whole earth,
> to show Himself strong on behalf of those
> whose heart is loyal (right) before Him."
> II Chronicles 16:9a

Wow! Let it be me Jesus! Be faithful in your financial

stewardship and watch not only your money grow but get ready to see and witness a greater capacity of joy and wisdom insight you've never witnessed before in your life!

Oh! We've got so much to live for when we're serving the Lord! Hallelujah!

**Chapter 9 Review**
**Lucy and the Offering Plate!**
*"Preachers and Finances!"*

In this chapter we've learned the following:

- Money is only a tool given to us by God to establish His work here on earth.

- Some people are reluctant to give to ministries due to skepticism of it's use or lack of sound Biblical teaching on finance and stewardship.

- It cost financially to preach the Gospel and God ordained that His people should be the chief supporters of His work.

- We should make sure we're giving into good ground.

- Some preachers steal the money not just out of greed but sometimes due to debt and lack.

- When we are needy and in lack we're more open to financial temptation and mismanagement.

- As pastors we don't have to steal but should practice excellent financial stewardship among the congregations we serve.

- A wise preacher will prepare financially for the future for himself/herself and family and not wait until a storm hits to get it together!

- God will promote us to bigger, better, and greater things if we begin practicing financial integrity in the small things!

- We still don't know who Lucy is! Huh! Got ya! Didn't I!

Celebrate a new beginning in your personal finances and in the life of the finances of your congregation!

Celebrate!

## CHAPTER TEN

# MY BABY DADDY! MY BABY MAMA!

## *"Preachers, Marriage and Family Relationships!"*

*"......one who rules how own house well,
having his children in submission
with all reverence
(for if a man does not know how
to rule his own house,
how will he take care of the church of God?)"*
I Timothy 3: 4-5 NKJV

*"This is the order!
God first. Then my husband. Then the ministry!"*
Compliments of the honorable
Rev. Mother Ella Mae Brown,
Senior Veteran and
General in the Gospel of Christ

[This chapter addresses 9-1-1 Emergency Help Cries 6, 13, and 14]

THERE IS A FAMILIAR SAYING that declares, "the family that prays together stays together." Oh! And how desperately today we need families that will stay together! In this chapter we're going to talk about preacher, marriage and family relationships. But first, let's start with the later, the family.

**The Power of Family!**

Today we live in a society whereas the family structure has been under severe attack like never before in history. More and more children are growing up without fathers and a two parent home with both mother and father is rapidly becoming a thing of the past. In today's world the definition of what a family looks like has been totally redefined.

*"The family is the most important
and powerful unit in all society."*

Parents today are generally younger and with so many $21^{st}$ Century technological distractions and options marriage is not so much a big deal as in previous generations. And people as a whole are generally getting married at later ages. (which is cool for some) However, so many of our children are being reared in an atmosphere that teaches it's ok to cohabit without the commitment of marriage. Thus, the idea of family is swiftly becoming an estranged word.

Nevertheless, we should always remember the family structure is the strongest force and unit in all society. Why? Because families make neighborhoods, neighborhoods make communities, communities make cities, cities make states and regions, states and regions make nations, nations make countries, countries make the world! All from one tiny family!

Very simply, to destroy a nation or even the world at large the method is very simple. Begin with the disintegration of the family and "BOOM!" there you have it!

A famous Ghanaian proverb says it like this,

*"The ruin of a nation begins in the homes
of its people."*

Just like one tiny cell in the human body can make a difference, so can one tiny family! The power of family is just that potent to the life and well being of any society.

## The Childhood is the Foundation of Every Life!

As a former health care clinician in the departments of mental health and social services, many of the ills we see in today's society and divers criminal behaviors can be traced back to the home. Yes! The childhood. Why? The childhood is the foundation of every life. Like cement that hardens, the things learned in the childhood will serve as a serious base in the further development and construction of a building.

Thus, the family structure or lack of such has been determined in psychology as a key source of major influence whether positive or negative in the life of an individual. And you know what? Preachers if we are serious about seeing real revival hit our communities, nations and world, it must first start with the family. We must be willing to roll up our sleeves, take off our clergy collars, move from the comfort and security zones of the 4 walls of our sanctuaries and be about the business of promoting healing, encouragement and uplift to families blown by the winds of life.

## Preachers, Our Ministries Will Be No Greater Than Our Ministry At Home!

Now when it comes to preachers and family, the total strength of our ministries will be no greater than our ministry at home. Why? Although we can fake it or cover it up, what happens in our home life and families will affect the strength of what we do in our pulpits to greater and lesser degrees. For this reason Paul writing to Timothy said,

> "For if a man does not know how to rule his own house, how will he take care the church of God?"
> I Timothy 3:5 NKJV

So charity does begin at home! Let's talk about this.

### A Lesson From Mother Brown!

At the top of this chapter I cited a quote from a dear and powerful preacher just a few years short of 100 years old in the person of Mother

Rev. Ella M. Brown.

This great old-fashioned Holy Ghost filled, prayer warrior and Mother in Zion is responsible for the countless conversions of untold persons to Christ. Not only this, via her ministry many pastors, teachers, missionaries, bishops and great leaders have been encouraged and birthed to greater Kingdom service through her witness. And most astonishingly, through her ministry great miraculous answers to prayer have been wrought, people delivered, souls saved, and many filled with the Holy Ghost!

A type of an American "Mother Theresa," and walking history, I would periodically visit this great woman to interview her, sit at her feet and gather golden nuggets of wisdom and know how that no money could ever buy.

An ordained minister in the African Methodist Episcopal Church and long time president of the renown Holy Ghost Crusader Prayer Band, (these holy ladies could literally bring heaven down to earth for those who feel Methodist folk don't operate in the Gifts of the Spirit) I was blown out the water by the integrity, success, physical health, and balance this old woman maintained in her life. She's simply a remarkable woman of God. I can't explain how unspeakably blessed and privileged I feel to have met her and be able to talk to walking history face to face.

So one day, I went to visit her and she told me the secret to her success in ministry. Here's what she said.

Using three fingers on her hand she told me success in ministry for her came in this order.

*"God first. Then my husband. Then the ministry!"*

Wow!

To be honest I wasn't expecting this answer because Mother Brown was always so busy on the field winning and helping souls, visiting the sick, conducting services, taking Holy Communion to people in hospitals, homes, and those who too were sick and shut in.
She was known by name throughout the city. Yet she revealed to me it was this order in her life that brought her unspeakable success. With all the ministry Mother Brown was doing she made it clear her first pulpit wasn't the church but her husband and home! Thus, she was able to reach the world! Why? Because she had balance!

PREACHERS LISTEN! We can learn so much form this great Mother in Zion. And by the grace of God Mother Brown is still alive to this day! Wow!

Reverends, are we too busy for our families?

## How Many Preacher's Kids Are Indifferent to Church and Ministry Because Too Much Time Is Spent with the Sheep?

Now here's a question to consider. How many preachers kids are indifferent to church because too much time is spent with the sheep? And here's another. How many preachers wives or husbands feel like the minister is the "other woman" or the "other man?" Let's understand the balance here.

### A Sad Story!
*The Preacher's Kid Who Killed Himself!*

I was once attending a clergy retreat scheduled for all ordained clergy who were a part of a particular jurisdiction of my denominational affiliation. It was a wonderful idea of an outstanding former bishop of mine to provide an opportunity for hard working clergy (about 400 plus) to get away from the hustle and bustle of ministry to get renewed, rejuvenated and refreshed. Try it sometimes! It will do wonders for your health and ministry.

Nevertheless, at this retreat there was a presenter who spoke to us about the importance of establishing balance in ministry. In his presentation, he told us a story about a pastor who really loved the Lord, his family, and of course, the congregation he served.

This pastor was very dedicated to this ministry to the point of being there all the time to answer every problem, call, and situation the ministry encountered.

One day, his son requested that he would spend some time with him. Loving his son with all his heart, this loving pastor and father agreed to do so. However, as time progressed, each time he promised to spend time with his son, a situation would arise in the ministry causing him to cancel his engagement with his boy. Over and over again this happened each time being interrupted by the demands of the ministry.

So one day this loving pastor/father promised his son their overdue engagement together would happen tonight! However, again, the duties of the ministry called. And this time it was serious. A member of this pastor's church had to rushed to the emergency room for a sudden life-threatening illness. Thus, again he had to cancel spending time with his son.

*"When Dad got home it was too late!"*

After tending to his parishioners in the hospital, this loving pastor/father rushed home to finally get to his son. When he got home, he noticed something very strange. All the lights were on in every room of the house. Rushing in to see what was going on to his great despair he found his son dead in the basement. His boy had committed suicide and hung himself.

Oh! Listen preachers! Listen!

**Don't Wait Too Late
To Spend Time with Your Family!**

While we're thankful that even in unspeakable tragedies such as this God is still able to mend wounded hearts there are some very serious lessons we can learn from this story. For starters, preachers don't wait too late to spend time with your family!

With deepest compassion and sympathy for both the father and the son my heart goes out to both.

First to the son because he lost his life! Something irreplaceable and priceless that perhaps could've been avoided. Evidently he was crying out for help (a "silent scream" remember?) but his Dad was too entrenched, unbalanced in the work of ministry to hear the cry. And when the father finally decided to spend quality time with his boy because he certainly loved him it was too late!

Secondly, my heart also goes out to the father in this story because only God knows the guilt he felt. It wasn't like this father was a dead beat dad at all. He really loved and cared for his son dearly. Perhaps he assumed his need to spend time with him couldn't be that serious. Perhaps he felt because he knew all his son's needs would be taken care of by him the need to spend time with him wasn't a dire emergency but could wait a little. I'm quite sure this father didn't know that his son was suicidal. However, and most sadly, he wasn't able to discern that the one that needed ministry most was his boy who perhaps daily sat across the kitchen table every day more so than the parishioner in the hospital.

Preachers in light of all this there is something we must all learn to do in our ministries and that's DELEGATE! When a man or woman is called to shepherd God's people, there is an agape love beyond words that the shepherd has for his or her sheep. It's a love to see the best for the souls of men, women, boys, and girls. It's a love that will cause us to get up at 3:00 AM to get someone out of jail. Or reach into our own personal bank accounts and pay off a bill for a sheep whose not even our blood family member. It's a love that compels us to stand with even the most difficult of sheep even sacrificing our own time with our own families and personal interest. However, I'm learning now it's so important that we train others to do what we do and help carry this load.

### FOOD FOR THOUGHT:
*"Besides traveling over the whole earth, land, sky and sea, have you taken the time to minister to your spouse, children and family who daily sit right across from you at your kitchen table?"*

To evangelize the whole world while our own immediate family is going to Hell in a hand basket is a travesty and out of order that will cost us serious regret in the end! From the Old Testament to the New, God has always been concerned about the health and well being of our families. And you know what? He still is today!

Like Mother Brown, our first pulpit is our home not the church!

Paul said it like this,

> "But if anyone does not provide for his own,
> <u>and especially those of his household,</u>
> <u>he has denied the faith and is worse than an unbeliever.</u>"
> *I Timothy 5:8 NKJV*

Preacher, want to run a revival? Start in your home!

### Your Family is Your Jerusalem!

Listen our families are our personal Jerusalem. Jerusalem in essence means peace. When a pastor's home, marriage, and children are in peace and order, it's easier to catapult to greater dimensions of Kingdom service.

Now world revival started where? In Jerusalem. After it hit Jerusalem it spread throughout the world! Now read between the lines here. When our home life is together, we are free to go around the world. Why? Because our base is solid! After all, how does it look for us to go around cleaning up everybody's house and our own home is junky? Physician heal thyself!

Let's consider the passage of scripture. Hear what Jesus said to the disciples about Jerusalem.

> "But ye shall receive power
> when the Holy Spirit has come upon you;
> and you shall be witnesses to me <u>in Jerusalem</u>,
> and in all Judea and Samaria,
> and to the end of the earth."
> Acts 1:8 NKJV

Now here, Jesus was talking to the disciples about the then coming decent of the Holy Spirit. The power of the Holy Spirit is still available for our generation today.

> "For the promise is to you and to your children,
> and to all who are afar off (that's us)
> <u>as many as the Lord our God will call</u>."
> Acts 2:39 NKJV

Preacher, are you called? Then the power of the Holy Spirit is available to you today for the asking and receiving!

> *"God always starts where we are
> before sending us abroad."*

However, the point I want to make here is this. Jesus said the disciples would be testimonies of redemption first in Jerusalem and then throughout the whole world! Jerusalem was where they were. Judea and Samaria were their neighbors moving them farther away from their starting point. However, they could do this because they completed their foundational start. See, Jerusalem was their launching pad to the global spreading of Christianity. So preacher, want to do global ministry? Start in your house first!

Likewise, if we make ministry to our own households first a top priority, I believe drama situations like 9-1-1 Emergency Help Cries 6, 13, and 14 can be avoided and diminished. I believe if we embrace this concept, not only will it send a powerful message of hope to the congregations we serve, (sheep are apt to take on the same spirit their leadership exemplifies) more importantly our own wives, husbands, and children will have a greater respect for what we do in the Kingdom of God. And who knows? Instead of feeling indifferent towards ministry and what we do, THEY MAY EVEN JOIN US! Without coercion! Why? Because what Baby's Daddy and Baby's Mama preaches on Sunday morning, they show it first at home! The kids feel confident, needed and valuable because now they don't feel left out. Further, wives no longer see the ministry as "the other woman" or husbands the ministry as "the other man" because the preaching spouse practices balance.

It's important as clergy that we remember our families are under pressure too along with us. Not only are we in the glass bubble of scrutiny and a 24 hour unrequested audience, so are our spouses and children!

*"First families are
not to envied! Huh!"*

Because our spouses and children are attached to us just by association alone they are prejudged, examined, and have to take hits just because we're related. Therefore, it's not enough for us to want them to understand what we go through as leaders alone. We must also take the consideration to understand what they're going through too! Just because we're called to preach doesn't mean they have to be preachers too!

This is why when families of pastors or some political dignitary such as the President of the United States are called *First Families*, it's nothing to envy. Huh! We're first alright. First to be talked about. First to be scrutinized. First to be held to standards higher than the moon itself! First! First! First!

However, when a pastor and his or her family are together on one accord, it's a beautiful and powerful force to be reckoned with.

Ecclesiastes says it like this,

"Though one may be overpowered by another
two can withstand him,
And a threefold cord is not quickly broken."
Ecclesiastes 4:12 NKJV

Preacher, does your ministry seem to be moving slow? No place to preach lately? Well you've been invited to do a service all the way in Jerusalem. Yes! It's a dinner meeting too. It's located right across your very own kitchen table. The precious souls of your very own family!

Pastor, go get your wife! Let her feel your embrace! Go get your husband! Treat him like your king. Go get that son! I know you may have youth ministry at your church but your boy needs you like never before. He's crying out for you. Please. Go get that daughter! She's growing up now and facing pressures we didn't as youth. Embrace her and show her the beauty of her being causing her to feel valuable and precious raising her self esteem. In doing so you'll cut off the need to search for love in all the wrong places. And if your children are already grown, reach out to touch them anyway. So what if there are mistakes made in your past. You can't change that. But THIS IS THE DAY THE LORD HAS MADE! You have today and it's a gift from God to you! Hallelujah!

Somebody's family is about to be healed right now!

Your family is your Jerusalem.

Rejoice!

## When Family Unity Becomes A Tremendous Challenge!

Now to be fair to this subject we also need to look at the other side of the coin. Although desired sometimes marital and family unity isn't that easy to obtain if at all sometimes! I've seen in my travels several situations whereas some clergy families just can't seem to get on one accord.

Let me give you some examples.

- A preacher really loves the Lord but their spouse is not a Christian or doesn't share the same faith or commitment to ministry.

- A clergy's husband, wife, or children have become apprehensive toward ministry because of hurt or mistreatment of their clergy loved one or they themselves by the congregation where they attend.

- A clergy's souse or children are non-supportive because of some hurt, violation, hypocrisy, wound, adultery, abuse, or disappointment inflicted by their clergy loved one themselves.

- The spouse or children of the clergy loved one is simply rebellious.

- The clergy couple is divorced and the children are pulled between two sides.

I believe in life there's a root cause to every behavior a human being can exhibit. Sometimes what looks like rebellion or indifference is a silent scream or a deep cry that shouts there's a need somewhere in that person's life not fulfilled. This is why as pastors and leaders we must make sure that we are meeting the deeper needs of our spouses and family members at home and not just simply preaching to them! Sometimes indifferent reactions are simply a cry out for love and attention.

However, in my years of ministry and counseling, I've found out this is not always the case. There are times when a clergy loved one is doing all he or she can do and still the battle never ceases. In each of these situations, GOD IS ABLE! However, there are some things we must consider.

Let's take it from the top.

**When A Married Partner Is Indifferent!**

For starters if a preacher is married to a spouse that doesn't share the same faith or commitment to ministry he or she has, realize that we can't make adults do what they don't want to or feel comfortable doing even if we're married! They're adults and no marriage can be successful without mutual respect. We are never to treat our spouses like they are children! This is the first step to a horrible marriage. Under no circumstances has God called us to be controllers or manipulators even if we feel we're right!

The best thing we can do is six--fold:

1. Seek to come to some peaceful agreement that will work for both of you.

2. Establish communication and lovingly discuss reasons or the source and cause for the indifference and seek peaceful and helpful resolutions.

3. Make sure you're taking care of all marital responsibilities at home and not neglecting them. Remember, your marriage is your first pulpit. In addition

strive to improve you! Too many couples at odds try to change their partner overlooking their own shortcomings. Improve "you" in the relationship.

4. Live the life of a sincere Christian before your mate. There is nothing tackier than talking Jesus, Jesus, Jesus, and your character is all jacked up!

5. Don't be so quick to give up on your marriage. Swallow your pride and seek professional counseling together. It will do wonders for your marriage!

6. Know that God is able, be patient, trust Him, and give God time to work. Give your mate time to process. Just because your mate doesn't jump up and down to your every beaconing call doesn't mean they aren't listening. Let your spouse know that you love them unconditionally. This means they don't have to act like you and who knows? One day you'll look up and they will willfully follow you to church. I've found in all my cases in mental health and ministry that very few people reject unconditional love.

Now God's best is that we take a long look at who we marry before we do so. We are encouraged not to yoke together with unbelievers because of the potential of such impending struggles. (See II Corinthians 6: 14-18.) God has called us to peace. Two can't walk together except they're in agreement.

However, when a person is already married to a spouse in such a state, that marriage by all means can still work out wonderfully and beautifully. Consider this passage of scripture.

<u>I Corinthians 7: 10-16. NKJV</u>

10. Now to the married I command, yet not I but the Lord: A wife is not to depart from her husband.

11. But even if she does depart, let her remain unmarried or be reconciled to her husband. And a husband is not to divorce his wife.

12. <u>But to the rest I, not the Lord, say; If any brother has a wife who does not believe, and she is willing to live with him, let him not divorce her.</u>

13. <u>And a woman who has a husband who does not believe, if he is willing to live with her, let her not divorce him.</u>

14. <u>For the unbelieving husband is sanctified by the wife, and the unbelieving wife is sanctified by the husband; otherwise your children would be unclean, but now they are holy.</u>

15. <u>But if the unbeliever departs, let him depart; a brother or a sister is not</u>

under bondage in such cases. But God has called us to peace.

16. For how do you know, O wife, whether you will save your husband? Or how do you know O husband, whether you will save your wife?

17. But as God has distributed to each one, as the Lord has called each one, so let him walk. And so I ordain in all the churches.

Wow!

The bottom line here is this, when a spouse is indifferent for whatever reason that marriage can still work. However, it's by choice only!

## Baby Did You Cook Dinner?
## Is the Bath Water Running?

As senior pastor in my ministry, I do lots of ministerial encouragement for both singles and married folks. I'm very hard on making sure saints have their home life together. Especially when they have family members or spouses who are not born again or are indifferent to ministry! We're the only Bibles some people will ever see! Everybody's not coming to church so we take the church to them!

I teach God is about holistic health and our families and spouses play a large role in this. Sometimes so many saints give God and Christianity such a horrible name by the way we conduct ourselves and handle our home situations. For example, wanting our loved ones to support us in ministry and we don't take care of our responsibilities at home doing simple things like making up our beds, paying for the phone bills we ran up, taking responsibility with the children.

Being a comedian pastor sometimes (I can't help it yall!) I often use humor to share powerful lessons about life. Listen in our ministry we have a ball! Check us out at St. Stephen AME! Ain't nothing like it! LIFE GIVING! We're not afraid to laugh in our ministry and preach holiness, righteous living and deliverance just the same! I often share some powerful words I borrowed from a dear friend of mine.

Check out what I tell them,

*"Don't get an "A" in church and flunk life!"*

Oh! That's a message! Thanks Desmond Pringle! You and Tanya are wonderful examples of couple unity, fun, and togetherness.

By the way, "What's up Tanya girl?"

Actually there's a lot of hidden wisdom in Desmond's statement. If we're getting an "A" in church, we should be getting an "A" in life also! Why? Because the principles we learn in church from God's Word are life giving! They're to be placed into practice outside the doors of the sanctuary!

> "Your word is a lamp to my feet
> And a light to my path."
> Psalm 119: 105. NKJV

Yeah Buddy!

So with all this said, in my ministry we have quite a few married couples whereas the spouse doesn't come to church. And this is what I always tell them!

*"Before you all come down here and spend hours in this sanctuary, don't come without first making sure your husband's or wife's dinner is cooked and the children taken care of! Come to an agreement with your mate! Make sure your spouses bath water is running! And whatever you do, don't be talking about Pastor Edwards in your home. Don't even bring me up! No man wants to hear his woman talking about another man all the time. Even it he is your pastor! No wonder some married brothers are indifferent to church! As a matter of fact, don't ever put me in your marriage! That's not my place and one where I refuse and will never go! My authority concerning your life ceases at the exit of the sanctuary doors. Besides, I don't want nobody showing up at my door with a shotgun saying, "You told Harpo to beat me! Huh!"*

I'm telling you! Order some of my CD's and video's. They will certainly be a blessing. Simply life giving and just keeping it real. And as a result, so many souls have been saved and lives changed to the glory of God!

However, here are a few tips and questions I encouraged married couples to consider prior to participating in ministry. Preachers, if we desire happy marriages, we need to consider the same!

## **Good Questions For Saints Who Want Good Marriages!**

- Have you ministered to your spouse first making sure all is well with them before leaving for church?

- Is dinner cooked? (How can you come to church, shout all over the place, and your husband/or wife is starving, and expect them to be smiling with you?)

- Are the children taken care of and covered?

- Are your bills covered and taken care of?

- Have you and your spouse discussed service times, what you do in church, and come to an agreement and peaceful understanding?

- Never compare your spouse to your pastor or anyone in any way, shape, or form. This is an extreme no-no! Not only is it unfair. It's rude!

- By your actions show your spouse that they are loved, special to you, esteemed very highly, your honey bunch and the ministry you're a part of is never a competitor but rather a catalyst to make your marriage even stronger!

Oh! If saints would do this, I believe whole families will come to Christ and join church!

Now being married is no excuse for missing services and not being consistent and faithful in the things of God! I've seen people use marriage as an excuse to the point that they spiritually just dry up to the point of almost backsliding.

Listen, Jesus comes first! However, truly putting Christ first in your life means that you will take care of these things! It's not an oxymoron! Sit down and have a heart to heart talk with your mate about your relationship with God and desire for spiritual growth. If you're interested in participating and attending certain ministries of your church, look at the scheduled times and discuss such with your mate. Even if they're indifferent to ministry, work together as a team, pray, and watch God move from there!

## Keep Romance
## In Your Marriage!

I said in the chapter on "Preachers and Sexuality" that sexual intercourse was God's idea and not the devil! Sex is celebration and preaches its own sermon of love and unity between a married couple! Preachers, keep romance in your marriage! Practice spontaneity! Learn to have fun! With laughter being the shortest distance between two people such will bring healing and refreshing to the both of you and your children will benefit!

Don't get so where you're just *"too anointed"* to have romance and love making with your husband or wife. Deny them this and somebody else may very well fulfill this need in their life all up in your place and face! This is where some saints flunk!

> *"Good romance begins
> with communication!
> Too many Christians are getting divorced"*

When it comes to married couples, sex, and romance, the Bible encourages couples to come to a mutual agreement concerning the timing being sensitive and respectful of each others concerns and needs. So in other words, good romance begins with communication! Hear this men! Communication! We can't just jump on our wives! Men and women are programmed differently. Communication! And women honor this too because sisters yall know yall can play hard to get! "Don't touch me! I'm in the spirit baby!" Now I'm talking to married folks here only! Holiness is still right! Huh! But listen. Too many Christians are getting divorced! I wonder why? It's sends a bad message to the unbelieving world!

Nevertheless, most holy sisters and brothers, if you decide to go on a consecration or fast plan your love making schedule. Come out the heavens and minister to your mate! They might cry out hallelujah! Oh! (I know that got you!) Actually, they might get saved!

The Bible says it like this,

> "Do not deprive one another (sexually)
> except with consent for a time,
> that you may give yourselves to fasting and prayer;

and come together again so that Satan does not
tempt you because of your lack of self-control."
*I Corinthians 7:5 NKJV*

Now consider this same passage in the Amplified Bible.

"Do not refuse and deprive and defraud each other
[of your due marital rights],
except perhaps <u>by mutual consent</u> for a time,
so that you may devote yourselves unhindered to prayer.
<u>But afterwards resume marital relations,</u>
lest Satan temp you [to sin] though your
lack of restraint of sexual desire.
*[Exodus 19:15]*

Wow!

There are times when sexual intercourse between a married couple may not always be convenient for a number of reasons including health issues. However, the key to keeping the devil out is to sit down, discuss your concerns and issues, and come out with a plan that will work for both of you!

Oh! This is good stuff! LIFE-GIVING!

## When Marital and Indifference Felt By Children Are Caused By Other Stimuli!

Now before we close out this chapter, let me also address this issue. Sometimes indifferences exist toward clergy support due to problems inflicted by a congregation or even because of a wound or abusive behavior inflicted by the clergy person themselves. We will actually discuss this in more detail in the chapter, *"The Congregation's Response to the Wounded Leader!"* However, let me say a few things.

In 9-1-1 Emergency Help Cry 13, a pastor's wife did not support the ministry because her husband was beating her! Now this is real! Now what is she to do? Domestic violence is a growing serious issue as the actual lives of people are at stake. Such a matter calls for immediate legal action by law enforcement and professionals of the criminal justice system. Why or how can we expect a person in such a predicament to support a ministry? They can be killed! In such cases a person must take the proper steps to ensure the security of their own safety and most of all GET PROFESSIONAL HELP AND ASSISTANCE IMMEDIATELY! I cannot give you advice here for legal reasons.

## When Indifference Is Because Divorce!

Let's face it. All marriages simply just don't work out. However, this still should not be the end of the world.

Too many Christians are getting divorced! And some people have legitimate reasons! Yes indeed! However, in my opinion some are simply because of our own stubbornness, self-centeredness, lust and desire for other things, peeping at the green grass in the other back yard, refusal to forgive, and unwillingness to reconcile and work together. But who am I to say? I'm just telling you how I personally feel. So please don't receive this as law! It's only my personal opinion from ministering and counseling firsthand to so many couples.

Nevertheless, while I believe that everything possible should be done to make a marriage work as divorce often carries unspoken long term ramifications, if divorce does occur ministry can still be successful.

First, the divorced couple should seek to come to a peaceful agreement and resolution how business should be handled especially if children are involved. Such matters need to be worked out with professional counseling and legal assistance to ensure proper insight and procedure.

Secondly, when it comes to ministry, family counseling is certainly a plus especially if children are involved who love both Mommy and Daddy and now are torn between which parent they will spend time with when, how, or even if the divorced couple remarries.

Nevertheless, praise God it's not the end of the world! Preacher you can move forward with your life and purpose knowing that great success lies full speed ahead!

Thank God!

**My Baby Mama and Daddy
Drama Can Be Avoided!**

### FOOD FOR THOUGHT:
*"When clergy can secure healthy spouse
and family relationships,
and practice balance in ministry,
that clergy person
will be free to accomplish great things
and catapult reaching untold destiny!"*
*A Brently Proverb*

As we prepare to close this chapter, out of all that's been said, "My Baby Daddy, My Baby Mama" drama can very much be avoided. And if we've had such in our lives, we can recover!

Clergy persons can indeed enjoy healthy marital and family relationships even while handling the business of ministry. All it takes is realizing that our marriages and children are our first congregation, then ministry and prioritizing from there.

When a preacher has laid the foundation of establishing a healthy home, come what will or may, the challenges that come with ministry won't carry such devastating blows and the launching pad for success will be laid.

So Reverends, LET'S GO GET OUR FAMILIES! Hallelujah!

Celebrate!

## Chapter 9 Review
### My Baby Daddy! My Baby Mama!
*"Preachers, Marriage, and Family Relationships!"*

- Families are important because they are the basic units of society.

- The destruction of a nation begins in the homes of its people.

- A clergy person's home life needs to be in order before seeking to oversee ministry.

- The total strength of a preacher's ministry will be tremendously affected and influenced by his or her marriage and home.

- Our marriages and children are our first pulpit.

- It's important that we understand the power of delegating ministerial responsibility to spend quality time with our families to curtail tragedy and devastating results.

- When spouses and children are indifferent to ministry we need to find out why and get the proper godly and professional help needed.

- When a minister's home life is healthy he or she has laid a solid foundation for great success.

- If we have failed in any areas of marriage and home life recovery and success is still available providing we reach for it!

## CHAPTER ELEVEN

# LORD, HOW DO I DEAL WITH JUDAS?
## *"Understanding the Controlling Minister!"*

> "......Assuredly, I say to you, one of you who eats
> with Me will betray Me."
> And they began to be sorrowful,
> and say to Him one by one,
> "Is it I?" And another said, "Is it I?"
> He answered them and said to them,
> "it is one of the twelve,
> who dips with Me in the dish."
> Mark 14: 18-20 NKJV

*"In ministry somebody somewhere is going to leave you hanging. But remember, the people we serve don't belong to us.*
*God only entrust them in our care as stewards.*
*They belong to the Lord!*
*Let God's people go and get on with your life!"*
*A Brently Proverb*

[This chapter addresses 9-1-1 Emergency Help Cries, 9, 10, and 11]

I MENTIONED EARLIER in this book how healthy pulpits make healthy pews. In this chapter I want to address the issue of the unhealthy pulpit and the controlling minister. I want to discuss some potential causes for such and give a few remedies how to avoid falling into this dilemma or recover if already ensnared.

## Control Defined!

According to *www.dictionary.com* the word, *control* means to exercise restraint or direction over. It's to hold in check. It's the act of power of regulation, domination or command. When one is being controlled, he or she is under the domination or command of another. There are some ministers who exercise complete control and domination over the people they serve extending even beyond the walls of the sanctuary.

## When Control Is Healthy!

Now there are two types of control. These are healthy and unhealthy forms.

As with anyone in leadership via any vocation such as a president of a cooperation, a coach over a football team, a manager of a busy restaurant, or a senior physician over a medical staff, there exist both healthy and unhealthy forms of control. Without healthy forms of control there would be total chaos as the need to establish order is paramount to the success of any business or organization.

*"Healthy control doesn't drive
but leads!"*

    Healthy control or regulation is when leader takes responsibility to make sure that the duties of his or her assignment and the holistic oversight of people under his or her care is carried out to the benefit of the vision and the well being of the people served. Providing healthy direction, accountability, and the establishment of boundaries that will produce productivity is a good thing!

    Healthy leadership doesn't drive but leads. It doesn't' push but motivates and inspires. It doesn't accept mediocrity but shows the way to excellence. And when a team member falls, it doesn't beat them down beyond recognition if at all. Rather, it rebukes and reprimands in a redemptive manner encouraging the wounded to rise up and live again! God has called us to be healthy leaders!

    The scripture admonishes us to obey those leaders whom God has placed over us with the boundaries they are walking after sound doctrine teaching of Christ and are providing healthy leadership. We are to "follow leaders only as they follow Christ" And we must make sure that it's truly Christ they're following and not some strange, erroneous, teaching or idea.

    Consider these passages for further insight and contemplation.

"Obey those who rule over you, and be submissive,
for they watch for your souls, as those who must give account.
Let them do so with joy and not with grief,
for that would be unprofitable for you."
Hebrews 13:17 NKJV

"But even If we, or and angel from heaven,
preach any other gospel to you than what we have preacher to you,
let him be accursed."
Galatians 1:8 NKJV

    Listen. GOD NEVER CALLS TO BLIND OBEDIENCE! We are only to follow leadership when it's healthy and sound in doctrine.

Doctrine is important because what we believe will shape our lives. This is why we must study!

> "Study to show thyself approved unto God,
> a workman that needeth not to be ashamed,
> <u>rightly dividing the word of truth</u>."
> *II Timothy 2:15 KJV*

Just because it's on television, comes across a pulpit, or has a large following doesn't mean it's sound! STUDY CHILD OF GOD! STUDY!

## When Control Is Unhealthy!

*"Control goes sour when it becomes possessive, manipulative, and dominant!"*

Now here's where the poison comes in. Here's when control becomes dangerous and lethal. It happens when we become possessive and we move from being healthy administrators to dominators! In other words, it's our way or the highway! When we're above taking sound advice, above being corrected or taught! It's lethal when we've made ourselves the final authority!

God has issues with shepherds who dominate over the people ruling them with an iron fist! To dominate someone is to steal their ability to choose, think for them, move for them, manipulate them by creating circumstances to cause them to bend to our will and wishes, and demand that their lives be swallowed up in ours! This even sounds drastic but it happens. Consider cult leader, Jim Jones!

Consider what Peter, the Chief Apostle of the 1st Century Church had to say on this matter.

<u>*I Peter 5: 1-4 NKJV*</u>

1. the elders who are among you I exhort, I who am a

fellow elder and witness of the suffering of Christ and a partaker of the glory that will be revealed:

2. Shepherd the flock of God which is among you, serving as overseers, not by compulsion but willingly, not for dishonest gain but eagerly'

3. <u>Nor as being lords (masters/dominators) over those entrusted to you, but being examples to the flock</u>;

4. And when the Chief Shepherd appears, you will receive a crown of glory that does not fade away.

I want to place special emphasis on verse 3. Preachers God has never called us to dominate nobody!

## What Makes A Controlling Leader?

In terms of the controlling minister, I believe there are several reasons why some pastoral leadership goes sour and become controlling.

Sadly, just in American history alone (but not limited to) we've seen instances whereas great leaders such as Jim Jones have led whole masses of people astray to their own death and destruction.

Perhaps in the beginning stages of his ministry he like many leaders started off on the right foot. But later became twisted and controlling.

In 9-1-1 Emergency Help Cries 10 and 11, we read two situations that often happen today which we want to avoid.

## Paying Attention to the 9-1-1 Help Cries!

In Help Cry 10, a preacher started off on the right foot and became very successful. However his success went to his head. Feeling powerful because of his many accomplishments in ministry his focus was no longer on Jesus Christ but himself. Thus, the congregation got hurled into new, strange, and false doctrines and total allegiance was demanded by all who are members of that ministry.

Oh! This is good stuff! Listen preachers! Listen!

In Help Cry 11, a preacher continues to preach the true Gospel of Christ with integrity and without deviation. He's very, very sincere. However, he is reluctant and refuses to delegate any ministerial assignments to the other ministers on his staff. He's afraid to trust anyone because like Jesus betrayed by Judas, one of his dearest spiritual sons in ministry hurt him real bad.

This spiritual son left him, started his own ministry and took tons of folk out of his church. Thus, rather letting trustworthy, proven staff help him with the many duties of the pulpit, he holds tightly onto everything never coming up for air in fear of being hurt again!

Based on these 2 Help Cries, I want to list 2 types of mentalities that carry the potential substance to create atmospheres that can possibly evolve into controlling situations among leadership. Secondly, I will give suggested keys in avoiding them!

## Potential Causes and Remedies For the Spirit of Control Among Shepherds and Leaders!

### Potential Cause 1. Feelings of Personal Inadequacy!

Inadequacy simply means not having enough to suffice, meet a standard, or a need. Whenever a leader feels in adequate it opens the door for him or her to battle with intimidation. Inadequacy and intimidation work together.

Intimidation is a torment that happens when we feel threatened by the success of potential of others. It's tormenting because it harbors the fear of some type of potential loss.

Inadequacy says, *"I'm not good enough."* And in ministry sometimes this happens because we may lack what we deem the necessary gifts, abilities, resources, favor, educational background, or experiences needed that another seemingly successful minster or colleague possesses.

In 9-1-1 Emergency Help Cry 9, we read how a minister felt intimidated by the fast growing mega ministry down the street. Feeling that his own method of ministry wasn't effective, he started to do the identical thing the church down the street was doing only to lose more parishioners. Bottom line: if we allow feelings of intimidation drive our ministries we will always lose and miss the blessings of God!

> *"When a leader is struggling with intimidation, it becomes difficult to celebrate the resources that God has placed in others to help him or her."*

If a leader leads while not healed from the spirit of intimidation it can open the door not only for the need to control and dominate but also for jealousy and competition. When this happens instead of being able to celebrate the resources that God has placed in persons surrounding that leader to help, they may begin to treat such with scrutiny and perhaps even minimize them before others to secure their position before the flock.

Thus, a root cause to becoming a controlling shepherd is often birthed out of a secret fear of loss. Secondly, the fear of rejection. If a leader fears rejection in any form then perhaps there are greater pains, hurts, and issues present which may even extend far beyond the walls of ministry but deeper into the personal life of the leader.

So here's the equation for the controlling leader:

- Inadequacy breeds intimidation.
- Intimidation breeds jealousy and competition.
- Jealousy and competition fight because of the fear of loss.

- The fear of loss is birthed from the fear of rejection.
- And the fear of rejection creates a need to control.
- And the spirit of control ensures the need of survival!

Wow! Makes sense?

Now there are other reasons why some leaders become controlling that may not be listed here such as greed and covetousness. But even these can still be traced back to this formula I've just presented to you.

## Suggested Remedy
## For Feelings of Personal Inadequacy!

Here are 4 tips you may find helpful.

1. <u>Learn to accept your own uniqueness.</u>

You are at your best being you! When God created you He didn't make a mistake. He doesn't need you to be someone else. He needs you to be you! Everybody has a gift, ability or talent form God. If you have only one, MAXIMIZE ON THAT and perfect it to the glory of God. Never compare or belittle yourself because your neighbor has 10! God rewards faithfulness not size!

"His lord said to him,

'Well done, good and faithful servant;
you were faithful over a few things,
I will make you ruler over many things.
Enter into the joy of your lord."
*Matthew 25:21 NKJV*

Awesome!

So celebrate your uniqueness and stop selling yourself short! You have more value and assets than perhaps what you give yourself credit for! For starters, YOUR STORY! Your story is your testimony to greatness how God brought you through and over! And if you've made mistakes from the past, learn from them. Don't dwell on them. Use such to propel you into greater wisdom and build. Besides, never underestimate the power of a seed. A seed my seem tiny and small but just one seed can feed a multitude!

Someone said it like this,

*"You can count the seeds in an apple
but no one has been able to count the apples in a seed."*

Wow! From this day forward, celebrate your own story to victory!

2. <u>Strive to better yourself and become more equipped for the task ahead.</u>

*"Complacency is the enemy to growth and progress!"*

Sometimes feeling of inadequacy occur in our lives because of the lack of proper preparation. However, don't fret. Growth is a process of evolving experiences.

Be encouraged and don't be afraid to work on improvements to make sure you have all the tools you need to be successful. This may mean having to go back to school, or enrolling in a class, or even setting long and short term goals for yourself. In other words, don't become complacent! It's the enemy to growth and progress. Keep moving and keep growing! Life becomes very boring standing still. There's too much work to do and too many souls and lives to reach!

I played around in college and flunked completely out due to falling into sin and backslided into depths of darkness unknown to me. But guess what? By the grace and mercy of God, I got up again! I went back to school, finished, got my degree and it's made all the difference. I even took time to lose weight and get in shape. It wasn't easy but certainly was worth it!

And here's a bonus. NEVER SAY YOU'RE TOO OLD! If you don't believe me, ask Abraham and Sarah!

"....Abraham was ninety-nine years old
when he was circumcised in the flesh of his foreskin."

*Genesis 17:24 NKJV*

"And the LORD said to Abraham,
"Why did Sarah laugh saying,
'Shall I bear a child since I am old?'
"Is there anything too hard for the LORD?
At the appointed time I will return to you
according to the time of life, and Sarah shall have a son."
*Genesis 18:13-14 NKJV*

So Preacher, IS THERE ANYTHING TOO HARD FOR GOD IN YOUR LIFE? Oh! What encouragement! It's not too late! Yes! Man and Woman of God, it's time for you to have a baby! Huh! (Spiritually speaking!) GO GET YOUR DESTINY!

3. <u>Stay Out the Rat Race!</u>

To overcome the spirit of inadequacy which leads to intimidation STAY OUT THE RAT RACE! What's the rat race? Competing with others! It's one of the fastest ways to becoming unhappy!

Never size yourself up to other people! This goes back to what I shared with you in point 1. When we place our lives in the unnecessary battlefield of competition, it becomes difficult to celebrate the success of others. Not being able to celebrate the success of others is a dangerous thing because God may want to use someone who is further accomplished in certain areas of expertise to bring us to higher ground. But if we're jealous, we'll bite them every time! Thus, we'll reject the elevation and help God sends our way and find ourselves wasting needless time reinventing a wheel that's already been successfully created.

4. <u>Realize people and the sheep you serve are not your personal property. Therefore, never treat them as such!</u>

There's a familiar saying that says,

*"Hurt people hurt people!"*

And how true this is!

Many times we become controlling because it's a way of compensating for wounds, hurts, and insecurities we may feel as leaders. Again, fear of rejection, abandonment, loss of status, fear of our vision not coming to pass, fear of not being able to support ourselves if we lose our following and supporters. So thus we clamp down hard on those who walk with us not letting them up for air!

But remember, the people don't belong to you or me, they belong to God and Christ purchased them with His own blood! And because they belong to God if we mess up just one, WE'RE MESSING WITH GOD HIMSELF!

> "But whoever causes one of the little ones
> who believe in Me to stumble,
> it would be better for him (or her) if a millstone
> were hung around his (or her) neck
> and he (or she) were drowned into the sea."
> *Mark 9:42 NKJV*

Listen in my years of ministry I've had a whole bunch of folk to abandon and walk out on me. And I'm telling you, many of these were people that I helped tremendous at my own personal expense with no desire for repayment or restitution.

And being honest, when people walk out on you especially with no sign and warning and you know your heart is right toward them in the Lord, it hurts! I used to struggle when people left the ministry especially when they were gifted and a tremendous blessing and load lifter.

However, as I began to mature in servant-leadership as a pastor, I came to the conclusion that the people belong to God not me. I had to remember that God loves them infinitely more than what I ever can and indeed has a plan for their lives even if it doesn't involve me. And guess what preacher? That's ok! Do you want the glory or something? Sometimes the Lord will allow people in our lives for a season. And then like a relay race, He may have someone else to take them to their next destination. This is the power of the Body of Christ having so many parts.

Paul said it like this,
> "I planted, Apollos watered, but God gave the increase."
> *I Corinthians 3:6 NKJV*

Yes!

And you know what? Even if people leave our ministries prematurely, like a shepherd leaving the 99 to find the one, let's reach out to them. However, learn to trust God concerning the lives of the people we serve. And you know what else? Life is not over! Sometimes we have to step back and allow people to find their own way. But we're never to force them. And while some folks we may never hear of again until we get to Heaven, there will be some who may be rebellious or indifferent today who later in life will come back to say two wonderful words to you,

*"Thank you!"*

However, even if they don't so what? Why get so bent out of shape? Why get all bound up, bitter, resentful? You have served the purpose God intended you in their lives! Rejoice in that and move on. Besides, there's a wonderful reward to be presented to you by Jesus Himself given face to face for all your hard labor and love! Listen I've been there! Let go!

Hebrews says it this way,

"For God is not unjust to forget your work
and labor of love which you have shown toward His name,
in that you have ministered to the saints,
and do minister."
*Hebrews 6: 10*

That's so awesome! Why not take a quiet moment right now to worship God and release and forgive all bitterness and resentment you may have towards those you love and have served who may have abandoned you.

Release them now to God. Now rejoice in that you have wonderfully served your purpose in their lives and God is pleased.

Now relax, breathe in the breath of God, AND LIVE!

## A Lady Told Me A Nursery Rhyme!

Listen. I've been there! Once I was just frustrated about some dear people whom I've imparted much into who flipped out on me, left the ministry and then dogged out my name. A lady that I didn't know came, approached me, encouraged my heart and told me a nursery rhyme.

She said,
*"Little Bo Peep has lost her sheep
And can't tell the way to find them.
LEAVE THEM ALONE!
And they will come home,
wagging their tails behind them!"*

Oh! At first I thought the woman was out to lunch! But then she made her point clear to me. The bottom line is let go and let God! He can do a much better job than you!

And again, if they never come home, GOD'S GOT IT ALL IN CONTROL!

Rejoice!

## Potential Cause 2.
## The Abandonment of Sound Doctrine!

Having said all this, the second reason or mentality that I believe contributes to the spirit of manipulation and control among shepherds is the abandonment of sound doctrine.

When we consider stories such as the Jim Jones cult of the 9-1-1 Emergency Help Cries, we discover if not careful a leader can become so lifted in his or her success he or she can get beside themselves. This is why I believer every pastor needs a pastor or someone in greater ecclesiastical authority pastors have to account to!

*"God cannot trust some people
with promotion because they
will flip out and get switched!"*

When people become so affluent that they forget the bridge that brought them over, the humble platform that got them to where they are today becomes obsolete and no longer needed! This is why God actually cannot trust some people with promotion because of such pride and abandonment from sound doctrine issues! They will get beside themselves, flip on the Gospel and get switched!

The Bible is very hard on false doctrine and teaching because of it's potent capacity to ruin lives as previously mentioned earlier. Furthermore, most people aren't Bible scholars so people trust pastors and believe in preachers. Although held in more skepticism than in earlier generations, on the most part people trust the preacher! And should be able to!

> "For the lips of a priest (preacher) should keep knowledge,
> And the people should seek the law from his mouth;
> for he is the messenger of the LORD of hosts.
> But you have departed from the way;
> You have caused many to stumble at the law.
> says the LORD of hosts."
> *Malachi 2:7-8 NKJV*

Wow!

Thus, with nothing being new under the sun, the Bible forewarns and promises severe judgment to those who ruin and mess up people's lives by requiring from them things God never requires and propagate strange, erroneous, and false doctrines.

Consider the following passages of scripture.

## **No Other Foundation**

> "According to the grace of God which was given me,
> as a wise master builder I have laid the foundation,
> and another builds on it.
> But let each one take heed how he builds on it.
> For no other foundation can anyone lay
> than that which is laid which is Jesus Christ."
> *I Corinthians 3: 10-11 NKJV*

## Don't Believe Everything You Hear!

"Beloved, do not believe every spirit,
but test the spirits, whether they are of God,
because many false prophets have gone out into the world.
By this you know the Spirit of God;
every spirit that confesses that Jesus Christ
has come in the flesh is of God.
and every spirit that does not confess that Jesus Christ
has come in the flesh is not of God.
And this is the spirit of the Anti-Christ,
(that which hates and opposes all that is Christ)
which you have heard is coming,
and is now already in the world."
*I John 4: 1-3. NKJV*

## Watch New and Strange Doctrines!

"For I testify to everyone who hears the words of the prophecy of this book.
If anyone adds to these things, God will add to him the plagues
that are written in this book.
And if anyone takes away from the words of the book of this prophecy,
God shall take away his (or her) part from the Book of Life,
from the holy city, and from the things which are written in this book."
*Revelation 22: 18-19. NKJV*

"But if we or an angel form heaven
preach any other gospel to you tan what we have preached to you,
let him be accursed."
*Galatians 1:8 NKJV*

When shepherds leave the foundational sound doctrine teaching of the Gospel of Jesus Christ, flies get in the milk and it becomes sour.

## 5 Suggestions To Get Back On Track!

1. Realize poisonous teaching brings poisonous results!

2. Be willing to repent, turn around and get back on track. The

promise of God still holds true.

> "If My people who are called by My Name,
> will humble themselves, and pray, and seek My face,
> and turn from their wicked ways,
> then will I hear from heaven,
> and will forgive their sin
> and heal their land."
> *II Chronicles 7:14 NKJV*

3. Be willing to accept the need for professional counseling and ministry for ourselves and our parishioners who may have received spiritual, emotional, and psychological damage due to erroneous teaching.

4. Be willing to resign, or sit down from ministry for the sole purpose of receiving the personal and intimate help, counseling, healing and renewal we may need. Continuing to minister while in pain and cloudiness may lead to further disaster.

5. Like never before in your life value the power of accountability and refuse to reenter or do ministry without credible oversight or as a solo project. I mean get an accountability system that will tell you the truth whether you want to hear it or not! People's lives are at stake at your mouth and leadership!

Remember, no matter how gifted again,

*"Every pastor needs a pastor!"*

It's the wisest thing we can do!

## So What Should I Do With Judas?
*Chapter Review*

In this chapter we've discussed issues concerning the controlling minister. In essence, what should we do with Judas?

I use Judas as a prototype because he was in leadership and walked very close to Jesus. Yet, Judas had control issues. He didn't like Jesus' method of ministry and his constant talk about His Kingdom "not being of this world." Judas wanted a piece of the pie right now!

Judas wanted thing to go his way so he manipulated the situation by betraying Jesus hoping to bring to himself some sort of satisfaction in leadership. Sadly, the results backfired to the destruction of Judas' own life.

Today as pastors and leaders with so many following us we must be careful not to fall into the same plight. While certain challenges accompany ministry, we must always be careful to do thing God's way and out our own. When facing problems whether personal or congregational, let's be careful not to dip our hands into the bowl of manipulation to domination in the attempt to reach a desired result. If we just pull back, honestly address our fears and the thing that bugs us with ourselves and the people we serve getting the proper godly professional counseling we'll do well.

So what shall we do with Judas?

Give him hope!

## Chapter Summary

*Lord, What Shall I Do With Judas?*
*"The Controlling Minister"*

- There are both healthy and unhealthy forms of control. Control becomes unhealthy when it turns into possessiveness, domination and manipulation.

- Judas is used in this chapter as a prototype of a frustrated leader who used manipulation to get what he wanted.

- God never commissions us to dominate over people at any time.

- We must always remember the people we serve are not our personal property but belong to the Lord.

- Most control issues in ministers are birthed out of some unfulfilled need for recognition, acceptance, or fear of some type of loss.

- When a minister or leader realizes that he or she is complete in Christ, the need to control and dominate over others loses its grip.

- Control issues and its aftermath can be overcome if properly addressed and the proper godly, professional help, counseling, accountability and guidance is adhered to.

# CHAPTER TWELVE
# SURVIVING THE CHURCH MAFIA!

## *"Preachers and Ecumenical Organizational Structures"*

*"Yet I have reserved seven thousand in Israel, all whose knees have not bowed to Baal, and every mouth that has not kissed him."*
I Kings 19: 18 NKJV

"I've never met one person in life whose chased the wind and caught it."
A Brently Proverb
(This chapter addresses 9-1-1 Emergency Help Cries 4, 9, and 15)

**SINCE THE DAY OF PENTECOST,** Christianity has evolved and spread to be the largest religion in the world although Islam is one of the currently fastest growing. Nevertheless, for a little over 2 centuries, Christianity has evolved from the original 12 disciples to 120 in the Upper Room at Pentecost. Then to about 3,000 in Acts 2: 41. Then to 5,000 in Acts 4: 4 and then to it's multi-million numerical status today.

And since the first century Christianity began to spread to new dimensions. The first 500 years of Christianity, the movement began to sweep the Greek - Roman world taking shape in organization and doctrine. During this time several momentous events and awakenings took place. There was the rise of monasticism, and between 500-1350 A.D. there was the Byzantine continuation, the Eastern and Western Churches, the effort to purify the Church through the Papacy, and expansion through Crusades.

Then later in time there came greater reforms and expansion around 1500-1790 AD. There were the Great Awakenings of the $16^{th}$ and $17^{th}$ Centuries including powerful people such as Luther and the rise of Lutheranism, John Calvin and Calvinism, the Catholic Reformation, the development of the Reformed and Presbyterian Churches, then reformers such as the Anabaptist, the English Reformation, and Protestantism. And let's not forget great leaders like Charles and John Wesley, founders of Methodism and Richard Allen, the founder of the first established denomination owned by people of African descent called the African Methodist Episcopal Church.

Then in the early 1900's there was a new wave of Pentecostalism that took it's first great explosion at a revival held on Azusa Street branching off into several new denominations composing of Holiness churches and ministries that placed greater emphasis on spiritual gifts. Then further in time again the Church began to evolve and people began leaving historical traditional denominations to establish several independent or non denominational churches. And now today we have tons of varied administrations within the Body of Christ since it's earliest beginnings. Methodist, Baptist, Catholics, Lutherans, Episcopalians, Moravians, Pentecostals, Adventist, and time does not afford me to list every different administration here.

However, my point in all of this is simply to say that the Body of Christ is huge with many diverse parts and administrations. And somewhere along the line we as clergy persons fall in somewhere even if our administration is independent of the traditional. In other words, even if we're doing our own thing!

Yet in this chapter, I want to talk about the importance of not losing heart if somewhere along the line we bump into some serious conflict within the administrations from wherewith we serve. Sometimes within our varied organizations, like Judas betraying Jesus there are spiritual mafia's who may seek to undermine us out! However, like Jesus, each of us must learn to stand. Thus there are 3 simple things I want to share with you.

**Perfection Cannot Be Found
On the Planet Therefore Seeking Such
Is A Waste of Time!**

Now I mentioned in a Brently Proverb at the top of this chapter that I've never met anyone who's been able to catch the wind. In other words, some things we do can be a terrible waste of time. Like trying to catch the wind!

The wind can be either a blessing or a curse. It can bring comfort or great hardship. Sometimes it can refresh us like a sweet cool breeze on a hot scorching day. Other times it can be a forceful hurricane or tornado tearing up everything in its path. But guess what? Either or, it's all the wind. And even when the wind is a blessing, we'll still never be able to confine it within our hands to determine what its next move will be.

In the same manner is working with people in the various organizations we may serve. There are bad winds and good winds. But what shall we do? Sometimes the organizations under which we serve are tremendous blessing to catapult us to new dimensions of service. Other times, just as in the historical past in the evolution of Christianity, groups or persons within our ranks will rise up like the Mafia to shoot us out the clouds!

In 9-1-1 Emergency Help Cries 4, 9, and 15 we see 3 clergy persons committed to ministry but are experiencing road blocks and challenges not at the hands of people off the streets but fellow colleagues who too are in ministry. Places where seemingly such challenges shouldn't even exist. At least not from such a source!

And in Help Cries 4 and 9, the clergy persons who are the recipients of such hardships allowed themselves to succumb to their situations. Like a foot on an ant they were spiritual aborted and cut off from fulfilling their God given destinies. They gave in.

In Help Cry 15, the clergy person didn't necessarily succumb to the blockage placed on their by fellow colleagues but was being forced to maintain a lower status of position being guarded by the gate keepers of the spiritual ecumenical mafia.

Working in any organizational structure these things can happen as it did to Christ. But preacher, you can't quit your destiny.

**3 Keys to Surviving Spiritual Mafia's!**

1. <u>First ask yourself, "Is it God's will for me to be a part of this organization?"</u>

This is key! Why? If it's not God's will then you're out of place anyway and won't prosper there. Get out and get in His will!

However, if it is God's will then you're in the right place even if under fire and challenge. But guess what? Anytime we're in the will of God, He will take care of us! And should His will lead us to the lion's den, He will deliver! Therefore, if you know that you're in God's will serving under the administration you are, know that what may seem like bricks to you will soon become stepping stones! Be patient!

2. <u>If in God's will, know that He doesn't send us into perfect situations but into places where we can bring light and hope into dead places He wants to resurrect and receive a greater glory!</u>

I often tell people, "stop looking for the perfect church!" Why? They don't exist. At least not yet. However, it's coming! The scripture promises that the Church will be perfected one day. But until then God uses us as salt and light to bring healing, preservation, flavor, taste, comfort, and insight into lives that may lack these elements. Challenges among our own people are character builders and can be instrumental in giving us hands on experiences to stability and overcoming obstacles that often come to challenge our destiny.

But the key again here is making sure that it's His will for you to be where you are.

### 3. If God has placed you on a certain assignment and you quit because the winds start to blow you may be denying yourself the greatest promotion of your life.

The scripture tells us that promotion doesn't come from the north or south but from the Lord! Always remember that we have an unseen enemy therefore are required to take the whole armor of God upon us to stand. (See Ephesians 6: 10 -18) Trouble is often an indication that something great is about to take place in your life. Like a pregnant woman in labor the pain is always greatest just before the baby comes.

You must always remember that what God has for you is for you and no one can stop it! Not even the mafia! And if it seems the ecumenical mafia is blocking some door for you to walk through, consider that God is in control and may have a better plan! Continue to learn to work well with people. Even those who may cause you the greatest pain. Stay faithful and don't deviate from the plan of God for your life and watch God take the very weapons the enemy uses to discourage and hinder you as a triumphant springboard to catapult you to greatness!

Remember, if you are in the will of God and know so, there's absolutely no one who can stop your blessings and what's yours! Stay faithful to your destiny and watch God even make the mafia behave! He may even allow them to come against you because there's a wonderful breakthrough, blessing, and transformation He wants to bring to their lives too!

After all, we are accounted as sheep for the slaughter! Let God use you. Now go and get the job done! God will be your promoter! Rejoice!

## Chapter 12 Review
## Surviving the Church Mafia!

*Preachers and Ecumenical Organizational Structures*

- The Church has evolved through many phases to get to where it is today.

- Because of such, there are many diverse parts to the Body of Christ and administrations.

- There is no administration that's perfect even if you're in an independent or non-denominational status.

- The key to victory is making sure that where you are is God's will for your life and that you're planted where God wants you.

- If you're in the will of God even the mafia can't stop your blessings so keep your focus.

- Trouble always comes before a great breakthrough! You'll never know what great things God is working out for your good in the midst of being challenged!

- **Stay faithful to the assignment God has placed on your life and even your enemies may get blessed!**

## CHAPTER THIRTEEN

# THE CONGREGATIONS RESPONSE TO THE WOUNDED LEADER!

*"And he said to his men, "The Lord forbid that I should do this thing to my masters, the LORD's anointed, to stretch out my hand against him, seeing he is the anointed of the LORD."*
*I Samuel 24:6 NKJV*

*"One of the greatest areas where the Flunk Monkey sits upon many congregations is our treatment of leadership when they fall"*
*A Brently Proverb*

*"It's been said we're the only army that kills its own wounded"*
*-Anonymous*

[This chapter addresses 9-1-1 Emergency Help Crisis 1&2]

YOU HAVE HEARD ME MENTION that healthy pulpits make healthy pews. Healthy pews make healthy pulpits. When both the pulpit and pew are healthy, that congregation can reach the world!

Well, in this chapter we're going to talk about what to do when the pulpit is not so healthy. In other words, what should be the congregation's response to the wounded leader and what can the pews do to ensure its own wellness?

## When the Shepherd Is Wrong!

Let's face it. There are times when the shepherds and leaders are simply wrong! No excuse. Our daily news media are often flooded with news of such. So what should we do? However, primary leadership falling into error in scripture is no new thing to history. Consider the following examples.

- Adam & Eve were wrong when they ate off the tree.
  Genesis 3:11-13

- Noah was wrong getting drunk after the flood.
  Genesis 9:21

- Father Abraham (Father of Nations) was wrong when he lied about Sarah being his sister
  Genesis 20:2

- Moses the Deliver was wrong when he smote the rock.
  Exodus 20:7-13

- King Saul was wrong when he became jealous of David
  I Samuel 18:6-9

- King/Prophet David was wrong when he slept with Bathsheba
  2 Samuel 12:7-10

- Judge Samson was wrong when he slept with Delilah
  Judges 16:15-21

- Peter was wrong when he denied Jesus
  Matthew 26:69-75

- You and I were wrong when we........................?

Huh!

All of these leaders were terribly wrong in scripture. Yet while they had to pay the consequence for their behaviors God never threw them away. As a matter of fact, these same leaders lived to make such a great positive impact in history that it can never be erased!

Suppose God got rid of David because of his errors and faults? We would never have the life changing beauty of most of the Psalms that we read and enjoy today.

Suppose God got rid of Father Abraham when he lied about Sarah being his wife? (Genesis 20:2) Then there would be no 12 Tribes of Israel and the great Jewish nation and also other nations wouldn't have been born!

Suppose God got rid of Peter because he denied Jesus 3 times prior to being crucified? (Matthew 36: 69-75) We would never be able to glean from the powerful sermon Peter preached on the Day of Pentecost recorded in Acts Chapter 2 or enjoy the great historical contributions that Peter made to the Church as chief apostle!

Suppose God got rid of you? Or got rid of me the moment we messed up or sinned? Suppose the stones of judgment and punishment were hurled toward you? Think about your life! Be honest! Where would you be today? Where would I be today? Think about this!

The point that I'm making is we all mess up from time to time and we must be very careful how we handle each other when we blow it. Suppose when we were babies our parents and guardians threw us out with the bath water when we boo-booed in our diapers? Huh! Got you there didn't I? See my point? There's a right and wrong way to go about the discipline of the fallen. And when it comes to senior leadership such as a pastor there are certain wisdom principles we should consider.

## A Greater Penalty Applied
## To Erroneous Leaders!

There's not a human being that's never done anything wrong. None! The Scripture is clear on this.

> *"For <u>all</u> have sinned and fall short of the glory of God."*
> *Romans 3:23 NKJV*

All means all! I think we too soon forget this when it's someone else's turn to be in trouble.

Nevertheless, while we understand that preachers are human too there's a greater penalty applied when one assumes a leadership position. Why? It's not because any sin is greater than others when committed by non-clergy. Rather it's the far reaching influence of the behavior. This is because actions by leadership go beyond affecting the leader personally but also influences the lives of others under that leadership either directly or indirectly.

Let me give an example.

Suppose an individual is driving a car, makes a bad turn and hits a tree. (God forbid) That individual's life will be grossly affected by such an incident. However, not only will the individual be affected but also all those who are in someway connected to that life. This is a bad situation.

Now while this situation is unfortunate, imagine if this same individual was driving a bus full of school children. Imagine he or she makes a bad decision in turning and hits a tree. The situation has just escalated and even become more complicated. Why? It's bad enough that the individual and those connected to him or her will be affected but now multiply that by doubles! Every life on that bus is now terribly affected by that individual's decision plus every person connected to those lives who aren't even on the bus!

In the same way it's sort of like this when leaders are in error at the driver's wheel. Whole lives are affected! Just like an airplane pilot must go to school before flying a passenger plane, a doctor to medical school before performing open heart surgery, an attorney to law school before practicing law, the scripture gives great wisdom instructions before ordaining people to shepherd a flock.

Consider these two passages.

> ".... Not a novice, (new convert or beginner) lest being lifted up with pride he fall into the same condemnation of the devil."
> I Timothy 2:6 NKJV

> "My brethren, let not m any of you become teachers, knowing that we shall receive a stricter judgment."
> James 3:1 NKJV

Why is the judgment stricter? Because we've got people's lives in our hands!

## So How Do We Handle Pastors in Fault?

Here's the answer plain and simple. WITH BIBLICAL UTMOST CARE AND CAUTION! I use the term "biblical" because there is serious wisdom from God's Word in such matters. Too many churches and organizations are making a grand mess in such matters and are running people away from both church and the Lord!

Such matters are to be a handled with utmost care and concern I say looking at the whole picture and not just one angle. While the Scripture is clear that we are never ever to follow erroneous leadership still there is a right and wrong way to handle such matters.

Tragically in my experience and I'm quite sure many of you out there too can testify the way some churches, ministries, and organizations handle fallen leaders is a disgrace, reproach, ridiculous, and presents a horrible witness for Christ. It's as if some people specialize or get a certain joy in killing our own wounded rather than enrolling such for healing and surgery. And then we have the nerve to want people to come to Christ after an unbelieving and skeptical world just watched us slaughter, barbecue and roast at flaming temperatures our own brothers and sisters at the stake. Again, God is going to hold us accountable for every soul lost at our hands!

And the amazing thing is many times the ones who inflict the greatest punishments upon the wounded or those in error soon get a taste of their own medicine because to their surprise fresh dirt comes up on them! Now they want the mercy THEY DID NOT EXTEND to the brother or sister found in fault. Remember what I said about boomeranging bricks in the beginning of this book? Swollen eyeballs! What goes around comes around!

Nevertheless, there are times when shepherds are just wrong. When this is the case, what should we do? Below, I've compiled 4 suggestions.

### 3 Suggestions To Handling Pastors At Fault

1.  Realize that pastors are still "God's anointed" and God's ultimate plan is recovery.

When we say that pastors are still "God's anointed" we're not talking anything spooky or mysterious. This simply means that God's Hand is still upon their lives and His purposes for that leader are yet to be unfolded. Because we are not God, we don't always know what God is working in that leader behind the scenes although at fault. Therefore, to take the place of God and come up against that leader can be as dangerous as coming up against God Himself! This is why in I Samuel 24:6, David refused to kill King Saul although Saul was acting a plum fool! Hear what David said!

> *"And he said to his men, "The LORD forbid that I should do this thing to my master, the LORD's anointed, to stretch out my hand against him <u>seeing he is the anointed of the LORD</u>."*
> *I Samuel 24:6 NKJV*

Check this phrase out: *"seeing he is the anointed of the LORD."* In other words, Saul was in error but David recognized that God's Hand was still on him! He realized that his knowledge about the life of erroneous Saul was only finite information and to kill Saul would be totally stepping out his league interrupting God's unknown agenda itself. We must be careful how we handle God's anointed. The Scripture says it this way,

*"Saying, do not touch My anointed ones,
And do My prophets no harm."
1 Chronicles 16:22 NKJV*

David didn't have to touch Saul! Why? Because David realized that God saw the whole thing and would judge righteously. And guess what? Saul kept acting up! David speared Saul's life twice! (See I Samuel 26: 1-11) This is telling us something!

David knew that he didn't have the right to pull the plug on Saul's life although he perhaps felt like it. Nevertheless, his finite mind didn't know what was in the God's mind concerning rebellious Saul. This is why we shouldn't be so quick to throw people away when they blow it! Remember the examples I gave about how people like Moses, Abraham, David, and Peter came to their senses and were mightily used of God to change history <u>AFTER THEIR FAULT?</u> The same holds true today! A leader may be in terrible and gross error today but we don't know what transformation God may bring forth in them tomorrow.

However, in the case of King Saul, he died a terrible death. He was a case of a leader refusing healing and recovery. But guess what? David wasn't the one to bring the judgment. It was God who knew rebellious Saul's beginning and how his life would end. And you know what? David's hands stayed cleaned the whole time and later became King of Israel. (See I Samuel 31: 1-13.)

Actually when a pastor or any one of us messes up, God's plan is not judgment but recovery. While Saul was rejected by God as King of Israel because of his gross rebellion, he didn't have to die the way he did! God gave Saul numerous times to repent but he wouldn't. He was overtaken by pride and jealousy. Thus, his own stubbornness plunged him to an early grave outside the will of God. Let us never forget that the plan of God is healing, restoration, forgiveness, and redemption, not judgment GOD HAS RECOVERY ON HIS MIND! But if we rebel, we'll shoot ourselves in our own feet. Let's not be so quick to want to throw leaders away the minute they fall.

Consider the following passages.

> *"Say to them: 'As I live,' says the Lord GOD,*
> <u>*I have no pleasure in the death of the wicked,*</u>
> *but that the wicked turn from his way and live.*
> *Turn, turn from your evil ways!*
> *For why should you die, O house of Israel?"*
> *Ezekiel 33: 11 NJKV*
>
> *"And that they may come to their senses and escape*
> *(recover themselves) the snare of the devil,*
> *having been taken captive by him to do his will."*
> *II Timothy 2:26 NKJV*

Wow!

And remember. Don't touch God's anointed!

<u>2. When the discipline of pastors/leadership is necessary it must be handled through the proper channels and by the proper hands!</u>

Now let's get to the nitty gritty. There are times and situations whereas pastoral discipline simply can't be ignored. And let me make this clear. <u>Although pastors and other leaders in the Body of Christ may be God's anointed erroneous behaviors must be dealt with</u>! This too is biblical! Failure to do so could cause disaster and casualties too costly to repair! God has never called us to be enablers of unhealthy behaviors that could have devastating consequences down the road.

However, still there is a right and wrong way to go about doing this and you and I may not be the one to provide the discipline! There are some disciplinary actions which require the attention of the church and the laws of the land.

Let me give some examples whereas as pastoral discipline or leadership is necessary. Here are a few examples:

- the rape or molestation of a child
- stealing and the misappropriation of funds
- infidelity or promiscuity between clergy and parishioners
- unhealthy religious practices that endanger the life and safety of

parishioners

When such acts are committed, there's no getting around it. Such must be dealt with and rightfully so! We are all pitifully unhealthy if we don't! The scripture tells us that we are to obey the laws of the land providing those laws don't entice us to ungodliness. We are commanded to give to Caesar (the government) what is Caesars and to God what is God's (See Matthew 22:21).

So when we violate God's Word, common sense and the laws of the land, we're going to get what's coming to us. Preacher or not! So, no need to complain or blame stuff on the devil. We know better! Again, there are some things that occur in ministry that will require the expertise of professionals especially in instances that touch legal matters. When things like the molestation of a child or the misappropriation of funds occur, we can get in some very serious trouble by putting our hands on situations we don't have the expertise to handle. In such cases we must let the proper authorities do the work.

As mentioned before, prevention is better than experience in such cases. We want to make sure that we avoid this type of drama and practice good stewardship over all God has entrusted to us. However, if a pastor or leader is caught in such, the church shouldn't just blackball the pastor but rather be mechanisms of support and prayer.
When I say "support," I'm not talking about being in agreement with the crime. No way! We're not called to be accompanist. However, we must remember that pastor is still a soul beyond the realm of ministry for whom Christ died and we should pray for God's will, healing, restoration, and the proper correction of the problem. We should also pray for persons who may be victims or casualties of the impediment who also may be in great pain.

Nevertheless, besides legal matters in pastoral discipline when it comes to issues that require decisions from the church, there are some guidelines we should adhere to.

Consider the following passages:

*"Do not rebuke an older man, but exhort him as a father,
younger men as brothers, older women as mothers,*

> *younger women as sisters with all purity."*
> *1 Timothy 5: 1-2 NKJV*

> *" Brethren, if a man (or woman) is overtaken in any trespass,
> <u>you who are spiritual</u> restore such a one in a spirit of gentleness,
> considering yourself lest you also be tempted.
> Bear one another's burdens, and so fulfill the law of Christ."
> Galatians 6: 1-2. NKJV*

While some mishaps by shepherds may require disciplinary action by the church, the scripture makes it clear that such is to be administered only by the <u>qualified</u> and <u>that in a redemptive manner</u>. The phrase, *"you who are spiritual"* indicates that person/s responsible for administering discipline and restoration in such cases should be persons of proven spiritual maturity, rank, and character. They must be seasoned in the things of God, not a novice, of sound godly judgment with the ability to properly discern and determine the mind and will of God with all fairness and wisdom in the given situation.

In other words, this is not a job for someone who doesn't qualify to correct a pastor or leader. For an example, it's out of order for a sheep (parishioner) to ordain a minister. This has to be done by a higher authority recognized by the organization in which he or she serves and also congruent with the state or laws of the land. The person/s administering church discipline must have the proper credentials to do so! Bottom line: everybody doesn't rank to correct a leader in ministerial etiquette and discipline.

Now today, various denominations within the faith are set up differently and have different methods of procedure to follow when a pastor or leader is in error. Some denominations have ministerial efficiency committees and other elders of higher authority such as presiding elders, district superintendents, bishops, or apostles to handle such.

Other organizational structures such as some independent or non-denominational ministries may have other types of systems in place to handle such matters. But woe to the pastor whose out there and his or her only system of accountability is him or herself! This is how Jim Jones got the people to drink the poison Kool–Aid! This is so dangerous!

Nevertheless, when those committed to applying church discipline are in due order with the proper credentials in place, the goal of such discipline is not to destroy but to bring the necessary correction so that the soul in trespass might come to real repentance, quit the error causing the problem, and find restoration in Christ.

3. The Way We Treat Wounded Shepherds is a Direct Advertisement For or Against Christ!

In the beginning of the chapter, I said that the way some handle fallen leaders is a reproach to the Kingdom of God and I mean it!

I say this because I've seen church folk act just pure ignorant! All on television and the neighborhood! And worse, some people actually think God is pleased with their behavior because they successfully rounded up a band to put the pastor out!

I was on the internet one day and a woman in a particular city hog-slapped her pastor dead slap in the face after a church disagreement. And guess what? THE PASTOR HOG–SLAPPED HER BACK! Huh! Oh! I hollered! It was a riot! I played that thing over and over again. I was truly amazed! I had to play that thing at least 6 -8 times! Hollywood has gone to the wrong place looking for actors! Oh! Yall we gotta do better!

Immediately the cops came on the scene. Someone recorded the incident and of course it was blasted all over the local news of that city and worldwide web! I said, WORLDWIDE!

Now how in the world can we expect people who are already skeptical about us to come to the Lord when we act like we've never met the Savior!!! I'm telling you again for the second time, God is going to hold each of us accountable for every soul that's lost, goes to Hell, turned off by the church, and rejects Christ as Savior because of our ignorant behavior! So don't get upset when our youth and others join cults and strange religions! When we act like this we push them there!

The same thing happened in the 1$^{st}$ Century. Paul had to get on the believers for handling the mishaps of falling believers before the unbelieving skeptical world!

> "Dare any of you, having a matter against another,
> go to law before the unrighteous, and not before the saints?"
> *I Corinthians 6:1 NKJV*

Saints lets do better! The way we handle the wounded and fallen is serious!

### FOOD FOR THOUGHT
With the world already being lost in sin,
who wants to get beat up in the world
and then come into the Church to get beat up again?
If we treat our own who have sinned with disgrace
—what will we do to them?
People aren't stupid! Let's get it together!"

But on the flip side, just imagine the powerful testimony of hope and grace we will give to a hurt and dying world if we go about church discipline the right way?

Wow! Let's get there!

## If Sitting Under Wounded Leadership What Should I Do?

***"Wounded leaders make wounded sheep!"***

Besides issues of discipline when shepherds fall, what should we do if wounds inflicted by leaders are on-going? Here are 4 suggestions I offer.

### 1. Pray & Intercede for that Leadership!

God can go places in the hearts and lives of people we never can. Thus, prayer is the first thing we must do. As a matter of fact, it's our greatest ministry and is more important than preaching, singing, ushering, board meetings, or anything we can do in the Church.

Secondly, we will get more accomplished through prayer and intercession than bad mouthing the preacher and spreading seeds of discord. Prayer will position us for God's next "suddenly" (see Malachi 3: 1-3) and enable us to hear God's will and directives in every situation.

> "Therefore I exhort first of all that supplications, prayers,
> intercessions, and giving of thanks be made for all men, (people)
> for kings and all who are in authority, that we may lead a quiet and peaceable
> life in all godliness and reverence.
> For this is good and acceptable in the sight of God our Savior,
> ……who desires all men to be saved and come to the knowledge of the truth."
> *I Timothy 2: 1-4. NKJV*

God still hears and answer prayer!

## 2. Don't Be A Vessel of Confusion But A Part of the Solution.

The familiar saying, "Talk is cheap" still holds true. The wrong thing we can do when sitting under wounded leadership is to add fuel to the fire by spreading discord by gossiping about the situation. "Do unto others as you would have them to do unto you!" Tell me, what are you going to solve by putting your shepherd's business in the street or all over the church? God hates confusion and discord.

When a shepherd is leading while bleeding, see what helpful thing you can do as a parishioner to help lighten the load. You may not be able to assist your pastor on a personal level but perhaps you can work with a specific department or organization in your ministry that's already in place to help alleviate undue ministerial struggle.

## 3. If You Have Personal Grievances with Leadership, Set up an Appointment for Helpful and Holistic Discussion.

Now here's where we need to be careful. Don't bug your pastor over petty things you can solve yourself or try to get in his or her presence because you have a hidden agenda. But if you have a grievance with leadership, set up an appointment so you can respectfully discuss such with your leader with the goal of reaching healthy and helpful solutions.

If angry about something, don't go with the attitude, "I'm going to give that preacher a piece of my mind!" But rather go in the respect, humility and dignity of Christ hoping to arrive at a peaceful resolve. As a great bishop once said, "you can draw more flies with honey than vinegar."

Thanks Bishop Vinton Anderson! What an inspiration you and Mrs. Anderson are!

Always remember, there are always two sides to a coin. Most pastors are already under a heavy load. Hear your shepherd out before jumping to conclusions. When the discussion is over seek to find a workable resolve.

Note: Because all ministries aren't the same, sometimes it may be difficult to get an immediate appointment with your pastor. If so, follow the proper protocol and chain of command. Leave a good message with the appropriate secondary leadership and go from there.

### 4. **If Wounded Leadership is Detrimental to your Life, Safety & Well Being —Leaving May be your in your best interest!**

Now, I'm very careful with this! I never encourage people to leave a ministry unless it's extremely necessary. You'll never get anywhere being a church hopper. People change churches today like they change clothes. This is a hindrance to spiritual growth. Like a plant with no roots, not getting settled will keep a plant from growing properly.

However, in extreme cases where the behavior of leadership becomes detrimental to your life, safety, and well being, leaving may be in you best interest. For example, if the people had left the Jim Jones cult in time, perhaps many lives would have been spared!

Now remember, I cannot counsel you. Seek the appropriate professional help in these matters. However, know that as a parishioner you don't have the authority to rearrange the furniture in someone else's house, even if you think it needs to be done! The worse thing people can do is sit under ministry when they are not in agreement. Even when leadership is bad, we cannot usurp authority. It's best to leave and continue to pray for the leadership and ministry. Again, if leaving is difficult due to the threat of physical harm or something, get the proper professional help and legal assistance.

## When Sheep Wound Shepherds!

### "It's not just the pastor. Wounded sheep make wounded shepherds too!"

Now here's the flip side of the coin. Healthy pews also make healthy pulpits. And guess what else? It's unfair to place all the problems in ministry on the pulpit. It's not just the pastor! Wounded sheep make wounded shepherds too!

In 9-1-1 Emergency Help Cry 1, we see a very well deserving pastor dying suddenly from extreme burnout. He was a good pastor! And again, all preachers aren't crooks!

However, the problem in this case wasn't the shepherd but the congregation he served. They didn't support him. They enjoyed and took advantage of his services but never poured back into him. They kept him both financially broke and exhausted until such an overload resulted in his untimely demise.

So after when we hear bad reports about ministries, the focus mostly is always on the pastor. However, while pastors take the lead in the overall well-being of a congregation, the pew also plays a very significant role.

## "Sheep, Shepherds need you to hold up their arms!"

### Realize the Pastor Cannot Function Alone!

Just like a head is no good without the body, so do leaders need the support of the flock. Consider this passage from Exodus concerning the pressures of Pastor Moses.

> *"<u>Thou wilt surely wear away</u>, both thou, <u>and this people that is with thee</u>: for this thing <u>is too heavy</u> for thee: thou art not able to perform it thyself alone.*
>
> *Moreover thou shalt provide out of all the people able me, such as fear God, men of truth, hating covetousness; and place such over them, to be rulers of thousands, and rulers of hundreds, rulers of fifties, and rulers of tens:*
>
> *And let them judge the people at all seasons: and it shall be, that every great matter they shall bring unto thee, but every small matter they shall judge: so shall it be easier for thyself, and they shall bear the burden with thee.*
>
> *If thou shalt do this thing, and God command thee so, <u>then thou shalt be able to endure, and all this people shall also go to their place in peace</u>."*
> *Exodus 18: 18, 21 -23. KJV*

Wow!

Listen. Pastor Moses was about to kill himself doing a good thing. He was serving the many needs of the people of God. However, there was one problem. HE WAS DOING IT ALL BY HIMSELF! Noticing this his father-in law Jethro told him that while what he was doing was a good idea, it wasn't a God idea. Moses was about to kill himself prematurely doing a good thing.

How many pastors and leaders today are plum burned out because of the shortage of help by sheep? Or sheep being apathetic to the vision or some sheep simply not caring at all what happens in the ministry? I'm telling you from experience! When the pew is negligent or refuses to help the pulpit especially when the vision and goals of the ministry are worthy ones, it wounds the shepherd!

## A Lesson From Rowing A Boat In Hawaii!

Mother Brown told us years ago, "You can't row this boat by yourself!" She certainly knew what she was talking about!

Just on last year I ran a revival in Honolulu, Hawaii. What an awesome time! Hi Pastor April and Jellico Bright! What's up yall! That revival was the bomb! God really moved and I am now totally in love with Hawaii! When God made Hawaii, He really showed off! To God be the glory!

Nevertheless, after preaching I had 2 extra days left free on the island. My adjutant and I decided to get on a long, narrow, skinny boat and push off into the Pacific Ocean. When we got in the water, the lady put me at the very front of the thing with a long paddle in my hand. Bro. Maceo, my adjutant was at the back and the lady was at the very end. Off into the ocean we went. I knew I could swim but I wasn't so sure about Bro. Maceo. Huh!

Being the comedian I am, all kinds of stuff was running through my mind. JAWS! All I could see in my mind was sharks all around and beneath us. I mean you could see straight through the water it was so beautiful and clear. I was thinking about what would happen if a shark appeared. I had already thought how I would somehow beat the shark up, rebuke it, knock it out, swim to safety and tell Bro. Maceo make it on his own! Huh! I was going to leave the Hawaiian lady too! Oh! Just teasing! We had a ball.

Nevertheless, on a more serious note, there's something very powerful I got out this experience. It took all 3 of us to maneuver that skinny boat through the water. To get it to go left, right, or to turn the whole thing around required specific instructions from the lady who was most experienced and the obedience of Bro. Maceo and I sitting at two completely different opposite ends. In other words, we had to work together as a team. If Bro. Maceo and I refused to obey her instructions on how to paddle that thing we could've capsize or end up way out in the ocean somewhere. Then the comedy would really begin!

But I'll tell you this. I was going to survive if I had to walk on water! Glory Halitosis!

All right let me be serious! However, there's a powerful lesson we can learn from this story in the treatment of pastoral leadership. In this story, the Hawaiian lady represents the pastor of a church and Bro. Maceo and I, the congregation. The boat represents the church or ministry itself.

As pastor, the lady had a deeper insight of the vision of what we were trying to accomplish and how to get there. To fight and buck against her would get us nowhere. However, no matter how great her vision, it would never come to pass without Bro. Maceo and I cooperating with her lead. So both he and I had to come to an agreement that we would cooperate with the vision otherwise there would be discord and the church (ministry) the boat would go nowhere. How many whole ministries are stuck today because people won't get on one accord and cooperate with the visionary?

However, when all components worked together the pastor and the congregation guess what happened? The boat (church) had smooth sailing and we all arrived safely back to land! And guess what else? NO CASUALTIES! No one fell off the boat and drowned! What a lesson for us to learn!

Moral of the story: many pastors are under great stress and turmoil today because congregants don't want to follow instructions in rowing the boat together. However, if done together great successes can be won! This is what Moses' father –in –law Jethro was talking about!

## Are You Holding Up The Arms of Your Pastor?

Likewise, in Exodus 17: 8-16, Israel was fighting against Amalek. Just like all ministries have challenges and enemies of some sort or another. However, when the people held up the arms of Moses as he stood on the hill with the rod (the proof of the power of God with him) in his hand, Israel won. When the people dropped Moses' arms they lost. Holding up the arms of a pastor means giving them all the necessary support they need to get the job done! Are you holding up the arms of your pastor?

> *"And so it was, when Moses held up his hand, that Israel prevailed; and when he let down his hand, Amalek prevailed. But Moses' hands became heavy; so they took a stone and put I under him, and he sat on it.* <u>*And Aaron and Hur supported his hands, one on one side, and the other on the other side; and his hands were steady until the going down of the sun.*</u>*"*
> *Exodus 17:11-12. NKJV*

Awesome! This is off the chain!

The Bible says that holding up the arms of Moses became tiresome and heavy. This is a sermon to us. In other words, it's not always easy assisting pastors in ministry. Nevertheless, the people had sense. They got a stone. Something or an idea that's solid, credible, and stable that would work so they could continue to hold up the arms of Moses without fail. In other words, they were determined not to let their pastor be without the resources and congregational support to do ministry. And guess what? They made sure the pastor lacked nothing! The Bible says they supported him on every side. And guess how long? As long as it took until the job was finished! And you know what happened? Israel won!

What they did was so powerful that even the LORD had something to say! Consider this passage.

> *"Then the LORD said to Moses, "Write this for a memorial in the book and recount it in the hearing of Joshua, that I will utterly blot out the remembrance of Amalek from under heaven. And Moses built an altar and called its name,The –LORD-Is-My- Banner;"*

*Exodus 17: 14-15 NKJV*

Wow! What a testimony!

People of God, are we allowing the arms of our pastors and leaders to drop? Are we giving them the support that God requires we should?

If we don't support our pastors and ministries, don't look for success in that house! Plain and simple!

*"You looked for much, but indeed it came to little; and when you brought it home, I blew it away. Why"?" says the LORD of hosts. "Because of My house that is in ruins, while every one of you runs to his own house."*
*Haggai 1:9 NKJV*

Wow! Let's be encouraged to support our pastors and ministries as the task is so great before them. Especially with the needs of this present generation!

## 5 Tips for Establishing Health Relationships Between Sheep & Shepherds

1. **Sheep, shepherds need your daily prayers for them. They have pressures on them like you wouldn't believe**.

2. **Free shepherds from all forms of burnout by making sure he/she has all the resources needed to shepherd the flock**.
-- On a natural job – They're going to make sure you have what you need to work with all benefits. The same should reasonably be proved for pastors.

3. Moses wasn't on the frontline of the battle Joshua was! **When we remove pastors from the battle planning room to the frontline of the battle, we risk losing that pastor to an early demise.** God forbid!

4. **When there are grievances in ministry, handle such carefully and go through the proper procedures to address and correct the problem. However, don't be a vessel of discord.**

5. **Don't leave your shepherd to the wind! Cover him or her .Remember Chapter 6! The wolf always focuses on the person left alone**

# Chapter 13 Review
*The Congregations Response
to the Wounded Leader*

- When shepherd's blow it, there's a right and wrong way to handle such situations.

- While much attention is often placed upon the shepherds who fall short, sheep also carry a major responsibility in the health of the congregation.

- Sheep too can kill shepherds!

- We are to follow leaders only as they follow Christ!

- We must always remember God's leaders are still his anointed and should be handled following the restrictions of the Word.

- When the pew does not support the pulpit properly and give them the necessary resources for shepherds to do ministry, we make the load heavier upon the shepherd, opening the door for various forms of leadership burnout that will affect the people served.

- When shepherds are leading while bleeding, sheep should pray, communicate concerns with the shepherd, and seek wisdom avenues to restore life and get the professional help the shepherd may need.

- The way we handle our wounded sends volumes of messages to a world skeptical of Christianity.

- It's never the sheep's place to usurp the shepherd's authority and run the church. This is out of order! However, if it's a situation where the congregation is endangered by a shepherd's behavior, go through the correct Biblical channels and proper protocol to address the situation. If this doesn't work seek the proper channels of professional assistance or leaving for one's own personal safety may be one's best option.

Somebody's pastor, church, and ministry is about to revived!

Rejoice! I FEEL REVIVAL COMING! Hallelujah!

CHAPTER FOURTEEN

# "WHERE DO PREACHERS GO WHEN THEY HURT?"

*Final Thoughts and Closing Prayer*

## WOW! WHAT A JOURNEY!

Finally we have arrived to the closing moments of our journey. My prayer is via our traveling together through the pages of location, discussion, and application that something you've read will have ignited a new and powerful flame of hope and a greater desire to see the health, healing, restoration, and wholeness of clergy all over the world to the glory of God! I pray that this book has wonderfully provoked pastors and congregants, clergy and laity, pulpits and pews, seminarians and interested persons of other vocations, to begin to engage in further positive discussion embracing the fact that WE NEED EACH OTHER AND WE'RE BETTER TOGETHER!

If this book can be found guilty of causing one precious soldier dying on the battlefield of life and ministry to find new hope and live, I believe Heaven will be pleased and my mission accomplished. If this book can be found guilty of propagating better relationships and understanding between both the pulpit and the pews, I know real revival is on its way! If this book can be found guilty of causing an unbelieving and skeptical world against Christianity to realize that there's more to us than what meets the eye then perhaps real evangelism can begin!

Is there no balm in Gilead to make the wounded whole? The answer is a resounding YES! However, the healing begins with each and every one of us.

In this book we've learned several priceless things! We learned:

- Preachers are human too and face deeper needs and issues not often discussed. As a result casualties among us have escalated.
- Preachers often have silent screams and non-verbal cries for help.
- Sometimes preachers internalize issues for fear of betrayal, scrutiny or ostracism.
- God has made provision for any and everything clergy persons may face enabling us to overcome obstacles and walk in victory.
- The journey to healing begins with talking and sharing what's really bugging us and finding the professional help we need in time.
- Healthy pulpits make healthy pews and the vice versa. When both are healthy that congregation can reach the world!
- Ministerial training and preparation is key before one assumes a leadership position in ministry.
- We should avoid having an isolationist mentality in ministry and

- embrace the power of accountability no matter how successful we become.
- Maturity in ministry is a process and not a one night stand!
- Experience is great but prevention is even better when it comes to avoiding pitfalls.
- God cares about our spiritual, physical, mental, emotional, and financial health.
- God cares and wants us to embrace healthy and proper attitudes about sexual intimacy whether single or married.
- God cares about our relationships with our spouses, children, loved ones and friends.
- There's no perfect organization in the Body of Christ. However, if we trust God and allow Him to guide us we'll bloom where He plants us.
- Controlling ministers often have issues with deeper insecurities. These can be overcome by embracing who we are and what we have in Christ.
- We learned that congregations must know how to properly and skillfully handle leaders who are in pain. If we do so, real breakthrough and victory can occur.
- The health of any congregation is not left up to the pastor alone. Teamwork is paramount and sheep must know how to hold up the pastor's arms as they play a major role in any ministry's vision.

## So Where Do Preachers Go When They Hurt?

Nevertheless, with all this said another pertinent question remains. *Where Do Preachers Go When They Hurt?* Let's finally answer this question.

One, we go to God and His Word. Two, we stand on our own faith. Three, we seek out the professional resources of help and assistance necessary. However, we learned going to God is not the issue although this we do! Being created social creatures by God, the greatest goal of this book is to get us to become more readily available to each other without fear of betrayal, scrutiny, or embarrassment. And whereas we may not all have the professional credentials to assist in every situation, as the Body of Christ we certainly can be life-giving suppliers of uplift and support as we transition to the healing and breakthrough needed! This is the greatest goal this book seeks to accomplish! It's to get us to hold hands. It's to release a greater understanding so we can come to each other as ordained by scripture in times of crises and need without any fear of scrutiny, betrayal, or undermining!

When a world in pain, who in recent decades have become more skeptical about Christianity due to our own bad PR and other worldly influences can see how we care and tend to our own wounded real revival will happen. When they can actually see us build bridges of hope and restoration instead of apathy, fighting each other over stupid things, abandonment, self righteousness, standing up for love, holiness, and integrity rather than passing mixed and diluted messages because we dare to be different, I believe innumerable souls will be added to the Lord and the Kingdom! Why? Like Peter and John at the Gate Beautiful, the world will be able to look at our dealings and not just hear a sermon but see one in living action!

So saints, brothers and sisters, let's get it together now. WE CAN DO THIS!

And you know what else? The question will no longer be asked, *Have Preachers Gone Wild?* Instead the Church of Jesus Christ having awakened out of sleep and having torn down the ancient walls that divide us will be able to shout, "THERE IS A BALM IN GILEAD TO MAKE THE WOUNDED WHOLE!" Then we'll be able to say, "No!" Preachers haven't gone wild. Instead, they have become the global ministers and representatives of healing to every country, nation, state, town and village!

And our youth?

Their indifference to church will cease, the deceptive, alluring, entertaining traps and tricks of the world used to satisfy a deeper hunger will be minimized and they will boldly proclaim..................

*"We've found something better! LIFE!"*

LET'S DO THIS!

## CLOSING PRAYERS!

Please pray these prayers aloud with me.

### I.
### Prayer for Pastors, Leaders, and all
### 5-fold Ministry Gifts)
(And for anyone who has been leading while bleeding!)

Dear Heavenly Father, thank you for all your grace and mercy. Thank you for another day of life allowing me a greater opportunity to become all that you want me to be! I worship You because Your love for me is unconditional and even when I'm facing my greatest pain, You are there to see me through it!

As a shepherd, pastor, and leader, I'm not ashamed to say that there have been times that I've been leading while bleeding. However, like King David, I stop by Your still waters today for the restoration of my soul. (Psalm 23: 3) Heavenly Father go into the deepest parts of my being and make me whole from the crown of my head to the soles of my feet. And show me now God Your wisdom to victory and the path You will have me take concerning this/these issues in my life.

I am willing and choose to forgive now all who've wounded and hurt me. As an act of my will I let go of all resentment, bitterness, deep hurt, and strife. I confess my total situation to You and am willing to cooperate with Your Holy Spirit and give up all grounds giving the enemy of my soul a legal right to keep my life in bondage. Through confession and repentance I break his grip and all strongholds in my life right now in the mighty Name of Jesus through the precious Blood of the Lamb!

Father if I need to make amends or seek godly professional counseling to further me in my deliverance please direct my path now on how to proceed. I am no longer afraid but go rejoicing and with expectancy from You! Free me now God so that I can be all that You've created me to be. And Lord, like the Apostle Peter, when I'm converted I will strengthen my fellow brothers and sisters.

Give me now the grace to serve Your people well pleasing in Your sight as a shepherd/leader with all integrity, clean hands, a clean heart, and with the joy and hope of a brand new and brighter day!

I praise You God for hearing my prayer and making me a new creature in Christ with a brand new beginning in You! Hallelujah! It is so!

In Jesus Name I thank You for the victory! Amen!

(Now take a quiet moment. Thank and worship Him for your victory and new beginnings!)

## II.
## (Prayer for Congregations and Sheep for Their Pastors and All Leadership)

Please pray with me now aloud.

Dear Heavenly Father, I praise and worship You for who You are and for all the mighty things You've done in my life and for all Your sons and daughters around the world. Thank You for this great, powerful gift and privilege of prayer and intercession. I thank You when the righteous cry, You always hear! Your Word says, "this poor man cried and the Lord delivered him out of all his troubles!" (Psalm 34:6)

Father in I Timothy 2:1-4, Your Word tells us to pray for all those in authority. Therefore, Father I come to You on behalf of my pastor/leader. He (or she) needs You so dearly right now. I pray that You will lead, guide, direct, comfort, strengthen, and give whatever grace, resources, and breakthrough needed for him (her) to be able to do all that You've called them to do with nothing aborted or miscarried in his (her) personal life and ministry.

Only You know God the unspoken pressures that my leader feels and encounters on a daily basis. Therefore, in the Name of Jesus Christ of Nazareth I intercede for him (her) now! Meet the deepest needs in their life to the honor and glory of Thy Name!

And Lord, as a sheep I repent of all sin, apathy, or any insensitivity

I've harbored against my leader during their time of trial and testing. Forgive me even if I haven't been praying for him (her) as consistently as I should. Give me wisdom too Lord! Forgive my sins too Lord! And most of all, show me how to hold up the arms of my leader as the saints did with Moses during the time of warfare and beyond! I await your wisdom now!

Thank You for receiving my prayer on behalf of my leader in the Name of Jesus Christ of Nazareth. Amen.

Amen!

(Now quietly begin to thank and worship the Lord for all His mercy and grace!)

## III.
## (Prayer to be Saved (Salvation) and to Receive Jesus Christ as Savior and Lord!)

Dear Heavenly Father, I come to You today praying the most important prayer that any human being can pray and that's the prayer of salvation. Where I will spend eternity and having a real relationship with You is a decision I must make while I'm alive and the blood is still running warm in my veins. (Deuteronomy 30:19, Hebrews 3:7-8, 2:3

Thank You so much Father for loving me unconditionally and desiring to share Your Life with me. God, I need You! I can't make it without You! I confess and acknowledge I'm a sinner and have not always done things Your way. Please forgive me. I'm sorry Lord. I'm also sorry for anyone I may have wounded along the way. According to Your Holy Word in Romans 10:9, I confess with my mouth that Jesus Christ is Lord. I believe in my heart that He died for my sins and You raised Him from the dead on the 3$^{rd}$ day! Save my eternal soul Lord! Come into my heart Lord Jesus and make me Your child. Wash all my sins away with Your precious shed Blood. I gladly welcome and receive You as My Lord and Savior. Walk with me. Talk with me. Lead me and guide me. Fill me with Your precious Holy Spirit and when this life is over, give me a home with You in Glory forevermore. Amen!

I thank You now upon the authority of Your Word in John 1:12 and Romans 10:9-10, 5:8-10, I AM SAVED!

(Take a quiet moment and give God praise for your salvation.)

Now that you've received Christ into your life it's important that you do the following:

1. Tell someone about your salvation! (Romans 10:9)
2. Find a sound doctrine (not a cult) Bible believing church so you can grow and develop and mature in Christ. (Hebrews 10:25)
3. Obey Christ command and be baptized in water. (Doesn't save you but is a public confession of an inward change!) (Matthew 28:19)
4. Pray and read your Bible everyday! (Knowledge and understanding is power! (II Timothy 2:15)

Welcome to a brand new life in Christ! The Bible says,

*"Therefore, if anyone is in Christ, he (or she) is a new creation; old things have passed away; behold, ALL THINGS HAVE BECOME NEW."*
*II Corinthians 5:17 NKJV*

And guess what else? In the midst of a world in turmoil, test, and challenges, THE BEST IS YET TO COME! Keep looking up! Please e-mail us at *brentlybooks@yahoo.com* and tell us of your salvation Welcome to wonderful new beginnings!

**Rejoice!!!**

# ABOUT THE AUTHOR!

Reverend Brent La Prince Edwards is an ordained minister and a powerful preacher of the Gospel of Jesus Christ! He is an author, an anointed and effective speaker, teacher, lecturer, facilitator of workshops, seminars, conferences and crusades. Such have afforded him opportunities to travel extensively and minister on both local and national platforms alongside several internationally known speakers, and contemporary voices of today. With much prayer and supplication, the Lord is raising him up to be an emerging voice both in secular arenas and an evangelistic, prophetic, and apostolic voice to the Body of Christ worldwide.

He is the senior past or of the progressive and life changing St. Stephen African Methodist Episcopal Church and the founder and CEO of the Helping Hands Community Youth Development Center, Inc. located in Mt. Gilead, North Carolina. The center is the first of its kind in the area and has made first time monumental history in the region expanding St. Stephen's to becoming one church in two locations. It serves the needs of both youth and adults alike. His work has gained the international recognition of the AME Church and was featured as a premier article in the May 7, 2007 <u>Christian Recorder</u> which serves as the official organ of publication in the global AMEC.

Reverend Edwards has served as a featured speaker in various arenas on both collegiate and university levels and has ecumenically ministered to a diversity of congregations crossing over both denominational and cultural lines. He has served both as a host and guest on both radio and television programs. As a keynote speaker on several prestigious platforms, his ministry has reached people from the streets and homeless to those of celebrity status. As a result, countless souls have been saved, delivered, set free, healed, transformed, filled with the Holy Spirit and encouraged and empowered to pursue excellence in every arena of life.

With a special passion for persons involved in gangs and "Thug Life," the congregation of St. Stephen's is known to be filled with persons who would never walk through the doors of a church! Bottom line: Pastor Edwards is a soul winner! His pastoral ministry and influence has caught the eyes of key politicians, educators, religious leaders and has gained such recognition because of the rarity of seeing a rural church make the vast economic, spiritual, and educational advancements greatly influencing that region. Via the ministry of St. Stephen's, blacks and whites, politicians and gang bangers, the young and the old all come together under one roof! To God be the glory!

Reverend Edwards is an "information" preacher and a deep thinker. God has given him the unique ability to take the abstract and convert the intangible into principles that are comprehensible to any audience. He is an ardent advocate against spiritual ignorance and procures the education and growth of the believer.

In addition, he holds several honors, awards, and recognition in several arenas. He graduated from Burke High School, Charleston, South Carolina (1983) and pursued his undergraduate studies via the historic Livingstone College, Salisbury, North Carolina where he majored in pre-med biology. He later transferred to the University of North Carolina at Charlotte where he earned a B.A. in the academic study of religion. (Religious Studies) In pursuit of his Master of Divinity he attended Union Theological Seminary Presbyterian School of Christian Education of Richmond, Virginia at the Charlotte campus. He was ordained an itinerant elder in the African Methodist Episcopal Church in 1995, Second Episcopal District and was inducted as a member of the Order of the FLAME (Faithful Leaders As Mission Evangelist) by the World Methodist Council of Churches, 1999. He has served faithfully as the "Tuesday" speaker at the Harvest Kitchen of Charlotte for several years where over 52,000 meals are prepared for the homeless annually. He has founded the Saturday Night Live Youth Evangelistic Outreach program and has served as a health care technician in both North Carolina Governmental Departments of Mental Health and Social Services in substance abuse and with BEH (behaviorally emotionally handicapped) adolescents. He has also served as a former key facilitator in the Ministry of Recovery Relapse Prevention Center also of Charlotte. In addition to belonging to several organizations he has also served as the former chapter president of the Gamma Mu Chapter of the Alpha Phi Alpha Fraternity, Inc.

Nevertheless, in the words of the famous late poet and writer, Rudyard Kipling, in spite of his many accomplishments Reverend Edwards has learned how to "walk with kings but never lose the common touch!" A true comedian at heart (even at the most serious moments) and a lover of people, he's never forgotten his family or the roots from whence he's come. It's this humility that causes people to readily connect with him. However, the greatest moment in his life happened when he had a supernatural experience with God and got saved at age 11 having received Jesus Christ as his Savior and Lord! This happened a year after being innocently drawn into the occult as a child by an unsuspecting teacher in the public school system. Via this experience, he has a tremendous passion for youth evangelism and warns the dangers of dabbling into the occult. Thus, a passionate lover of God, he gives God the glory for any and all blessings upon his life. Reverend Edwards is the second son of the honorable Mr. and Mrs. James and Gloria La Prince Edwards. He currently resides in North Carolina.